SCREWING
UPWARD

SCREWING UPWARD

KEITH FRANCIS

iUniverse, Inc.
Bloomington

Screwing Upward

iUniverse books may be ordered through booksellers or by contacting:

iUniverse
1663 Liberty Drive
Bloomington, IN 47403
www.iuniverse.com
1-800-Authors (1-800-288-4677)

ISBN: 978-1-4759-6810-1 (sc)
ISBN: 978-1-4759-6811-8 (ebk)

Library of Congress Control Number: 2012923765

Printed in the United States of America

iUniverse rev. date: 1/03/2013

CONTENTS

Author's Note

The Society for Cosmic Wisdom, which provides the background for this story, is not intended as a representation of any actual spiritual movement. Like the characters depicted herein, it is entirely fictional.

The town of Glastonbury, of course, is not fictional. I have merely presented it with a Grammar School and a hotel that it did not previously possess.

I

Characters

(1)

The young blonde sat up in bed and spoke very seriously to the old man beside her.

"Look, Klaus, I know it's kind of humiliating for you, but for God's sake, you're eighty-four, and it's not surprising if you can't get it up the way you did fifty years ago. Anyway, I've got packing to do, and I think you need a rest."

The scene was a room in a brownstone on Manhattan's Upper West Side, but the accent would have been more a home in London's East End. The reply came with a mild German accent.

"Perhaps we could try again later—you know how important it is for me to reach . . ."

"Orgasm—yes, and if you want to know the truth, I sometimes wonder if you're really the spiritual savior of the world and not just a dirty old man with a passion for young girls."

"My dear! You know that I have never made such a claim. Dr. Goerner . . ."

"OK, I'm sorry. You're very kind and at least you stick to one girl at a time. But I don't believe old Goerner ever said anything about sex in his life. At least, not the way you mean."

"That is true—it is simply a very well known and universally acknowledged fact that . . ."

"A good lay makes your clairvoyance work overtime."

"My dear Halcyon, I beg you not to keep interrupting. I was only going to say that sexual fulfillment helps to awaken one's spiritual faculties."

1

"OK, I'm sorry again. We can try again later, but maybe it's just that now I'm eighteen I'm getting too old for you. It wasn't a problem when I was sixteen."

Klaus looked thoughtful.

"I do not remember that you found my attentions distasteful."

The young woman called Halcyon smiled and kissed the old man on the top of his head.

"It's true. You were just like those old pictures of God—all white hair and bulging muscles—and I was all blue-eyed innocence, and nicely developed for a kid of that age. We really turned each other on, didn't we? But maybe you really do need somebody new."

"And you? Do you need somebody new?"

She kissed him again.

"If I don't get on with my packing, we'll never make it onto that plane tomorrow morning, and we'll miss the blasted conference, and you won't get to make your speech. I s'pose Alison is packing for you."

"Yes, I believe so."

"Maybe it wouldn't be a bad idea to go down and say something nice to her."

Klaus looked faintly puzzled, but he went to the door and as he opened it the sound of a not very amicable conversation reached them.

"I do wish that she and Imre would become more friendly."

"Don't count on it—Alison may be a bit funny, but she's really a sweetheart, whereas Imre's a sleaze-ball and I still can't figure out why you took him on as your secretary. Anyway, you'd better go down and see what's up—but put something on first. I know everybody knows what's going on but . . . Well, you know what I mean."

The voices from downstairs got louder.

"Imre, will you get the hell out of my room?"

"But Alison, I only wanted to . . ."

"I know what you wanted."

A door slammed.

Klaus went to his room for his ornate dressing gown, while Halcyon reached for her bathrobe, caught sight of herself in her dressing table mirror, liked what she saw and grinned at her image. It grinned back encouragingly at her, so she decided against the robe and pulled a suitcase out from under the bed.

"And the four of us are going to be stuck together on that plane for six or seven hours", she muttered. "Klaus will tell us everything Goerner ever said about flying, Imre will spend the whole time saying, 'Yes Sir, no Sir, three bags full' while he's ogling Alison, she'll keep on snubbing him and I'll just keep quiet and hope for it to be over. OK, Glastonbury, here we come."

(2)

From *Barnett's Guide to the West of England*:

The town of Glastonbury (population 9,000) is notable for the myths and legends surrounding the hill at its south-eastern corner, Glastonbury Tor, which rises five hundred feet above the generally flat landscape of the Somerset Levels. These myths concern Joseph of Arimathea, the Holy Grail, King Arthur, whose body the monks of Glastonbury were believed to have discovered, and a Celtic hero called Gwyn ap Nudd. The Tor can be approached from the Chalice Well at the foot of its western slopes or from the meadows on its eastern side. The climb to the distinctive tower at the summit is rewarded by views of the Mid-Somerset area, including the drained marshland of the Levels. From there it is easy to see how Glastonbury was once an island. At certain times of the year, the surrounding moors are often flooded, giving that appearance once more. It is an agricultural region with open fields surrounded by ditches lined with willow trees, and dotted with small hills. Glastonbury is less than a mile across the River Brue from the village of Street.

*

Tom Dexter met Alison on a sunny Thursday afternoon in July 1988, two days after Klaus and his entourage landed in England. Tom, who was nearing the end of his fourth year as a physics teacher at Glastonbury Grammar School, had been pondering some of the facts of teenage life while he walked home from school. The first of these was that most teenagers are not very interested in physics. And it's not fair to blame them, Tom thought—it's perfectly natural for kids to find Isaac Newton's Laws of Motion less interesting than their own physiology and personal appearance. It seemed that Newton hadn't bothered much with such things, but Tom had to admit that Newton was really a bit of a freak—a freak of great genius, but still a freak. Maybe the kids were right about the relative importance of things. Newton's Laws might be useful for calculating how long a runway had to be to get a 727 off the ground, but they had never done Tom much good, except to provide him with a moderately interesting job.

Well, that wasn't quite fair either, since many people thought that Newton could take a lot of the credit or blame for the way modern civilization had turned out. Tom, however, was more interested in the kind of physics where Newton's Laws didn't work. Einstein and Heisenberg were his heroes, and he found the weirdness of space and time and the odd behavior of things like electrons and photons endlessly fascinating. As he walked along, he was so deep in the idea of getting the kids interested in the strange problems of modern physics that he became completely oblivious of his surroundings.

All pie in the sky, he told himself. Teenagers were what they were, the curriculum was what it was and the work he was doing was OK enough—it just wasn't very inspiring. Furthermore, he had to admit that in some ways he still felt very much like a teenager himself. This didn't prevent him from being a very good teacher, but at the age of twenty-six his physiological processes still gave him a lot of pleasure, and his personal appearance was one of the keys to allowing them to perform their proper functions. So when the sight of a girl with a hammer and a stack of posters startled him out of his preoccupation, the immediate result was probably more predictable than the future path of an electron encountering a photon, although the further ramifications were not.

She was really a woman of about the same age as Tom, but she was a foot shorter than his six foot four, slim, dark-haired and dressed in very brief, bright blue running shorts and a yellow sleeveless shirt. Now she was busy tacking a poster to a tree, reaching as high as she could, so that her shirt parted from her shorts and, being of some stretchy material, made it abundantly clear that she had nothing on underneath. Tom couldn't see her face, and from his angle of vision she looked about sixteen. His first thought was to regret that she was below his preferred age-group, but he stopped to see what the poster was about.

"Are you interested in education?" it asked, under a large heading advertising the "Archway Schools Triennial Global Conference". "Modern education addresses only the intellect. Would you like to hear about a worldwide movement that has as its goal the education of the whole

4

human being, a movement in which the intellectual and the artistic go hand in hand with the development of practical capacities? If so, why not come to the Archway Schools' Public Forum and Concert at the Wolfgang Goerner School (an Archway School) on Sunday July 11th at 3 pm?"

Her tacking finished, the young woman turned, and Tom was relieved to see in her nicely tanned face a combination of youthful charm and adult experience that placed her much closer to his own age. She looked up and saw certain features of Tom's personal appearance that he couldn't do much about, namely his ginger hair, freckles and slightly snub nose.

"Hi", she said, with an agreeable touch of New York in her voice. "Are you interested in education?"

At that moment Tom's physiology seemed inclined to go into overdrive, so it took him a few moments to reply.

"Well, I'm a teacher", he said.

"Not necessarily the same thing, is it? What's your name?"

"Tom."

"I'm Alison. You should come to this. It's free and you get something to eat."

"Will you be there?"

"Sure, I'm one of the faithful. I'd stop and talk, but I still have a whole stack of these to put up."

"Do you always dress like that when you're putting up posters?"

"You mean, am I the Archway sex symbol?"

"Well, I wasn't thinking that, but now you come to mention it . . ."

"No, it's just that I like to jog from tree to tree like a dryad. What do you teach?"

Alison picked up her stack of posters and gave one to Tom.

"Physics mostly—and don't you find jogging rather awkward with all these posters and a hammer?"

"It is, a bit. Where do you teach?"

"At the local Grammar School."

"Will I see you on Sunday?"

"Why not tonight? I know some very nice pubs."

"I can't—we have all kinds of committee meetings and . . ."

"And what?"

"I'll see you Sunday."

"Only if you promise to sit next to me."

"OK, I'll keep a place for you. You can have one of these—all the directions for getting there are on it."

Alison jogged off. In spite of the posters and the hammer she managed it quite gracefully and without excessive jiggling in the upper storey.

Tom was still standing by the tree in a pleasant daze when Alison's voice came from a couple of hundred feet along the road.

"Tom what?"

"Dexter."

He was about to shout, "Alison what?", when he heard a chorus of giggles from across the street and realized that he was being watched by several of his female students.

"Nice legs, Mr. Dexter!" one of them called out.

Something about Alison had interfered with Tom's usual poise, and he wasn't in the mood for badinage, so he gave the girls a grin and a wave and went on his way. Looking at the travel directions below the main text of the poster, he realized that the forum was to be held at a place that he knew quite well, since he had been born there.

*

Tom's father, James, Duke of Brueland and Street, was known to the general public by one of his lesser titles, Lord Otterill. The Duke, who looked like an older edition of his son, had been a widower for over twenty years. After the death of his wife he had sold his ancestral home in Somerset and made the transition from being one of the smarter and more durable relics of the feudal system to being the owner of a very successful chain of newspapers. His ginger hair and freckles had faded somewhat, but they were still well known to the public, frequently being made the subject of little jokes about some bygone Duchess and a red-haired milkman. Otterill maintained that one of his ancestors had insisted on marrying a young woman from Swansea, who had been introduced to him by the then Prince of Wales, but no one could be quite sure whether or not this was a joke.

Tom had spent most of his boyhood and adolescence at boarding schools, where it had been decided that it would be better for him if his identity were kept secret. Later on, he entered Cambridge University as plain Tom Dexter. Father and son agreed that while there was no particular reason why the boy should follow his father into the media world, it

6

wasn't a good idea for him to live a life of pleasant unemployment. So, following his inclinations and the path of least resistance, Tom took his degree in physics and returned to teach in his native county. He felt that a background of enormous wealth might be a social disadvantage, so with the cooperation of his father, a great deal of effort and a certain amount of luck, he continued to keep his lineage secret, telling his friends and colleagues that his father worked for the *Daily Sentinel*, without mentioning that he actually owned it. After cultivating this mild deception for four years he had come to the point of almost believing it himself, which made his occasional surreptitious visits to Lord Otterill's resplendent mansion in London a little uncomfortable. This wasn't because of any difficulty with his father, with whom he was on the friendliest terms, but because he had become unused to luxury and the presence of servants who kept up all the traditional appearances of class distinction. He had tried to explain this to the butler, Fortescue, and had been gently reproved for his pains.

"Well, you see, Your Lordship, we like to know where we are, and being servants protects us in a way, if you see what I mean. All we're responsible for is doing as we're told, so we don't have to make decisions, and if it goes wrong it's not our fault. Your Lordship and His Grace have your private lives and we have ours, and when you start mixing them up there's trouble. It's the same with me and the lower servants. If I get too familiar with them the whole system is liable to go to pot."

Appreciating the wisdom of Fortescue's explanation, Tom found that the old butler responded well to humor, and that friendliness and mutual esteem were possible without undue familiarity.

Not wishing to spoil his boyhood memories, Tom had avoided his old home in Somerset. He knew that it had been purchased by an educational foundation and turned into a school, but the Archway Schools were just a vague rumor. He knew nothing about Wolfgang Goerner.

(3)

Dr. Wolfgang Goerner had been dead for more than half a century, but he was still a strong presence in the conversation of Alison and her friends. Like Albert Einstein, Goerner was born in Ulm, Germany, in 1879, but there the similarity ends. Most people have heard of Einstein, and some of them can say $E = mc^2$ as if they know what it means, whereas Goerner, believing that energy had a different origin, never produced a formula for it, and so for most of the world he isn't even a name. While Einstein's theories triumphed over the initial scepticism of the scientific world and produced sensational results, Goerner's vision of the truth came from some region not recognized by science. His esoteric history of the world and his handbook for spiritual research were generally ignored, derided as the delusions of a misguided fanatic or dismissed as hodge-podges of gleanings from earlier mystics; but people who actually met him often had a different response.

Goerner was not your average mystical ascetic with a lean frame, a gaunt visage and a far-away look in the eye. He was short and plump, and looked at you with a merry twinkle. People who had vaguely heard of him were surprised to find that he had had an orthodox scientific education, could talk clearly and to the point, and was very fond of dubious jokes. His father, a Roman Catholic, and his mother, a converted Jew, were the jovial proprietors of the Red Hedgehog, a large inn near the center of Ulm. Their suburban house happened to be next door to the residence of the Schmidt family, owners of the great Suddeutscher Brauerei, the South German brewery that supplied inns, taverns and families all over Europe. Papa Schmidt and his family were strict Lutherans, so while relations between the two families were never less than civil, there was a distinct lack of warmth. Large quantities of Papa's best products were consumed at the Red Hedgehog, but the *Brauerei* had plenty of good customers, so he didn't feel under any obligation to the Goerners.

Wolfgang grew up feeling that the Schmidts were lofty and unapproachable, so he kept his jokes to himself and nothing much happened to change the situation until 1901, when Papa and Frau Schmidt needed a tutor for Johann, their twelve-year-old only child. Wolfgang, who had recently returned from Berlin with a degree in science, was working at the local newspaper, while keeping his spiritual researches strictly under cover. When Frau Schmidt, who had always found the lad mysteriously charming, insisted on engaging him, Papa Schmidt reluctantly agreed. Goerner turned out to be such a good teacher that within a year Johann was able to keep up with his work without the young man's help. Delighted that his Lutheran castle was rid of this potentially popish influence, Papa was shocked to find that in spite of the ten year age difference, Johann and Wolfgang had become close friends. Things got worse when Goerner began publishing his esoteric histories and spiritual guide-books, but by that time Johann was sixteen and his father's health was failing. Goerner might be a heretic and a heathen, but there wasn't much Papa could do about it. Frau Schmidt became the head of the brewery, but she soon began to consult her son on major decisions, and at the age of twenty-one he became the *de facto* CEO. He had also committed himself heart, soul and bankroll to his friend's spiritual aspirations for the world, which was just as well since Goerner had been politely removed from his job at the newspaper, on the ground that his opinions were incompatible with editorial policy.

*

With Johann's backing, the first meetings of an informal society began in 1910. Goerner lectured on an astonishing variety of subjects, always beaming with pleasure at his audience and peppering his presentations with sly allusions and bad puns. Behind all this *bonhomie* there was an austere message: the human race, materialistic and egotistic, was heading for a cataclysm in which evil, fallen spirits would take over the human soul and destroy all freedom of thought and action. The only defence and the only hope for the future would be for people to follow the true path of spiritual knowledge, to realize that human history and human destiny could be understood only in terms of reincarnation and karma, and to wake up and be aware of the danger. Of the two dozen or so people usually present, some received this message with deep seriousness and inner resolve, some were intoxicated by the sensation of being members of an elite group who possessed special knowledge and carried the responsibility for the salvation of the world, and some thought the whole thing was sheer fantasy.

Johann encouraged Goerner to create a formal society with a home of its own, but the outbreak of the First World War and the subsequent chaos put everything on hold for a long time, and it wasn't until April of 1927 that the foundation meeting of the Society for Cosmic Wisdom took place. The society's Newsletter (Volume 1. No. 1) reported the founder's opening address as follows, tactfully omitting the puns and multiple references to cow shit:

"Dr. Wolfgang Goerner was introduced by Herr Johann Schmidt, the owner and Managing Director of the Suddeutscher Brauerei, and greeted with heartfelt applause by the 72 founding members. After thanking Herr

Schmidt for his spiritual and financial support, Dr. Goerner spoke about the early stages of the path to esoteric knowledge.

I am an enthusiastic gardener and I expect that many of you are, too. I have always found that one of the most exciting times of the year is the moment in the spring when everything is freshly dug, raked and weeded, and ready to receive the seeds of a new beginning that will lead to a harvest of leaves, flowers and fruit. It is such a beautiful sight that it seems almost a pity to disturb it, but we know that, left on its own, it will soon grow another crop of weeds; so we get on with our planting and mentally prepare for the hard work of tending the garden and helping the being of nature to bring our labors to fruition. Perhaps while doing so we hum a few lines from a great old hymn:
"We plough the fields and scatter the good seed on the land,
But it is fed and watered by God's almighty hand."
It is just so with the meditative work we do when we try to free our souls of the evanescent whims and nagging anxieties of everyday life. Some weeds can easily be removed with the hoe, while others are deep-rooted and have to be dug out one by one. So it is in the human soul, and while we are performing this necessary cleansing we are transforming our inner soil with a rich compost of great words from the seers of the past and present. If our inner seed-bed is empty of distractions and full of transformed wisdom, then the spiritual world may speak to us. We cannot, however, compel it to do so. One requirement for progress along the path of knowledge is enormous patience. We may feel that we are ready, but the still, small voice works according to its own timetable.

Such work, Dr. Goerner, said, may eventually bring us awareness of our previous incarnations and their karmic consequences. He promised to elaborate on this theme at the Society's next meeting, and the meeting ended with the first public performance of the new art of *Bewegungskunst.*"

Among the many omissions was Goerner's remark, *a propos* the matter of compost, that if cows could fly it would solve the whole fertilizer problem and greatly decrease the country's dependence on the mineral deposits at Stassfurt and imported birdshit, by which he meant *guano,* while having beneficial results for the manufacturers of umbrellas. The report did, however, give a full description of *Bewegungskunst,* praising Goerner for the creation of a new art of movement that transcended dance and, although still in its infancy, had the potential to take music and drama to a higher level than ever before.

It was realized that the German name for the new art would be too much of a jaw-cracker for the English-speaking world, so *Bewegungskunst* soon became known as euphonics.

*

Good German beer would always be in great demand, no matter what happened to the currency, but Johann Schmidt had other aspirations besides turning a profit. By 1929 he felt that while the world seemed to be descending once more into chaos, Goerner might be able to help save something from the wreck. Concerned for the welfare of his workers and their children, Schmidt asked his friend about the possibility of creating a school which would provide a good standard education and something extra, namely independence and the strength to stand up to adversity. Goerner soon gathered a miscellaneous group of people, including Johann's cousin Walter Schmidt and a young man called Klaus Hübel, who would become the faculty of the first Archway School. While they worked enthusiastically throughout the first half of 1930, the political scene changed rapidly. By the time the school opened its doors for the new academic year, the Nazi Party had become the second largest in Germany.

Walter, who at thirty-two was the chief chemist at the *Brauerei*, became the school's first chemistry teacher. Klaus, who was six years younger and had the advantage of a large supply of inherited wealth, studied euphonics and worked as a general assistant and dogsbody until 1932, when he took over the First Grade. His class included Walter's daughter Maria, eventually to be Alison's mother. Klaus was tall, athletic, articulate, responsive to the children's needs and utterly committed to Goerner's philosophy; Maria, small, dark-haired, high-spirited and precociously smart, soon became his darling. One of the features of Goerner's system was that the teacher advanced with the class, so Maria was with Klaus for several years.

As the school in Ulm prospered, Archway Schools opened in several European countries and as far afield as New York. People generally assumed that the name "Archway" symbolized the passage from dependent infancy to independent adulthood, but the reason for the name was really much simpler. The first school was housed in an old building in Ulm with an ornate covered entrance, flanked by twin towers and leading into a courtyard. This building had been known locally as "The Archway" for donkey's years and the name stuck to the school.

After the Nazi takeover of 1933, the German Archway Schools were threatened on two fronts. Goerner had not been afraid to air his opinion that Germany was primarily responsible for the carnage of the First World War, and had voiced his opposition to the Nazi party, so the staunchly independent Archway Schools were not popular with the new regime. Furthermore, he and several members of his faculty had Jewish connections. Walter's wife was Jewish, and it was in one of the small rooms over the Archway that he met with Klaus one evening in 1935 to discuss the future. It was clear that Walter and his family would have to leave Germany, and that Klaus, who could not bear to be parted from Maria, would go with them. They decided to hold on as long as they could, but a few weeks later they learned that a minor bureaucrat had informed the authorities that Goerner's mother was Jewish. The writing was on the wall in very large letters.

Klaus, Walter and Walter's family made it out of Germany on the pretext of attending an educational conference in Belgium, and by the fall of 1935 the two men were established as teachers at the Wolfgang Goerner School in Manhattan. Goerner developed a progressive disease that was never clearly diagnosed, and died in 1937, the year in which the Nazis closed the Archway Schools.

*

By August of 1946 most of the German Archway Schools had reopened. Maria and Klaus returned to Ulm in 1950, Maria to study euphonics and Klaus to play a major part in restoring the city to its position as the center of the Cosmic Wisdom and Archway Movements.

Things were more difficult in Eastern Europe under the communist regime, where any form of independent education was almost impossible, but little groups of enthusiasts studied Goerner's work. In 1956 the movement towards democracy in Hungary made it possible for Bela and Elena Takacs to obtain permission to spend six months in England at the Glastonbury Archway School, taking their six-year-old son Imre with them, with a view to starting a school in Budapest when they returned. After the October uprising and its violent suppression by the Soviet Union, they were granted political asylum in England. A few months later, they decided to move to Ulm and study at the fountainhead. This, to all intents and purpose, meant Klaus, but they also met Maria. Elena was short, spherical and phlegmatic; Bela was only a few inches taller but he was wiry, dark-haired, full of vitality, and something of a mathematical genius. Imre, who was roughly the same shape as his mother and had very little German, entered first grade at the Archway School, where he had a very hard time.

As his German improved, other things did too. He did quite well with his work and learned his own particular ways of defending himself. As far as the other students were concerned he remained a marginal, odd kind of figure, but he had carved out a niche for himself and was very upset when, in 1962, his parents decided to move to New York, where he had to go through the same painful process again. He was not consulted, and many years elapsed before he understood the real reason for the move.

II

Alison and Tom

(4)

Tom Dexter liked teaching because in the classroom he was more or less his own boss, he got on well with the kids, and he was on vacation for twelve weeks in the year. He disliked it because he had to go through the motions of teaching all those boys and girls as if they were destined to become scientists, while knowing that once they passed the age of eighteen, 98% of them would never see the inside of a lab again. The problem was that since there was no way of telling which ones would eventually make a career out of science, they all had to be put through the same mill, a procedure accepted gracefully by most of the brighter students and with anything from good-humored acceptance to sullen reluctance by the others. It was a bit like the salmon, producing millions of ill-fated eggs, except that the salmon presumably doesn't know what minute proportion of its spawn will ever come to anything, and the eggs don't talk back. So he wasn't altogether impervious to the idea that some German philosopher might have thought of another way of doing things. It was Alison, however, who really made the sap rise, and he was preoccupied with her for the rest of Thursday evening and a certain amount of the night.

Friday was an ordinary school day until lunchtime. Tom was at the faculty table in the cafeteria, about to tackle his meat and two veg, when Flossie Howe, the school secretary, tapped him on the shoulder.

"Here's a message for you. It sounded like a young woman, and she said you would know who it was from. It doesn't make much sense but here it is anyway."

Flossie, who was round, motherly and secretly entertained hopes for Tom and her daughter Wendy, waited for a moment and observed the slight tinge of color that appeared on Tom's face with a mixture of

14

disappointment and gratification. It might mean nothing at all, and at least it offered material for some minor gossip, so she just happened to wander into the kitchen for a chat with her friend Maisie Robinson, the cook.

Tom reread the message: "Small committee meeting this afternoon 4:30 pm. Same place. No hammer."

"No hammer" was as good as a signature and "same place" presumably meant the tree with the poster. Alison must have assumed that Tom passed that point every day on his way home. This was an unwarranted assumption since he had no fixed routine, but he was uncomfortably aware that some of his students did have very predictable paths and that he might well be subjected to more teasing from the gaggle of giggling girls who had seen him on the previous afternoon. Guessing that the committee would consist of two people, he resolved to whisk Alison out of sight as rapidly as possible. For once he regretted his habit of walking to school on fine days, since this would be much easier if he had his car. Well, there was just time to go and get it before the end of the lunch hour. To the surprise of his colleagues, he hastily swallowed a few mouthfuls and hurried from the room.

*

Alison was wearing jeans and a purple tee shirt with ARCHWAY printed across the front. She was discreetly loitering a little distance from the tree, but she had already been spotted by some of the girls who had seen her on the previous day. Tom pulled up rapidly in his old green Morris Minor, leaned over, opened the passenger door and said, "Get in and close the door quick." Alison did as she was told and although the car didn't exactly speed off, since Morris Minors were not built that way, the whole process was completed rapidly enough to leave Marilyn Robinson and her friends open-mouthed.

"Well", said Alison, "that was pretty efficient."

"News travels fast around here. You leave a message with Flossie, she passes it on to me over the lunch table and then has a nice little talk with Maisie the cook. Maisie happens to bump into her daughter Marilyn, who happens to have seen us yesterday, and Marilyn spreads the good news. Hence the reception committee. Speaking of committees . . ."

"OK, I admit it—there weren't any last night."

"So why . . ."

"Well, you see, when you said 'How about it?' I wanted to say 'Yes', but I'm only here for a week and I thought I'd better not get involved in anything."

This sounded a bit lame, but Tom went along.

"What made you change your mind?"

"Well, I spend so much time with these Archway people, I thought it would be nice to get away for a few hours."

"That's not very flattering."

"You mean to them or to you?"

"Both."

"I'm sorry. OK, the truth is I woke up in the middle of the night and wished I was with you, and it's unusual because I don't go in for fantasizing very much."

"That's funny—the same thing happened to me."

The sap was rising so fast that Tom's first impulse was to stop the car and take Alison behind the nearest convenient hedge. This was tempered not only by the fact that it was five o'clock on a Friday afternoon and the countryside was fairly well populated, but also by the feeling that this might be the beginning of something beyond a one, two or three night stand. The civilized thing to do would be to take her out for a meal, which seemed an especially good idea since he had eaten very little lunch.

"Are you hungry?" he asked.

"Yes. People working at the conference only get what they call natural vegetarian food."

It was a bit early for dinner, so Tom drove into the middle of Glastonbury, parked opposite the Anglican church, and conducted Alison decorously into one of his favorite eateries, a little café known as the March Hare.

"Nothing fancy and only a little mad", he said. "Same menu all day and I can thoroughly recommend the fish and chips. They're served with real peas."

"If that's what you're having, I'll have the same. What's the difference between real peas and fake peas?"

"The fake ones come out of a tin and taste as if they were synthesized from old cardboard. This is an old-fashioned place, so it includes tea and bread and butter. Are you able to drink tea or do you want to risk the coffee?"

"I think the safest thing is to have whatever you're having."

"OK—Mirabelle, two chish and fips please and don't make the tea too strong."

"Comin' up", Mirabelle yelled from behind the counter. She was blonde, broad and fortyish as to both her age and her bust. "Got another new friend, I see."

"Now then, Mirabelle, watch that naughty old tongue of yours. If you start letting out my secrets, I might have to start going elsewhere."

Mirabelle approached the table with glasses of water.

"Don't you take any notice, Miss. He's a nice lad and I'd trust him with my own daughter, 'cept I haven't got one."

As she turned away, she added, "Well, I couldn't get anywhere with him myself."

Alison's eyebrows had gone aerobatic.

"She didn't really . . ."

"No, not really. She has a warm heart and likes to flirt a bit, but it's just make-believe. Her husband's the cook here and understands her perfectly, and she adores her children."

"No daughters?"

"Identical twins, male. How about you?"

"How about me what?"

"Children."

"Heavens, no! Why, do I look matronly?"

"No, just irresistible."

"OK, if that's how it works, why are you on the loose?"

"Why shouldn't I be?"

"Well, you seem very eligible?"

"How do you judge eligibility?"

"Well, you're good-looking and you have a good job."

"I'm not good-looking. I have carroty hair, freckles and a snub nose."

Alison laughed.

"Well, you look good to me. I don't trust tall, dark and handsome."

"Two chish and fips! Here's the bread and butter and the tea's just comin' up. I hope you two aren't quarrelling already."

Mirabelle put the plates in front of them with an exaggeratedly elegant gesture and retreated with a mock bow.

Tom grinned at her.

"Just an opening skirmish—not to worry."

Turning to Alison, he added, "It's quite edible."

"I like it—it makes me feel really English. Well in a way I am English. It seems that I was conceived just a couple of miles from here."

"Sounds like an interesting story."

But Alison seemed to regret having sent the conversation in this direction.

"Well they met at a conference here and then went back to New York. Nothing very interesting about it."

Tom looked at her curiously. He thought that there probably was something interesting about it and that Alison wished she hadn't mentioned it. He broke the awkward silence by asking her how she got involved with the Archway movement.

"Well, my parents were both Archway teachers, so I didn't really have much option. I started in kindergarten and went right through twelfth grade. Then I decided I wanted to be a teacher so I went and studied in Germany . . . Could we please skip the Archway stuff? If you come to the conference on Sunday you'll hear all about it. Tell me your life story."

"Something's wrong, isn't it?"

"Yes, but I can't talk about it—not yet, anyway. It's true what I said. I needed to get away and forget it for a little while, and I wanted to see you again. Tell me about yourself or teach me some physics or tell me some jokes."

"Well, I was born at an early age . . ."

"I know", Alison butted in, "I've heard that one. The first thing you remember is a man in a white coat slapping your feet and saying 'It's a boy.'"

"It wasn't white, it was green."

"OK, now tell me something real."

"Well, if you insist. I was born near Glastonbury, but we moved to London when I was little. When my father realized that I was a genius, he packed me off to Cambridge and I got a degree in physics and came back to teach here."

"That's what they call a brief bio. What kind of people are your parents?"

"Very nice, only my mother got very ill after I was born and she died when I was five."

"I'm sorry."

There were tears in Alison's eyes, and Tom had the impression that they weren't just for his mother.

"Did something happen to your mother?" he asked.

"Yes . . . What does your father do?"

"He works for a newspaper."

"Reporter?"

"Not exactly. Have you been up the Tor?"

"No, but I'd like to."

"Will you be requiring any dessert, Sir and Madam", Mirabelle asked in her fanciest tones. "You can have jam roly-poly or spotted dick."

"Don't be coarse, Mirabelle", said Tom, with a wink to Alison.

Alison smiled and added, "The fish and chips were lovely", to which Mirabelle replied, "Well, maybe he has his own ideas about dessert."

*

Tom's lodgings were on Ashwell Lane, which leaves the A361 just southeast of Glastonbury and leads to the path up the Tor from its east side. The first half mile was flanked by highly respectable homes, some of which had been adapted as mini-hotels to provide bed and breakfast for the tourists who swarm over the Tor in the summer months. Tom occupied the top floor of a house belonging to an elderly couple whose concept of respectability included the notion that it would be grossly improper for one of their tenant's female friends to go beyond the ground floor. Tom, they kindly intimated, might entertain in the drawing room without arousing the prurient curiosity of the neighbors, but that was the limit. "Drawing room" was a posh term for what the lower classes usually called the "front room", in which a settee and two armchairs were customarily grouped about an empty fireplace, providing a chilly and antiseptic environment of uncertain seclusion and decidedly antipathetic to love-making.

This was of some relevance, since Tom had a feeling that he would end up in bed with Alison, but there was something in the atmosphere that suggested that tonight probably wasn't the night. He parked in his usual spot in front of the house, waved to his landlady, who was peering through the lace curtains, and set off with Alison along the lane.

The houses were soon left behind, and they made a left turn into Basket Field Lane, which was so narrow that they had to squeeze themselves into the hedge to allow cars to go by. Occasional gaps on the left allowed a good view of the Tor, but the local farmers had left plenty of indications that there was no public access that way. Another left turn into Stone Down Lane brought Tom and Alison quickly to a wicket gate that led to the stone path up the eastern side of the hill. As they passed through there was a moment when they faced each other. It seemed symbolic of something, so they kissed impulsively.

When they broke, Alison said, "Tom . . ."

"I know. You mean, not too fast."

"Yes."

Alison led the way up the steep and narrow path, and Tom was impressed by the ease and grace with which she accomplished the climb. It was still a couple of hours before sunset, but it had been a warm day and the air was already becoming misty. The green of the surrounding meadows was so intense as to be almost unbearable, and the little hills that dotted the plain were merging into a blue-green haze. St. Michael's Tower stood like a great exclamation mark against a milky sky at the summit of the Tor.

They sat on the grass just below the west wall of the tower, where the path continued on its way down to the Chalice Well, and looked towards Bristol and beyond that sprawling city to where the Welsh mountains would have been visible on a clear day. His arm was around her and his hand closed over her breast. She took it, pressed it tightly against her and then gently removed it.

"I'm a little bit lost", she said. "Are you?"

"I wasn't", Tom replied, "but I think maybe I am now. Let's hop, skip and jump and try not to worry about it."

So they hopped, skipped, jumped, dawdled and ran a bit here and there, all the way back to the car, where they kissed uninhibitedly and failed to notice the agitated gyrations of Tom's landlady's lace curtain.

*

Tom was expecting to take Alison back to her lodging, but when they got to the center of town she asked him to stop.

"I'll walk the rest of the way", she said.

"Why, don't you want me to know where you live?"

"Don't be silly—I just want to arrive looking fairly normal, which I won't if I've just finished kissing you."

This time the kiss was more subdued, but it left neither of them looking or feeling quite normal.

"I'll see you on Sunday', Alison said. "Then you can take me all the way."

"Home?"

"What else did you think I meant?"

"Whatever you thought I might think."

(5)

The Archway Public Forum was the prelude to a week-long conference of teachers which was held every third year at Glastonbury, partly because the ancient town was the site of legendary happenings that the Archway people took very seriously, and partly because of the Archway School and its strong local following. To many of the inhabitants of Glastonbury, Gwyn ap Nudd, King Arthur, Joseph of Arimathea and the Holy Grail were tourist attractions of mostly economic importance, but for the people who had founded the Wolfgang Goerner School they provided an almost tangibly present spiritual background.

On Sunday morning Tom woke up with the kind of sensation in the pit of his stomach that he had felt before his finals at Cambridge, and it took him no time at all to figure out where the butterflies came from. Alison had got under his skin in a way that he hadn't experienced since he had his teenage romance with Sandy What's-her-name from Street. He grinned—Sandy had been a lot of fun and very well informed as far as sex was concerned. Unfortunately she hadn't been well informed about anything else. Tom had no idea what to wear at an Archway Conference, but judging by Alison it was probably pretty informal, so he decided on jeans and an old sweater—clean, since he was quite fastidious about such things, but definitely showing their age.

He set out along the main road to Wells in his elderly Morris Minor, a vehicle that helped him to keep up the fiction that he was plain, impecunious Tom Dexter and that his father worked for a newspaper in London. Twenty minutes later, after several miles on a minor road, he turned into a short narrow lane between high hedges that led into the school parking lot. The ancestral home was still standing, but the front of the building had been extended to form a new structure with a large vestibule fronted by three wide steps and a pair of glass doors. As he was getting out of the car he saw Alison. She was wearing a long, loose purple dress with a high collar and walking between a blonde girl, also attired in deep purple, and a tall, elderly man with an unruly mop of white hair. As Tom watched she burst out laughing. The old gentleman waggled his forefinger at her, but seemed to relent and kissed her on the cheek. They walked towards the glass doors and by the time they entered the vestibule Tom was close behind them.

"Good luck, Klaus", Alison said, "You'll be fine."

"So will you, my dear, as long as you behave yourself."

Klaus and the blonde turned aside to join a little group of extremely well dressed people. Alison passed through double wooden doors into an unexpectedly spacious auditorium with a wide, open stage. Tom followed, hastily thanking the elderly lady who pressed a program into his hand, and feeling rather conspicuous in his jeans and disreputable sweater. Alison went straight to the front row, sat down next to the center aisle, put her handbag on the seat beside her and looked over her shoulder.

"Hi, Tom, I knew you would come but I was scared you wouldn't."

"Hi, Alison, I was scared too. Silly, isn't it? I still like you. Do you still like me?"

"Yes, dummy, of course I do. Look out, here comes someone."

A plump, rosy-cheeked woman with flaming red hair trotted up to the podium at the center of the stage. Her dress was as long as Alison's but it was mauve.

"I wish she wouldn't", Alison muttered.

"Wouldn't what?"

"Her hair—it's out of a bottle and it doesn't go with her face—not like yours."

Tom found her whole shape and color scheme a bit overpowering, but she spoke with a pleasant accent from somewhere south of the Mason-Dixon Line, introducing herself as Jane Malone, General Secretary of the World Association of Archway Schools, and welcoming everyone to the International Conference. She talked of the foundation of the first Archway School in 1930, when the great philosopher, visionary and founder of the Society for Cosmic Wisdom, Dr. Wolfgang Goerner, had been asked by the owner of the Suddeutscher Brauerei to start a school for the children of his employees.

"Now that there are Archway Schools all over the world", she continued, "it is our great good fortune to have in our midst one of the few remaining teachers from the original foundation, Dr. Klaus Hübel. Since his retirement from teaching, Dr. Hübel has become one of the leaders of the Society for Cosmic Wisdom, and has played a major part in promulgating the philosophy on which our educational methods are based. He will give the opening address, so let's give him a warm welcome."

Hübel turned out to be the elderly man who had greeted Alison in the parking lot. Tom calculated that he must be well over eighty, so he was impressed when the old gentleman strode energetically up to the podium. Amid polite applause he shook hands with the red-haired woman, who then retired to a seat at the back of the stage.

In spite of his accent, Hübel spoke excellent English, giving his view of the state of education in Europe and the United States, and noting the problems, the chief of which seemed to be that although the teachers were doing the best they could, they had no true understanding of the real needs of the growing child and the maturing adolescent. The knowledge these teachers lacked, he said, was exactly what had been provided by Dr. Goerner.

It was at this point that Tom began to feel uncomfortable. This was supposed to be a public forum, but Hübel began to talk as though the audience were already familiar with Goerner, Cosmic Wisdom and the Archway schools. He stopped looking at his notes, and his discourse morphed into a continuous rhapsody delivered in a resonant, bell-like tone, in which he spoke ecstatically about Goerner's spiritual researches and what they meant about human evolution, child development and education. Tom came from a nominally Christian family in which no one believed anything in particular, and his mental apparatus included a sceptical streak that incoming ideas had to evade or penetrate. So when Hübel started talking about etheric and astral bodies and asserted that it was impossible to understand life on earth without the knowledge of reincarnation and karma, his remarks bounced off Tom's barrier, generating unsympathetic vibrations within and leaving him with the question of how Alison could possibly be involved with what looked like turning out to be a bunch of cranks. He turned and saw that she was biting her lip.

"Please don't leave yet", she whispered as the speech ended and Jane Malone returned to thank the speaker. "Klaus gets carried away sometimes."

Meanwhile, Jane was making an announcement.

"If you haven't already signed up for a workshop, you'll find the list on the bulletin board in the foyer. After the workshops there will be some refreshments in the cafeteria. Then we'll return here for a euphonics performance and some closing remarks."

Tom looked questioningly at Alison. She was still looking anxious.

"I forgot to tell you about the workshops. There's one on science that might interest you, although . . ."

"Although what?"

"Never mind—you'll see. Anyway, I'll be involved in something else for the next couple of hours but if you're still here I'll see you at the euphonics performance."

"What on earth is euphonics?"

"It's too hard to explain. I hope you like it."

"OK. Same place?"

"Just be here and we'll see each other."

Tom could get no more out of her, so he went off to the science workshop feeling vaguely disturbed and wondering what the "although" meant.

*

Major architectural changes had been needed to create the auditorium, but the rest of the big house had been left very much as it was when it was Tom's family home. Rooms that had seemed spacious to Lord Otterill's guests looked cramped when viewed as classrooms. Twenty-eight feet by twenty may seem ample for a bedroom but the situation is different when twenty-five desks are crammed into the same area. Joining twenty other people in a laboratory half the size of his physics lab at the Grammar School, Tom concluded that it was a general purpose lab, since there was a cabinet full of chemicals, another with miscellaneous electrical apparatus and a wall chart showing the different orders of invertebrates. After the opulence of the auditorium, this gave him the impression that science was not high on the list of priorities at the Archway schools.

The session was opened by a short, pudgy man who was wearing the usual dark suit and looking very uncomfortable in it. He had loosened his collar and tie, his jacket hung open and his curly brown hair flowed over his ears and down his neck. Tom couldn't identify his accent, which was an equal mixture of Hungarian, German and generalized American, and placed him incorrectly as a superannuated hippie. His name was Imre Takacs, and he talked a lot about how modern science was preoccupied entirely with measurements, numbers and abstract theories, whereas in the Archway schools there was a great effort to bring students into contact with the real essence of things, to dwell on what they actually see, hear, taste, touch and smell, before plunging into theories of atomic particles and such.

Tom, having arrived last, was forced to sit right in front of the speaker, and he was still digesting this last remark when a voice from the back bench said, "Surely atomic particles *are* the real essence of things."

Recognizing the Welsh inflections, Tom looked over his shoulder and saw Elwyn Davies, his friend and colleague from the Grammar School chemistry department. Davies, a tall, dark-haired native of Llandudno, continued in his best lecture room manner:

"All these sights and sounds are purely subjective impressions. An objective science has to be quantitative. When properly pursued, it will eventually explain all our sensations and feelings."

Takacs, unprepared for this sudden assault, was quite flummoxed. There was a long silence before he managed to pull himself together:

"We want our boys and girls to live into the actual phenomena and feel at one with them. Our science is phenomenological, not merely theoretical."

Davies was not to be put off.

"It seems to me that we have different ideas about what is or isn't phenomenological, and I don't know what you mean by 'merely theoretical.' It sounds as if you think a theory is just something that hasn't been proved, whereas if you're any kind of a scientist you must know that it's really a whole body of rules and principles with broad applicability to a wide range of phenomena."

Tom winced. He knew that Elwyn was no respecter of persons, and that when he got going he would be off into the history and philosophy of science and way over the heads of most of the other participants. He was still wondering what could possibly have brought the pragmatic Davies into this circle of idealists when an earnest Germanic voice spoke from the side of the room.

"My name is Carolina Ende. I am for the European Archway Schools the Science Coordinator. I believe it is at cross-purposes that here we speak. Dr. Goerner has said that the quantitative mathematical study of nature is essential and that our students should study the modern science. But he considered that they should before this be encouraged to see on the basis of their sense impressions how far they could proceed so that they would not in the end only in terms of atoms and molecules see things."

"But things *are* only atoms and molecules . . ."

Tom realized rather vaguely that he wasn't listening any more—he was thinking about Alison and wondering if she had anything on under her purple dress. Having seen Imre Takacs he thought he understood the reservation implied when she had said "although." He pulled himself together just in time to catch Frau Ende's parting shot. For some obscure reason, it stayed with him.

"A science that denies the validity of sense impressions must in the end contradict itself."

(6)

The signs to the cafeteria led to the back door of the main building and along a gravel path across a wide expanse of well-worn grass, which was obviously the playground. The dining area was big enough to accommodate twenty round tables with eight chairs apiece, and was separated from the kitchen by a wall containing a door and the serving hatch. Fruit bowls and plates of bread and cheese had been set out, and a round, russet lady with a Somerset accent was serving soup from a steaming vat on the counter. Large windows allowed the late afternoon sun to sparkle on the soup tureen and create flickering shafts in the aromatic steam. It was all very gracious and appetizing, but there was a little problem affecting Tom's digestive system; he wanted to know where Alison was and what mysterious activity she was up to. So when he bumped into Elwyn Davies he didn't feel like talking. Elwyn would say, "Hello, Tom, what are you doing here?" and Tom would have to mumble some kind of reply.

Elwyn did that and Tom mumbled, "Oh, I was just curious."

Brightening up a bit, he added, "What's more to the point, what the hell are you doing here? Not really your cup of tea, is it?"

"I take it you don't know anything about this gang and you haven't realized that everything you do in the classroom is wrong. You're teaching the wrong science by the wrong methods at the wrong time of day, and when your pupils get dyspepsia, asthma and arthritis at the age of thirty-five it'll be your fault."

"It's true I don't know anything about it. I just happened to meet someone and they seem like nice people so . . ."

"They're cranks and cranks usually are nice people. But they're also dangerous. If you'd read the works of this chap Goerner you'd know . . ."

"May I introduce myself? I'm Anne Weston—Faculty Chair at the Manhattan Archway School."

The speaker was a grey-haired woman of middle age and medium height, and Tom wondered why all the Archway women he had met wore some variety of mauve or purple.

"You are Thomas Dexter, aren't you, but I don't know your friend."

"Tom, not Thomas. And this is Elwyn Davies—he teaches chemistry at Glastonbury Grammar School. How do come to know my name?"

"Well, it seems we have a mutual friend. Alison Hübel told me all about you. She said you're a physics teacher"

Tom was struck speechless by this revelation. So Alison was the old gentleman's daughter or, more likely, granddaughter, and she had been talking to this New Yorker who seemed to be in charge of a school on the other side of the ocean, if that was what Faculty Chair meant. Tom had never heard of a Faculty Chair.

Getting his voice back, he asked, "Where is Alison now?"

"I assume that she's preparing for the euphonics performance that's due to begin in a few minutes."

"Euphonics", Elwyn broke in, "You're all very keen on that, aren't you?"

There was something in Elwyn's tone that Anne didn't like, but before she could reply Tom said, "What's euphonics?"

Anne had got as far as saying, "Well, I really wanted to talk to you about teaching . . ." when someone sounded a gong and announced that it was time to go back to the auditorium for the concert. Tom promised that he would talk to Anne later and hurried off to make sure he would get his old seat in the front row. It was beginning to dawn on him that Alison might have an ulterior motive.

*

At the left side of the auditorium five musicians finished their tuning. The house lights were dimmed and the curtain opened. The five women who stood on the stage seemed at first to be dressed only in long, filmy

27

flowing veils, but from his vantage point in the front row Tom could see that they actually did have something on underneath. Four of them were young and stood at the corners of a square, while an older woman with a stern expression stood at the center. The music began, something slow and solemn, and the women started to move. Tom realized with a shock that one of them was Alison.

"So that's what she meant when she said we should see each other", he thought.

The veils were various shades of magenta, red, orange and yellow and, with the motion and the changing light, gave the impression of a flickering fire. All moved lightly around the stage, with undulating motions of their arms, but the older woman remained the central figure. There was a momentary pause and the music changed to something merry and dance-like. As the women began to move with more flow and animation, one of the younger ones became the central figure, and Tom recognized her as the young blonde he had seen with Klaus Hübel and Alison earlier in the parking lot. They still didn't exactly dance, and no trace of enjoyment appeared on their faces. Tom appreciated the sheer beauty of the spectacle, and sensed that the whole thing in some way mapped the music, but after a while he began to feel that there was a quality of randomness about it that reminded him of Brownian motion. Alison passed in front of him several times without appearing to be conscious of his or anyone else's presence, but as the music showed signs of coming to an end, she leaned slightly forward and gave him the shadow of a wink.

The dancers, if that's what they were, retired gracefully to hearty applause, in which Tom joined, but nobody took much notice of the musicians, who took their instruments and their stands and disappeared quietly through a side door. When he came in Tom had been too preoccupied with Alison to bother with his program, but now he looked at it and saw the following:

Mozart: String Quintet in G Minor—Finale

The New York Euphonics Ensemble

Tom figured out that the Euphonics Ensemble were the people on the stage and not the musicians, and saw that next item was a poem by Wolfgang Goerner. After a fairly long pause, the stern-faced lady reappeared in different colors, and someone began to speak in a sepulchral voice from the side of the stage. Alison slipped back into her seat next to Tom, who had no idea what the poem was about, since it was in German. The sensation of Brownian motion absent, and now there was a feeling of strength and purpose.

"That was Kara Henkemens", Alison whispered during the applause. "I think she's the world's greatest euphonist."

"How about you? You looked pretty good."

"Oh, I'm only a bit-part player. They think I don't take things seriously enough."

This was said ruefully and without rancor.

The conversation was interrupted by the start of Mozart's Turkish Rondo, done as a solo by the blonde girl, who was now dressed in what looked like some form of Central European national costume. This time she really did seem to be dancing. Her twirling skirt revealed that she had nice knees to go with her classical figure, and her hair, escaping from its tightly twisted bun, flowed down over her shoulders and sparkled in the ever-changing light.

*

After the concert Kara Henkemens gave a short talk in which she explained that euphonics had been developed by Dr. Goerner in an effort to make the inner workings of speech and music visible to the outer eye. This didn't exactly set Tom on fire, since his interest in music and poetry was of the casual sort, but he paid enough attention to get to the point of wondering why anyone would want to do that. An elderly gentleman with a Somerset burr introduced himself as Bill Graveney, the chairman of the Trustees of the Wolfgang Goerner School. He expressed the hope that visitors had enjoyed themselves and found something to think about, and he thanked all the participants, especially Klaus Hübel and the euphonists. As the applause started, Alison nudged Tom and said, 'Let's go."

"I didn't want you to get caught", she said, as they made their way to Tom's car. "I know Anne Weston has her beady eye on you and there might be other complications."

Tom found this a bit puzzling but, before he could say anything, Alison went on.

"What do you think?" she asked.

29

"I think you're very beautiful."

Alison laughed.

"That wasn't quite what I meant, but I'll take it."

"It's only eight o'clock. We could walk down to the river and have a bite of bread and cheese at the Ship Inn. Then you could tell me all about it."

"OK, this might be tricky but give me a minute and I'll be with you."

Alison ran back to the school entrance, and disappeared. She was gone so long that Tom began to think she must have changed her mind. When she eventually reappeared she looked anything but cheerful.

"I just had a scene with someone, but let's go anyway. Don't worry about it, but could we drive? I don't want to have to talk to anyone else."

So they drove out of the main gate, watched by a grinning Elwyn Davies and unaware that Imre Takacs was peering out at them from among his brown curls with a furious expression on his fat face.

(7)

The Ship Inn had the advantage of being just down the road from a thoroughly spoilt English pub. "The Lady of the Lake" had once been "The Queen's Arms", a nice rustic inn with the traditional public bar for the lower classes and a private bar, latterly known as a "lounge", where the more affluent could pay an extra threepence a pint for their beer and enjoy a little peace and quiet. Now the public bar had been replaced with a posh dining room, the lounge was adorned with television screens, and the whole place was crowded with sight-seers. People who preferred an old-fashioned atmosphere took the narrow lane down to the stream that shared the name of Otterill with Tom's father, and enjoyed the peaceful delights of well-worn stools and benches, home-brewed ale, quiet conversation and the little *thups* of the dart board. The Ship lay only a foot or so above flood level, but in the middle of summer no one seemed to worry about this.

Tom and Alison were silent for the five minutes it took to drive to the Ship. There were no class distinctions, so they made straight for the bar and Tom asked Alison whether she could drink English beer or preferred something stronger.

"I'll have a double Scotch", she said, "as long as this is a Dutch treat. And let's leave the bread and cheese until later."

"I gather something unpleasant happened", Tom said after buying the Scotch and his pint of bitter. "Let's go over to the corner and if you want to you can tell me about it."

They settled in the corner where oak window benches met at right angles and red and white hollyhocks peered in through the window, still bright in the setting sun. Alison said, "I think I'd better tell you the whole story, if you're willing to hear it."

"I've been wondering if there was a story. This isn't by any chance a recruiting trip, is it?"

"No, it just sort of happened. There you were and you were a physics teacher and you made a pass at me. I don't usually respond to passes from total strangers but you did it rather nicely and for once I thought yeah, let's go, only . . . Well, things were just too complicated."

"And then they got uncomplicated? And you don't need a physics teacher after all?"

"I want to tell you the whole story, Tom, only I'm scared you might decide that you don't want to have any more to do with me."

"It would have to be pretty bad for that to happen. Anyway, I can't stand the suspense, so you'd better tell me the worst."

"It *is* pretty bad, but I truly don't think I've done anything wrong. I work at the Archway School in New York . . ."

"Where Anne Weston is Faculty Chair, whatever that means—what does it mean?"

"Only that we don't have the usual kind of principal. We elect one of the teachers to do the job. We do need a physics teacher, but I'm not really a complete airhead. I know you have a job here and you'd never heard of Archway. It's just that we had been discussing what to do if we couldn't get anyone, and I turned around from that tree and there was this big hunk with a funny face and a humorous expression, and it just popped out. When I got home I was thinking I'd much rather be in a pub with you. They started talking about finding a physics teacher, and I said I had just met one. They wanted to know all about you, and I told them I didn't know anything. So they said I should find out."

"Who's 'they'?"

"I'm staying in the same house as Imre, Klaus and one of the euphonists. Anne Weston was there too."

31

"So they sent you out to make a reconnaissance the next day? I thought it was because you wanted to see me."

"It was. I told them you'd be coming to the conference and I'd talk to you here—they don't know I saw you on Friday. And you never told me how smart I was to get that message through to you."

"I'm sorry—I was so excited at seeing you and whisking you away that I forgot all about it. How did you do it?"

"Well, I told them I was going to the town library to do some research on Glastonbury. Imre said he was interested and wanted to come with me, so I told him I had a headache and wanted to lie down for a while first. When he wasn't looking I just snuck out. I found one of those nice red phone booths, looked up the school number and left a message. I thought Imre would probably look for me so I didn't go near the library. I just went and waited for you. When I got home he asked me sarcastically if I'd found out anything interesting about Glastonbury. I told him I had, which was true."

"You were very smart and I love you very much, and I don't believe you've done anything bad."

None of this was the real trouble, Tom was thinking, so he asked Alison what had upset her after the show.

"Well, first of all, Klaus saw me wink at you. You're not supposed to show any sort of emotion or feeling or anything when you're performing. Klaus got very annoyed—he's what they call very 'echt' in CW circles, takes everything very seriously and thinks winking is definitely not kosher."

"Well he'll get over it, surely."

"I expect so. But then there's Imre. He was furious when he found out that I was going to the pub with you."

"Why should Imre be furious? Does he have his eye on you?"

"Well, it's all very complicated. You see Klaus is the real problem."

"Klaus? You don't still have to worry about your father's opinion, do you? Or is he your grandfather?"

Alison looked forlornly at Tom.

"He isn't my father or my grandfather. He's my husband."

(8)

Tom had been living in a wonderful new world for the past couple of days, and the bottom had just dropped out of it. He stood up.

"Come on", he said, "I'll take you back to your husband. Will he still be at the school?"

"I don't know. For God's sake sit down and listen. This isn't one of those movies where I say, 'I can explain everything' and you say, 'I don't want explanations.' Maybe after you've heard the story you'll still like me a little bit."

Tom sat, still quivering inside.

"Talk", he said, "and you'd better make it good. Why didn't you tell me you were married?"

"Because I don't really feel like I am, and because I wanted to see you and get away for a few hours. Only you don't know what I was trying to get away from."

"All right, I'll listen."

"OK. You heard Jane talking about how Archway got started. Well, Klaus and my grandfather taught at the first Archway School and they were both totally purple."

"Purple! What the hell is it about purple, not to mention mauve, lavender and lilac?"

"Well, something Goerner said gave people the idea that purple was the proper color for human beings to wear. I don't think he meant it like that, but it got to be a sort of badge, so when you say someone's purple it means they're hook, line and sinker CW. It's really the same as saying 'echt'."

Tom could see that this was going to be a long explanation and he wasn't sure how much of it he could take, so he decided just to concentrate on staying relaxed.

"Anyway", Alison continued, "my mother went to the school as a little girl and Klaus was her class teacher, and then nearly everyone went to America because of the Nazis. Someone had started an Archway school in Manhattan, and they all descended on it and more or less took it over. There was a big fight and the original people went off to Massachusetts and started another one. So my grandfather taught chemistry in Manhattan, my mother went into the elementary school and Klaus was her teacher through eighth grade. What's the matter, Tom—you're not going to faint, are you?"

"No, I'm just practicing deep breathing. I just wanted to know why you married Klaus and why you didn't tell me about it, and now you're telling me your whole life story."

"I'm sorry. I think it's the influence of CW—everything always has to go back to the creation. Please be patient with me—I'll be as quick as I can."

"OK, I'm working on it. How did Klaus get to be a big wheel?"

"Well he did a lot of things besides class-teaching, but the biggy was that he was the first male euphonist."

Tom had been having association problems with the word "euphonist", and now he had a mental image of Klaus festooned with multicolored veils and playing a huge euphonium. He told Alison about it and she apparently didn't find it funny.

"Have I dropped a brick?" he asked.

"No, it's just that it suddenly struck me as a bit too symbolic—the big euphonium seems kind of Freudian. Anyway, the purple rubbed off on my mother, so when she was in high school she decided she wanted to be a euphonist like Klaus. After the war Klaus went back to Ulm and Mom decided go and study with him. He was very sweet on Mom, but he was twenty-three years older so he really didn't have much chance. OK, I know that sounds stupid in view of what happened later. Can I have another drink? Here's some money."

"Same again?"

"No, I'll have some of your warm English beer."

Tom returned with Alison's beer and her change and a refill for himself.

"For your information it's tapped up from the cellar at about 55 degrees."

Alison sipped.

"It's just right and it seems to have real hops in it. Klaus gave up on Mom and married a euphonist who was even younger. He took over the Euphonics School and wound up as head of the CW Governing Council. After my Mom qualified, she taught at the Ulm school for a long time. Then she came here for the summer conference in 1961 and met my father. In those days there was just a little elementary school in an old farmhouse and people slept in the barn or in tents. My Dad was teaching in the New York school, and he came over and they really hit it off. Mom had to go back to Ulm for a couple of months while they found another euphonics teacher, and when Dad met her off the plane at JFK she was pregnant."

"And that was you?"

"That was me."

"Are you telling Mr. Dexter your life story, my dear?"

Tom and Alison had been so involved in their conversation that they didn't notice Imre Takacs until he was standing right over them.

"You think it right that he should know that you were—how do you say—a shotgun baby? I thought you were going to talk about education."

"Imre, get the hell out of here and mind your own business. And I'm not your dear."

Takacs sat down very close to Alison, put his hand on her knee and said, "You may not be my dear but I *am* minding my own business."

"Come on, Tom, we're leaving."

The Hungarian's hand was now on Alison's shoulder, making it hard for her to stand up.

"I do not think that this is wise", he said.

Alison shrugged him off and made for the door.

Tom paused for a moment. Looking down at the plump little man he remarked, "I'd enjoy knocking your block off if I could reach that low."

He followed Alison back to the car in the pleasant dusk of a warm July evening.

(9)

Tom saw Takacs emerging from the pub, so he started his engine and drove slowly up the lane.

"Can't you just tell me why you married Klaus? He must be about sixty years older than you are."

"OK, I'll try. After Klaus went back to Ulm he came to visit us sometimes in New York, and everyone thought he was awesome. By the time I was twelve I had an acute case of hero worship for him and I had no idea how old he was. I was so much like my mother that I think he felt as if I was a new little Maria. So I decided I wanted to be a euphonist, and when I was fifteen I started asking my parents if I could go and study with him in Germany. My Dad thought that Klaus was the most spiritual thing ever created—after Goerner of course—but Mom wasn't so sure and she didn't want me to go."

"My Mom died when I was sixteen. A few months later my Dad met someone from the Massachusetts school and decided to move there. She was twenty-five, very pretty and really with it. They soon got married, and

35

I thought it was my opportunity, so I told him I wanted to go to Europe for the summer before college and he didn't argue. I went to see Klaus and he persuaded me to stay and study with him, and I have to admit that I didn't take much persuading. He was on his third wife by then and they had a big house with a studio and lots of spare rooms, so I moved in with them. I don't know whether you can understand this but I was seventeen and Klaus still seemed like God. So if he wanted me and said it was our destiny, that was it as far as I was concerned."

Horribly detailed pictures of an old man and a young girl flooded Tom's imagination, making it difficult to drive, but he thought that the headlights behind him belonged to Takacs, so he kept going.

"We're being followed", he said.

"Imre is such an idiot. The trouble is we're all staying in the same house, so if you take me home I'll have to talk to him, and if you don't he'll know I'm out with you."

Tom had the advantage of knowing the countryside. He accelerated as hard as he could in the old Morris, made a hair-raising turn into a narrow lane and switched off the lights. Takacs had also accelerated but, unprepared for the turn, he had to keep going. By the time he had found somewhere to turn around, Tom had driven into another lane, opened a five-barred gate and backed into a field.

"Well", said Alison, "You're more of a daredevil than I expected. Are you going to seduce me now or later?"

"Probably both."

Tom's arms were already around her, but the design of the car, with the gear lever between bucket seats, made this rather uncomfortable, so they moved into the back seat.

"You may find this hard to believe", Alison said, "but I've never done anything like this before. When I ought to have been doing it Klaus had already swept me off my feet."

A pair of headlights seemed for a moment to point straight at them, but then they moved off slowly into the distance.

"With any luck he'll get lost. OK, go on. I don't like the story but I need to hear the rest before—only . . ."

"Only what?"

Tom had been exploring Alison's body almost absent-mindedly.

"Don't you ever wear a bra?"

"Well Klaus told me it inhibited the way I moved, and anyway I happen to be blessed with what they call a boyish figure, so I don't bounce when I walk. It's like some men don't wear underpants. And before we get any hotter I think you'd better know what kind of scene you're getting into. I mean, I guess you don't make a habit of screwing married women"

"That's true and I expect you're right—but I'm still holding on to you, and I absolutely don't want to know about Klaus's underpants."

"It's good you can see the funny side of things. Klaus laughs quite a lot but he doesn't really have a sense of humor—well, not like that. Are you still angry with me?"

"Well, I have a feeling that I might go off bang at any moment, but I don't think I'm angry with you. It's sort of hard to tell."

"I'm afraid you're going to get angrier before I've finished. Anyway, if you get involved with CW you'll find we're pretty much like everyone else when it comes to self-justification, but we have the advantage of being able to say 'It's our karma.' And it's mostly pure B-S. Klaus was overwhelming and he didn't need to talk much about karma, but his wife did. She was only about ten years older than I was, but she knew from experience what was going on. At first she thought it was her destiny to share him with me, but when Klaus stopped sharing, which happened pretty soon, she got fed up and moved out. It split the euphonics school from top to bottom. She went off somewhere in Austria, taking half of them with her, while the rest stayed in Ulm and talked gravely about *Schicksal*."

"*Schicksal?*"

"Destiny."

"So Klaus thought it was your destiny to marry him?"

"Yes, although marriage was a bit of an afterthought. His wife was very uncooperative at first, but before long she hooked up with someone nearer her own age and they arranged a convenient divorce."

"Didn't it seem, well, strange—I mean with someone that age?"

"Well, I didn't have much to compare it with, and if you want to know the truth, I still don't. Klaus was pretty athletic for an old man, but he was kind and gentle and somehow made it seem natural. And he was always very careful to make sure I didn't get pregnant. But lately he's begun to slow down so I've gradually changed from a kind of deeply spiritual lover to a paid companion and soon I guess I'll switch to being his nurse. Anyway, as far as sex is concerned I've already been playing second fiddle for a while."

37

"Not that young blonde who was dancing, or whatever you call it, with you? The one who looks like Hollywood rendered by a Greek sculptor? She looks about seventeen."

"She's nearly nineteen and when he first spotted her when she only fifteen."

Tom was genuinely shocked.

"I think", said Alison, "that the older he gets, the younger he needs them to turn him on. Well, maybe that's not quite fair. He gets genuine grand passions, and his excuse is that we rejected his spiritual guidance in previous incarnations, so now we have to fulfill our destinies through sex. This girl was a scholarship kid at the Archway School in London, and one time when Klaus was visiting he spotted her doing euphonics. He told her parents she was so talented that he would finance a year in Germany. He said it would be good for her development, which was kind of funny considering how well developed she was already. Anyway, she went to school in Ulm, learned a bit of German and a few months later she moved in with us so she could have what he called intensive training, which she certainly got. And I think he was genuinely besotted and not just using her for exercise"

"But didn't it cause a scandal?"

"Most people either don't know or turn a blind eye. Some of the really purple people say Klaus is so far above the rest of us in spiritual development that we can't even attempt to judge his actions."

"What do you think?"

"Well, at first I believed everything he told me, so I completely bought it. Now I'm not so sure, and I'm beginning to think that he isn't either. One certain thing is that you won't find anything like that in Goerner."

"And what about his new girl—I mean, doesn't she think the whole set-up is weird?"

"Well, as I said, there's a lot of glamour about being Klaus's wife or lover. It makes you feel very spiritual and important. But it wears off after a while, or it did for me at any rate. And I think it's beginning to wear a bit thin for Halcyon."

"Halcyon!"

"It's not her real name, but it's what he calls her, so now everyone else does, too. He even makes them print it on the programs."

"Why don't you divorce him?"

"I'm thinking about it, but I'm afraid he'll make it very difficult. He says our destinies are linked with his in different ways. She's the Mary and I'm to be the Martha and the funny thing is that I don't think she's the Mary type. She's very good-natured and down to earth, loves clothes—just a good wholesome girl who happens to be totally out of this world when she's doing euphonics, and doesn't spend a whole lot of time sitting at his feet and absorbing wisdom. I like her very much. Actually you were right in a way—he treats me a bit like a naughty daughter who is useful around the house and needs to be kept in line. He doesn't seem to mind what I do, as long as I'm there to attend to his needs and don't screw up when I'm performing."

"You mean he wouldn't mind if he could see us now?"

"Well he might, but not for the usual reason."

"What other reason is there?"

"It's Imre, and you've seen what he's like—a very weird mixture of smart and dumb and he's had his eye on me for years. Can you imagine? He went to the Archway School in New York, went all bug-eyed about Klaus, and eventually followed him back to Ulm. He studied chemistry with various CW dignitaries and somehow managed to get a job at the Ulm school. He never got a degree in anything, so he just hung around for a long time, teaching this, that and the other. The Massachusetts people think he's the great scientific authority, which is nuts, and every so often they implore him to go and give a course to the teachers. A few years ago Klaus kind of adopted him as unofficial secretary and yes-man, which I never understood because I don't think Klaus likes him. When Klaus retired from the Euphonics School the year before last, they needed a euphonist at the New York school, so I took the job. When we moved back to Manhattan Imre came along too, and we all live together in a brownstone on the Upper West Side. Anyway for some God-forsaken reason Klaus has decided to kind of farm me out, or leave me to Imre in his will, and Imre already wants to take possession."

"Klaus must be crazy. What about Halcyon?"

"He told her parents that a year in New York would widen her horizons, and he didn't tell them how much he'd already widened them, so she came along too and went into the 12th Grade. By the time she graduated she was eighteen, and she told her parents that she wanted to stay there for a while. I think it's really just her mother—she's always telling me things that her mother says, and Mom seems to take a very liberal view of life. You may find it hard to understand, but in spite of all this I'm still committed to Archway, CW and euphonics, and I'll be going back to New York next week. But I'm not committed to Klaus anymore. It's probably going to make a complete mess of my karma, but now you know the worst could we please get on with the seduction?"

"OK", said Tom, "but I warn you that when we've got all this sorted out I'm going to marry you."

The night was warm and pleasant, the air was balmy and relatively bug-free, the grass was thick and soft, the voluminous old raincoat that Tom kept in the back of the car guarded them from the possible perils of the cow pasture, and there was no one for miles around to overhear the sounds of their enjoyment.

An hour or so later they drove back to Ashwell Lane and crept upstairs to Tom's apartment. His bed was just wide enough to accommodate two people who were not averse to physical contact, and they managed to keep the dubious future sufficiently at bay to sleep contentedly for several hours. In the middle of the night Tom woke up and muttered to himself, "I wonder what the hell Klaus and Imre are doing."

Alison murmured sleepily, "Klaus is asleep and Imre is still sitting up."

Waking up a little she added, "Now I think it's my turn to seduce you."

It turned out that all three of these observations were correct.

(10)

Tom got up at 5:30 and made coffee and toast. He kissed Alison on the nose and said, "Hello, do you remember who I am?"

"Yes, you're King Solomon and I'm your newest concubine. Is it really time to get up?"

"You're better than all the other ten thousand put together, but it's Monday morning. I have to teach and I don't suppose you want to meet my landlord and landlady. There's no shower, I'm afraid, but there's a bathtub and plenty of hot water."

"Which is what I'm likely to be in soon."

By six o'clock they were out on the lane, sitting in Tom's car.

"I have to be in school by half past eight", he said. "Is there anything we can do for a couple of hours or do you want to go back and face the music? Surely Imre won't have sat up all night."

"I expect they're all asleep except for Halcyon. She gets up early to meditate, or that's what she says—I think it's really just to get away from Klaus for an hour or two. Anyway it would be nice if I could slip in without anyone seeing me. Do you still want to marry me?"

"Well . . ."

"No teasing!"

"Yes, of course I do, and I don't want to wait until Klaus dies? Couldn't we just live in sin? No one else seems to worry much about the conventions."

As if in response, the front door of the house opened and an elderly female voice called out, "Mr. Dexter!"

"Oh Lord", muttered Tom, "It's my landlady."

He got out of the car and said politely, "Good morning, Mrs. Trathgannon."

Mrs. Trathgannon opened the door a little further and revealed herself as a tall, grey-haired, desiccated woman in a long faded blue housecoat. Now that she had Tom's attention, she continued in a stage whisper:

"Be so kind as to come here for a moment. You may leave your paramour where she is."

While Tom was still deciding how to respond, Alison was already out of the car.

"Hi, Mrs. Whatever-your-name-is that I didn't quite catch, we weren't expecting you to be up so early or we'd have made a social call."

"Sssshhhh", hissed the landlady, looking apprehensively around at her neighbors' windows. "Mr. Dexter, I must ask you to keep this young woman in order and remember that this is a respectable neighborhood. Mr. Trathgannon and I have our reputation to keep up."

Deciding that a conversation with his landlady on the subject of her moral standing was not a good way of starting the day, Tom took Alison's arm and said, "We'd love to talk but we have an urgent appointment. I'll see you later, but don't worry—I'll be moving out soon."

"Nice to talk to you", Alison added as she got back into the car, which was out of sight before Mrs. Trathgannon could think of a suitable reply.

Tom's question was still hanging in the air, so he drove to the parking lot of the Grammar School.

41

"There won't be anybody here for at least an hour", he said. "Now, as I was saying when I was so rudely interrupted . . ."

Alison answered obliquely.

"You see, I'm third generation CW and I really caught the old fervor from my parents and Klaus and all the others—where we all thought we were specially privileged because we knew all this stuff from Wolfgang Goerner, and other people didn't believe what we knew. So we could do whatever the spirit moved us to, and the rest of the world could go to hell and probably would. There are still plenty of CW people who think that if it didn't come from Goerner there must be something wrong with it, but some of us have realized that the rest of the world isn't as dumb as we thought it was. And then you get someone like Klaus who's a marvelous euphonist, knows everything that Goerner ever said and quite a bit that he didn't, and seems intensely spiritual, and we all take him at face value as if he were the messenger of God. I can't tell you how privileged I felt. It was almost like having sex with Goerner himself."

"And now you wish you hadn't? You think Klaus is just a dirty old man taking advantage of innocent kids?"

"I'm not sure about that. I believed him when he said it was our spiritual destiny, and I think he believed it too. And then again, maybe he just conveniently convinced himself. I'm not even sure I wish it hadn't happened. I mean, I think if he were just a D. O. M. I'd find him as disgusting as Imre, only in a different way, and I don't. I just wish I weren't married to him."

Alison broke off, looking anxiously at Tom.

"I really want you and it's not just because you're smart, healthy, funny and never heard of Goerner. Something just kind of clicked inside me and the problem is, like I said, I'm damaged goods and confused and maybe a bit ashamed into the bargain."

Something inside Tom felt as if it had been dragged through the wringer. He knew that the only remedy would be for the two of them to take complete possession of each other.

"It isn't that I don't care about your past, and you know I'm not exactly pristine myself, but I'm head-over-heels in love with you and I think if we were together the past wouldn't really matter."

"Let's try it, Tom. There's lots of things to figure out but yes, let's give it a whirl. O God, I'm trying to be calm and rational but I'm so excited

I can hardly see straight. I just hope Klaus will agree to a divorce if he realizes I'm leaving anyway."

"What about Imre?"

"Imre doesn't come into it—that's just Klaus's funny idea. But I really hope I can get a divorce. It would be kind if nice to have a regular, conventional marriage."

"We weren't exactly conventional last night."

"I don't know. I think having a date and ending up in bed with each other is socially acceptable."

"Even if one of us is married?"

"The way things are with Klaus I sometimes forget I'm still married to him."

"How do you think he's going to take it when you tell him what's up?"

"He'll probably go very quiet, and then he'll give me a long lecture about the spiritual implications, but he won't fly into a rage. And I really do believe that everything we do has spiritual implications—it's just that I don't automatically believe Klaus's version any more. And Imre already knows what I think of him."

"It strikes me he has a nasty streak in him—maybe I should come with you."

"Well, I guess he does—maybe it's something to do with having had a very difficult time as a kid in Ulm and New York—and he has a sly way of insinuating himself with unsuspecting CW's. But I'm not scared of him and Klaus wouldn't let anything bad happen."

Tom looked surprised and Alison said, "I know—it's really weird how Klaus is. He's obsessed with young girls and Cosmic Wisdom, but apart from that he's just a kind old man who wouldn't hurt a fly. And is it OK if I tell Halcyon about us? She may not look it, but she's as strong as a horse and very down to earth. If anything unpleasant happens we can deal with it together."

"OK, you can tell her. Maybe she'd like to be a bridesmaid, or have you got zillions of sisters?"

"No sisters—my mother had a very bad time when I was born and she couldn't have any more children. How about you?"

"I'm an only. What about your parents?"

"There's only one. My father's second marriage only lasted a few years, and after the divorce he went all withdrawn and introspective. Will you wait for me if Klaus makes things difficult?"

"Of course I'll wait for you, but if it takes too long I'll just tuck you under my arm and carry you off. And waiting doesn't mean not seeing each other. I mean, after last night how long do you really think we can leave each other alone?"

"Not very long, Tom . . . We'll find a way."

This was a kind of resolution and eventually Alison said, "I think I'd better go back and start sorting things out. What time do you get out of school this afternoon?"

"Four o'clock."

"Can you meet me at the Ship at six? We have meetings all day, but we have the evening off."

"OK, I'll be sitting next to the hollyhocks."

"I don't think there's any way you can call me, but I'll leave a message for you at school if something happens."

"OK. Flossie would love to talk to you again. She's very sweet really and has an eligible daughter and seems to think I need mothering."

As Alison was getting out of the car fifty yards from the residence of a certain Mrs. Eleanor Barrington-Smythe, Tom said, "I had a little bit of a fling with her once—just so you know . . ."

"Who—Flossie?"

"No, bird-brain, Wendy, her daughter—very sexy at first sight, but on closer acquaintance almost as motherly as her mother."

"Well, I hope you're not expecting me to mother you. Here goes, wish me luck!"

It was just starting to rain, so Alison did a skipping sprint to the front door. As she was carefully closing it, it occurred to Tom that he ought to have told her what kind of family she would be marrying into. Well, he could take care of that later.

(11)

Archway conference delegates from foreign countries usually arrive in London, travel to the adjacent town of Castle Cary by way of British Rail, and make the final hop to Glastonbury by bus. For most of them, car rental is financially out of the question, so once they have been deposited at the bus stop, they are dependent on their hosts for transportation around the town.

Klaus, Imre, Alison and Halcyon were staying in the house of an elderly widow who was one of the benefactors of the Wolfgang Goerner School. Klaus could easily have afforded a rental car, but Mrs. Barrington-Smythe had a temperamental old shooting brake, an antique, wood-paneled version of the modern station wagon, which he and Imre found amusing to drive. While their hostess was taking the waters a hundred and fifty miles away at Harrogate Spa, Klaus and Halcyon occupied her blameless bedroom, Imre slept in the second bedroom, and Alison slept on a camp bed in the box room.

When Alison got back she found the house absolutely quiet, so she tiptoed upstairs to her little room, only to find Halcyon wearing a short diaphanous violet nightie and sitting on the camp bed with a book in each hand. One of them was a Bible and she quickly tucked the other under the covers, but not before Alison saw the name "D. H. Lawrence" on the cover.

"So that's what you read when you get up early in the morning—and I always thought you were studying Goerner."

Halcyon started to say something disrespectful about Goerner, but changed her mind.

"I had a dust-up with Klaus last night. He doesn't want me any more and he wants you to start sleeping with him again. So he said I was to sleep here and tell you to go to him when you got home."

"And you're reading that just to get even with him?"

"Sort of—I read a bit of Laurence and a bit of the Bible just to balance things up." Halcyon began to cry.

"Sorry", she said after a while, "I'm not crying because Klaus has turned me out of his bed—it's really a relief. It's just that I'm so messed up I can't think straight. You've been through this, haven't you, except that you're actually married to him? What do I do now—just pack up and go home?"

"You'd better tell me how it happened. I mean, what was the dust-up about?"

Halcyon's story came out in a continuous, breathless, unpunctuated stream.

"Well, it was about you, as a matter of fact. You went off with that carroty hunk and Imre went chasing after you and Klaus said not to worry, you were just trying to get a physics teacher, but I had seen the two of you together and I said, 'Oh yeah, and why is Imre following them and how are we going to get home?' He didn't say anything—just went and talked to Jane Malone and they squeezed us into their car and he didn't say a word all the way back. When we got here he told me he wanted some coffee, so I made it for him and he told me to go to bed. Half an hour later he came up and said I would be sleeping in the box room for the rest of the time, so I said what about you and he more or less told me to mind my own business. So I said considering what I had given him I had a right to know what was going on and he said what I had given him was nothing to what he had given me and that my karma had been to fulfill his physical needs so that he would could range freely in the spirit and my task was now complete so I could go and sleep in the box room and spend the rest of my life being grateful for the privilege. Well, he didn't say that last bit but you know how his mind works. And now you're supposed to sleep with him and between you and me I don't think you have to worry too much about his physical needs—I think the old boy is getting past it. He says my aura has become too active for him and yours is much more restful. So I asked him what's going to happen when we get back to New York and he said not to worry, he would make sure I was taken care of, so at that point I lost it. I told him I used to think he was so bloody spiritual that he might be taken up on a fiery chariot at any moment and now I can see he's just a nasty old man with a hyperactive penis only now he can't get it up any more and it's like having sex with your great-grandfather. And the worst of it was he didn't lose his temper, he just went so pale I thought he was going to faint and he got more and more gentle and told me I'm the most wonderful euphonist he's ever had and I should stick to that and not try to think too much. He said it was my destiny to do my thinking in my next life. So he made me get my things and come in here and tell you to go to him as soon as you got back. Only I don't think he was expecting you to be out all night. Anyway, I was just trying to get to sleep when Imre got back, so I opened the door and listened a bit. They went into Klaus's room and shut the door and this time Klaus did lose his temper and so did Imre, but I couldn't really hear what they were saying—it was just a lot of shouting. After a few minutes the door opened and they went on shouting and Imre said, 'Never say I haven't warned you' and Klaus said, 'I can't keep her under lock and key—if you want her, you will have to use your own powers of persuasion, and if she seems not to care for you

I do not find that surprising.' And Imre said, 'Don't forget, just don't forget', and Klaus said, "One day you will suffer the consequences of my forgetfulness", and slammed the door and I got into bed and Imre came in here and looked at me. I can't tell you how scared I was. I thought he wanted to rape me but after a minute he shook his head and went away. I heard him prowling around the house for hours and I thought, No, Mr. Takacs, he's taking Alison back and he said you could have me if you can get me, so just you try, and I waited till it got quiet and crept down and got the rolling pin from the kitchen."

Alison laughed.

"You shouldn't have bothered, Halcyon, it's not you he wants."

Halcyon pointed at Alison.

"You? But I didn't think that was serious."

"I know—you thought he was just trying it on. Well he doesn't want to rape me, although I'd love to get him with the rolling pin. He wants me to be Mrs. Takacs, so rape wouldn't quite fit into his plans. Anyway, none of it really makes sense. I guess you didn't know Klaus was planning to pass me on to Imre, so why he wants me back now I can't imagine, unless it's just to nurse him till he dies. You're a good kid, Halcyon, and I think your best bet would be to go back to London and talk nicely to your parents."

"But I like it in New York."

"Maybe, but do you really want to live in a madhouse?"

"Klaus said I would be taken care of . . . Look out, here he comes."

Klaus appeared at the door in a dressing gown of deep purple silk.

"Good morning, Alison, I trust you slept well."

"Good morning, Klaus, very well indeed. And you?"

"Not so well. And your friend Mr. Dexter—did he sleep well?"

"I really don't know", said Alison, which was quite true since she had slept exceedingly well when not actively engaged. "You'll have to ask him. And how about Imre? He seems to have kept Halcyon awake most of the night."

"Imre was with you?" Klaus said to Halcyon in a startled tone.

"Well, I thought you told him he could have me if he could get me. But you were right, I don't like him very much and neither does Alison."

Klaus turned on his heel and marched straight into Imre's room. Finding it empty he went downstairs, followed closely by Alison, with Halcyon trailing in the background. Imre presented an unlovely sight, sleeping fully dressed on his back on the drawing room sofa, with his mouth open and a tangled mess of curly hair obscuring most of his face. Klaus was about to give him a good shake, but Alison took his arm and said, "For goodness sake don't wake him up—I want to talk to you. Let's go in the kitchen."

Seeing Halcyon standing in the doorway, Klaus said, "You must go to your room and wait for me."

"I'm not sure which is my room."

Klaus was momentarily flummoxed.

"My room. The room where we have customarily slept—I have changed my mind."

"Well, all I can say is I hope the new one's an improvement."

Halcyon started up the stairs and stopped halfway as Klaus and Alison disappeared into the kitchen. She crept down to the bottom step and was still sitting there several minutes later when she heard a loud snort. A moment later an extremely disheveled Imre stumbled out of the drawing room.

(12)

Alison thought that she was going to do the talking, but as they sat down at the kitchen table Klaus got his blow in first.

"I begin to feel very old. You are my wife, and it is your duty to provide for the needs of your husband. And, as I have told you, when I have passed over, Imre will take responsibility for you. Why do you laugh?"

"I can't help it, Klaus—there must be at least six different reasons. First of all there's this string of teenage girls you've had providing for your needs, which have been pretty remarkable for an old man, and when we're too old for you at the age of twenty-something you get a new one and find some way of disposing of the old one. You just need something new, shiny and inexperienced to turn you on, and the funny thing is I think maybe you sincerely believe that it's all for the sake of your spirituality. Well, when I was seventeen you convinced me, and you persuaded Minna it was time to move along. So when I reach the advanced age of twenty-three you ditch me, and the baton, to give it a polite name, passes along to Halcyon, who is a nice kid and a genius at euphonics. Now at the age of eighty-four you suddenly discover that it's you who's too old. You're losing your sexual prowess, so you want me back as a live-in nurse. And to put the finishing touch on it, as soon as you start expanding into the celestial regions and don't need me any more, Imre can have me. You saw him a minute ago. Can you imagine how disgusting it feels to be wanted by Imre?"

Klaus maintained his dignity.

"My dear child, there are, as you know, spiritual realities that make these strange relationships necessary. If you do not fulfill your proper destiny in this life, your suffering in your next incarnation will be terrible."

Alison had stopped laughing.

"I don't know about Halcyon, but I've decided to do my thinking in this incarnation. Maybe you seriously believe all that stuff about sex and our destinies, but I don't think you got it from Goerner. I don't trust your advice and I'm not taking orders from you. I can understand why you want me to stay and nurse you until you leave, and I don't think there's anything particularly spiritual about it. Since you switched your attentions to Halcyon, why don't you get her to nurse you? And as for Imre, there's no explanation for that idea except senile fantasy."

Regretting the harshness of this last remark, Alison added, "I'm sorry, Klaus. Incredible though it may seem I still have some affection for you. I'll help you if I can, but I have a life of my own and I can't make any promises."

Klaus was clearly shaken. His shoulders sagged and he now he spoke more as a parent might and less as a spiritual authority.

"You must do as you think best, child, and it comes to me now that perhaps you are right. I have begun to see more clearly my imperfections as a human being and to be less confident in my spiritual powers; but, if you will believe it, I love you more than anyone else in the world. And you must not think that I am senile. There will be great risks involved in this life, as well as in the next, if you do not do as I have said."

Klaus sat up straight and looked searchingly into Alison's face.

"Yes, you are strong, brave and gifted with insight—a little flighty, perhaps, but that may be an advantage. You must be very, very strong."

The door opened and Klaus looked around.

"Now here is Imre", he said.

Alison noticed that he didn't ask Imre how he had slept.

(13)

Tom taught his first two classes that morning in something of a daze. When he went to get his cup of tea at the mid-morning break, the first person he met was Elwyn Davies.

When Tom and Elwyn were not discussing scientific or educational matters, their conversation consisted mainly of cheerful badinage, so Elwyn's first remark was, "Hello, Tom, how's the romance going?"

"What romance?" Tom asked defensively.

"My spies are everywhere. Not only did I see you driving off with that gorgeous euphonist yesterday, but I also happen to know that last week you were dallying with a very sexy girl wearing next to nothing."

"Not true—I was fully dressed, and let me guess; Marilyn Robinson and Janet Jones."

"Holed in one", said Elwyn. "They were having a good cackle together before school, so I made the mistake of asking them what it was all about and they described this sexy young athlete in the most lurid terms. They said you had gone all goopy and it looked like love at first sight, and furthermore they saw you drive off with her at an amazing speed on Friday."

This was so close to the truth that Tom couldn't think of anything to say. Realizing that he might have put his foot in it, Elwyn said, "Sorry, old chap. She looks like a terrific girl and I hope it goes well."

"That's OK. I may want to tell you about it some time, if you can stand it."

Elwyn tried to put the conversation back on its usual light-hearted footing.

"Euphonics seems to attract desirable women. I don't suppose you could get me an introduction to that other young one—the one who looks like a kind of Venus de Marilyn Monroe and seems to go under the name of Halcyon. She really makes things stand up and take notice. OK, I wasn't serious and I don't think my wife would approve. Tell me what you think of these Archway people."

Tom pulled himself together.

"A lot of this Archway stuff sounds like pure mumbo-jumbo, but every so often someone says something so sensible that I wonder if they're really on to something. You know I'm not particularly satisfied with what we're doing here. Why did you say these people are dangerous?"

Seeing the look in Elwyn's eye, Tom added, "Not a whole dissertation—we only have three minutes."

"Well, you know I think the only way to save the human race is to cut out all this so-called spirituality, which is a mixture of fraud and sentimentality, and make a complete commitment to science. To cut a very long story very short, although Goerner sometimes says that it's very important for people to understand modern science, when you come down to the details you can see that he thinks that it's completely up the pole. You heard the way those people were talking yesterday. Goerner thinks atomic science is pure codswallop and that nature works through etheric forces governed by planetary influences—whatever that means. It's easy to dismiss them as a bunch of cranks, but the trouble is they have schools all over the world where this stuff is being preached, and they have influence, not only on the usual crop of old maids but on a lot of young people too. Some of the schools are supported with government money, so resources that ought to be used for real education and research are being used to promote this antiscientific agenda."

"Do you think there's some really sinister purpose behind all this? I mean, you make it sound like a nuisance and a pain in the neck, but is it really dangerous?"

"I think it would be if it ever reached critical mass."

"And you don't think there's any possibility that some of this stuff might be true?"

"My God, that girl really has turned your head!"

The bell rang for the end of morning break, and the two men had to hurry off to their respective labs. Just for a moment Tom was thinking about Halcyon, instead of Alison. Elwyn had made a neat allusion to the Venus de Milo, but from what Tom had seen on the stage, Halcyon was really not the voluptuous, lips-and-bust Marilyn Monroe type at all; more like Doris Day, perhaps, and probably capable of being a Calamity Jane. It was a pleasant thought, but it didn't last long. Alison was soon back in full command.

Tom had the pleasure of a double period with a small class of students who would shortly be taking their exams in advanced level physics. Nearing the end of a survey of everything they had studied over the past two years, they were reviewing the list of particles discovered in the twentieth century.

Marilyn and Janet were both in this class and, when not giggling over matters romantic, they were quite serious students. Janet was very gifted but it was only by sheer determination that Marilyn kept her head above water, so while Tom was patiently explaining something that Marilyn hadn't grasped the first time around, Janet was thinking about what it would have been like to be a scientist in the early years of the century.

When the explanation was finished, she raised her hand and asked, "It couldn't happen like that now, could it, Mr. Dexter? I mean, a huge discovery made by one man in a little lab with a few assistants. Now it takes billions of pounds, a place like a factory and scads and scads of scientists."

"That's true", Tom said. "And if you go back a bit further, to people like Faraday and Dalton, it's usually pretty much a one man show."

Another student said, "It really seems as if being a scientist is nowhere near as much fun as it used to be—it's so impersonal, like a lot of ants running around finding things out but it's only the queen ant that really knows what's going on."

"Except it's usually the king ant", Janet added ruefully. "And I sometimes wonder whether it's really all true. I mean, when you meet an attractive girl, do you really think she's just a configuration of atoms and molecules? That's what Mr. Davies says."

"No, I don't", said Tom, with touch of feeling in his voice, and hastily added, "Now it's time to move on to Alison's discovery of the positron."

"Alison's?"

"Oh, I meant Anderson's."

Tom's face turned a deep red and someone tittered in the back row.

(14)

There was no message from Alison, so Tom drove out to the Ship through the on-and-off showers that had persisted all day. He bought himself a drink and waited in the corner by the hollyhocks. His previous amorous excursions had always been casual and uncomplicated, and he felt some resentment that the joy of his new love affair was tainted by such a malign collection of problems. This was not the kind of courtship he had imagined. Klaus would say that it was the working of karma, and Elwyn would talk about the results of statistical processes and self-replicating super-molecules, but Tom could think only of Alison and the highly problematical circumstances in which he had met her. Alison had called herself damaged goods and Tom could see in a way that this was true. His sense of sexual morality was pretty relaxed and he had never expected to marry a virgin, but it still seemed to him that Klaus's treatment Alison, not to mention Halcyon and his former wives and mistresses, was scandalous and bound to leave emotional scars. Tom was fairly confident that the best cure would be an extended period of monogamy, but it seemed that all he could hope for at present was an illicit romance of uncertain duration, with all its attendant anxieties.

Well, if Alison could stand it, so could he; but where was Alison? Time had gone on while he sat and thought and sipped his beer. It was now twenty past six, and Tom was the victim of a new set of worries. Had something happened to her, or had she simply changed her mind? Maybe she had decided that the whole thing was too complicated. Or maybe Klaus and Imre were making things difficult. He got up and went outside.

The narrow lane was empty and silent, and the Otterill made its lazy, meandering way across the flats with scarcely a ripple. Tom had been expecting that Alison would walk from the school to the pub. He still hoped that she might appear in the lane at any moment, but the conviction was growing in him that she would not come. It started to drizzle again, so he got into his car and drove slowly to the Wolfgang Goerner School.

Just as Tom pulled in, Anne Weston emerged from the front door of the school. After carefully closing the door behind her, she went to the only car left in the parking lot. Tom was tempted to keep moving and drive out again, but on a sudden impulse he drew up beside her car, got out, and stood in the rain while Anne lowered her window. Without any preliminaries he said, "Hello Anne, I understand you need a physics teacher. I've become very interested in the Archway movement and I'd like to talk to you about the position."

Anne smiled distantly, as if she had more pressing concerns on her mind. As she focused on Tom, it struck her that there might be something disingenuous about his interest in Archway. At the same time, however, she could not ignore the possibility that this man might be able to fill a gaping hole in her school's faculty roster.

"Certainly, Thomas. I'd be very glad to speak with you. It would also be good for you to meet Mr. Takacs, who is a very experienced science teacher. Perhaps the three of us could meet here tomorrow afternoon."

Tom didn't bother to correct Anne's mistake about his name, but he had to swallow hard to accept the idea that he would have to talk to Imre.

"I teach all day", he said, "but I could meet you here any time after five o'clock."

"Good, let's make it five then and I'll make sure Imre is here."

"I'll look forward to it", said Tom untruthfully. He got back into his car and drove off as decorously as he could manage. Once in the lane he put his foot down and shortly after seven o'clock he was knocking on the front door of Mrs. Barrington-Smythe's elegant residence. The door opened immediately and he found himself facing Halcyon, who was wearing a bright red cotton mini-dress, flared and nipped in at the waist.

"Come in quick", she said, not bothering with introductions. "The others are out and I want to talk to you. Come up here."

Tom followed her up the stairs and into the box room. Halcyon shut the door and stood with her back to it.

"Something bad happened this morning", she said. "Alison's gone."

"Gone? Where?"

"I don't know. Maybe she's on her way back to New York, but it might be anywhere. Here, you better sit down."

Tom's world seemed to have gone into violent rotation and sitting down on the low, unstable camp bed required some care. Halcyon sat next to him, just as she had sat next to Alison earlier in the day, showing a lot of thigh but apparently unconscious of the effect it might have had if Tom hadn't had other things on his mind. Tom seemed incapable of speech, so Halcyon went on with her story in her usual high-speed fashion.

"I guess Alison told you about the set-up here, so you know she's Mrs. Klaus Hübel and Klaus has this habit of picking up a new young girl every few years and ditching the old one. Well the funny thing is that last night he decided to ditch me and take Alison back and I don't think he's ever done that before and when she showed up this morning and I told her she sort of said not bloody likely and told me I should go back home to Mummy, which would be kind of nice in a way. What was I saying? Oh yes, Imre was sleeping like a pig in the drawing room and Klaus told me to go upstairs and he and Alison went in the kitchen, but I sat on the steps and listened, which I shouldn't have, but you know I like Alison, she's OK and in a funny way we're friends. I never realized this before but Klaus wants to hand Alison over to Imre when he's finished with her and

Alison more or less told him to bugger off—not exactly in those words but she has a way of getting her point across. Imre woke up and heard them talking, and he didn't see me. He listened for a while and then went into the kitchen. He said something like, 'Perhaps there is something that Alison ought to know that you haven't told her.' Then he closed the door behind him and I could still hear them talking but I couldn't hear what they were saying. After a while I went and put my ear against the door, but it got very quiet and all I could hear was Imre talking in a very low voice. I thought Klaus was trying to make him stop but he wouldn't. Then all of a sudden Alison screamed—well it wasn't exactly a scream, more like a cross between a scream and a gasp and she came out and ran past me upstairs. The door opened so fast that I fell into the room and Alison had to jump over me. Imre was still sitting at the table with a smirk on his big fat face and Klaus started to get up to follow her, so I got out of there in a flash and ran after Alison and she said, 'Help me, Halcyon, I've got to get out of here.' I asked why and had they tried to hurt her and she said no but she wouldn't tell me anything else. We just crammed her things into a suitcase in two minutes flat and she's left God knows what here. I asked her where she was going and she said to the bus stop and I said how are you going to get there, it's a long way and neither of us can drive the old wagon. So I helped her and we were going to walk all the way in the rain but someone picked us up and when we got there there was a bus just about to leave. She asked me if I had any money so I gave her all I had and then the poor thing remembered she had a credit card and gave some of it back. She got on the bus and I don't think she even knew where it was going and that was the last I saw of her. That's really all, except that I had to walk all the way back in the rain. When I was about half way, Imre came along in the old car and when he saw me he stopped all of a sudden and stalled the engine. He started to get out of the car so I ran away, and when I looked back he was getting out the starting handle. I walked the rest of the way and put on some dry clothes. I passed Klaus on the stairs and he looked terrible and wouldn't talk to me. He just muttered something and went out. We were all supposed to go to the conference today but by then it was too late anyway. Later on a copper came and knocked on the door and I pretended I wasn't here."

Tom stood up.

"Where is Klaus?"

The rage in his voice was contained but potent. Halcyon thought she could see where this situation was going, and she was frightened.

"I don't know—he's not in his room. I haven't seen him since he went out this morning, but I'm scared he might pop up at any moment. Tom, he's not much more than a silly old man. If you ask me, this is all Imre's doing, and he's gone."

"Maybe Klaus came back."

But when Tom went downstairs, closely followed by Halcyon, there was no one to be seen.

Halcyon muttered, "What the hell am I going to do now? Imre's taken the car and he's not coming back. I'm stuck here and there isn't even a phone."

"Show me their rooms", Tom said.

They went back upstairs and looked in Imre's room, which showed all the signs a hasty departure—drawers left open, bed rumpled and oddments left lying around, but no suitcase or outer clothing.

"Yep" said Halcyon. "He's gone after Alison."

Klaus's room was different—everything neat and tidy, bed made and suitcases empty. On the bedside table there was a portrait of Wolfgang Goerner. "Well he's coming back", Halcyon said. "He wouldn't have left without that."

Tom tried to get a grip on himself and resist the impulse to drop everything and set off in pursuit of Imre and Alison. He had no idea what Imre could possibly have told her, and it was mere conjecture that she was heading for New York. One thing he was sure of was that she didn't need him to protect her from Imre. If it came to the point she would be able to handle him herself. Anne Weston would be expecting Alison to be back at school in September, living in the same household with Klaus and Imre, but that was two months ahead and seemed grotesquely unlikely. Alison probably had friends in England, so she might decide to stay on this side of the Atlantic. The outlines of a plan formed in Tom's mind. Preparation for the exams at his school would be complete by the end of the week, and surely there would be some word from Alison. If not, he would have to assume that she had gone back to America, so he would keep his appointment with Anne tomorrow and try to establish a base of operations at the Archway School in Manhattan. Now he knew why Anne had been so reserved in their brief conversation—she must have been wondering why Alison, Imre and Klaus had not shown up at the conference. This brought him back to Halcyon, who obviously hadn't been there either. He asked irrelevantly, "Why are you wearing that red dress?"

She managed a wan smile.

"I was so mad with all of them, the way they treated me and Alison, and I suddenly had this feeling that I don't want to have any more to do with any of that lot. So I stuck all my purple dresses in the bottom of my suitcase and put this on. I'm really just an ordinary girl, nothing special. Do you like it?"

"I think it's very nice. Maybe Alison was right and you should go back to your parents."

"What a brush-off! OK, I wasn't really coming on to you, but maybe you could help me figure out this mess. Or maybe Klaus will come back and I can tell him what I think of him."

"I'm sorry—you're a darling and a sweetheart, and if I weren't otherwise engaged you could come on to me as much as you liked. Let me see if I can get my brain working. You said Klaus tried to stop Imre, but he kept on talking until Alison screamed?"

"Yes."

"So it was something Imre said that's so bad that she can't talk about it and has to get away . . . If Imre assumed that she was going back to New York, he probably drove to London or to the nearest railway station."

"Maybe he couldn't start the car".

"Right! Let's go and look. This time you don't have to walk."

(15)

At nine o'clock every morning at the Archway Schools Conference, the hundred-and-fifty or so delegates met to hear an introductory verse by Wolfgang Goerner, sing some rounds and hear the main presentation of the day. They then dispersed into a dozen groups for discussions of the topic, which, on Monday, had been school administration. This was followed by lunch and an hour of artistic activities such as painting, singing, and euphonics. The afternoon's work ended with a plenum, in which the chairs of each small group reported on the discussions, and a summing up was given by the morning's speaker.

Monday had started off reasonably well, since Anne Weston was the speaker, and the non-arrival of Klaus, Alison, Imre and Halcyon had caused some concern but not panic. Anxiety mounted, however, when a messenger who had been sent to the Barrington-Smythe residence to find out what was going on returned with the news that there was no one there and the car was missing. A call from Anne to the local police yielded the information that no traffic accidents had been reported and the obvious suggestion that the car had broken down somewhere. Glastonbury being a small town, the duty officer was familiar with the vehicle in question.

"That'd be Mrs. Barrington-Smythe's old shooting brake wouldn't it? Brake's the word, Ma'am, to put it bluntly. It's broke down so many times I wonder she don't get herself something a bit more modern, even though she don't drive any more. Yes, I'll let you know if we hear anything. Archway School—yes I've got the number."

Nothing further was heard, however, and the conference had to go on. For the morning sessions it was easy to substitute for Klaus and Imre, who had been expected to chair small groups, but by lunchtime people had begun to ask questions to which the organizers had no answers. Since euphonics was a very popular choice, two groups had been planned, one with Kara Henkemans and the other with Klaus. When it was announced that one of the younger euphonists would take Klaus's class, there was a general wish to migrate to Kara's group and a certain amount of discord when this was not allowed because it would have made the group too big. Several people decided that they would prefer to go for a nice walk in the country, only to discover that it was raining heavily. The remaining alternative was to sit in the cafeteria and wait for afternoon tea to appear. Before it did so, a tall, prosperous-looking man of late middle age walked into the room on the off chance that a cup of tea might already be available.

Harry Grainger was a former Archway teacher who had retired from the movement when he was elevated to the position of General Secretary of the Society for Cosmic Wisdom in Great Britain. As a person of some importance, he frequently excused himself from participating in the humbler activities of the rank-and-file CW's and Archway people. After an earnest conversation with Anne Weston and Jane Malone, he had agreed to give the opening address on Thursday morning if Klaus wasn't available. Harry was genuinely concerned about the missing quartet, but his admiration for Klaus was strongly tinged with professional jealousy, and he had a very low opinion of Imre. To balance this he had a great weakness for attractive young women, especially blondes like Halcyon.

Suspecting that Klaus was up to something, he welcomed the opportunity to speak about a subject that was very close to his heart—form, order and discipline—feeling sure that he would make a better job of it than Klaus would have done.

Although Harry had no official standing at the conference, his aura of self-importance often gave people the impression that when they wanted to know something, he was the one to ask. He was in the middle of a cautiously reassuring statement about the missing conferees when the gong sounded for tea, and Bill Graveney, the old gentleman with the Somerset accent who had closed the opening session on Sunday, came in. Looking very grave, he spoke to Harry in an undertone.

"We've just had a call from the police—they've found the car. When the officer Anne spoke to went off duty, he thought he'd take a look at Mrs. Barrington-Smythe's house, and on the way he noticed the car parked at the side of the road. There was no sign of anyone in it and there was no one at the house. One slightly odd thing was that the ignition key had been left in."

"What did he do with the key?"

"He left it there. The car is legally parked, and for all he knew the occupants would be coming back and expecting to drive off. In fact he had no authority to do anything except report that he'd seen it. Anne and Jane know about this, and we think we should make an announcement. Here they are."

The room was filling up rapidly, but it remained quiet. Everyone could see that the organizers were discussing some serious matter, and few had any doubt about the subject of their conversation.

"All right", Harry said rather reluctantly, "but let's keep it as low key as possible. Who's going to do it?"

"We'll wait a minute till most of the people are here. Then I'll sound the gong and Jane will speak."

But people were already anxiously crowding around the little committee, so Bill went over to the gong, gave it a discreet pat with his open hand and asked people to be seated.

"All I can tell you", Jane said, "is that we have no further information about Klaus, Alison, Imre and Halcyon. It seems probable that they left the house this morning in Mrs. Barrington-Smythe's car, but the car has been found parked in Glastonbury and there is no trace of its occupants. The police have no information about anything unusual happening in the town today. We shall remain in touch with them, and if there is no news by tomorrow morning they will take some action. We must remember that Glastonbury is a small town and resources are not available for a large-scale search. Harry Grainger is prepared to give Thursday's nine o'clock talk, but we feel that four grown-up people can't suddenly disappear without a trace, and some explanation will soon be forthcoming. If there is no news by tomorrow morning we may wish to change our plans and look for ways of helping the police to find our friends. We must remember in any case that there are invisible presences fostering our movement and that we can ask for their help. As you know, the rest of the afternoon is free for artistic activities, ad hoc committees and discussion groups. I ask you to continue in the confidence that we shall be guided by the spirits who work for the healthy evolution of mankind, which is the true purpose of our movement."

Everyone looked properly serious, but it wasn't long before sandwiches, cakes and cups of tea began to disappear at the usual rate.

III

Tom and Halcyon

(16)

Tom and Halcyon found the station wagon standing forlornly at the side of the street, just where Halcyon had last seen it. It had been there for twelve hours, but there was still a smell of gasoline, from which Tom deduced that there was probably nothing wrong with the car beyond a flooded carburetor. "Look, the keys are still there, but if you can't drive a car with manual transmission I think we'll have to leave it until tomorrow. What we need is to find Klaus and make him tell us what happened this morning."

"I can drive a car with manual transmission", Halcyon said in a miffed tone. "It's just this one. The synchro only works on the top two gears and then only sometimes. Imre just crashes it in by brute force."

It was nearly eight o'clock when they got back to the house. Klaus still wasn't there, but Anne Weston had passed by and left a note taped to the door. It was addressed to Klaus, but Halcyon had no compunction about reading it. It was very brief; Anne and the other dignitaries were extremely concerned. The remainder of the conference was greatly dependent on the presence of Klaus and Imre and they were asked to contact her as soon as possible.

"I guess they're not worried about me and Alison. Do you think we should go and tell her what's happened?"

"OK, you do the talking."

Halcyon rummaged among her belongings and eventually found the list of delegates and their addresses.

"William Graveney", she said, "I think it's just round the corner"

*

Bill Graveney wasn't one to take liberties, so he addressed Halcyon by her real name.

"Ah, Miss Tompkins, do come in. We've all been very worried about you. And Mr . . . ."

"Tom Dexter."

"Bill Graveney, but everyone calls me William. Mrs. Weston will be glad to see you, especially if the two of you can tell us anything about what's happened to Mr. and Mrs. Hübel and Mr. Takacs."

They were ushered into a drawing room containing the usual array of two armchairs and a settee grouped around a fireplace. Anne Weston, Jane Malone and Carolina Ende were scrunched together in a big purple patch on the settee, and Harry Grainger occupied one of the armchairs. He rose rapidly to his feet at the sight of Halcyon.

Graveney performed the introductions.

"Miss Tompkins, I don't believe you've met Mr. Grainger, but he has seen . . ."

"And admired . . ." Grainger interjected.

"You from a distance." Graveney completed this composite sentence as if nothing had happened. "Mr. Dexter—Mr. Grainger; Mr. Grainger is General Secretary for the Society for Cosmic Wisdom in Great Britain. I believe you know Mrs. Weston and you probably saw Mrs. Malone and Frau Ende yesterday at the Conference."

There were handshakes all round, but Tom said nothing about distant admiration.

Graveney courteously placed Halcyon in the vacant armchair and brought chairs for himself and Tom. So Tom ended up between Grainger and Carolina Ende and more or less opposite Halcyon, from which vantage point it was clear that the depth and backward slope of her armchair made it impossible for her to disguise the fact that she was wearing pale green panties under her highly abbreviated mini. She solved the problem as best she could by sitting forward on the extreme edge of the seat and folding her hands across her lap. Unfortunately the seat was of polished leather and sloped in such a way that she had to maintain continuous tension in her knees in order to avoid slipping backwards. Graveney placed himself between Halcyon and Anne Weston and they all stared at the vacant fireplace for a few moments before several people started talking at the same time.

Grainger's voice was the loudest and most insistent, so the others soon dropped out, but as soon as he had the floor to himself he adopted a friendly and informal tone.

"Halcyon, I understand that you, the Hübels and Mr. Takacs have been staying in the same house. We're very relieved to find that you are safe and sound, but we are extremely concerned about the others. We'd be extremely grateful if you could shed any light on the situation."

Halcyon was momentarily at a loss. Although she didn't want to tell the whole story, it seemed necessary to let these people know that Alison and Imre had left and that she had no clue as to Klaus's whereabouts.

"Alison packed and left this morning. I think she must have had some bad news or something. I helped her carry her things to the bus stop."

"You mean you walked all the way to the bus stop? Why didn't someone drive her? And how did she get this bad news?"

"Neither of us can drive that car, and she didn't seem to want anyone else. I don't know how she got the news, but she had just been talking to Klaus, so maybe he told her to go back to New York. You know how he is—he just tells you what to do and you do it."

Halcyon threw up her hands in token of resignation and slipped all the way back in her armchair in a confusion of arms, legs and panties, while the gentlemen opposite her politely shifted their gaze elsewhere. With a "What the hell" gesture she continued.

"Imre left before I got back. I looked in his room and all his things were gone. I couldn't get to the school because there was no one to take me. Klaus went out just after I got back and I haven't seen him since. He looked ill and he just ignored me. And that's all I can tell you."

Grainger turned to Tom.

"This is all extremely disturbing", he said. "I understand that Alison Hübel has had some discussions with you about your possibly becoming interested in the Archway Movement. Do you know of any incident that might have precipitated these events?"

As far as Tom could tell, none of these people except Halcyon knew that he had spent the night with Alison, so he replied as non-committally as possible.

"We talked for a long time about the Archway schools, and I thought I might be able to see her again this afternoon, but when I got to the school everyone had left except Anne Weston. So I went to the B-S—I mean

Mrs. Barrington-Smythe's house—to see if she was there and Halcyon told me what had happened."

"How did you know where she was staying?" Anne asked suspiciously.

"As I already mentioned, we had a long conversation after the concert yesterday."

"It seems to me", Jane Malone put in, "that our immediate objective must be to find Klaus. He must know the reason for Alison's and Imre's extraordinary behavior."

Grainger agreed.

"Exactly. Furthermore, Alison and Imre are young and vigorous and we have some idea of their intentions, but Klaus is elderly and apparently not well. His disappearance is unaccountable and he may need help."

"But the conference—how are we to continue if Imre is gone and Klaus is not to be found? It was today extremely difficult and embarrassing."

This was Carolina Ende, in a kind of despairing Germanic moan.

Although Grainger was not officially one of the conference organizers, the three women on the settee all looked at him.

"It's now past eight o'clock", he said, "and we must first find out if Klaus has returned, in which case there may be a simple explanation for what has happened. If not, we must insist that the police take some action immediately."

Anne Weston seemed to regret her acquiescence in this appeal to the dominant male.

"I think that's a bit premature now that we know more about what happened this morning. He was up and about earlier in the day—what time was that, Halcyon?"

"It must have been about ten o'clock."

"He may be old but he's livelier than a lot of people half his age. I mean, what could possibly happen to him?"

No one had noticed that Bill Graveney had left the room after hearing Halcyon's story, but now he returned and coughed politely.

"For your information, I've just telephoned the police station and there's no further news—no traffic accidents or anything else significant. They said they would keep their eyes open but it was much too soon to think about search parties and the like. You should realize that 'insisting' doesn't go down very well with our local constabulary. Some of you know Alison, Imre and Klaus much better than I do, but my instinct tells me that there must have been a real how-d'you-do this morning."

Seeing several looks of incomprehension he went on:

"I mean a bit of a scene, a bust-up of some sort. Alison was so upset that she had to get out of there immediately; Imre, who seems to have a possibly reprehensible interest in her, followed her, and Klaus is so disturbed that he has gone off on his own to think about it. I think Miss Tompkins could tell us more about what happened if she had a mind to."

Halcyon struggled out of her armchair and stood by the empty fireplace, looking very pale and defiant.

"OK", she said, "you've asked for it, only it's amazing to me that some of you hadn't already realized what was going on with Klaus and his youth parade."

Anne looked resigned, Jane scandalized and Carolina linguistically bemused. Grainger said, "Such conduct is not necessarily reprehensible among spiritually advanced individuals. Some of this was common knowledge."

Halcyon was not impressed.

"And most of it is bloody humbug! Klaus liked young girls, specially if they were convinced that he was God and they were going to heaven with him. That's how he got his four wives and all the others who never made it to the altar with him. Only the novelty seemed to wear off every few years. Well, I didn't know this until today, but when he got tired of Alison he decided to pass her on to Imre, who is a disgusting pig, and Alison didn't want to be passed on, so she scarpered and Imre is chasing her—except she knew that already, so there must be another reason. And, yes, Klaus is probably somewhere trying to walk it off. And, by the way, he's tired of me now and he wants to get Alison back to nurse him in his old age, and how he was going to do that and give her to Imre at the same time I haven't a clue. And what I really don't understand is that I feel a bit sorry for the old sod and I don't want him dying of exposure out there. What I really want is to give him a piece of my mind."

She looked at Tom.

"Now I wish I could to go home. I mean real home, not the B-S."

"Halcyon's parents live in London", Anne explained.

"That's a very good idea", said Graveney, who seemed to have the most practical notion of the situation. "But there ought to be someone waiting for Klaus at Mrs. Barrington-Smythe's house. For all we know he may be back by now. We have no idea where he is and it's not practical to go looking for him, so we should set a deadline, say ten o'clock, and if he's not back by then we should have another go at the police."

Halcyon offered to act as a messenger.

"I can't very well leave tonight, so I'll go back now, and if he shows up I'll come and tell you. It's only a five minute walk."

"Is there anything I can do to help?" Tom asked.

There was an awkward pause while everyone waited for someone else to answer. Eventually Halcyon spoke.

"Could you come and wait with me for a little while? To tell the truth, I'm a bit scared."

(17)

Tom and Halcyon sat in Mrs. Barrington-Smythe's kitchen, listening to the rain as it splashed over the gutters and poured into the big steel tank at the corner of the house. Tom was thinking about Alison, half wishing that he had been as impetuous as Imre, but knowing that it would probably have been a fruitless endeavor. Now, unless there was a message from Alison, the next few days would be a nerve-racking agony in which he could do nothing but wait and hope for the best. Well, when he came to think of it, there were things he could do. First he would have to do the right thing by his students at the Grammar School. Also, he might be able to take advantage of some of his father's connections. As a newspaper magnate, he must have a whole investigative department at his disposal that might be able to track down an individual traveler. So he would try to get his father on the job, even if it meant going into awkward explanations. Meanwhile he would talk to Anne Weston, express a deep interest in CW and Archway, and ask if he might spend a few weeks visiting her school.

"Halcyon", he asked on an impulse, "what do you really think of Goerner and Archway and all that stuff?"

"I don't know. It sort of creeps up on you. Why, are you getting interested?"

"Maybe. Listen, you may be able to help me, so I'd better tell you what's up."

"Maybe I know already", Halcyon said with a wry smile. "You and Alison hit it off in a big way. You want to go after her and one way would be to get a job in New York. What I don't get is why you didn't go after Imre straight away. Surely you want to find her before he does."

"I don't think he stands a chance against her, and in any case, can you imagine going to London and trying to find Alison at the airport when we don't even know if that's where she went? Do you know if she has any special friends anywhere—anybody she might stay with?"

"Well, there are half-a-dozen Archway Schools in England, and she knows people at most of them. Some of them are here for the conference. But my guess is that she doesn't want to be with Archway people, or CW's for that matter. I still think she's gone back to New York. And look, it's nearly ten o'clock—what the hell is Klaus up to?"

"Maybe he's still out there walking.

"But he's been gone since ten o'clock this morning and look at the weather. Oh hell, I've just remembered something. When he's here and he needs to think he likes to go up the Tor. He's probably been sitting up there all day in the rain. He's such a stupid old idiot."

Tom stared at Halcyon.

"You still love him, don't you?"

"Sort of . . ."

"And does Alison still love him?"

"I don't know. Come on, let's go."

Tom borrowed a raincoat that he found in the hall closet, and Halcyon put on a white, translucent, hooded plastic Mac that came down almost to her knees without quite obscuring the red mini. It had the odd effect of making her look sexier than ever.

*

Klaus Hübel, who believed that Goerner had given true and practical interpretations of the universe and its inhabitants, had spent a large part of his life trying to follow his late mentor into regions of experience where enlightenment was to be found. Goerner's writings undoubtedly contain a great deal that is wise and helpful, but to the outsider there is also much that appears to be pure mumbo-jumbo. Klaus had absorbed both the wisdom and the apparent mumbo-jumbo to the point of being able to speak almost with the voice of his master. The result of this, together with his strong personality and his outstanding skill as a euphonist, was that in the Cosmic Wisdom movement, old hands and novices alike found him overwhelming, and placed him securely on a pedestal. It was only when he passed the age of eighty that he began to have doubts about his spiritual capacities and to feel that he might never be able to enter the realms of pure spirit for which he ardently longed. He even began to wonder whether he might possibly have been mistaken about Goerner. While this inner crisis was developing it was dawning on him that the young women in his life were no longer generating the sexual energy that he had always striven to transmute into power for his spiritual endeavors. So when the catastrophe had taken place that morning, the aged exponent of Cosmic Wisdom was already in a vulnerable state.

Alison and Klaus had still been sitting at the breakfast table when Imre entered the kitchen. He sat down opposite them and, in spite of Klaus's protests, spoke softly for several minutes. When Alison rushed out of the kitchen, Klaus tried to get up from his chair to follow, but Imre reached across the table and grabbed his arm. The old man, suddenly energized, turned and with amazing force punched his tormentor in the mouth. Imre stood up and tried to speak, but his mouth was a mess of blood and teeth and he tottered over to the kitchen sink for water and paper towels. Klaus stood still for a moment, looking in astonishment at the bleeding knuckles of his right hand. The impact had produced one of the most satisfying moments of his life, very much akin to a sexual release; but there was no afterglow. He felt as old and tired as he had before striking out at his adversary. Realizing that it would be useless to try to reason with Alison, he left Imre sniveling over the sink, went slowly up to his room and locked his door. He heard the sounds of Alison and Halcyon packing in the box room, and he heard them go and slam the front door. A few minutes later, a barrage of abrupt and frenzied noises broke out in the room next to Klaus's, where Imre was hurling his things randomly into a suitcase. Klaus sat mute on his bed while Imre shook his door, banged on it and croaked bilingual imprecations through damaged lips. Eventually Imre clattered noisily down the stairs, and the front door slammed again. The engine of the old station wagon started and stopped, started and stopped again; then repeated cranking and high-pitched cursing, a frantic search for the starting handle and a tremendous roar and back-firing, as Imre gunned the ancient engine mercilessly in an effort to keep it going; and, finally, the sound of the old car hiccupping into the distance.

Klaus still sat on his bed in a state of diminished consciousness. Time drifted by and he was aware only of still images of scenes in the kitchen and a deep emptiness in his soul. Now someone was coming up the stairs. It didn't sound like Imre, so Klaus unlocked his door and looked out. It was Halcyon, and seeing Klaus looking pale and ill, she said, "What's been happening? What did you do to Alison? And you look as if you need a doctor."

Klaus shook his head and said, "What have I done . . . For the love of God let me pass . . ."

Halcyon stood aside and something impelled Klaus to go to the kitchen, mop the table and chair that had been spattered with Imre's gore, and clean up the mess in the sink, after which he left the house and walked in the rain for a long time without any clear objective. Pictures of episodes in his life came into his mind unbidden, causing him intense pain. Was everything he had always believed, or thought he had believed, about the link between sexuality and spirituality merely an elaborate system of self-deception, fabricated from various sources and having little or nothing to do with Wolfgang Goerner? And not only self-deception; had the dozen or so girls who thought that they were setting him free to range in the spirit also been deceived?

And then there was Alison. She was so much like her mother that Klaus couldn't see her or even think about her without seeing Maria—only in Alison there was nothing of the coquette. As a little girl it had taken Maria only a few days to figure Klaus out, and she had had him on a string for the next twenty-five years, letting him have his way when it suited her and keeping him at arm's length when it didn't. Klaus had found consolation in his succession of wives and girlfriends, but when Maria felt like it all she had to do was snap her fingers. Well, that had all ended when she went off and married Phillip Johnson, after allowing Klaus a farewell performance that he didn't look back on with much pleasure. It wasn't surprising that Maria hadn't wanted Alison to go to Ulm.

*

Klaus's path took him along High Street, down Chilkwell Street, and past the remains of the old Abbey and the Chalice Well. A little further on he came to the stone footpath that leads to the top of the five-hundred foot eminence that towers over the damp plain. It was raining harder now and the path was steep, but, bare-headed and soaked to the skin, he kept on walking. Few people were sight-seeing on a wet Monday, and there was no one to wonder at this strange old man who stood in front of the ancient roofless tower that crowned the Tor, gazing out over the plain while water soaked his mass of white hair and dripped from his nose and chin. His thoughts turned to King Arthur and his knights, and it came to him for the first time that they would not have been pleased with his performance. But, also for the first time, he found himself thinking that the exoteric historians might be right about Arthur. There was nothing in Goerner about him and his entourage. Could it be that CW people believed the old legends because they liked old legends and disliked modern scholarship? Then, in the wind and rain, Klaus came to a different kind of certainty. Something of great moment had happened in this little enclave. He could feel it in the earth, the water and the air, and in the still fiery embers of his soul. Great deeds had been done, people had made stories about them, and perhaps it was true that Christ had walked here. But the real thing was such that no story about it would ever convey its wholeness, purity and potency. Likewise, what Goerner had given the world did not have to be true in every detail, but now there was no doubt in Klaus's mind that his spiritual master had tapped into the fundamental being of the cosmos, and had allowed a stream of spiritual reality into human consciousness that was ultimately more powerful than hydrogen bombs.

These visions of a new stage of understanding stayed with him for a long time, exciting his imagination so strongly that he almost forgot the evil situation that he had created. When his consciousness returned to the light of common day he felt deathly tired, so he sat with his back to St. Michael's Tower and fell asleep; but when he woke up his first thoughts were not of Arthur but of Alison.

"I must find her", he muttered. "What is wrong with me that I am up here indulging myself when I ought to be looking for her?"

He thought of Imre spitting blood and teeth into the kitchen sink. Goerner and Arthur were real, but not as vividly immediate as that. And if Arthur hadn't had a sword handy he wouldn't have scrupled to use his fist. The physical world had to be given its due—Goerner had said so—and Klaus had certainly done that in his own way. Realizing that he was in danger of falling into another fit of philosophizing, Klaus scrambled to his feet and immediately fell over. It was getting dark and still raining, and he seemed to have lost the use of his legs. Crawling on hands and knees he eventually found the path, but he still couldn't stand up.

When Tom and Halcyon found him he was half way down the hill, and still on his hands and knees. It was all they could do to get him down the narrow path as far as Tom's illegally parked car.

(18)

Bill Graveney had lit a fire in the drawing room. Harry Grainger, who had taken up a commanding position in front of it, was at his most pontifical.

"We must get him into hospital immediately; otherwise I shall take no responsibility for the outcome."

"No one has asked you to take any responsibility, my dear Harry, and if you would be kind enough to move a little to one side I should be able to get more benefit from the fire."

This was Klaus, speaking with some of his accustomed resonance from a recumbent position on Bill Graveney's sofa. Grainger moved hastily to one side and became unusually quiet. Klaus continued:

"I shall be perfectly all right. Mr. Graveney, do you by any chance have some brandy?"

Frau Ende was shocked. "Brandy! But Dr. Goerner has said . . ."

Graveney was not interested in what Dr. Goerner had said.

"Certainly, I was just going to suggest it myself—it'll help you get the circulation going again now that you can see the fire. I suspect that you're not the only one in need of a drink."

He looked at Tom and Halcyon, whose wet clothes were dripping on the drawing room carpet. They were standing by the door, looking as if they weren't quite sure if they belonged.

"Come on in, you two, and let me hang up those wet coats for you. We owe you a great deal. Klaus might never have found his way back if you hadn't gone to the rescue. I have beer, scotch and several other varieties of alcoholic beverage—also tea and coffee, which I believe Dr. Goerner has said are allowable under certain circumstances."

This last remark was accompanied by a twinkle.

"I'll just get Klaus his brandy and then you can all place your orders."

So the two young people sat down on the rug in front of the fire, Halcyon making a splash of color at the feet of Harry Grainger. Tom was wondering why Grainger could be Harry when he had to be Thomas and Bill Graveney had to be William, but Halcyon still had her wits about her.

"Klaus", she demanded, "What happened this morning. Why did Alison run away?"

"Not now, my dear, please not now."

The reply came in a murmur and Frau Ende, nervous about the forthcoming libations, turned to Harry Grainger.

"Now that we know that Klaus is safe, it is perhaps time that we should leave."

Jane Malone didn't agree.

"But Carolina, we've been talking for a long time and we still have only a tentative schedule for tomorrow's activities. A lot will depend on how Klaus feels, and we still have the mystery of Alison and Imre. Klaus, you must know what the situation is. Can't you shed a little light on it? And yes, William, I'd like some scotch."

Klaus spoke from the depths of the sofa.

"The brandy is excellent and I shall take no further part in the conference. I shall instead devote myself to ensuring that my wife is safe and well. As far as Imre is concerned, he is nothing, and so I have nothing to say."

Having made his statement he promptly appeared to fall asleep. Halcyon took the brandy glass from his hand before it fell to the floor and shook him angrily, but there was no response.

"He's not asleep—the old so-and-so doesn't want to talk and he's just shamming."

Klaus opened one eye and spoke softly to Halcyon.

"There are times when it is better not to talk. Since I believe that I am the only one who can help Alison, I shall devote myself to doing all that I can for her."

Raising his voice a little he added, "You must make your plans for the rest of the conference on the assumption that Alison and I will not be here. As for Imre, I advise you to have nothing further to do with him. Now I shall sleep."

There was a stunned silence during which everyone looked at Klaus, who was breathing easily and didn't look as if he was going to expire any time soon. Eventually it was broken by Anne.

"I think I'd like some scotch too", she said, to the surprise of those who knew her. Grainger maintained a disapproving silence while Halcyon asked if she should leave since she would not be expected to take part in the discussion. Anne had other ideas.

"You had better stay for a while, Halcyon. Since Klaus will not be available, we may ask you to assist Kara in some euphonics classes. Harry has agreed to speak at the plenum and Carolina will lead Imre's workshop, but there are many details to be worked out."

Halcyon muttered in Tom's ear.

"I'm not going back to that house with Klaus—God, that's funny—or on my own. And I'm scared Imre might come back."

Tom gave her hand a squeeze and whispered, "Don't worry"

Aloud he said, "Perhaps I could be helpful", he said. "I'm very interested in your school movement and my car is just outside, so I can take people home when you finish."

Harry Grainger started to say "I don't think that will be necessary . . .", but Anne headed him off.

"That's very kind", she said, "but Jane and I are staying here, and Harry has a car, so he can take Carolina home. I think if William agrees, Klaus should stay the night here. He looks very comfortable and we can keep an eye on him. Also he may change his mind, and it would be helpful to know as early as possible. But you and Halcyon might be helpful in other ways and I think it would be good if you both stayed for a while."

*

"Well", said Tom as he followed Halcyon through Mrs. Barrington-Smythe's front door, "I never expected to be giving a talk on modern physics to the delegates at the Archway Conference."

"And I didn't expect to be teaching euphonics instead of going home to Mum. At least they've given you a day to figure out what you're going to say. I s'pose you wouldn't like to stay and have a cup of tea or something."

"I don't think it would go down very well on top of Bill Graveney's scotch. It's past midnight, and I have a pile of exercise books to mark before I go to bed."

"I'm still scared, Tom. I mean I think I could deal with him, but being alone in a dark house and not knowing . . ."

Tom knew that it was no use telling Halcyon that there was nothing to be scared of, but he would be teaching again in the morning and he had to go back to his apartment for clean clothes. The exercise books would probably have to wait, but he couldn't show up at school looking like the wreck of the Hesperus. He thought of Mrs. Trathgannon and his sense of humor took over.

"OK, get your toothbrush and something to wear. Just make sure my landlady doesn't see you."

(19)

Before settling down to sleep in Tom's bed, Halcyon insisted on a goodnight kiss, pulling him down on top of her and making a very thorough job of it. Tuesday was Mrs. Trathgannon's cleaning day and she was due to arrive at nine o'clock the next morning, so Tom took his alarm clock from the bedroom and set it for 5:30. There was a couch in the living room, but it had not been built for someone of Tom's height, so he got out a pillow and his old sleeping bag and dozed for a while on the rug.

There was too much going on in his mind to allow real sleep. He and Alison were in love. Alison's body was wonderful. Her mind moved quickly and meshed delightfully with his. She was married to Klaus, but the marriage was morally over. Klaus wouldn't divorce her and had been keeping her for Imre. Imre, who must have realized that she wouldn't take him at any price, had told her something so shocking, disgusting, shameful or frightening that she had fled without even leaving a message. He had no idea where she was or what had happened, and he wanted the dawn to come quickly so that he could start trying to find out. Somewhere out there was Imre, who had become a sort of Mephistopheles figure in Tom's mind. The only possible explanation for Klaus's weird agreement with Imre was that Imre had some hold over him—otherwise it was perfectly unintelligible. What kind of things were the Cosmic Wisdom Society and the Archway Schools if they harbored people like this? There must be something good there or Alison wouldn't be involved. After several circuits of this merry-go-round, Tom fell into a troubled sleep, only to be awakened by the suppressed rage that had been brewing inside him all day while he tried to keep calm and reason things. He sat up with a start and finally allowed full play to his seething anger, cursing Klaus, Imre, Goerner, the Archway schools, Cosmic Wisdom and everything connected with them. It was only when he gradually began to run out of fire that he realized that someone was holding his hand.

"Halcyon—I'm sorry, I didn't know you were there."

"Come on", she said, and led him into the bedroom. "I'm on the pill and it'll do you good. Just let it all out. I don't mind if you hurt me."

*

The alarm clock, which was on the floor in the living room next to Tom's sleeping bag, duly went off at half past five, but it didn't disturb the sleepers in the bedroom. So at nine o'clock, when Tom ought to have been starting his first lesson, a loud exclamation at the untidy state of the living room woke Halcyon, and she was still sitting up, trying to figure out where she was, when Tom's landlady put her head round the bedroom door. The sight of her tenant in bed with a naked young woman, not to be identified with his previous night's companion, was too much for Mrs. T. With an even louder squawk she rushed out of the room.

Tom's reactions were a little slower. Halcyon's generosity had enabled him to sleep, but his first thoughts were of Alison and the fact that within twenty-four hours of swearing that he would marry her he had been unfaithful. As his anger returned, Halcyon became one of its targets. He got out of bed and faced her, an angry, naked young man facing an unrepentant, naked young woman. The trouble was, it was hard to be angry for very long with Halcyon sitting there grinning at him.

"You look good with nothing on", she said.

It was only then that Tom noticed the time.

"God damn you", he said. "You've made me late for school."

"And damn you too—Anne Weston was supposed to pick me up at eight thirty to go and teach euphonics."

Tom collapsed onto the bed and, holding on to each other, they laughed until they wept ambiguous tears.

*

The only telephone in Mrs. Trathgannon's house was downstairs by the front door, and Tom absolutely refused to venture into that hostile territory. So he and Halcyon made some primitive ablutions, got dressed, crept to the side door, ran to the car and made their getaway before that outraged lady could catch them.

On the way to the call box on the street corner, Tom said, "I haven't got time to take you out to the conference so I'm afraid you're going to have to go back to the B-S house".

"I know, but it's not so bad now it's daylight. Will you come and see me after school?"

Tom hesitated, feeling that he shouldn't but knowing that he would.

"Come on", said Halcyon, "Be a pal."

"OK, Halcyon, as long as you understand the situation. I'm just afraid that someone's going to get hurt, or even more hurt than they are already. Whether it's you, me or Alison I don't know."

Halcyon spoke very seriously.

"Probably all of the above. When I was just plain Doreen Tompkins—it seems ages ago—I used to worry a lot about the future. But since old Klaus turned me into Halcyon, everything's been so weird that I don't even think about it any more. I just take everything as it comes. Sometimes it's sugar and sometimes it's shit, but it just happens and there's nothing much I can do about it. So don't worry about me. I'm here if you want me and maybe by the time you and Alison are married I can figure something out. There's the telephone."

Tom got out, called the school and spoke to Flossie, giving a severely edited version of what had happened. He took Halcyon home, made sure that she was safely inside and that the house was otherwise uninhabited, and set off for school.

*

Tom's story, that he had overslept after being out very late searching for an old gentleman on Glastonbury Tor, was accepted with some reserve by the headmaster of the Grammar School, and with derision by some of his colleagues, including Elwyn Davies.

"So young Tom straggles in after another night on the tiles!"

"Shut up", Tom snapped with more than usual vehemence. "If you'd had to straggle down the Tor with that old man at midnight in the pouring rain, you'd be the worse for wear in the morning."

"OK, OK, so I put my big foot in it again. What do you think of the paintings of Van Eyck?"

"They reveal the artist's total ignorance of human nature. When I've got some idea of what's going on I'll tell you about it. Meanwhile I have to go and bully a class of subnormal sixteen-year-olds into learning enough stuff to pass an exam without having the faintest idea what they're writing about."

After school Tom went in search of Mrs. Barrington-Smythe's old station wagon, which was still where Imre had left it. Tom knew enough about old cars to be confident that the engine would start easily enough if he was careful not to flood it. After thirty-six hours the carburetor had dried out, the battery had regained a little and the car started after a couple of turns of the handle. Tom parked his own car and drove the wagon back to the B-S house.

Halcyon, modestly dressed in jeans and a tee-shirt, was sitting in the front room, looking out of an open window. She hadn't seen a soul all day.

"Hello", she said. "There isn't any real food in this house and I'm bored stiff and starving. Can we go out and get something to eat? And listen—Klaus came here early and cleared out. All of his stuff is gone and there was just a letter for me. You'd better read it. Wait a minute—I'll come out."

Halcyon emerged from the front door with the letter in her hand.

"Let's start walking", she said. "They're just about finishing at the conference and someone's probably going to show up and ask me what the hell I've been doing all day. There's a tea shop just round the corner and you can read it when we get there. And here's his front door key. You better take it."

Tom couldn't wait, so he put the key into his pocket and read the letter as he walked.

"Dear Halcyon", it said, not in Klaus's usually flamboyant hand but in an untidy scrawl; "I find it necessary to return to New York immediately. Here is your ticket and some money, but I shall understand perfectly if you decide to remain in England. It is impossible to explain further, since there is much that you do not and should not know, but I should tell you that if you do go to New York, I may already have left by the time you arrive. However, your room in the brownstone will still be available for you.

"I realize that my behavior has been open to reproach. I can only say that when the present crisis is over, I shall offer you any assistance that you are willing to accept in developing your outstanding talent as a euphonist, or in any other endeavor you wish to pursue. Thank you for coming to the rescue last night; please convey also my thanks to Mr. Dexter. He is a young man of considerable resource and moral fibre, and may be the best friend you have at this time.

"I shall be in your debt for whatever remains of this life and in future lives."

Tom looked up and was not surprised to see tears in Halcyon's eyes.

"He's not really such a bad man, Tom. He looked after us and we were kind of settled in a weird sort of way. It was kind of comfortable even though we knew it couldn't last. Have you got any idea what's going on?"

"Only the vaguest outline."

"Then listen. Klaus did a pretty good job of cleaning up before he left. He did the kitchen and he even tidied up Imre's room, but he forgot to empty the kitchen garbage so when I went to throw away my teabag it was full, and what do you think it was full of?"

This turned out to have been a rhetorical question, so Tom's profession of total ignorance died on his lips.

"Bloody paper towels!" Halcyon continued.

Busy with his own thoughts, Tom was about comment that this wasn't surprising when Halcyon again forestalled him.

"I mean paper towels soaked with blood, only it wasn't fresh—it was mostly dried up and going brown, and it was a lot, not like just cutting your finger with the carving knife and I think I know whose it was. It couldn't have been Alison's or Klaus's so it must have been . . ."

"Imre's?"

"Yes—no wonder I was scared to stay there."

"He seems to have been well enough to pack and drive to the station. Do you think Klaus did something to him?"

"Yes, I think he got pissed off and gave him a fourpenny one. Did you see his hand last night?"

"Not particularly."

The tea shop was called "Cakes and All", and they sat at table in the window while Halcyon went on talking.

"Well, I thought there was something funny about the way he was drinking his brandy. I've never seen him drink left-handed before and when he was sleeping, his right hand was hanging down in front of me and it looked all swollen and scabby and that letter looks like he wrote it left-handed. I want to have a whole toasted teacake. What are you going to have?"

"OK, so Klaus punched Imre on the nose because of something he said. I'll just have a cup of tea."

"Come on, Tom, you'll be found dead with nothing in you. That's what my mum says. I don't suppose it helps much, but thinking about Imre with a broken nose makes me feel better."

"Me too, but I don't think you hurt your hand that much punching somebody on the nose. Maybe he hit him in the teeth. OK, I'll have a teacake and you can help me finish it. Listen, I can't stay in my apartment—I haven't seen Mrs. T but she's going to throw me out anyway. How long are you going to stay here?"

"I guess I'll stick it out until the end of the conference. That's Sunday, and then I'm not sure whether I'm going home or back to New York. Do you want to move in with me till then?"

"Yes, only . . ."

"Only you don't want to sleep with me?"

"Well, you see . . ."

"That's not very flattering. I thought we had a good time last night."

"Yes, but . . ."

"And I don't think Alison would mind—I'll just be keeping you warm for her."

Tom grabbed Halcyon and kissed her uncompromisingly.

"That's the only way I could think of of shutting you up. I do want to sleep with you—things don't hurt so much—but I don't think it's a very good reason and it really isn't very flattering to you."

"Like you're taking me instead of a couple of aspirins? Well I don't care—I'll just borrow you for as long as I can. I'm going to be in Klaus's room and you can sleep anywhere you like, only if it isn't with me I'll be very upset."

(20)

When Halcyon had finished her teacake and half of Tom's, they bought some milk, apples and sausage rolls at the adjacent grocery and went back to the B-S. Telling Halcyon that he might be gone for a few hours, and being told to mind what he got up to, Tom took the old station wagon and drove to Mrs. Trathgannon's house. His landlady was on her knees, weeding the front garden. At the sight of her errant tenant she stood up as quickly as her elderly joints would allow her to, put her hands on her hips and opened her mouth to speak. Tom was just quick enough to forestall her.

"Good evening, Mrs. Trathgannon. I'll be moving out by the end of the week and I'm going to start taking some of my things now. I'll pay you an extra month's rent in lieu of notice."

Mollified by the prospect of a little free money, Mrs. T cancelled the dissection of Tom's morals on which she had been about to embark, but couldn't resist a final jab.

"Well, Mr. Dexter, I think that will be satisfactory. I expect you will find somewhere where you will be able to conduct your affairs without offending your elders."

"Yes, Mrs. T. You and your husband will be left in peace, knowing that other people's affairs are their own affair. Now, if you'll excuse me, I'll get on with the job."

None of the furniture in the apartment belonged to Tom, so his main purpose was to take essential personal possessions and everything he needed for school. While he was picking out a few books his eye fell on his old copy of Francis Bacon's *Novum Organum*, and it gave him an idea for his forthcoming lecture at the conference.

After several trips up and down the stairs he was packing the last items into the back of the wagon when Mrs. Trathgannon came and stood beside him.

"I'm sorry you're leaving, Mr. Dexter. You've always been such a good boy and I can't think what's come over you."

"Probably not as good as you think, Mrs. T, just more discreet. But, you know, things happen and you can't always do much about it. You understand? It's not just casual."

But Mrs. T didn't really understand. Perhaps she didn't remember, or had no way of knowing that people's morals had been pretty much the same fifty years ago as they were now. But she did see the pain in Tom's face.

"Well, I hope things will turn out for the best."

Tom nodded, got into the car and drove off, not to the B-S residence but to a cottage on the outskirts of the town, where Elwyn Davies lived with his wife and small son. By this time, he thought, they would have finished their evening meal and Mickey would be in bed. When he arrived, Elwyn was in the kitchen, washing the dishes, and Diana was still upstairs, singing the baby to sleep.

"Just in time", said Elwyn, handing Tom a tea towel, "and careful with the best china. What shattering emergency brings you here? Woman trouble?"

Unlike Tom, Elwyn and his wife really did have to make ends meet on a schoolmaster's salary, so the "best china" came from Woolworth's.

"You can make that plural", Tom said.

"Women or troubles?"

"Both."

"And you want some advice from Uncle Elwyn?"

"Sort of—and maybe Aunt Di, too. It's partly a question of trying to guess what a woman would do under certain circumstances."

Diana had come downstairs and heard the last remark.

"According to you guys we're totally unpredictable."

Diana was as short, round and fair as her husband was tall, thin and dark. She was a Londoner, a professional clarinetist, and had spent a summer at Tanglewood as a student. Elwyn, who had a fine baritone voice, always said that Diana had fallen for him because she heard him before she saw him, and when she woke up on the morning after the wedding she took one look at him and said, "Elwyn, for God's sake sing!"

Elwyn pointed out that as scientists, he and Tom were used to working with statistics and probabilities, and maybe they could figure something out, to which Tom replied that statistics weren't much use when you were dealing with just one event.

"I suppose the main thing is that I'd just like to talk the whole thing out. The other thing is that I need to use your telephone. I'd like to ask my father if someone at the Sentinel could do a bit of detective work."

He described the sequence of events from the tree and the posters to the rescue of Klaus, including Halcyon's account of all the goings on between Klaus, Imre and Alison. After that he was a little more circumspect. He explained why Halcyon had spent the night in his apartment, but he didn't mention her method of helping him to sleep. Elwyn, who had already taken a strong dislike to Imre because of his performance at the science workshop, was very curious about the blow-up in the kitchen.

"Sounds like a real bastard, but what could he have said to put Alison into such a flat spin? She may be a bit impetuous, but she looks pretty self-possessed."

"Something about her parents", Diana suggested. "Maybe her mother—she never said what happened to her, did she?"

"No, all she said was that her mother died when she—I mean Alison—was about sixteen. She didn't seem to want to talk about it. And I have feeling there's not all that much fatherly love for her."

"That might be important—otherwise the first thing she would do would probably be to go back to her dad. I think you should see if you can find out what happened to her mother. I expect the *Sentinel* could manage that. But listen, Tom, are you sure you want to get all lathered up about a girl you've only known for a couple of days? And what about this other girl? It sounds a bit as if you've fallen for her too."

Tom was silent for a few moments.

"That's true", he said finally. "When she's doing euphonics she's breathtaking and when she's being good old down-to-earth Doreen Tompkins she's funny and generous and much more intelligent than you might have thought. If I hadn't met Alison first . . . I can't explain it, but Alison's just something altogether different. I don't think she ran away because she's afraid of something. Whatever it was, I think I helped precipitate it, and I can't go on without knowing."

Elwyn looked disapprovingly at Tom.

"So you're contemplating giving up your job here and flying off to America on the off chance that you'll find her and she'll have cooled off enough to explain herself and still want to marry you. Come on, Tom, you know how evanescent these things are."

"Really?" said Diana. "You didn't seem to think I was evanescent."

"Well, you didn't scream and disappear into the sunset."

"I'll have to try it next time you . . . Well, never mind that. I'll tell you what I think, Tom. It's not just your feelings for Alison and it's not just a mystery that you want to solve. It's something you're up to your neck in and you won't be happy until you find the answer—or answers. It's the physicist in you, I suppose, but the idea that you're somehow responsible for what happened is just silly. You meet this girl, you fall for each other and go to bed together. This upsets the malevolent Imre so he says something nasty to the girl and she scoots. It's not even as if he was the outraged husband."

Having finished with the dishes, Elwyn was opening a bottle of Tarragona, a very useful drink for people of modest means. He propped himself against the kitchen sink, Diana sat on a tall stool, Tom hoisted himself on to the counter, and the bottle started on its triangular rounds.

Diana looked at Tom and raised her glass. "Here's to you and a happy ending, and this is what I think. If it had been something ordinary, she would have come to you or maybe to Halcyon. She ran away because it was something she was ashamed of or something she couldn't explain that made it impossible for her to have any kind of relationship with you. Do you think she's an honest girl?"

"I think so. She wanted me to know all about her past."

"Then Imre must have told her something that she didn't know before, or she would have told you already—maybe something that she did but never knew the consequences of, or something about her parents."

The bottle went round again and Tom said, "I suppose out of all the possibilities the most likely one is that she's gone straight to her father, even though he doesn't seem to care that much for her. And I think she needs time."

"That's all very well", Elwyn chipped in, "but what about Imre?"

"Imre is short, fat, slow-moving and probably has a damaged face. Alison could run rings round him. And he has the same problem I have. He gets off the train at Heathrow and what does he do next? He has no more idea than we have where to start looking. And Alison can't write to me because she doesn't know my address—in fact I don't either at this point. Mrs. Trathgannon objects to my entertaining young women in my flat."

"Imre goes straight to Heathrow", said Elwyn. "It's a dead cert. He knows it's a bit stupid because there must be dozens of flights to New York, but it's his only chance. He wanders round all the check-ins on the off chance of seeing Alison. He hops on a flight to New York, can't find her there and turns up at her father's house a day later. What does he do then? Bang on the door and demand to see Alison, or confront her father with a bit of unpleasant information? What does he hope to get out of it? Either he's out of his mind or he has something up his sleeve. And if you're short of somewhere to stay, we have a spare room."

"Thanks all the same but I'm going to stick around Mrs. B-S's house until the end of the conference."

"You mean you're moving in with Halcyon for a few days. Getting the best of both worlds?"

Tom had reached a kind of provisional working relationship with Halcyon, but when Elwyn put it as baldly and disapprovingly as that it made him feel acutely uncomfortable, so he abruptly changed the subject.

"If you had to give a talk on modern physics to a bunch of Archway teachers, what would you talk about?"

"Indeterminacy", said Elwyn promptly.

"That's a bit advanced, isn't it?"

"They think everything is determined by karma. You can put the two ideas side by side."

*

The bottle now being empty, Tom thought it was time to try calling his father. It was at this point that he realized that in spite of all his efforts he still hadn't been thinking very clearly. He could certainly ask Lord Otterill if his staff could trace a young woman called Alison Hübel through London Airport, but he also wanted to find out what had happened to her mother, and he had no idea what her mother's name was. Well, perhaps Halcyon or Anne Weston would know. In the meantime he could get on with the first objective. So he made the call, only to be informed by Fortescue that Lord Otterill was in Canada and would not return to England until the end of next week.

"Where exactly is he now?" Tom asked.

"I believe he is in Montreal, whence he will travel to Toronto and finally to New York. Is there any way in which I can be of assistance?"

"You could tell me when he's expected to arrive in New York and where he'll be staying."

"Certainly, your Lordship, all the information is at hand. He will arrive in New York on Monday of next week and stay with his friend Ted Murdoch, the proprietor of the New York Evening News and, I believe, sundry other publications. 825b Park Avenue, Sir, and the number is 212-536-1101."

"Thanks very much. And do you happen to have the number of Jack Peterson?"

"I'm afraid not, but you should be able to get him *via* the main office in the morning."

Jack Peterson was the sports editor at the Sentinel and the only one of Lord Otterill's employees Tom knew well enough to ask a favor.

*

When Elwyn saw Tom to the front door he appeared to have something on his mind. Eventually it came out.

"What was it like with Halcyon?"

"What do you mean?"

"Come on, you know what I mean. You said she was generous, so how generous was she?"

Tom hesitated long enough to make the answer obvious. In the end, all he could say was, "Goodnight, Elwyn. Thanks for the help."

With several glasses of Tarragona inside him, Tom drove very slowly back to the B-S house. Taking a suitcase with him, he let himself in through the front door. The place was very quiet, so he found a sausage roll and an apple and sat at the kitchen table. Now he knew what he was going to do, and he wanted to tell Halcyon. So after finishing the sausage roll and depositing the apple core with the bloody paper towels he went upstairs. Halcyon was asleep in Klaus's bedroom and Tom had forgotten to bring pajamas, so he simply took everything off and got into bed. It looked as if he'd have to explain things in the morning.

Halcyon stirred sleepily and said, "Hello, big boy, do you want your sleeping pill?"

Tom didn't say anything but Halcyon's arms were already around him.

(21)

It was all very confusing. Imre was a fat, slow-moving nucleus and Alison could run rings round him. Did that mean she was an electron? No, that was all wrong—Imre had no charge, so he must be a neutron and a neutron wouldn't attract an electron. That didn't work either—Imre was repulsive and had a damaged face, and a neutron didn't have a face. It just blundered around making a nuisance of itself—well, maybe that was right after all. Tom gradually regained consciousness at three o'clock in the morning. He had a mild hangover and dimly felt that he had been dreaming about Imre. It took him a little while to remember where he was and who was in bed with him. He felt amazingly comfortable. Fantasies drifted through his mind, of giving up his job, buying a little cottage and staying in bed with Halcyon all day and all night. He thought that this must be her way of mothering him, and this reminded him of Flossie and her daughter. The comparison seemed so comical that he chuckled and Halcyon woke up.

"What is it, Tom? Are you OK?"

"I'm OK—just thinking about something."

"What?"

"You."

"Oh! Do you love me, Tom?"

"Yes."

"I love you. Do you still love Alison?"

"Yes."

"What shall we do?"

"I don't know."

"You could become a Mormon. I think I could get used to it. Come to think of it, Alison and I are sort of used to it already."

Tom tried to include both women in his fantasy of bliss in a country cottage, but somehow it didn't seem to work. It's like the three-body problem in mechanics, his associative mind said—there are no exact solutions.

"If I don't hear from Alison, I'm going to New York next week. Will you come with me?"

"What happens when we find her?"

Tom's euphoria was turning sour on him and he could make only a feeble restatement of the impossible problem.

"I don't know. It's one of the things I have to find out. And I don't want to make you unhappy."

"It looks as if I'm going to be unhappy anyway. And it's not your fault—I did kind of throw myself at you. OK, I'll come with you."

*

At seven o'clock the next morning, having run out of sausage rolls and apples, Tom and Halcyon took everything they needed for the rest of the day and drove out to an all-night café on the main road to Wells, where they sat side by side at the counter and treated themselves to eggs, bacon and coffee.

"Do you know what I'm doing?" Halcyon asked. "I'm pretending that we're a couple and we're having breakfast together and then we're going to work and then we'll come home and be a couple together and do nice things in the evening and go to bed and get up in the morning and have breakfast again. Like that, you see?"

She began to cry.

"I'm sorry, I thought I was being really brave and strong and all that, but I love you so much it hurts, even when I don't think about what happens when you find Alison."

Tom had been about to ask Halcyon whether she knew Alison's mother's name, but now he hesitated and could find no words to comfort her. Her fantasy was so much like his own that a big part of him wanted to say, "OK, let's let Alison go and just take care of each other." But his feelings were in a state of complete confusion and his rational mind seemed to have switched itself off.

Smiling through her tears, Halcyon said, "Well, aren't you going to say something? You could at least put your arms round me and give me a kiss."

Which Tom did.

"Well done, mate!" said the man behind the counter. "I was wondering when you'd get round to it."

*

When they got to the Wolfgang Goerner School it was still only eight o'clock and the parking lot was empty. The weather had turned fine and warm, so Tom suggested walking round to the lawn at the back of the building, where there was a garden seat.

"Halcyon, it's very hard to say this, but maybe it would be better if I just cleared off and got out of your life."

"Is that what you want?"

"No. I want you with me—I need you and I don't know what I'd do without you but . . ."

"I know what the 'but' is. Now listen. Alison is my friend too. We lived in the same household for three years and we were both euphonists and we talked a lot. I want to know what's happened to her, so I'm not doing this just to oblige you. So we'll be partners until we find her, and after that—well, we'll see."

This was a new element that Tom hadn't expected, and he really didn't like the idea of two women fighting over him. He wasn't exactly a modest man but he didn't have that kind of vanity.

"OK", he said. "We'll fight it out together. Do you know what sleeping partners are?"

"Not really, but it sounds like a nice idea."

"That's what I think. I'd better go. Are you coming to my lecture?"

"Yes, but I probably won't understand a word of it."

"Don't worry, I probably won't either. Do you know the names of Alison's parents?"

"Yes, her father is Phillip Johnson. He teaches in Pittstown, Massachusetts and her mother's name was Maria. I've seen their pictures in an old school yearbook and Alison looks just like her mother. Now you come to mention it, it's funny she never had any pictures of them—well, none that I saw."

They walked back to the parking lot just as Harry Grainger and Carolina Ende were driving in, closely followed by Anne Weston and Jane Malone.

"Is it OK if I kiss you in front of all these people?" Tom asked.

"Why not? They've already put one and one together."

(22)

As Tom drove back to school he thought of the old saying about a bird in the hand. On this occasion there was only one in the bush, and maybe a rather dubious one at that. He tried thinking of the situation in reverse. Suppose he had found out something dreadful or humiliating about himself; would he have immediately run to Alison for comfort or advice? Perhaps not, but he wouldn't just have vanished from the scene. Well, to make it fair, suppose it had happened in New York when he was three thousand miles from home; would he have immediately rushed back to Somerset? Most unlikely, he thought, but then he remembered that he didn't actually know that Alison had gone to New York; as far as he knew she might still be somewhere in England. He had to recognize that he couldn't weigh up the situation until he knew what it was that had caused her precipitate flight. He thought about Alison and he thought about Halcyon, and all it did was to make him more confused.

He was free in the second period of the morning, so he called Jack Peterson, who wasn't very optimistic about finding a colleague who would undertake to locate a passenger on an unknown flight at an unknown time on an unknown airline. He did think, however, that there was a reasonable chance of finding out something about a Maria Johnson who died in 1978 in New York City. This was somewhat promising, so Tom set out for the faculty room to fortify himself with a cup of coffee and spend the rest of the period trying to decide what he would tell the Archway people about modern physics. Elwyn's idea of juxtaposing indeterminacy and karma might be a good one, the main problem being that while he knew a great deal about the former he was clueless about the latter. On his way to the coffee urn he encountered Janet Jones, sitting on the floor in a corner of the corridor and having a good cry.

Squatting down beside her, Tom asked, "What's the matter, Janet, and why aren't you in class?"

"Oh, it's just something really stupid", she said between sniffs.

"Boy trouble?"

"Sort of."

"Where are you supposed to be now?"

"In maths with Mrs. Paget, but Marilyn is in there too and I just suddenly couldn't face being in the same room."

"Could you face it now?"

"I think so."

"Well, take a minute to fix up your face and I'll write a note for Mrs. Paget."

"Will I get into trouble?"

"Probably not—Mrs. Paget thinks you're a very good student and nothing like this has happened before."

While Tom was writing the note ("Please excuse Janet; not well—will explain later.") he was thinking that that was what we all thought until life knocked the conceit out of us: nothing like this has ever happened before in the whole history of the human race. Now the highly intelligent, self-possessed Janet has had her nose put out of joint by her dim but diligent friend Marilyn, and it might take several days or even weeks for the tragedy to dissipate. The best thing to do was to refuse to admit any association between Janet's problem and the one he was involved in, but somehow there was a grain of comfort to be found in sharing other people's agonies. Now, about that lecture . . .

*

Ideas buzzed through Tom's mind at high speed. Except for the ones that reminded him of his tangled love life, they disappeared without leaving much of a trace. Most equations have no solutions, so we have to invent imaginary numbers to deal with them. His personal problem seemed to have no solution and he didn't seem able to imagine one. We can calculate the orbit of the earth around the sun or the moon around the earth, but put all three bodies together and we can only get approximations. If he was the earth, which was the moon—Alison or Halcyon? Somehow the assonance between their names made the thing even more confusing. There were other bodies in the picture—Klaus, who seemed to be an unusually refined specimen of the class of Dirty Old Men, and Imre, who was a particularly odious middle-aged one. According to Newton all the bodies in the solar system attract one another, but Imre didn't attract anybody. Klaus apparently still did but the attraction had weakened. Perhaps his large size suggested a low specific gravity. Or maybe he was like Jupiter and had a lot of moons, and whatever Alison's problem was, he was in the middle of it. Alison's mother had hovered for a long time but had apparently been reluctant to go into orbit with him. Perhaps Alison and Halcyon had come out of their orbits around Klaus and simply attached themselves to the next reasonably dense object they encountered. Tom came out of his daydream and sat up in a hurry. He knew that he was attractive to women, but they had not always made a habit of jumping into bed with him at the earliest opportunity. The auditorium at the Wolfgang Goerner School had not been crowded with eligible-looking young males. Was that all it was? The old song about a ricochet romance started going through his head.

"I don't want a ricochet romance, I don't want a ricochet love
If you're careless with your kisses, find another turtle dove."

Maybe it was time to let the instinct for self-preservation put its two cents in.

I have plenty of money, I don't need a job, I can do whatever I want. What I want at the moment is to find Alison and see what's up with her—maybe it was just an infatuation and maybe that's what it is with me. And if Halcyon wants to get involved—well she's old enough to make her own decisions and if that's what she wants it's OK with me. And it may be helpful to get in with these Archway people. Now then, what was it that Bacon said about atoms?

All of which was of some help in tackling the immediate task, but it didn't even scratch the surface of his inner confusion and it concealed the ambiguity of his motivation. Was he more interested in finding Alison or in figuring out which woman he wanted and getting her?

*

Halcyon was sitting under an oak tree at the edge of the parking lot when Tom arrived at the Wolfgang Goerner School. As he caught sight of her the instinct for self-preservation took rather a knock.

"Everyone else is guzzling tea and *stollen*", she said. "Here, would you like this?"

She produced two slices of the delicious hybrid of bread and cake, wrapped in a napkin. Thinking of Janet and the whole world of boy-girl miseries, all he could say was, "Thank you", in a very muffled voice.

"What's the matter? Now listen to me, Tom Dexter, I want you to be in love with me, but I won't have you feeling sorry for me. You got that?"

"OK, OK, damn your eyes!"

But somehow he couldn't help feeling sorry for her.

*

Harry Grainger introduced Tom's lecture.

"Dear Friends, as you already know, Imre Takacs has been called away on urgent family business. We're delighted that Thomas Dexter has consented, at very short notice, to take his place. Mr. Dexter, who is a graduate of the University of Cambridge, will speak about a subject which our founder would certainly have considered to be of the greatest possible interest—the relationship between modern physics and human destiny."

As Tom stepped up to the podium to polite applause, he was still wondering why these people simply wouldn't believe him when he said that his name was Tom. Getting his mind back to the immediate subject he took out the one sheet of paper that constituted his lecture notes. His talk was going to be largely improvised, and he had been warned that his audience, which had been expecting a nice, comfortable talk on the qualities of metals in relation to the planets, would be quite apprehensive. Most of its members were up to their necks in things like reincarnation and karma, but were as ignorant of modern science as they were of Goerner's interest in it. All Tom knew about karma was the smattering obtained from a brief conversation with Halcyon while falling asleep the night before, so he had decided make his talk as informal as possible and take as his theme something that he had already done a lot of thinking about—the enormous gap between quantum physics and relativity theory on the one hand, and ordinary life on the other. He introduced his lecture with a passage from Francis Bacon, the Lord Chancellor of England nearly four hundred years previously, who had tried to revolutionize science and had received a great deal of posthumous abuse for his pains.

"Bacon's chief concern was to create a practical kind of science that would be of great benefit to his fellow human beings. He thought that the science of his time concerned itself far too much with the very big and the very little, whereas, in his own words, 'utility and the means of working result entirely from things intermediate. Hence it is that men cease not from abstracting nature until they come to potential and uninformed matter, nor, on the other hand, from dissecting nature till they reach the atom; things which, even if true, can do little for the welfare of mankind.' It's an interesting fact that Bacon's strictures apply to the two areas of physical science that are hardest for most people to understand today—the theory of relativity and the quantum theory. The "things intermediate", which we find in our living rooms and garages, obey ordinary, old-fashioned physical laws. It's only when we get involved with things far beyond the range of our normal human senses that bewilderment sets in.

"So, as a practical man of science Bacon had little use for atomic theories and high-flown discussions about matter, space and time, and he would have been astonished at the enormous influence these apparently abstruse matters have on our daily lives. It remains true, however, that in all our daily doings we are totally unconscious of atomic particles and the relativistic kinks of the universe."

Tom picked up his piece of paper and put it back into his pocket.

"Well, folks, that's the end of my notes—now I'm going to give you a brief report on something that emphasizes this great gap between modern physics and ordinary experience—something quite well known and not all that modern. In fact it had its fiftieth anniversary several years ago. I'm speaking of what is usually known as Heisenberg's Uncertainty Principle."

Someone in the audience groaned and several people chuckled. Somehow this gave Tom a little more confidence. He talked about the fact that with a thing like teapot or a car you can tell where it is by looking at it, and looking at it doesn't seem to have any effect on it. If we want to know where a tiny, invisible particle like an electron is, we have to illuminate it with a ray of light and catch the light that it reflects in some kind of instrument. The trouble is that the electron is so tiny that the impact of the light ray knocks it into the middle of next week, so the information we get tells us where it was but not where it is now. That, Tom said, is just a very rough example of the kind of thing that brought us to the idea of indeterminacy. Scientists in the 1920's found several different ways of arriving at this idea, and most agreed that for many purposes it was not practical to work with individual particles, and that physics would have to become a matter of probabilities and statistics. The reason why we could predict the behavior of matter in bulk so accurately was that we were dealing with such large numbers of particles that the probabilities became close to being certainties. There was, however, still plenty of uncertainty around, and no one believed the old idea of determinism in which if one knew the present state of the universe exactly, all future states could be predicted and so must be predetermined. In any case, he said, it's impossible in principle to know the state of anything exactly, even apart from the uncertainty principle.

A hand waved in the audience and Tom paused.

"Surely there must at all times be an exact state of the universe, even if we can't know what it is."

Tom smiled encouragingly.

"That is what common sense tells us, but modern physicists often find that they have to ignore common sense, and work with happenings and probabilities instead of particles and their movements. So the things that could be stated precisely would be probabilities, not traditional measurements. One of the basic ideas is that anything that can't be observed has to be ignored—if we can't measure it, we mustn't talk about it—and this brings me to the point that I wanted to make; in spite of all this uncertainty, many scientists seem to be working on the assumption that they are on the road to a complete explanation of the universe, including the people who live in it. But some think that our decisions about the kind of information that we allow into the system mean that modern physics is in some ways subjective and that really objective experience eludes it. A lot of scientists have written about such things in books about physics, philosophy and religion. They tend to contradict one another quite a bit, and it's hard to know who's right. As some of you know, until last Thursday I had never heard of Wolfgang Goerner; but I do know that since Heisenberg's principle was announced, the problems of modern physics have only become more acute, and I'm ready to explore any path that seems to offer the prospect of a more effective way of looking at nature."

Tom was trying to tell the exact truth while steering his talk in a direction that would help him to infiltrate the Archway movement. Everything he had said was correct, to the best of his knowledge, but there was a definite slant that he intended to push a little further.

"At the time when Heisenberg's Principle was introduced, a great astrophysicist named Eddington put forward an idea that, as far as I know, has never been properly explored. He said that although the uncertainty principle seemed to destroy the old idea of determinism, it didn't replace it with anything significantly better on a human level. He pointed out that calculations based on the statistics of atomic particles worked as long as their behavior was random, but would not work if there was any influence that gave their behavior any kind of unity. He believed that in the human brain there is a region where such an influence exists and creates what he called conscious matter. He said that the purely objective world is the spiritual world. It is only because we are spiritual beings that we recognize matter, and perhaps the spiritual field is strong enough in us to change random particles into conscious matter. It may be that the spirit is so strong in us in the juiciest and most unconscious parts of our being that it can flow into the dry area of the brain where greatest consciousness is needed. Eddington died in 1944 and since then his ideas have generally been ridiculed, but it seems to me that he pointed to an interaction between spiritual and material that might well be explored from this side of the fence. In other words, if there is really any possibility of a bridge between the kind of work done in the Cosmic Wisdom Movement and what is happening in university physics departments, this might be the place to start building it.

"That's all I have to say this evening. I apologize for not having talked about karma but I excuse myself on the ground that I prefer to speak about things that I know something about. Thank you for listening."

This time the applause was more enthusiastic and Tom felt that he had made a modest hit. Harry Grainger thanked him for a thought-provoking and insightful speech and Kara Henkemens closed the session with a euphonics performance of a verse by Wolfgang Goerner. This was in German, so Tom didn't understand much of it. He let his thoughts dwell on the question of how much he believed of what he had just been saying, and how far he had taken Eddington's opinions beyond anything that the great astrophysicist had actually said. He was very thankful that Elwyn wasn't present and he returned from his fit of abstraction just in time to hear the last word of the verse, which was "Schicksal". Did these CW people really believe that everything was a matter of destiny? Tom didn't know what they believed, but he did know that he couldn't just sit back and let destiny have its way with Alison.

(23)

Several people wanted to shake Tom's hand and Anne Weston was very anxious to have another talk with him. Halcyon would be waiting in his car but he couldn't avoid giving the Faculty Chair a few minutes. The conversation took place on a somewhat artificial basis; Anne couldn't mention her suspicion that if Tom's primary interest wasn't Alison it must be Halcyon, and Tom was at pains to be as honest as he could while concealing his motive for wanting to cross the Atlantic and failing to mention that he intended to leave for New York at the earliest possible moment.

"Well, Thomas, that was a highly inspirational talk and I'm quite sure that your ideas will be of great interest to the scientists at the Goerner Institute. What I wanted to talk to you about is the need that we have in New York for a physics teacher, and I must say that what we have just heard from you has convinced me that you are exactly the kind of person that our movement needs—someone with deep spiritual insight and a profound knowledge of modern science. So let me ask whether you would consider the possibility of coming to America."

Did Anne really believe what she was saying, or was she just spreading the butter—or was it soft soap?—with both hands. In any case Tom didn't want to give the impression of jumping in with both feet.

"I'm willing to consider it, but you have to remember that I know virtually nothing about the Archway Movement and its methods. I certainly want to find out more, and I'd really have to do that before making a commitment."

"Well, as far as the methodology of teaching is concerned, we have an in-service training program which includes the study of Goerner's insights into human development. At the same time, I can see what a tremendous step it would be for you to leave your present job at such short notice and start a new one on a new continent a few weeks later. What do you think of us, from what you've seen so far?"

"That's very hard to say—I mean, if I put it bluntly, you haven't represented yourselves very well. Klaus Hübel's talk started well enough but soon got into stuff that meant absolutely nothing to me or anyone else who wasn't already into Cosmic Wisdom, and I wasn't very impressed with the science workshop. Then there was all the coming and going on Monday . . .

"That makes it hard to understand why you have any interest at all."

Tom couldn't very well explain that he was in love with two euphonists.

"There are two reasons. One is that I'm not particularly satisfied with the work I'm doing at the Grammar School. The other is that in spite of everything, I have the feeling that Goerner did get hold of something real and true. What I'd like to do is to see if I can take a leave from the Grammar School and spend a few months in America, visiting your school and maybe some others. I'd like to get a feel of what the movement is really like, and I could study Goerner's educational works while I'm doing so."

"Well, I think that's a very sensible approach. When would you expect to arrive in New York?"

"I'll have to talk to my headmaster before I can say anything definite, but all being well I'd like to have a couple of weeks to get acclimatized before school starts in September."

"I suppose there's no chance that you could come over sooner than that."

"How much sooner?"

"Well, we have a summer program for teachers that starts next Wednesday in Manhattan, but I imagine that's out of the question. In any case, that may be a bit problematical, as we were expecting Klaus, Alison and Imre to take part."

"I'm afraid that is a bit too soon. What will you do if Klaus, Alison and Imre are not available?"

"That remains to be seen. Frau Ende will be there and there are people from our own faculty and the Pittstown school who might be able to help out."

"Well, the best of luck with it and I hope to see you in August."

"Wonderful—then you could come to some of our opening faculty meetings, as a visitor, of course, and I could arrange for you to visit some classes and have some sessions with the teachers who run the training course. I'll be in Glastonbury until Monday, so please let me know what you decide."

*

"Well, I sort of understood what you were getting at, and everyone else seemed to like it. But I did wonder a bit if you believed everything you were saying."

"You know, Halcyon, you're much too smart—you can see right through me."

"That's what love does. I don't buy that bit about it making you blind."

"Are you sure you really love me? I couldn't help wondering if it was just the relief of getting away from Klaus."

"Can't you tell? I'm not just a promiscuous baggage, you know. And except for this business I haven't cried for years. How can you love anyone who cries all the time?"

Tom was busy kissing her tears away when he heard a step at the side of the car.

"Oh, I'm sorry . . . I'll see you in the morning."

It was Elwyn.

"Can we go home now?" Halcyon whispered.

On the way back, Tom phoned the headmaster and arranged to see him at half past eight the next morning. He offered to take Halcyon out to dinner but she said that she didn't feel like it. She sat in the car while Tom stocked up again at the local grocery and when they got home she said that she wasn't feeling well and wanted to go to bed.

"Kiss me good night, Sergeant Major", she said with a little flash of humor.

Tom kissed her gently and managed to avoid asking her what was the matter. He thought he knew exactly what the matter was, doubted whether it was PMS, and felt miserably guilty about it. He was also feeling too exhausted to do anything useful and too jittery to go to sleep. When he went upstairs an hour later, Halcyon was sitting up in bed, reading *The Evolution of the Sexes* by Wolfgang Goerner. She was wearing a long mauve flannel nightie and looking a little more cheerful.

"It says here that the sexes evolved because of the fall, only it seems that there was more than one fall and none of them seem to be the one in the Bible. My Mum told me that the serpent was really Adam's dick and if Eve had offered Adam a Brussels sprout we wouldn't be here now."

Tom went downstairs and brought in another suitcase from the old car. He took it upstairs, opened it in front of Halcyon and took out a suit of striped panamas. Carefully avoiding exposure, he put them on and asked, "Please may I sleep with you, Halcyon?"

"I don't know. I'll have to think about it."

Tom wasn't sure how seriously to take this and the pause lasted long enough to cause something to turn over in the pit of his stomach.

"I still don't know, so I want you to do something while I make up my mind. Go down to the kitchen and bring two glasses and then go to the box room and look in my big suitcase. Take something from it and bring it here. Then I'll tell you."

Tom brought the glasses and the bottle of dry sherry that he found in Halcyon's suitcase. When he got back to the bedroom he found that Halcyon had pulled the covers right up to her chin and appeared to be asleep. He was wondering what to do next when she murmured, "Now pour out the sherry, take off those stupid pajamas and get into bed."

It was only then that he noticed that Halcyon's mauve nightie was lying neatly folded at the foot of the bed.

"This is sort of a celebration, or you might call it a parting shot—starting tomorrow I want to be just a kind of business partner until this whole thing gets settled. So make it good."

Halcyon sat up and took a swig of her drink. Tom felt as if something inside him was being put through the wringer, but there was something comical about the sight of Venus sitting up in bed and drinking sherry out of a kitchen tumbler, and he couldn't help laughing.

"What's so funny, big boy?"

"I don't know. How long have we known each other?"

"Several years, I think."

"I know—it seems like that, but really it's fifty and a half hours unless you count Sunday when I saw you on the stage and you didn't see me."

"Yes, I did, and I thought who's that big guy sitting in the front row? He doesn't look like a CW. And then I saw you with Alison."

"What did you think then?"

"Don't embarrass me. I thought some things. And I think you're right about bouncing off Klaus, but it doesn't mean I don't really love you. Can you drink and make love at the same time?"

"I don't know—I've never tried."

"Well, I'm going to talk to the serpent while you finish."

Halcyon's head disappeared under the covers. Tom drained his glass, forgot his troubles for a while and went with the flow.

*

It was still daylight and Halcyon's arms were still around him, but Tom was thinking about Alison. It occurred to him that Jack Peterson was probably still in his office and might have some information. As he gently detached himself, Halcyon opened an eye and said, "What's up, big boy?"

"I have to make a phone call."

"OK, I'll still be here when you get back."

Admirable young woman, Tom thought, not to ask who he was calling and how long he would be. Then he thought, well maybe she doesn't care, and then, but I'm sure she does. He put some clothes on, kissed her and went down to the phone box on the corner. He arranged his supply of coins, dialed the number and hoped for the best. His luck was in.

"Hello, Jack. If you've got anything for me please talk fast—I might run out of coins."

"Nothing on your Hübel friend", Jack said, "but we have a report on a traffic accident that took place in Manhattan in 1978. A woman called Maria Johnson was giving her daughter a driving lesson when the kid hit the accelerator instead of the brake. The car shot through a red light and was broadsided by a truck. Johnson was killed and her daughter received minor injuries."

"Does it give the daughter's name?"

"No—the victim's age was given as fifty-one and the daughter's as sixteen. The only other information is that it happened on West 96th Street and that the police expressed the opinion that driving instruction should be left to professionals."

So Alison had been reluctant to speak of her mother's death because she was still carrying a load of guilt, but this couldn't be the subject of Imre's revelation. It must be something different and worse. Tom thanked his friend and asked him to keep trying on the Hübel front—Alison or Klaus.

*

At six o'clock the next morning, Tom was awakened by the sound of someone clattering in the kitchen and the smell of burning toast. Like his quarters at the Trathgannons', this house had a bathtub but no shower, and he was on his way there when he almost bumped into Halcyon, who was wearing slippers, a green pinafore and nothing else, and carrying a tray loaded with tea and toast.

"I'd have been up sooner only the B-S toaster is almost as old as she is and thinks it's an incinerator. Do you like my new dress?"

"It's very becoming—I think you should wear it for your next performance."

Somehow it didn't seem to be the moment for the serious talk that Tom thought they obviously ought to have. Halcyon seemed to have the knack of heading such things off, so he gave himself a quick scrub at the wash basin and got back into bed.

"You smell very nice", he said.

"Well, I got up early and had a bath. Is the toast OK? Sorry there's no marmalade. If we were married I'd bring you breakfast in bed every day."

"If we were married we could have each other for breakfast every day. Now that you're just my business partner, do you want me to move out? I could probably go and stay with Elwyn."

"I wish you wouldn't be so goddamn calm and considerate about everything! It's OK for you, you're having the best of both worlds—a nice romantic adventure to find Alison and plenty of sex on the side with me. What I want is something that I can't have. I want Alison to disappear without a trace, and now I come to think about it, why the hell am I trying to help you find her? I have to keep reminding myself that I started this—otherwise I might start feeling used and get seriously angry. OK, I know, I'm sorry—you're just as mixed up as I am. And that thing about being a business partner seemed like a good idea, only I can't do it—I think maybe you really do love me and I just want you to hold me tight and talk to me about Heisenbugger's Principle. I'm not as dumb as I look, you know—if I'd had you for a teacher I might really have got somewhere."

Tom was thinking that if she really wanted him to leave, she probably wouldn't be wearing just a pinafore. Damn all this science—it turns you into an observer instead of a participant, and then what you observe is never really what you thought it was.

Halcyon had only stopped talking for a moment.

"I guess if we're to have any peace we have to find out about Alison. Can you take me to school and come back and pick me up again afterwards? When we've finished breakfast, I mean. And is it OK if I keep changing my mind?"

"You know, I really think you're the best person I've ever met."

"Don't be silly, Tom", Halcyon said as she took off her pinafore, adding in a confidential undertone, "But I do think you're the best person I've ever had sex with."

(24)

"Come on, you little nympho, you've made me late again."

Halcyon, who was compromising by wearing a slightly longer purple version of her red mini, was indignant.

"I'm not a nympho, I just want to make the most of you while I've got you. Anyway, you could always say No, and I want to see how fast you can drive."

"I'm just a guy who can't say No", Tom sang in his deep bass rumble as the old Morris Minor whizzed through the streets of Glastonbury. He had an obvious reason for feeling high, but it might also have had something to do with the fact that while taking his bath after finally getting out of bed he had decided on a clear course of action, which had been triggered by his talk with Jack Peterson and a review of the facts.

Maria Johnson was born in 1927, attended the Archway School in Ulm, got out of Germany around 1935, and went to the Archway School in Manhattan until about 1945. After college, so presumably about 1949, she went to back to Ulm, stayed there for twelve years and met Alison's father, Phillip Johnson, at Glastonbury in 1961. Alison was born in New York in 1962 and Maria died there in 1978 as a result of a crash that happened when she was giving her daughter a driving lesson. Klaus had been a constant presence in the story, but where did Imre come in? Well, he must have known Phillip Johnson when he was a kid in Manhattan, and he probably met Maria, but he graduated from High School and left for Ulm while Alison was still a child. Alison had said that he often visited the school in Massachusetts, so he must have seen quite a bit of Phillip since his remarriage. Somewhere in all this there was a fact—or maybe just a guess that could be presented as a fact—with such powerful implications that it seemed to have destroyed Alison as a person. Since Imre had had at most a passing acquaintance with Maria it was a reasonable guess that his source of information was either Phillip or Klaus. Klaus was almost certainly back in America at this moment. So, presumably, was Imre, and now it appeared to Tom to be much more likely that Alison was there too. And Phillip might be the focus of their attention. Tom stopped singing and explained all this to Halcyon.

"I want to leave for New York tomorrow. Can you come with me, or do you really have to stay till Monday?"

Halcyon was silent for a long time. Finally she said, "Poor old Alison, no wonder she never talked about her parents. I guess I can get away—I thought I was supposed to help Kara, but I just stand there like a lemon while she does all the talking, so they don't really need me. But I'm scared of what will happen. Will you take care of me?"

Tom was also scared of what might happen. He felt irremediably split, but while his brain was paralyzed, his emotions apparently weren't.

"Yes, I'll take care of you."

"What if you're too busy taking care of Alison? All right, I'll come. I don't know why I'm crying—I just can't help feeling that something bad's going to happen."

Tom thought that Halcyon was probably right, but now that he had a plan, action could displace anxiety, at least to some extent.

"I'm going to the travel agent after school, so I won't be back till after five o'clock. Now I have to rush back and see the headmaster, and God knows what he'll say. 'Bye, my darling, I love you."

Halcyon responded to Tom's fervent hug but could think of nothing to say. She didn't really believe that Tom could be in love with two people at the same time and she thought that, given the choice, he would obviously take Alison. She got out of the car and stood forlornly watching it disappear up the lane.

"Good morning, Miss Tompkins—or may I call you Halcyon?"

Halcyon turned and found Bill Graveney looking sympathetically at her.

"Good morning, Mr. Graveney. You can call me Doreen. It's my real name and I don't think I want to be Halcyon any more."

"Forgive my asking, but has that young man upset you? And you can call me Bill if you like."

After living with Klaus for several years, Halcyon was deeply suspicious of the sympathetic attentions of elderly gentlemen.

"I'm not upset, Mr. Graveney."

"Oh, I'm sorry, Miss Tompkins. Nice morning."

Halcyon realized that she was still wiping the tears from her eyes and that Bill Graveney might possibly be a nice old man.

"I'm sorry—Bill. It's just things. It's not his fault. Do you think it's possible to be in love with two people at the same time?"

Bill remembered seeing Tom with Alison on Sunday evening, and thought it much more likely that Tom was simply playing fast and loose.

"Well, I can't say it ever happened to me. Do you want to talk about it?"

"Yes, please. Maybe we could skip singing. Do you think there might still be a cup of coffee in the cafeteria?"

They sat with their cups of tepid coffee in the corner of the cafeteria while the other participants drifted off to the auditorium, but they were not free from interruption.

"Good morning, Halcyon. Good morning, William. Not singing today? Perhaps I might join you."

This was Harry Grainger. Halcyon was pretty sure that whatever reservations she had about older males would apply to him, so she spoke up.

"Good morning, Mr. Grainger. I'm consulting Mr. Graveney on a personal matter, so . . ."

"Oh, I see."

Harry didn't see at all and was rather miffed, but he accepted defeat as gracefully as he could.

"Well, I'll see you later. I hope you're not going to miss today's keynote address."

"Oh, who's giving it?" Halcyon asked innocently.

Harry was momentarily taken off-guard, so Bill answered for him

"Mr. Grainger is giving it. I'm sure it will be most enlightening."

Bill grinned at Harry's retreating back, and Halcyon thought that perhaps she had found a new friend. She plunged straight in.

"Tom was very upset when Alison ran away and I . . . I don't know how to say it."

"You offered yourself as a substitute?"

"Yes. It was just a sort of friendly impulse at first, but now I'm terribly in love with him."

Halcyon told Bill as much of the story as she could. She didn't say much about sex but the implications were clear enough.

"Do you think I should go with him?" she asked.

"How old are you, Doreen?"

"I'm eighteen."

"Well, for a girl of your age you've already seen quite a bit of life and some of it must have been quite difficult. If you want my advice I should say 'Go ahead.' Treat the whole thing as an adventure that you don't want to miss. You're very young and resilient, and although it may make you unhappy it will be experience and it may bring wisdom. Sorry if that sounds hifalutin but I don't know any other way to say it. Tom is an unusual young man and you may end up with a broken heart, but there are other unusual young men about. I read somewhere that young people average at least three broken hearts apiece, and it's the best time of your life—it's all downhill from there. So make the most of it. And I don't know the answer to your original question, but I have heard of threesomes getting along quite well."

"Have you ever been in a threesome?"

"No. I married my boyhood sweetheart and we lived happily ever after—well, for over fifty years—so you're probably asking the wrong person."

Halcyon hesitated; Bill had evidently lost his wife and she felt that she should say something sympathetic. Graveney helped her out.

"It's all right, my dear, I've learnt to cope. I don't feel that she's very far away and it can't be for long now."

Halcyon was afraid she was going to cry again, so she did her best to pull herself together and went on with the conversation.

"You know, Mr. Graveney—Bill, this isn't quite the kind of advice I expected from you. I thought you would be kind and fatherly and . . ."

"Tell you to go home to your Mum and Dad?"

"Yes."

"But I don't think you would be very happy if you did that. You've seen too much already and it isn't in your temperament. Why don't you want to be Halcyon?"

"I don't know—for some reason I just took naturally to euphonics, but the rest of this CW stuff mostly goes right over my head. You have to read so many lectures and know what Goerner said about everything under the sun, and talk in such a superior way . . . I do sometimes want to get clean away from it."

"What could you do if you didn't do euphonics?"

"Nothing much. I could go home and get a nice boring job at Woolworth's. OK, I know when you put it that way it sounds awful, but I don't know what else I could do. I'm not the studious type, you see. Tom says I'm smart, but I'm not smart that way. That's why I said Woolworth's. But I was forgetting that Klaus said he would help me. Maybe I could go back to school and do something practical, like nursing."

"That's a very good idea. I've known Klaus on and off for quite a number of years. Whatever you may think about him as a lover, he'll keep his word about helping you."

"But do you still think I should go with Tom?"

"Yes, I do. I'm not a hook-line-and-sinker CW person, but I think there's something here that needs to be worked out, and the perfect Goernerite would call it karma. If you don't go you may spend the rest of your life wishing you had."

"Last night I told him I'd go as a kind of—I don't know—assistant and we wouldn't sleep together until the thing was sorted out. And this morning I realized I couldn't keep it up."

Bill laughed.

"I'm sorry, my dear, I know it seems like life and death to you. I can't unravel it, and all I can say is, don't try to look too far ahead. No one knows what's just round the corner and all we can do is to make ourselves as strong as we can so that we can deal with whatever turns up. We don't know what happened to Alison, and when you find her she may not be the same person. And we mustn't forget that she's still Frau Hübel. So I'll stick to my advice, but I'm not going to tell you whether you should sleep with Tom."

"You said it's all experience, so I'm going to sleep with him as long as he wants me and I think maybe I'll still be Halcyon. You're very kind and I think my Mum would like you. She didn't have a whole lot of education, but she really understands things. Do you think it would be all right if I went for a walk now?"

"I think that's a very good idea. I suppose I'd better go to Harry's lecture, although I know exactly what he's going to say."

Halcyon gave Bill a hug and a kiss, and he gazed wistfully after her as she ran to the doorway.

(25)

David Pryce-Jones, the headmaster of Glastonbury Grammar School, was outraged when he heard Tom's plan for the immediate future, the more so since his physics master could give no rationale for his decision to leave at a few days' notice. It wasn't illness or a family emergency, or even a sudden decision to climb Mount Everest.

"So something has happened in your private life, about which you can give no explanation, and which makes it immediately necessary for you to catch a plane and set off for New York. Meanwhile, your colleagues will have to substitute for you for the last three weeks of the school year and I shall have to hunt for a new physics master at the worst possible time. If you can't guarantee that you'll be back in September this talk of a leave of absence is all moonshine. I find this absolutely unacceptable and can only assume that you have taken leave of your senses, an assumption made more plausible by your idiotic offer to pay for a substitute. Even in your present state of irrationality you must have known that things don't work that way in a state-run institution."

Tom pointed out that the General Certificate exams would be starting the following week and that whoever substituted would have very little teaching to do, but the headmaster was not appeased.

"You know as well as I do that people who have worked hard throughout the year look forward to a little relaxation in the last few weeks, and it's too bad of you to deprive them of it. Now go away and leave me in peace to work on the mess that you have created."

Tom went to the staff room for a quick cup of coffee before assembly, and had an embarrassing moment when he found Elwyn standing by the urn. They looked at each other and neither seemed to be able to think of anything to say. As far as Tom was concerned it wasn't just a matter of a somewhat dubious speech and an encounter with a young woman who wasn't the one he had consulted Elwyn about a day or so earlier. What Elwyn didn't know was that for the next three weeks he was going to have to spend most of his free periods substituting for Tom.

Eventually Tom said, "Can we talk at lunch time? I'm not quite such a bad person as you think."

And then, remembering about the substitution, he added, "Or maybe I'm worse."

Meanwhile, Mr. Pryce-Jones had picked up his intercom and asked Flossie to step into his office.

"Do you know what that young idiot Dexter has just told me? We'll have to put an advertisement in the Times Ed immediately."

*

Tom and Elwyn took their plates of sausage, mashed potatoes and cabbage to the prep room next to the chemistry lab, where the overcooked cabbage chimed well with the mousy smell of the acetamide that some students had been preparing. Elwyn kept his room in good order, so there was a clear space for two people to eat side by side at his work bench.

"Do you want to talk first or shall I?" he asked.

"I'd better tell you the worst. I'm in love with two women. I slept with one on Sunday and the other on Monday, Tuesday and Wednesday. The first one has disappeared and the second one is going to help me find her. We're going to New York on Monday, and if we find the first one I have to decide which one I'm going to marry—that is, if either one still wants me. Meanwhile I've given a dubious talk to the Archway people in the hope of getting in with them in case it turns out to be helpful. This morning I told the headmaster I'll be leaving tomorrow and he's furious. I expect you'll be furious too—you'll probably have to substitute."

Elwyn worked industriously on his sausages. There was a long interval before he spoke.

"I always thought there was something a little bit funny about you. Now I realize you're absolutely crazy. Right now I'm stunned and later on I expect I shall be very angry. What a stupid waste of a damn good physicist! Are you coming back, by the way, or will you be gone for good?"

"I wanted to make it a leave of absence but I don't know when or if I'll be back, so the HM's looking for a new physics master."

"You mean to say you actually proposed a leave when you didn't know if you were coming back? No wonder the old boy's furious. And what the hell are you going to do for money? You won't be paid for August and you ought to return your July check. Are you going to sell your Minor? You might get twenty quid for it."

This was a very embarrassing question. Tom hesitated and finally made up his mind to let Elwyn in on his guilty secret.

"I have an allowance from my father."

"Good God! I didn't know Lord Otterill paid his employees that well."

"He doesn't. You see, he's my father."

"Wait a minute. Who's your father?"

"Lord Otterill."

"I don't believe it. You're kidding."

"No—it's absolutely true."

"You mean it, don't you? Well I'll be damned!"

This was too much for Elwyn. He chuckled and the chuckle turned into a guffaw which rapidly became an uncontrollable fit of giggling. It was several minutes before he could speak.

"So, you bastard, you're the Honourable bloody Thomas bloody Dexter."

"Tom, not Thomas. It's what I was christened and you're as bad as the CW's. And, in any case, my father's really a top-quality duke, so I'm actually Lord Leyford."

This set off another round of hysterical laughter.

"Do your women know about this?"

"No, I keep forgetting to tell them."

"I suppose this alters matters. Maybe you're not as crazy as you seem, or maybe you're crazier. I can sort of see why you wanted to keep your family connections quiet and you seem to have made a pretty good job of it. You've actually been living within your income, haven't you?"

"Yes, so the allowance has been building up."

"Well, well, well! That was a bloody awful talk you gave yesterday."

"OK, tell me exactly what was wrong with it."

"Well, of course, one of the worst things was that a lot of it was true. Then you used the correct bits to bolster up all that rot from Eddington and to make matters worse, you misrepresented him. Fortunately that doesn't really matter since nobody takes him seriously any more."

"Not true", said Tom. Five minutes were spent on a heated argument about Eddington's status before Elwyn returned to the real topic, which he did with some heat.

"Listen, Tom. You're making a bloody fool of yourself. I know you don't need the money, but you're a damn fine teacher. You know your stuff and the kids love you. And what you're proposing to do is guaranteed to end up in pure frustration and broken hearts all round. Alison is back in America getting over whatever it was and thinking it was a great one-night-stand she had with you, and Halcyon is just a kid. She's the same age as some of the kids you've been preparing for university entrance, and you have no right to involve her in something like this? What's going to happen to her when this all comes unstuck? For God's sake go to the HM and ask him to forget what you said this morning. Then you can wait for Alison to come back, which she will if she really wants you, and try to make a gentle break with Halcyon, who's probably much too good for you anyway."

This all made such admirable sense that Tom could find little to say in reply. He was uncomfortably aware that even the most ardent love is apt to evaporate and leave not a rack behind. If he persuaded Halcyon to pack up and go home they would both get over it in a few weeks, and maybe Alison had already recovered from whatever it was and was having a good time on the other side of the Atlantic. That was how it looked from the outside, and it was impossible to explain how it felt on the inside.

He told Elwyn what he had heard from Jack Peterson.

"Well, it's a terrible thing to happen to a kid of sixteen", Elwyn said, "but from what you've told me she seems to have handled it as well as could be expected. I can't see that it alters anything as far as the present is concerned."

"Maybe not, but it must be part of the puzzle."

"Which doesn't have to be your puzzle. You're a complete mess, Tom. First it's love at first sight, then it's a yen for this crackpot Cosmic Wisdom stuff, then it's love at first sight squared and in and out of bed like a pendulum, and a meretricious speech about physics from a guy with a degree from the bloody Cavendish, and now a completely irresponsible decision to go off and leave the rest of us in the lurch because you have to satisfy your bloody curiosity about a woman who's probably promiscuous and enjoying herself somewhere in little old New York. And for God's sake send that other little nympho back to her parents."

Tom had called Halcyon a little nympho only a few hours previously, but that had been in fun. Now the anger that he felt at Elwyn's use of the phrase brought home to him the strength of his feelings for the girl. Restraining himself with difficulty he said, "One moment she's much too good for me and the next she's a nympho. She's got under your skin, hasn't she?"

Looking at Elwyn he realized that he had scored a hit, although not a very welcome one. He suddenly felt very hungry, so instead of saying any more he applied himself to his sausage and mash. Eventually he stopped chewing long enough to say, "Go to Hell!"

Elwyn got up and left the room. He was so agitated that he forgot to take his empty plate, so when Tom had finished he picked up both plates and set off for the kitchen. Along the way he met Janet and Marilyn, who were walking arm in arm and having an animated conversation. He smiled and would have gone on by, but Janet stopped him with her free hand and said, "Mr. Dexter, thank you for being so nice to me yesterday. Guess what, we're starting an anti-male society, only it doesn't apply to you."

"You mean whoever it was let Marilyn down as well? That was quick."

"Got it in one. So we've decided that men are all unreliable and irresponsible and women aren't. All this dating and who's going with whom is a stupid waste of time. So we're going to stick together and concentrate on our work and . . ."

Janet petered out so Tom added, "And wait for Mr. Right to come along?"

Marilyn put her two cents in.

"We don't believe in Mr. Right; he's just an artifact of the male imagination."

Janet laughed.

"Marilyn has been reading Women's Lib stuff."

"Yes", said Marilyn, "I gave it up a few days ago but Pete made a fool of me yesterday and I'm taking it up again."

Standing in the corridor with the residues of lunch in his hand, Tom was afraid he might have to hear the whole story so he said, "Well, I'm glad you're friends again, but I hope you're wrong about Right."

Janet smiled.

"We'll take those plates for you, Mr. Right—I mean Mr. Dexter."

(26)

Mr. Barrell (stress on the second syllable, please), Glastonbury's solitary travel agent, resembled his name (self-referential, Tom had thought, the first time he met him) and he was cheerfully pessimistic.

"Starting your summer holiday early, Mr. Dexter? I don't know, though—getting a flight on a Saturday at this short notice . . . Now if you were flying first class . . ."

"OK, we'll fly first class."

Mr. Barrell, aware only of Tom's middle class *persona*, smiled indulgently.

"Now, if you were willing to wait until Monday . . ."

"I said we'll fly first class", Tom repeated with unexpected brusqueness. "We'll need a room at the Ibex Hotel for tomorrow night and the earliest possible flight on Saturday morning."

"Did you say a double room?"

Mr. Barrell's eye's shone with the anticipation of scandal.

"I believe I mentioned that there are two of us."

"Yes, Mr. Dexter, certainly."

Mr. Barrell was meeting a different Tom Dexter from the one Glastonburians were accustomed to. This was what you might call the London or cosmopolitan Tom Dexter, who knew his way around and carried the kind of heavy metal credit card that was available only to the wealthy.

*

Tom had no idea how long he would be away from Glastonbury, and he still had the problem of what to do with all the belongings that he would not be taking to New York. Some were in the old station wagon, and there was still a lot of stuff in his old apartment. He had intended to ask Elwyn if there was room for a trunk and a few other items in his garage, but in view of their lunchtime conversation this didn't seem such a good idea, so he went to see his former landlady. It was just about teatime when he arrived and, to his surprise, she invited him in for a cup. Sitting among the teacups and cucumber sandwiches he explained his idea, while Mrs. T.'s better half dozed in his armchair.

"Something totally unexpected has cropped up and I have to go to America, probably for about three months. I'd like to continue renting the flat until I come back. If this suits you, I'll pay you another four months' rent in advance."

"Are you intending to marry one of those young women?" Mrs. Trathgannon asked tangentially.

"Yes, I am", Tom said, without mentioning that he wasn't sure which one.

"Well, I hope it's the second one. Mr. Trathgannon always says I'm a great judge of character, and that first one was much too snippy. You know I don't approve of your goings-on, but if you were married it would be different and the flat would make a nice place for a young couple to start their married life—well, till the children start coming along. Will you be having children?"

"I certainly hope so."

Tom hadn't thought about children but Mrs. T probably approved of them, provided that they were kept in their proper place.

"Well then, I think we can agree on that, as long as you put it in writing that you undertake to remove all your belongings by the end of the year if you decide not to return."

Tom paid the rent through December 31st, gave the required undertaking, thanked his hostess for tea, and told her he would be back later to replace some of the items he had removed earlier.

*

When Tom arrived at the Wolfgang Goerner School he found Halcyon dancing round the oak tree at the edge of the parking lot. She stopped dancing and hugged him enthusiastically.

"Hello, what's got into you?" he asked.

"We're going on an adventure and I'm not going to worry any more. When do we start?"

"Tomorrow. I leave school at four o'clock and pick you up here. We drive to Castle Cary, take the train to Paddington and Heathrow, stay overnight and get on the plane to New York early next morning. How did you manage to stop worrying?"

"I have a new boyfriend and he advised me."

"Anyone I know?"

"Yes and he's very handsome."

Tom went over all the possibilities and asked, "Is he much older than you?"

"Yes, but he's not as old as Klaus."

"Oh, I see. Did you just walk up to him and say, 'Now, you see, I have this problem.'?"

"No. If you want to know, he saw me crying. He's a very nice old man."

"Come on, there's no such thing—I bet he likes your legs."

"Yes there is, and it's OK if he likes my legs. I kind of like them myself. Can we go to the teashop again?"

"Wouldn't you like some real dinner? How about pretending we're tourists and getting chicken in the basket at the Lady?"

So they drove sedately to the Lady of the Lake, parked the battered Morris between two middle-class Hondas, and wandered out to the umbrella'd and betabled lawn where the local songbirds vied for their attention with golden oldies and miniskirted waitresses. It occurred to Halcyon that if she ever needed a job, this might be the perfect place, and this brought the question of money into her mind.

"Tom, how are you going to pay for all this? I mean, I have a little money, but not much, and maybe I can get something back on the plane ticket that I don't use. But all these train and plane fares and dinner here into the bargain, and the way you walked in and ordered, anyone would think you owned the place."

Tom had already told his secret to Elwyn, but he was afraid that Halcyon might find it intimidating.

"Well", he said, "there's a little bit of money in the family. My grandparents were very careful people and my father made some good investments."

"Oh, that's very nice. My old man never had anything to invest, so what you see is what you get."

"You're a treasure, Halcyon, and one day I'll tell you more about it."

"I get it—you're really a king's son out of a fairy tale but you want to stay incognito and you're afraid I won't love you if I find out the truth. Well, that's OK—it just makes the whole thing more exciting."

Tom explained his agreement with Mrs. Trathgannon and suggested that it might be a good idea if he went on his own to return his belongings to his old apartment. Halcyon had other ideas.

"I don't care if she does ask questions. I'm pretty good at making up a fib on the spur of the moment and I don't see what harm it could do."

After dinner they collected the station wagon and drove to the old lady's house.

"Well, here you are", she said and, turning to Halcyon added, "Hello, my dear, I'm glad it's you and not the other one. You're awfully young, though. What's your name?"

Halcyon was equal to the occasion.

"Doreen", she said, reverting to her native Stepney accent, "and I'm older than I look."

"Do your parents know what you're up to?"

Halcyon put her arms round Tom.

"My Mum knows everything, and she thinks Tom's the bee's knees."

"And when are you going to get married?"

Tom thought it was time for him to butt in, but Halcyon beat him to it.

"We have a special license and we're going to the registrar's office before we go to New York. Then we'll do the job properly when we get back."

Mrs. Trathgannon sighed romantically and then pulled herself together.

"Well, I hope by then you will have learnt to dress like a respectable married woman. All right, then, I mustn't keep you gossiping any longer now, but I shall expect to see you when you get back, and still happily married I hope."

*

A few trips carrying boxes up the two steep flights of stairs left Halcyon looking flushed, slightly out of breath, incredibly young and inordinately desirable. Tom looked at her and thought, "How can I do this to her?" and "How could I possibly let her go?"

"Why are you looking at me like that? Are you mad with me?"

"No, I was just thinking."

"Well, you'd better stop thinking—it makes you look too scary. Where are we going now?"

"I think I ought to go and see my friend Elwyn. We had a bit of a row this morning."

"Can I come?"

"What would you say if I said 'No'?"

"I'd say 'I'm coming anyway.'"

"That's what I thought. OK, maybe he won't be so angry with me if you're there."

"Why is he angry with you?"

"Well, he saw me first with Alison and then with you, and he heard me give that talk yesterday, which he thought was really bad. He thinks

CW and Archway are nutty and full of cranks. When I told him I was leaving, he told me I was crazy and walked out of the room. And the worst of is he'll probably have to substitute for me for the rest of the term."

Elwyn was polite to Halcyon but made no secret of the fact that he was not pleased to see Tom. It was different with Diana.

"Hello, Tom, I gather you're in Elwyn's doghouse and you'd prefer it if the sun didn't go down on his wrath. He told me the whole thing in lurid detail, and I don't think you stand much of a chance. Hi, Halcyon, sit down and have a drink with me, and let's send these two naughty boys into the kitchen to try and settle their differences."

Neither Halcyon nor Elwyn really approved of this arrangement, but it would have been very awkward to resist, so Halcyon sat while Elwyn and Tom filled their glasses and did as they were told. Elwyn went on the offensive immediately.

"What you're doing is immoral and stupid and if you haven't got anything to add to what you told me at lunchtime you might as well leave now."

Tom was patient at first but his patience wasn't going to last long.

"OK, explain exactly where the immorality comes in."

"You mean you have to have it explained? Leaving your job at a moment's notice and on a feeble excuse, so the rest of us get landed with three weeks of substituting—is that moral behavior?"

"I don't think the excuse is feeble. I seem to remember doing you some good turns in the past. You haven't been exactly a model of morality yourself."

"The excuse is rubbish, and what about the kids you're leaving in the lurch?"

"You know damn well the exams start next week and after tomorrow there's nothing more I can do for them. What else have you got that's eating you?"

"I never went around seducing schoolgirls."

"Schoolgirls—what the hell are you talking about?"

Elwyn pointed at the living room.

"That girl. She's not much above the age of consent and she ought to be at home with her parents, not satisfying your gross sexual appetite."

"My what?"

By the time Elwyn got to the seduction of schoolgirls, the quarrel had become so loud that it was plainly audible in the living room.

"Sorry, Diana", Halcyon said as she got up from her armchair, "but I'm not letting him get away with that."

Opening the kitchen door just as Elwyn was saying, "You heard me—your gross sexual appetite", Halcyon planted herself, hands on hips, in front of the tall Welshman, like a Cockney sparrow confronting an oversized pigeon

"What's all this about seduction? As far as I know, Tom never seduced anybody. It just happens that we like each other and we both like sex. Is there anything wrong with that?"

"Nothing whatever."

The voice was Diana's.

"Come on, you silly old jerk, or you'll wake the baby. I can see what your problem is, and why I still put up with you I can't imagine. Sorry about this, Tom and Halcyon, but I think I'd better deal with him on my own. You may get an apology from him one day, but don't count on it. 'Bye, Halcyon, come and see me some time and tell me all about euphonics. What Tom has done to deserve you is beyond my comprehension."

"Did you get what all that was about?" Halcyon asked as they got into the car.

"Yes. Elwyn has the hots for you, and I can't say I blame him, even though, as far as I know, he's only seen you twice."

"I can. Diana is lovely and he ought to be thankful and behave himself in his own house, specially when there's a baby upstairs. I hope he's not going to be like Klaus."

"No, the last one was about thirty-five—he usually goes for the motherly type."

*

Tom and Halcyon spent most of the night packing and house-cleaning, which included tidying Imre's room and finding some shopping bags for all the oddments he had left behind. These they left in the box room. Halcyon collected a few stray items that Alison had missed, and they eventually got to bed around three o'clock. They were bone weary and slept like a couple of logs.

IV

Alison, Imre and Klaus: Glastonbury to New York

(27)

Alison's bus took half an hour to get from Glastonbury to Castle Cary, and everything was still churning inside her when she got on the train to Paddington. She had just one clear objective; she must go to Pittstown and see her father as soon as possible. What Imre had said must not, could not be true, and Phillip would clear it up; but by the time she reached Heathrow she had lapsed into a "What if it's true?" stage where horrible thoughts about her mother, her husband and herself chased each other uncontrollably through her mind. She became acutely conscious of every atom of her body, and every single one of them hurt. Her consciousness was all inner and she walked like a sleep-walker or someone under hypnosis. People at the airport kept saying, "Are you all right, Miss?" and "She looks as if she might faint at any moment." Alison murmured repeatedly, "I'm all right, thank you", and clutched the little bag containing her passport and her money as tightly as she could. She remembered that someone had told her that if she ever needed a flight in a hurry, Air India was the best bet. She stood on line for along time and found that she could get a seat on a plane leaving at 8:00 p.m. This meant waiting four hours until it was time to board. A young man who helped her check her suitcase became very attentive. "I'm sorry", she managed to say, "I need to be left alone. Please leave me alone." She wanted to cry but couldn't. She tried waiting in one of the restaurant areas, but the smell of food was unbearable, so she sat in the lounge as close as possible to the gate. If she could make it onto the plane and find her seat, it would be wonderful to lose consciousness for a while, but she had tried to sleep on the train and it hadn't worked.

When it was time to board there was a big crowd and a lot of laughter and jostling. Getting out her ticket and passport was difficult, and the woman had to help her. Inevitably she asked, "Are you sure you're all right?" and Alison said, "Yes—just very tired." "Well, you'll be able to sleep on the plane." No, she wouldn't be able to sleep on the plane, and when she was finally seated, the faint odor of curry renewed her anxiety about nausea. When she tried deep breathing, the expansive lady in a sari next to her patted her hand and said, "Don't worry, Duckie, it's as safe as crossing the Old Kent Road. We'll be in little ol' New York before you can say 'Jack Robinson.'" Disconnected thoughts drifted through her mind, of Minna and Klaus, of her mother, bright and vivacious, and of her father, energetic and purposeful when Alison was young, but fading into nonentity after his move to Pittstown. Somewhere there must be someone who would be good to think about. It wasn't sleep that was overtaking her but something more like concussion. Now there was Tom, but he was very far away and not looking at her. And behind him there was Imre. How odd—it was Imre who had told her about Air India. She sat up with a start, sweating profusely. The plane began to move.

*

Alison went with the crowd at JFK, and it took her mechanically through customs and down to the baggage claim area. It was nearly midnight in New York, five o'clock in the morning in Glastonbury, and she had had nothing to eat since half past five the previous morning, when Tom had given her toast in bed. Watching the stream of bags and cases made her feel dizzy, as if they were standing still and she was floating along backwards. The same cases kept going by and she found it difficult to remember what hers looked like. At last she saw it, all by itself with the little wisp of flame-colored veil that she had tied round the handle for a joke. Anyone could see that it belonged to a euphonist. A middle-aged, professional-looking man helped her with the case and saw the label.

"I'm going to the Upper West Side too. We could share a cab."

"No thanks . . . I . . . I . . ."

He looked at her sympathetically.

"I'm totally harmless and, if you don't mind my saying so, you look a bit wobbly."

"I'm sorry. I'm OK . . . But, yes, thank you . . ."

"My name's Nick", he said as they got into the taxi, "and I noticed that you're Alison."

Alison could think of nothing to say.

"I'm sorry—I don't think I can talk."

When they got to West 88th Street Nick said, "I'll just wait till you're safely inside", and Alison realized that she had no idea where her keys were. She searched her suitcase, couldn't find them and, at last, began to cry. She wanted Nick and the taxi just to go away and leave her on the sidewalk, but they wouldn't. She could see that Nick was repacking her case, but she felt too dizzy to do anything about it. All the lights flickered and went out.

When Alison came to she was in the taxi again. They stopped just around the corner on Central Park West at an awning in front of a building with a brightly lit vestibule. The doorman said, "Good evening, Dr. Perlman. Welcome home", and Nick said, "Thanks, Jose, everything OK? Give me a hand with this young lady, she's not feeling very well."

"I'm really all right", Alison said feebly.

"I don't think you are. Just for the moment I'm appointing myself as your physician and I'm not leaving you out on the sidewalk at this time of night. Furthermore I don't think you're well enough to survive the emergency room."

While Jose took the suitcases, Nick took Alison's arm and together they made it up to the eighth floor. Nick opened the door of his apartment and called out, "Hi, Chris, I'm home and I've brought a young lady with me."

"Oh, no, not another one! I guess you'd better bring her in."

The voice was male, and there was enough humor in it to take the sting out of the words.

*

At three o'clock the next afternoon Alison woke up in a strange bed in a strange room, wearing a man's striped shirt that was much too big for her. In her dreams she had been standing alone on the slope of a green hill, watching the sheep and cows in the fields below, and she urgently wanted to get back there, where there were no people and there was no memory. She slept again, but now there was a tower at the top of the hill and men were looking at her through binoculars. The sun flashed on the lenses and she woke up again with a start. On the table beside her she saw a telephone, a plate of cookies, a glass, and an ice bucket with a quart of milk.

At that moment the door opened and Dr. Perlman asked her how she was feeling.

It took Alison a long time to try to figure this out.

"I don't know—pretty awful, I guess. How did I get like this?"

"Well, once we got you inside you fainted again and we had to put you to bed. Don't worry, Chris and I are physicians, and women undress in front of us all the time. It's all very professional and you seem perfectly healthy except for exhaustion and not eating for a long time. So now you have to take some nourishment and then you can tell us what you want to do next. We can deliver you back to 88th Street or anywhere else within reason. Will there be someone there to let you in or will we have to send for a locksmith?"

"I don't want to go back to 88th Street. Couldn't you please just let me go?"

"My dear young lady, you can get up and go whenever you're ready. Do you have any relatives?"

This was said rather stiffly and Alison realized how ungracious she had sounded.

"I'm sorry. It's all been so weird, wonderful bits and mostly horrible bits, and I can't talk because I don't want to think. You're one of the wonderful bits because you're very kind and you don't want anything from me. I mean you don't want to marry me or use me as a nursemaid in your old age or prove that I'm really a bastard or something much worse. And the only relative I have is my father, only he isn't my father. Well, then I have a husband only . . ."

Her voice became very weak and shaky.

"I thought I would just go somewhere where nobody knows me and start over, but I'm frightened it'll never go away. Isn't there some way of stopping it, like a lobotomy or something? I had a feeling on the plane that I might just be able to open a door and step outside and kind of dissolve into the atmosphere. Don't you think that would be a great way to go?"

"Frankly, no. If you jump out of plane at a height of seven miles you fall for about three and a half minutes before you hit anything, so you have all that time to think about it. Why do you want to commit suicide?"

Alison tried to speak, but the scene in Mrs. Barrington-Smythe's kitchen rose up before her in all its monstrosity—Imre with his simian smile, inexorably squeezing all the juice out of his horribly believable story, and Klaus, ancient and exhausted, his protests lacking conviction and easily turned aside by Imre's quiet insistence. It wasn't, it couldn't be true. Klaus would say the word that would end this dreadful recital and dismiss it to the four winds. But Klaus didn't . . .

"I . . . I don't think I can talk about it."

"It might help if you did."

Alison made another effort and the words came out in a matter-of-fact way that bore no relation to her inner turmoil.

"Because I killed my mother and married my father. I'm a female Oedipus and that way around I think it's much worse. Women have killed themselves for less than that."

Nick took the phone from the bedside table and dialed a number.

"Chris, can you come up for a moment? Spare room? I only have a few minutes and it's important. OK."

He put down the phone. "Look, Alison, I can't physically stop you if you decide to leave, but now that you've started talking about suicide it changes the whole situation. It was a matter of luck that I looked in just when you woke up, but I have to get back to the hospital and I'll be there for hours. Chris is a psychological counselor, so when I said that bit about women undressing, it was metaphorical in his case but not in mine. He's just finishing with a patient and I strongly advise you to talk to him. You'll have to talk fairly fast because he only has about twenty minutes, but he may be able to help you figure something out. I mean, for a start, how much danger you're in. Will you talk to him?"

Alison spoke hesitantly and without much conviction.

"OK, I'll do my best."

"Now, just tell me this; what did you mean when you said you had killed your mother? I take it it wasn't what would normally be described as murder."

"I might as well have murdered her. She was giving me a driving lesson and I hit the accelerator instead of the brake. Hello, I think you met me but I didn't meet you."

Christopher Ginsburg had entered the room. At first sight he looked like Nick Perlman's identical twin—the same suit, the same slightly stooping figure and look of encroaching middle age, gray and tired-eyed.

The voices were different, however. Nick was a baritone and Chris was a deep bass.

"Yes. How are you feeling?"

"That's what Nick asked me, and I still don't really know. I guess totally messed up is the best description."

"Drink some milk and eat some cookies", Nick said. "We'll arrange about some real food later." Turning to Chris, he added, "Alison thinks that she might be better off dead, so I asked her if she would be willing to talk to you about it."

He gave Alison a firm handshake and hurried out of the room.

There was no bedside chair, so Chris sat on the edge of the bed.

"I gathered from what you were saying when I came in that you feel responsible for the death of your mother. Did someone tell you that you had done it out of a deep, subconscious motivation?"

"No, but I've read stuff like that. Some people seem to think that everything comes from deep, subconscious motivations."

"That may or may not be so, but if it is, you should realize that your motivation may equally have been to kill yourself. When was this?"

"Ten years ago, when I was sixteen. I loved my mother and I don't think it matters whether I did it for some reason that I don't know about. The fact is I killed her."

"Then you've been living with this fact all that time and it hasn't made you suicidal. What else has happened?"

Alison tried to speak, but choked on it. Eventually she found her voice.

"When I was seventeen I went to live with an old man who had been a friend of my mother's. We were lovers and then we got married. Yesterday I found out that he had an affair with my mother and he's my father. Can you imagine what that feels like?"

"I can try. How do you know he's your father?"

(28)

Alison didn't respond to Dr. Ginsburg's question, so he repeated it.

"How do you know he's your father?"

Alison still didn't want to think about it, but she forced herself to explain who Imre was and to describe the scene at the kitchen table in Mrs. Barrington-Smythe's house.

"Imre was very pleased with himself, like a kid who knows a naughty secret about another kid. I didn't believe it, so he told a story about hearing my father—I mean Phillip Johnson—and my stepmother talking in the doctor's office, and then getting it straight from my stepmother. Phillip had some congenital defect and wasn't capable of fathering a child. Imre said that Klaus had known about it for four years and that he and my mother had had an affair that lasted right up to the time when she met Phillip. Klaus had been trying to stop Imre, but when I asked him—Klaus I mean—if it was true, he just sat there looking at me, and for a moment I caught this look on his face as if he couldn't deny it and was a bit proud of it. That was when I screamed."

Ginsburg was not convinced.

"Listen, Alison, there's one thing we need to get straight here. Questions of paternity are very complicated—it would be fairly unusual for a doctor to examine an apparently normal man of fifty and say for certain that he couldn't have fathered a child twenty years previously."

Alison told him everything she knew about her family history that had anything to do with the question. It turned out to be not very much.

"I didn't know Klaus and my mother had been lovers, but now I can see that that was why she didn't want me to go to Ulm. I suppose she may have wondered if I was really Klaus's child, but she couldn't have any more children and there didn't seem to be anything the matter with my father. And I looked so much like my mother that no one could have told who my father was."

"Where is your father now?"

"Phillip lives in Pittstown, Massachusetts. I have no idea where Klaus is. Probably still in Glastonbury."

"I meant Phillip, although we'll need Klaus as well. There's just a chance that if we knew all the blood groups we could eliminate some of the possibilities. How would you feel about that?"

"Somehow I know in my gut that Klaus is my father. But I suppose it would be good to check. Anyway, I can tell you right now that Klaus and I are both Group O, rhesus positive. We found out when we went to give blood together and I said something about monkeys that Klaus didn't approve of."

"Well, I'm afraid that means it's unlikely that we can find anything out this way. Almost anybody can produce an O positive child. The only thing we can be sure of is that if Phillip is AB he can't be your father, and that's a fairly rare type. Do you know if he ever had a blood transfusion?"

"I don't think so."

"How would you feel about going to Pittstown and asking him about his blood type?"

"I don't want to see him. When Imre said all that stuff I didn't believe it at first, only then Klaus wouldn't deny it, so I thought I would go straight to Phillip and get the truth out of him. But even if the doctor was wrong, he *thought* I must be Klaus's daughter and he didn't say anything. He just let me go on being married to Klaus for another four years. And there's something else I want to tell you. Last Thursday I met someone that I really liked. We fell for each other in a big way and slept together on Sunday night. Klaus had lost interest in me and he has his new girl, so Tom and I thought we would be able to get married and I could get away from this weird kind of life I've been living. Imre saw us go off together, and I think it must have made him insanely jealous, so he got his revenge the next morning. And the worst of it is I don't want to see Tom either. I think I still love him, but I can't bear the idea of sleeping with anyone any more."

"Does he know?"

"No, I left without seeing him. I just needed to get away from Klaus and Imre as fast as possible. If Tom knew the truth he wouldn't want me any more—I mean I don't think anybody would."

Ginsburg thought Alison might be mistaken about this. He wondered whether she had thought about what Tom might be going through now, but he didn't want to pile on the guilt, so he asked, "And what exactly is Imre's angle on this?"

"That's the weirdest thing of all and you'd have to know Klaus to understand it. He decided that when he'd finished with me he'd pass me on to Imre and I more or less told him to go fuck himself—well, I told him he must be crazy and he told me that if I didn't marry Imre, bad things would happen. Right at the end he seemed to give up and that was when Imre walked in."

"So Imre wanted you, and when he found he couldn't have you he spilled the beans. Did you figure out that he had been blackmailing Klaus? 'I'll keep quiet if you make sure I get Alison.'"

"Sort of, and it only makes the whole thing worse. Why didn't Klaus just tell me when he first found out? And why didn't Phillip tell me? And why did Klaus go after me in the first place if he knew I might be his daughter? Imre is just a kind of animal trying to get what it wants, but Phillip and Klaus seem like rational human beings . . ."

"Yes, being human does seem to give us obligations that are too difficult to fulfill. Things like sex, love, parenthood and religion often put too much strain on our rational faculties, which is one reason why there's so much mental illness. Sorry, I'm talking like a book and I try not to do that. It's not your rational mind that wants you to commit suicide. You feel dirty and tainted and there's no way of ever getting clean, as if you had been out in the garden and accidentally picked up a big, slimy slug. You know you can physically remove every trace of slime from your hand, but the feel of it is still there. That may be only a weak analogy, but just for the moment try to think of the whole thing as a slug and imagine what it will be like when you feel clean again."

"It didn't work for Lady Macbeth."

"Well, she was a murderer."

"And I guess nobody told her about the slug."

Chris laughed.

"I have a patient waiting for me downstairs. There's the phone and there's the number to get me if you feel scared. You can't jump out of the window because the AC is on and it's locked. I'd like you to stay here for a couple of hours until we can talk again and decide what to do. In the meantime I'll send someone up with a sandwich and a newspaper. Now before I go I'd like your own assessment of how much danger there is of your hurting yourself."

"Now that I've talked to you I'll be OK for while. I don't feel so locked up in my body. I don't suppose you've heard of Wolfgang Goerner and the Cosmic Wisdom Society, but we generally think suicide is not a good idea. It messes up our karma."

Alison made this last comment with a smile, so that it seemed half humorous, although it was inwardly wholly serious.

"Yes, I have a couple of Goernerite patients—they seem to be very anxious that their friends shouldn't know they're seeing me."

"Anyway", said Alison, with a flash of her old spirit, "if I do commit suicide it will only be after a lot of thought, and I promise not to do it in your apartment."

Chris appreciated the gallows-type humor, which was rare among his patients.

125

"OK, I think I can trust you. I'll be back about five o'clock and don't forget the telephone. Your suitcase is in the bottom of that closet and there's a bathroom with a shower. There's also a coffee maker—we don't bother much with food in this establishment, but there's a little store on the first floor, next to the entrance."

"Thank you. Everyone I know always seems to have some point of view or axe to grind, so I really appreciate being treated kind of objectively—professionally, I suppose I should say. Which reminds me, there's a medical card somewhere in my suitcase."

"Good, I was going to ask about that. And if I didn't insist on proper professional relationships I'd be out of my mind in no time flat."

Chris left and Alison lay back on her pillow. There was some relief in having told her troubles to someone kind and objective, but she doubted whether it would do any good in the long run, and she still felt exhausted, ill and nauseated. It occurred to her that it would solve the whole problem if she just died in her sleep. Unfortunately she was now very wide awake. She sat up again and resolutely tackled the milk and cookies. The phone rang and someone called Helen asked her what kind of sandwich she would like. Her mind went blank, so out of sheer bravado she asked for roast beef on a roll with butter, lettuce and tomato. Yes, a little salt please. She didn't think there was a ghost of a chance that she would be able to eat it, but she had spotted a little fridge in the corner of the room and she thought perhaps someone else would like it later. She went to the closet, opened her suitcase and took out some clean underwear, jeans and a shirt. There was the long purple dress. It reminded her of Tom and she didn't want to think about him. Tom wasn't perfect, but he seemed clean and she didn't want her dirt to rub off on him. Maybe it would be better after she took her shower. Something gleamed in the bottom of the suitcase. It was the bunch of keys that she had been unable to find and that now she absolutely didn't want to use. She picked them up and put them on the bedside table next to the telephone.

When the sandwich and the newspaper arrived, Alison was sitting in an armchair in the corner of the room trying to read Goerner's *Reincarnation and Karma*.

"Sorry it's the Post—they were all out of the Times."

Helen appeared rotund, comfortable and soothing, but she had a careful, appraising eye, and Alison knew that she was being given a professional once-over. Helen soon left, so apparently she had passed the test. She put the sandwich in the fridge and opened the Post at random.

"NFL Star Kills Girlfriend and Shoots Self . . . *continued from front page.*"

Well, it was the continuation that mattered, although not perhaps for the girlfriend. Getting murdered in the heat of the moment might not do anything terrible to your karma, but killing someone and then messing up your suicide probably put you in a hell of a position. Alison applied herself again to Goerner, but she hadn't really been reading before and now she still wasn't.

It was the question of dirt that was occupying her mind. It seemed like a good metaphor but it wasn't the whole story. It was as if everything inside her had been twisted into the wrong shape. "Bent out of shape" was what people often said, but it didn't usually seem to mean very much—well, not like this. Everything in her body and soul was in a state of acute distortion, and the effort to get it all back where it belonged only increased the pain. That might be the problem—maybe it couldn't be pushed. If she could let go and relax enough it might go back on its own. Halcyon's mum had an expression that was a good fit for the way Alison felt: "all screwed up like a fart in a bottle." She smiled. The two euphonists had been good friends in spite of the oddball circumstances in which they had met, and Alison thought how comforting Halcyon's presence would have been—just a thoroughly good person who understood things with her heart. Dr. Ginsburg was fine and helpful, but Alison had a feeling that he didn't really get it. Looking at the book in her hand, she had the same feeling about Dr. Goerner. His great sweeping insights made sense of world history and evolution, but he didn't seem to have any experience of the intimate details of ordinary cockeyed relationships between actual people.

Well, Halcyon was thousands of miles away, and Alison would have to work it out for herself. She decided to make a start by tackling her sandwich, which she did with only moderate success. After a couple of bites she had to put it back in the fridge. Feeling rather discouraged, she started thinking about Goerner again. Presumably he hadn't given any meditative techniques for dealing with the trauma of incest, but surely a Cosmic Wisdom person must be able to do some form of meditation that would calm things down. Unfortunately the person who knew more about CW than anyone else was the one who had caused all the trouble, and in any case, Alison knew she would have to get calm before she could start meditating. "It's all too hard", she thought. "If only I could just get clean away—just me, myself, no one and nothing."

She began to picture herself working at a MacDonald's in Peoria, Illinois, and it had a curiously calming effect that lasted until Chris Ginsburg reappeared around half past five.

(29)

"Hello, Alison, still here, I see. Well, that's promising. Have you eaten anything?"

"Hello, Chris. A little milk, six cookies and two bites of a sandwich. I want to go and work at MacDonald's in Peoria. Or something like that . . ."

"Do you have any money?"

"A little—not very much, but I could go on a bus. Not very practical is it?"

"Not really, except that your husband ought to support you. How would you feel about that?"

Alison didn't answer directly.

"I've been trying to figure out what I think about all these people. I despise Imre and I'm very angry with my father—Phillip, I mean—and with Klaus. But the weird thing is I almost feel sorry for Klaus. He's been the kingpin of Cosmic Wisdom and Archway all these years, and always so sure that he was following Goerner straight into the spiritual world, but now I think maybe he doesn't believe in himself any more. When we were talking just before Imre came in, he said he loved me more than anyone else in the world. He said I was facing great risks and I had to be strong. And he said he thought I would make it. It was kind of generous after the way I had spoken to him about his obsession with sex and young girls. He always told us that we were helping his spiritual whatever, and I think he was realizing that it had all been a bit of a sham. Well, maybe everything he says is a sham and in any case that was before Imre said his piece, so I guess it doesn't really count. Anyway, I don't want to see him."

"Never?"

"I don't know. Do you think I'll get better?"

"You'll certainly get better—I just don't know how much better."

"You see, the thing about money is that I have a room in a brownstone just around the corner on 88th Street, but Imre and Klaus live there and I can't stand the thought of meeting either of them. And I have a job at the Archway School, and either of them might show up there at any moment. And I can't expect . . ."

Alison was getting agitated again, and Chris understood the incomplete sentence.

"There's nowhere for you to go and you can't expect to stay here. Is that right?"

"Yes."

"Well, it's true we can't take you in as a boarder, but we won't throw you out on your ear. Nick and I occasionally take on what you might call projects, and they have to be worthwhile projects. I'm not sure what motivates him, but in my case it's a little bit of return for the obscene fees that I extract from wealthy patients who have time on their hands and like to spend it talking to me. He should be home around seven, and then the three of us can have something to eat and see what we can figure out. That leaves you an hour and a half to fill in."

"I'd like to go for a walk in the park."

"Can I trust you to behave yourself?"

"I won't jump in the reservoir, if that's what you're worrying about. As I told you, if I do kill myself I'll do it very privately."

"You're serious, aren't you?"

"Yes. Tell me something—do you get many female Oedipuses here?"

"No—you're definitely the first. Why do you ask?"

"It's just that you make it seem as if it was all in a day's work."

"Well, in a way it is, but let me assure you that I have seen many women far more messed up than you are with far less cause. Frankly, I'm a little surprised that you hung in there so long even before this bombshell hit. You said he stopped sleeping with you four years ago and soon found himself another girl, so why didn't you leave then?"

"I don't know. I suppose it never occurred to me. He was our spiritual leader and I was and, if you must know, still am a true-blue Goernerite, and I think that most people in the CW Society don't even know what that means. He was very kind to me . . ."

"OK, you can go for a walk, but I'm sending Helen with you."

*

Except for her figure, Helen was a little bit like an American version of Halcyon, very good at her job, down-to-earth and unpretentious. Alison was curious about her exact position in the Perlman-Ginsburg establishment.

"Well", she said, "I do a bit of everything. I'm a trained nurse, secretary, receptionist and housekeeper. In case you hadn't noticed, those two are what's known as an item."

Alison hadn't noticed and it took a moment for the penny to drop.

"Oh. Am I supposed to know this?"

"Well, you'll be staying another couple of nights and you could hardly miss it."

"I will?"

"Well, of course, only if you want to."

"I think I do want to, but . . ."

"You're not sure if you ought to?"

"Something like that. I still keep thinking that if I could be on my own I could figure it out."

"Take the advice of an old lady . . ."

"You're not old—you're about forty-five"

"An old lady", repeated Helen, who was fifty-three and only mildly flattered. "They won't solve all your problems, but they can help a bit. They're doing this because you're worth helping, and if you kill yourself it'll be a waste of a good person. And at least you know it's not because of your sex appeal."

This was an aspect of relations between the sexes that Alison had never considered. She found it oddly comforting.

"Isn't it rather awkward for them?"

"Well, so far it doesn't seem to have been. They have separate offices downstairs, and one of Chris's chief problems is keeping some of the old ladies out of his underpants."

This was not such a pleasant thought, so Alison suggested walking through the Shakespeare Garden and up the steps to Belvedere Castle. Everything seemed a bit dusty and care-worn, but when they got to the top and looked across the pond to the Great Lawn, they saw half a dozen softball games being played with enormous gusto by people who had probably just come off a hard day's work. Alison momentarily fell into the illusion of wishing that she could be as carefree as that. "No", she thought, "there's no evidence that they're carefree—maybe it's the other way around."

Then for a moment she fell into the cognate illusion that she could solve her problems by throwing herself into some energetic, mind-numbing activity like . . . Like what? Euphonics? Or throwing hamburgers in Peoria? She laughed.

"What's funny?" Helen asked.

"Oh, I was just thinking about Peoria."

"What about it?"

"Oh, I don't know . . ."

Yes, that was it. Just thinking; doing anything else just put things off. But she couldn't think all the time—it would be OK to take a rest from it occasionally. Perhaps euphonics wasn't such a bad idea.

*

Helen stayed to dinner and the four of them sat down to a selection of dishes from the nearest Chinese restaurant. Alison didn't have much appetite but she no longer felt nauseated, so she nibbled away at a bowl of chicken fried rice while the others ate energetically and discussed the upcoming election. Feeling, as she did, that the world as she knew it had come to an abrupt end early the previous morning, she was a little shocked to find that the situation was exactly the same as it had been a few days ago, when she last taken a serious look at a newspaper. It was also slightly surprising to discover that while the two doctors were democrats, Helen was a staunch republican. Alison had taken no part in the conversation, so she was quite nonplussed when Helen asked her who she was going to vote for in November. This was difficult since she didn't want to say, "Well, I've been thinking of killing myself before then, so I haven't really thought about it." Could these people possibly have staged this conversation so as to make her think about something four months down the road? It didn't seem likely but, deliberate or not, it had the effect of making her picture herself at a concrete time in the future. Oddly enough, she wasn't in a polling booth, but standing in front of a class of small children in the euphonics room of the Archway School on West 90th Street. She realized that Helen was still looking at her, so she gave an answer that millions of Americans might well have given.

"I don't know. Does it make any real difference?"

"We sincerely hope so", said Chris. "Anyway, we've been doing a bit of plotting and we need to know about your secretarial skills."

"Why", Alison asked. "Do you have something in mind?"

"Yes, it's the vacation season, and temps are very much in demand. Here's the plan. You can sit with Helen in my office for a couple of days, After that I can place you with a professional associate who will take you on as a temporary receptionist for a week, provided I can certify that you're up to the job. It would mean a certain amount of miscellaneous typing and being sufficiently on top of things to answer the phone intelligently. Helen will know the answer to that when she's had you for a few hours. Will you give it a try?"

"The trouble is, when I try to figure out something like this none of it seems to mean anything. Please don't think I'm ungrateful . . ."

"Please don't think about gratitude at all, or you'll start feeling guilty about this as well as everything else. This is something practical you can do to help make the worst days go by, and it will spare us from having to make harder choices, like recommending that you check yourself into a mental hospital."

"All right—I'll do it. I'm not really such a bad person."

"Oh, shit!" said Nick. "You're not a bad person. In fact we have an idea that you may be a specially good person, otherwise we might have packed you off to Bellevue right away. You probably need some things from your room in the brownstone. Helen noticed that you'd found your keys, so we've told her about the other occupants and she's volunteered to go and get a case-full of things, if you'll tell her how to find your room and what to look for."

The list Alison gave Helen included her boom box and a case of tapes.

(30)

On the previous morning, at the time of Alison's arrival in Castle Cary, Imre was still trying to restart Mrs. B-S's car. He didn't lack persistence, and kept cranking until his arms hurt so much that he had to stop. Finally, with another string of curses, he hurled the starting handle into the back of the old station wagon, grabbed his suitcase and started running. The case was heavy and he was out of condition, so the run soon lapsed into a dogged walk. He reached the bus stop, soaked with rain and perspiration, just in time to see another bus to Castle Cary receding into the distance. When he eventually got there he found that he had just missed a train to Paddington. It was nearly seven o'clock when he arrived at Heathrow, and by this time he was sick and tired of being asked if he'd been in a fight. Like Alison he had to wait on line and the best he could do was to be put on standby for Air India's next available flight. He reached the gate area just in time to see Alison disappearing into the gangway. He assumed that she would be in Manhattan by midnight and spend the night in the brownstone. Imre was familiar with the bus schedule to Pittstown—two per day, leaving Manhattan at 9 a. m. and 6 p. m. Alison would probably catch the early one and get to her father's house in Pittstown in the early afternoon.

After a very uncomfortable night in the lounge, Imre made it onto a plane at six o'clock the next morning, which was Tuesday. Arriving at the brownstone at 11 a. m., New York time, he wasn't surprised to find it deserted. Since Alison's room showed no sign of occupation, he concluded she must have gone straight to the bus terminal and waited there overnight. He was so overwhelmingly preoccupied with Alison that it never crossed his mind that it would be very smart to see a dentist and take some time to think things over. Leaving his suitcase and taking a small bag with his overnight kit, he rushed out of the house and hurried over to the car rental at 96th Street and West End Avenue. Getting the paper work done seemed to take for ever, and it was midday before he was on the road. Knowing that the bus went a long way around and that Alison would have quite a long walk from the bus stop to Phillip Johnson's house, he was still hoping to get there first or maybe to intercept her on the way.

It was only when he was some distance up the Sawmill River Parkway that it dawned on him that he had no idea what he would do when he found her. His passion for her had been so consuming that it was only now that his brain began to work well enough for him to realize that he had played the one card that he had, and that she would never under any circumstances become Mrs. Takacs. What Imre wanted was Alison, and it was Alison that he was not going to get. He pulled over onto the grass verge and began to feel exceedingly sorry for himself. This seemed to be the time to make use of the small bottle of cognac that he always carried in his overnight kit. The combination of a sleepless night and some generous swigs of brandy had its natural effect, so when the patrolman pulled up behind him he was flat out with the empty bottle on the seat beside him.

133

Imre spent most of Tuesday at a police station in Yonkers, where he was charged with driving while intoxicated. The fact that he wasn't actually driving carried no weight at all, and the presence of an open liquor bottle was particularly damning. The state of his mouth made the breathalyzer test very difficult and painful, and when he eventually managed to get a reading it had him at twice the limit. The rental car was an infuriating problem. Imre could no longer drive it, since the insurance papers that he had signed included the statement that he was not under indictment for such things as DWI, so he had to pay for it to be towed in from the parkway.

Pondering all this in relation to the larger picture, he had to admit that for the sake of a momentary triumph he had stupidly fouled his own nest—his comfortable billet as Klaus's so-called secretary. Now his main hope was that rather than becoming the center of a major scandal, Klaus would settle down quietly with Halcyon, and Alison would simply disappear from the Archway scene. Under those circumstances he could probably get a job as a chemistry teacher in almost any Archway school in the country and pick up some worthwhile additional income as a science consultant and lecturer. This might eventually lead to a prominent position in the movement, like science coordinator for North America. In any case, Klaus still had several days of the conference to deal with and could hardly be back before the following Monday, so the most comfortable thing for now would be to go back to the brownstone and wait a few days for the dust to settle. Fortunately there was a convenient train service from Yonkers to Manhattan.

While trying to comfort himself with these thoughts, he still cursed himself for being such a fool. If he had played his hand more carefully he would still be in England, getting ready to deliver his deeply (as he believed) Goernerian lecture on the metals and their planetary properties. Sitting in the train on the way back, he told himself that his desire for Alison was merely carnal and could soon be satisfied in other ways. This was 90% true but the odd 10% wouldn't go away—the need for something fresh, green and fragrant that might deodorize his inner life, although he didn't think of it that way. He was just acutely conscious of wanting Alison, and the thought of her filled him with misery. His ill-disciplined mind wandered over the whole sequence of events that had led to the present situation, starting with his dim memory of Alison as a child and his first encounter with her as a young woman eight years earlier in Ulm, soon after she had moved in with Klaus and Minna Hübel.

Not yet aware of Klaus's proclivities, Imre had set his sights on Alison, but she had remained sublimely indifferent to him. When the truth dawned on him he was devastated to find that he had been beaten to the post by someone nearly half a century older than himself, a man whom he had regarded as his spiritual stepping stone into the upper reaches of the Society for Cosmic Wisdom. As long as Minna was still around, Imre had hoped that the affair was a temporary infatuation and that he might be able to get Alison when Klaus had finished with her. After Minna left and Alison became Frau Hübel, Imre had tried to console himself with the thought that Klaus was very old and that a young widow might soon seek comfort from the nearest presentable male object.

Soon after this he had become established as a regular visiting teacher at the Pittstown Archway School, and one afternoon in January 1984 he found himself, by an evil chance, waiting in the doctor's office with Phillip Johnson and his young wife Eileen. Imre had stepped on a rusty nail and was there for a tetanus shot, but Phillip and Eileen seemed to have something weightier on their minds. Their conversation was subdued, but with his sharp ears and inquisitive streak Imre soon realized that they were there to get the result of a fertility test. When they emerged from a long session with the doctor they looked very unhappy.

Phillip said, "I don't understand. If what he says is true, how could I . . ."

Eileen quickly shushed him and reminded him that whatever it was must be kept entirely confidential, but as they were leaving she said, "I'm sorry darling, but I think it must be true", and Phillip said, "Then what about Alison? And what about Maria? God in Heaven!"

The door closed on his final sentence. "It can only have been . . ."

For the rest of his stay in Pittstown, Imre had cultivated the Johnsons as unobtrusively as possible, without raising any difficult issues. He also chatted with several older faculty members about the history of the school and spent a couple of days visiting the Manhattan school. By the time he returned to Ulm he felt that he had enough information to put a little scheme into operation. A couple of weeks later, sitting at the coffee table and telling Klaus about his trip to Pittstown, he mentioned quite casually that he had heard something odd about Phillip Johnson. Klaus had his mind on higher things and wasn't interested in gossip, but Imre pressed on.

"I hear he isn't capable of producing children."

There was no response from Klaus, so Imre added, "And never has been."

Klaus stared into Imre's eyes.

"Why are you telling me this?"

The intensity of Klaus's gaze was frightening, and for a moment Imre felt very small and nasty.

"I thought you ought to know."

"And why did you think that?"

Imre had no reply, so Klaus continued.

"And why should I believe you?"

Still no reply.

"Now, get out of my sight."

Imre pulled himself together.

"I imagine that you would not wish this to become public knowledge, especially since it is widely believed that you were Maria Schmidt's lover. It also seems to me that with all your responsibilities you really need a secretary."

Klaus stood up and Imre left the room hurriedly; but the other members of the household noticed that the great euphonist and master of Cosmic Wisdom treated his new secretary with a surprising degree of deference.

When he was invited back to Pittstown in June, Imre found that his previous efforts soon paid off. Dropping into Eileen's office for a chat he saw that her desk was covered with legal papers. She tried to cover them but gave up.

"Well, I guess everybody's going to know soon. I hate it and it's killing me, but Phillip and I are getting a divorce."

"But why?" Imre asked, with genuine interest and well-feigned astonishment.

Eileen was too distressed to contain herself.

"Because I want to have kids and Phil can't."

Here it was, straight from the horse's mouth. Imre could hardly contain himself.

"So what about Alison?" he asked much too eagerly, and Eileen saw the friendly smile transformed into a ghoulish leer. It was such a shock that she put her hands over her eyes and almost screamed.

*

Imre's mind didn't come back to the present until half past five, when his train pulled into Grand Central Station. Now the rational view of his future that he had painfully worked out on the train dissolved into nothingness, and his desperate need to see Alison returned with even greater force. Unable to help himself, he forced his way through the rush hour crowds and got on the shuttle to Times Square, where he faced a long and steamy walk to the Port Authority Bus Terminal. The Pittstown bus was due to leave at six o'clock, and he was too late to buy a ticket upstairs, so he went down to the gates. Seeing some familiar names on the placard at Gate 15—White Plains, Danbury, Norfolk—he got on the end of a long line. It was just six when he asked for his ticket.

"Sorry, Sir. This route's been changed. The Pittstown bus leaves from 17. That's it, just pulling out. Next one's at nine o'clock in the morning. Have a nice evening."

Imre's exertions over the past thirty-six hours had caught up with him, and it seemed like several miles to the Eighth Avenue Subway. The rush hour was still in full spate. Everyone seemed exhausted but grimly determined to get on whatever already overcrowded train came along. It took Imre several attempts before he happened to be in just the right position to be pushed through the door by the crowd behind him. Getting off at West 86th Street was nearly as difficult, and he was almost reduced to crawling on his hands and knees by the time he got to the brownstone. He staggered upstairs, collapsed on his bed, and passed out immediately and comprehensively.

(31)

Having spent Monday night on Bill Graveney's couch, Klaus woke up very early on Tuesday morning and made ample use of his host's telephone. He left his heavy luggage with Bill and took a taxi to Castle Cary, arriving in good time for the express train to Paddington. Enough money and useful connections enabled him to fly comfortably in Lufthansa's business class, and by 5 p.m., Eastern Daylight Time, he was standing in front of the brownstone on West 88th street and noting with some concern that the front door was wide open.

Like Imre, he went first to Alison's room, but he was not surprised to find it empty and apparently undisturbed. She might have wished to take some different clothes and repack her bag, but she wouldn't have wanted to stay there. It was clear that Imre had been in his room, although probably not for long. Klaus pictured him racing through the house, finding no one, grabbing a few things from his room and hurtling out without bothering to shut the door.

Klaus knew exactly what he wanted to do. Four years ago, Imre's allegations had given him a rosier view of his last session with Maria, which he had hugged to himself without feeling any desire to check up on the facts. The facts, after all, might have been awkward. Now the situation had changed. Phillip Johnson might be willing and able to provide confirmation, so first he would go to Pittstown, find Phillip and persuade him to talk. The thought that he might really be the father of Maria's child was still very gratifying, but it was fighting a losing battle against his realization of the load of guilt that his behavior had heaped on him.

"Since I am responsible for this evil situation", he thought, "it must be my karma to do whatever can be done to find Alison and bring her to some kind of resolution."

Deeply disturbed and having no idea what kind of resolution would be possible, he still had enough faith in his spiritual knowledge and wisdom to feel some hope that he could find a way. So, being the man he was, he dined well at his favorite French restaurant before returning to his room in the brownstone, where he read a chapter of Goerner's *Summa pro Cosmosophia* in preparation for a good night's rest.

Unfortunately it didn't work out that way. He had not forgotten the thoughts that had come to him during his vigil on Glastonbury Tor, but they had moved to the middle distance of his mind. Out the depths of sleep he woke up and started thinking about reincarnation, which was one of the fundamental tenets of Cosmic Wisdom, and he realized that in spite of all his efforts, he had only a few glimmers of personal knowledge of it. What he did know was that reincarnation and karma provided the only hypothesis that made any sense of the seemingly random, vicious sequence of events usually known as history. As Goerner had written in Chapter III of the *Summa*, speaking experientially and not hypothetically:

"In spiritual science, as in orthodox science, we must learn to expect contradictions. As Emerson remarked, 'A foolish consistency is the hobgoblin of little minds.' Unfortunately, the Sage of Concord forgot to tell us how to identify foolishness, so we must rely on our own resources in deciding whether consistency is desirable in any particular case. As mere mortals we rightly condemn the use of foul means to arrive at fair ends, although ideal behavior is much easier to formulate than to emulate. If, in the spiritual world, things seem to be different it is because of our almost ineradicable habit of seeing things in terms of only one incarnation. It seems quite right and understandable that in our individual lives we have to go through very bad times in order eventually to achieve some sort of redemption; in the larger context we can preserve our sanity only by seeing the undeserved agonies and extinctions suffered by whole groups or even nations and races as belonging to a great cycle in which origins and consequences work themselves out over successive incarnations. This does not mean that we condone evil acts of persecution, murder and genocide. We know that we must do everything in our power to prevent them, and that in so doing we may alter the course of karma for the persecutors as well as for the victims. But we also have some consolation in the knowledge that when the intentions of the good spirits are subverted by the activities of those who have their own ideas about the evolution of the human race, the evils which result can be turned to good, even though the process may take centuries or millennia."

Klaus had never wavered in his belief in reincarnation, but now he was old, tired, afflicted with feelings of guilt such as he had never experienced before, and facing the prospect of death in at most a few years. It was two o'clock in the morning. He was uncomfortably aware of the *coq au vin* that he had eaten a few hours previously, and the chapter from Goerner's *Summa* was showing signs of becoming equally indigestible. What reason was there to suppose that history was not the random, vicious tale of rape and slaughter that it seemed to be? By what rule could anyone assert that it had to make sense? If fifteen million Ukrainians and six million Jews, not to mention Huguenots and Armenians, could speak, they might have the same question. Well, reincarnation did make sense, and there were sane and intelligent people, including Goerner, who seemed to have knowledge of their previous incarnations. Klaus, however, didn't, and furthermore he had seen that a belief in past and future incarnations sometimes led to a slightly cavalier attitude towards the present one. He had heard people say light-heartedly, "Well, I can't manage that now but I'll get it right next time around." Sometimes, when they spoke of their current actions as being karmic necessities, they were referring to the necessity of doing exactly what they wanted. None of this meant that Goerner was wrong—only that Cosmic Wisdom provided immense opportunities for self-deception.

Klaus chewed these uncomfortable ideas over for a long time. In his heart of hearts he still believed that Goerner was fundamentally right, and he knew, more surely than ever, that he had misused Goerner's rightness. Now he compared himself with the Children of Israel, who received divine revelations but could not avoid backsliding, and frequently had to be called to account. He had had a kind of revelation on the Tor. He had thought that he understood and would act accordingly, but he had really made himself much too comfortable. He ought to have gone straight to Pittstown, where he might by this time have found Alison and could at least have talked to her father. All he could do now would be to telephone Phillip Johnson, get his car out of the garage on 97th Street as early as possible in the morning, and try to make up for lost time. Alison might already have come and gone by then, but it was possible that he would get some idea of where she was going. Mentally he had not succeeded in digesting the indigestible, but he had identified his problems more clearly. The *coq au vin* was less intractable, and Klaus slept soundly for a couple of hours, unaware of Imre's unconscious presence on the next floor.

V

Phillip Johnson

(32)

Phillip Johnson's great-grandfather's name had been Johannesen, and when the family decided to make things easier for everyone, they didn't succeed in erasing a persistent Nordic strain of blue eyes and fair hair. Phillip's father worked at a bank on the Upper West Side of Manhattan and often took his lunch break in Central Park, where he entertained himself by watching teachers and children from the Archway School. One day he got into conversation with a teacher, and the next day she enthusiastically presented him with a fat brochure. His children seemed to be happy enough at public school, however, and Archway looked expensive, so when he got home he parked the brochure on the nearest bookshelf, where it stayed for the next eighteen years.

Phillip wanted to be a writer, so when he went to Manhattan's Hunter College in 1947 he ignored everyone's advice and majored in English Literature. After graduating *magna cum laude* he realized why people had advised him not to be a literature major. There seemed to be zillions of literature majors with *summa* degrees from Harvard, Yale, Princeton and Columbia, all looking for jobs with publishing houses and, failing that, newspapers. Needing to find some way of supporting himself, Phillip split his time between serving hamburgers and studying for his MA in elementary education. He ended up teaching third grade in a rundown public school in Long Island City, where he learned to appreciate the enormous efforts of his colleagues to instill the basic elements of literacy while keeping things at an acceptable level of order. People were helpful in small practical ways, and it was nobody's fault that when he returned every evening to his apartment, he was exhausted and had very little on

141

his mind beyond the question of how he would get through the following day intact.

He had left a lot of his belongings at his parents' home. One weekend in 1959 they decided that too much stuff had accumulated, so Phillip was set to work on a large bookcase. It was some time before anyone noticed that he had been sitting on the floor for over an hour reading *The Archway Schools—Wolfgang Goerner's Approach to Education.*

The author had wisely refrained from trying to give the whole works on Cosmic Wisdom, which might seem anything from exciting and unorthodox to totally kooky, depending on the reader's frame of mind. What appealed to Phillip was that each school was an independent entity, and that Goerner had given a curriculum in outline and left the teachers to fill in the blanks. There was a great deal more that anyone contemplating becoming an Archway teacher would eventually have to absorb, but the book had triggered Phillip's imagination, and he felt that he had stumbled on something more important than being a writer.

*

Several visits to the Archway School in Manhattan convinced Phillip that in spite of its oddball philosophy and the perception that almost everyone seemed to think that they knew better than everyone else, something real was happening there. Having decided that he could live with the philosophy and deal with other risk factors as they arose, he signed on for a year as an apprentice teacher with a training program attached. On the third day of school, Phillip had to replace the fifth grade class teacher, who had been mugged and seriously injured on her way home from a late faculty meeting the previous evening. In view of his youth, good looks and classroom experience, people were ready to overlook his ignorance of Archway and Cosmic Wisdom, and by the end of the 1960-61 school year he had made such an impression that the faculty asked him to continue with the class. He set off enthusiastically for the Archway summer conference in Glastonbury, where, at a euphonics performance in a converted barn with a bovine redolence that would have delighted Dr. Goerner, he saw Maria Schmidt for the first time.

Phillip was fascinated by the small, dark-haired euphonist with twinkling eyes and a ready smile, so on the second day of the conference he joined her workshop and asked her to explain why euphonics was so important for young children. She said they could talk later, which they did for a long time in Maria's sleeping bag, a procedure that they repeated on the remaining five nights. Klaus showed up on the last day of the conference and gave a performance and a lecture. Phillip found Klaus very impressive, and Maria assured him that her little fling with her old mentor was over and hadn't amounted to much anyway. She had to go back to Germany for several months, but they had already decided that they would get married in New York at Christmas. At the end of October she reported that she was pregnant.

Alison was born late in the following May, and the complications were such that Maria had to avoid any further pregnancy. The baby was healthy, however, and the older she got, the more she resembled her mother. Phillip continued as a class teacher for the next seventeen years while Maria taught euphonics in the lower school. Neither took much notice of a plump Hungarian high school student called Imre, who graduated in 1968 and whose father was often seen at Maria's adult euphonics classes.

After the death of Maria, Phillip went into his shell and didn't begin to emerge until a couple of months later, when the Manhattan and Pittstown Archway Schools had some joint faculty meetings and he met the dark, mysteriously Celtic-flavored Eileen O'Rourke, who would shortly be taking the position of school secretary at Pittstown.

Phillip spent only one more year in Manhattan before moving to Pittstown and marrying Eileen. Alison went to Ulm in the summer of 1979. Phillip had not been expecting her to stay there but, of course, she did.

*

After a couple of years in Pittstown, Phillip was elected Faculty Chairman. Eileen, who was more than twenty years younger than her husband, caused a certain amount of alarm and despondency among the more *echt* members of the community by habitually wearing her skirts a foot shorter than the Archway norm and avoiding purple dresses, Birkenstocks and grey wool socks. The two of them basically ran the whole show, and it was not to be expected that serenity would reign for very long. The few who had not been enchanted tolerated the situation for a few months, but overt grumbling and covert whispering soon began. Phillip had a way of stating things clearly, saying exactly what he meant and avoiding innuendo, which the grumblers found disconcerting and used as a pretext for complaining that their chairman was "too intellectual"; but for a year or so the most serious criticisms of Phillip were kept under the table.

Eileen was a more obvious target. Her flamboyant way of dressing was equated with an excessively liberal attitude to sex, and it was a fact that she had been propositioned by several boys and at least one girl in the senior class. She was certainly popular with students of both sexes and there was a lot of anxiety about her influence on the young. When a deputation of teachers admonished Phillip about his wife's behavior, he told them that he liked the way she dressed, and if they objected they could speak to her about it. This they failed to do, knowing that Eileen's power of repartee was much greater than theirs.

Phillip made no announcement of his daughter's marriage to Klaus in 1982, and when the news trickled in it caused a combination of disbelief and malicious amusement. To have a son-in-law twenty-five years older than yourself is, to say the least, unusual, but the anti's were unable to find a way of exploiting the situation.

Halfway through Phillip's fourth year as Chairman, people began to notice a change. He became more and more distant and preoccupied, while Eileen seemed attentive to him in a different way, as if he were more of an aging relative than a vigorous husband. It was assumed that Phillip was ill, so everyone was startled to hear in the middle of the following summer vacation that the couple had divorced and that Eileen would not return to the school. The beginning of Phillip's decline had coincided roughly with one of Imre Takacs's visits to the school, and Imre was back again in June to give one of his spurious chemistry workshops. On a couple of occasions he had been seen chatting with Eileen, an observation that supplied a lot of grist to the rumor mill. Eileen, however, had no interest in Imre. She simply disappeared from the scene, while Imre continued to make his periodic visits.

Phillip continued for a while as Chairman. There didn't seem to be anything wrong with his health, but he had lost his inspiration as well as his wife, and he soon gave way to the counter-revolutionary party. He stayed on as a class teacher for several years but was increasingly plagued by depression, and in June of 1987, a year before Alison met Tom in Glastonbury, he retired to his small, white-painted cottage just off the main road north of Pittstown, where he concentrated on growing vegetables and keeping his front lawn weed-free and green. He still had friends, including his next door neighbor and former colleague, Virginia Reddick, who had joined the faculty about the same time as Eileen left, and had become his confidant.

Virginia was a square, gruff woman of indeterminate middle age who had abandoned a career as an industrial chemist to become a science teacher in the Archway movement. Some anticipated wedding bells, but Virginia already had a partner, having brought along her former technical secretary, Michele Weiss, and Michele's thirteen-year-old daughter Amy. Virginia and Michele were firmly established as lovers, and the worldly-wise Amy was under the impression that she understood the situation perfectly. Virginia taught chemistry in the upper school, Michele worked as a secretary in town, and by 1988 Amy had completed her high school education.

As a new teacher, Virginia had been obliged to accept Imre Takacs as a mentor, so Imre found himself spending a fair amount of time with someone who knew a great deal more chemistry than he did. Virginia took care to maintain a proper professional relationship with him, and Imre departed under the impression that Virginia was a good friend and ally.

*

Phillip occasionally heard from Alison but had lost touch completely with his son-in-law, so he was surprised to receive a phone call from Klaus early on the day after Klaus's arrival in New York. After listening carefully to what Klaus had to say, he sat down at his desk and wrote two letters. On his way outside he remembered that the front lawn needed cutting, so he went to the back of the house for the lawn mower. It would only take a few minutes and he didn't want to leave a mess. He completed the task, put the mower away, called at the grocery store to pick up a quart of milk and five hundred aspirins, and slipped one of the letters into Virginia's mailbox on the way back.

(33)

Having talked to Phillip, Klaus knew that Alison had not yet been to Pittstown. Thinking that she might still be on her way, he continued with his plan and at one o'clock on Wednesday afternoon he rang the front door bell of Phillip Johnson's cottage. The place was silent and remained so, but the lawn had been freshly mown and the smell of cut grass was still in the air. It seemed that there must be someone around, so he rang several more times before opening the door and going inside. Getting no response to his calls, he opened the first door he came to and immediately saw Phillip. He was sitting in a deep armchair with his right arm on one of the rests and his head on his arm. There was an envelope on the side table next to him.

Shouting and calling Phillip's name had no effect. He seemed to be barely breathing, so Klaus ran back to the telephone in the front hall and dialed 911. He explained what he had seen and gave the address. No, there were no signs of violence or any disturbance at all, and no bottles or medicines were visible.

Klaus left the front door open and hurried back. Phillip's breathing was almost imperceptible. An ambulance drew up at the gate and two emergency medics ran up the garden path. Klaus glanced at the envelope on the side table, saw that it was marked "personal" and addressed to Alison, and quickly put it into his pocket.

"I don't think it's cardiac", one of the medics said. "Could have OD'd on something."

"Nothing visible", the other commented. "Pulse very feeble—better not move him. Here's the doc. I'm going to look in the kitchen."

The police surgeon was Dr. Frazer, the physician who had given Phillip the result of his fertility test four years previously. It didn't immediately occur to him that there might be a connection between that event and the present situation.

The EMT returned a moment later with five empty aspirin bottles in his hands.

"Tidy kind of guy. Took his medicine in the kitchen and put the bottles in the trash."

The doctor looked up and said, "Must have been quite a while ago. He's nearly gone. Any sign of a note?"

The medics shook their heads and Klaus said nothing. There was a step at the door and Virginia Reddick said, "Can anyone please tell me what's happening? Oh, dear Heaven, no!"

"Stand back, please", said one of the medics. "The doctor needs room and we'll have a whole team here in a minute. Take the lady into the next room, would you, Sir."

Klaus did as he was told and said, "I am afraid it looks very bad."

"Suicide?" Virginia asked.

"It seems to be. I believe that I am to blame."

Virginia had never seen Klaus, but the truth dawned on her at this moment.

"Are you Klaus?" she asked.

"Yes."

"Then may God damn you and may you rot in Hell."

*

Phillip Johnson died without regaining consciousness.

(34)

One of the odd things about Klaus's relationship to Alison was that he was apt to forget that his marriage to her made him Phillip's son-in-law. This lapse of memory, together with the inner devastation caused by his father-in-law's suicide, Virginia Reddick's violent condemnation and his desire to avoid any enquiry into Alison's past, resulted in a rather garbled statement to Sergeant Gerstman of the Pittstown police.

"Yes, I have known Phillip for a long time, but I haven't seen him for several years. No, there was no particular reason for the visit except to renew an old friendship."

"Did Phillip have any close relations?" the sergeant asked.

"Yes, he had a daughter."

"What was the daughter's name?"

"Alison."

"Any siblings?"

"No."

"Was this daughter married?"

"Yes."

"Do you happen to know her married name?"

"Yes."

"Well then, what is it?"

"It is Hübel."

"Isn't that your name, Sir?"

"Yes."

"Oh, I see. You must be her father-in-law."

This was mere politeness—Klaus looked more like a grandfather-in-law.

"No, I am her husband."

Coming out as it did, this piece of information caused a sensation. This elderly gentleman, who had given his age as eighty-four, was the son-in-law of the fifty-nine-year-old deceased, and seemed to have tried to avoid mentioning the fact. Perhaps his memory was failing, but he seemed quite sharp about other matters, and it was certainly an odd thing to forget. Klaus realized that he had started on the wrong foot and had better go back to the beginning and concoct a plausible story that didn't mention the reason for Alison's precipitate flight from Glastonbury.

"Alison Johnson and I were married in Germany in 1982. We now live in Manhattan and were attending the Archway Schools Conference in England. On Monday, Alison returned to New York and I followed yesterday. I wanted to consult Phillip on some educational matters, and I telephoned him early this morning. He seemed to be perfectly all right then. No, I didn't see a note of any kind."

The doctor and the investigating officers had no reason to doubt that Phillip had committed suicide, but the absence of a note was a little unusual. This fact and the oddness of Klaus's statement gave Sergeant Gerstman enough reason to ask him to remain in the station while he talked to Virginia Reddick.

"How long have you known Mr. Johnson?" he asked her.

"About four years. We were colleagues at the Archway School. I joined the faculty soon after his wife left."

"Have you noticed anything unusual about him recently? Has he been worried or depressed?"

"He's been depressed most of the time I've known him, and it's gradually been getting worse. This letter was in my mailbox."

Virginia handed over the letter and this is what Sergeant Gerstman read:

> "Dear Virginia,
>
> You have been a good friend and without you I wouldn't have lasted as long as I did. The enclosed check is for my cremation. Please do your best to ensure that it is done with no religious trappings and that no representatives of the Archway Movement are present. I hope you will be there,

however. It is also my wish that there should be no memorial service.

  With my thanks and best wishes,

       Phillip."

"The check is for $5,000", Virginia said. "And do you know the most amazing thing? He was out there at nine o'clock this morning, mowing his lawn. He was like that, you know—unlike a lot of his colleagues. He never wanted to leave a mess for someone else to clean up."

"Do you know if he's been seeing anyone about his depression?"

"No—only our school doctor."

"Did you ever worry that he might take his own life?"

"No, I'm very surprised. It's not something that people with our philosophy would consider."

It seemed to Sergeant Gerstman that a philosophy that precluded suicide might be worth investigating, but not at this moment.

"Can you think of anything that might have precipitated this action?"

"Yes."

"And what would that be?"

"You'd better ask Klaus Hübel, and if he won't tell you, I will."

"I'm afraid I'll have to ask you to be more forthcoming."

Virginia had kept this indigestible secret for several years and, once it was released, the words came tumbling out.

"Very well. Do you know why Phillip's second wife divorced him? It was because he was not capable of fathering a child. According to the doctor it was a congenital defect and he couldn't possibly have been Alison's father. But his first wife, Alison's mother, couldn't have any more children so he didn't find out until several years after his second marriage. He and Eileen loved each other, but she wanted the chance to have her own children, and he understood. I know all this because Phillip told me. After the divorce he went through a terrible period of depression and he needed someone to talk to. That's all I'm going to say. Now bring that man back in here and tell him what I said."

The sergeant's calm was shaken by a wild surmise, but he kept his tone level.

"This might make more sense if you could tell me who was Alison's father."

Klaus had been standing by the open doorway for several minutes and now he spoke.

"I see that this must all be known and I was foolish to think otherwise. I believe that I am Alison's father—in fact it now seems to be certain. I was her husband too, but that I am no longer, except in the eyes of the law. I wish to add something to my statement. At the time when Alison and I were married, I was unaware that she was my daughter. As soon as the possibility was raised I ceased intimacy with her."

"Excuse me, Sir", Gerstman interposed. "Are you sure you want this to be part of your statement?"

"Yes. I am very old and have been much too satisfied about the way in which I have lived my life. It is because of Alison that I have begun to realize my deficiencies. Now my one concern is for her well-being. I have here a letter addressed to her by Phillip Johnson, which I have read and now hand to the police on the understanding that its contents will remain confidential."

"I'm afraid we can't make any promises about that, but you can rest assured that we'll be as discreet as possible."

Klaus paused. When he went on, his measured tones were replaced by a kind of controlled desperation.

"I do not know where Alison is. I thought she would have come to see Phillip."

"Why did you think that, Sir?

"She had no idea that Phillip was not her father until early on Monday morning, when my secretary, Imre Takacs, told her in a very sudden and malicious way. She left precipitately and it seemed most likely that she would immediately come and ask Phillip to confirm or deny the story. She was utterly distraught and I fear greatly that she may . . ."

"Become suicidal?"

"Yes. I telephoned Phillip this morning to find out if Alison was here. He was appalled when I told him what had happened. He said that he had known the truth for several years and that he had always felt that it would be better for Alison never to know. He told me that he felt enormous guilt, and said that he realized that he ought to have told her as soon as he found out. I tried to convince him that he was not at fault, but he blamed himself bitterly for taking the easier course and I believe he could not face seeing Alison."

Virginia didn't altogether agree.

"I'm not sure it was the easier course. He could have just told her and then washed his hands of her. The trouble was that he still wanted her to be his daughter—I mean his *real* daughter—even though she couldn't be, and it was just one long struggle to live with the situation. He had been a handsome, proud and vigorous man. He felt his sexual inadequacy very keenly, and couldn't bear the thought of talking with her about it. Well, I don't know; perhaps it was the easier way."

"Very often there is no easier way."

Virginia and Klaus looked at Sergeant Gerstman in some surprise, and he got back to business.

"Once it's established, as I'm sure it will be, that Mr. Johnson committed suicide by swallowing a large quantity of aspirin, it should be possible to close the case without any damaging revelations. We shall have to try to find his daughter, since she is legally his next of kin, no matter what the truth is about her parentage. I can see that this is a very complex and distressing matter, but from the police point of view it seems very straightforward. The autopsy will establish the cause of death and every scrap of evidence points to suicide. I have your addresses and telephone numbers and I don't think there's any need to keep you here longer. Obviously it's vitally important to find Ms Johnson—I mean, Mrs. Hübel—as soon as possible, and I must ask you, Sir, to let us know if you locate her."

As they were leaving the station, Virginia said to Klaus, "I don't approve of your way of going on, which is common knowledge among Archway people, but now I think maybe you're just a naughty, misguided old rascal. We need to talk and figure out what to do about finding Alison. I'd invite you over for a cup of coffee, but we have a teenage girl in the house and I'm not sure you can be trusted."

"I can assure you that my opinion of myself is more severe than yours. The young lady has nothing to fear from me, but I understand your caution. I believe I should tell you what Phillip wrote in his note to Alison, since you are mentioned."

Not bothering with coffee, they sat on a bench under a maple tree in front of the police station.

"It was quite brief", Klaus went on. "First he admitted that he had known the truth for four years and bitterly regretted having allowed her to continue as my wife for all that time."

Interrupting himself, he asked, "Why was he so sure that I was Alison's father? Did he know that Maria and I had been lovers?"

"Yes, he told me all about it. When he and Maria spent their first night together they told each other about their previous lovers. They were so rapturous, he said, that it was a bit of a joke to recall these past affairs and how insignificant they seemed."

For a moment Klaus was far away.

"I wonder what she said."

"Well, if you really want to know, she said that for an old man you were quite a lot of fun and you performed pretty well when you weren't explaining her karma. She told him that she had tried to end it, but when you found out that she was leaving you were very upset and she took pity on you."

"Phillip told you all that?"

"Yes—later on it seems to have worried him that Maria had still been doing it with you only a few days before she met him. When the fertility test came back he drew the obvious conclusion."

"Yes, I'm afraid he was right. In all those years when Maria lived in Ulm I was her only lover. It is true that she told me that she wished to end our relationship, but on the night before she left for England . . . Do you wish to hear this? We are almost complete strangers, and if I were a Roman I should be speaking to a priest."

"Now that you've said so much I'd like to know the rest, but remember, I'm not going to say 'Ego absolvo te' when you get to the end. I might go back to damning you to hell."

"You may be justified. On that last night she was extremely passionate and we were not as careful as usual. And then she told me that she loved me as much as ever but, if I express it very simply, that she wanted to find a husband before it became too late, and live a normal married life."

"Why didn't she marry you? Oh, of course, you were already married and . . ."

"Yes, she had seen what being married to me meant."

"So you knew there was a chance that you were Alison's father and yet you married her. That's not what you told you told the policeman—now you're saying that you knew there was a possibility. I don't understand how you can sit there calmly and tell me this stuff. What possible excuse is there?"

There was a long silence before Klaus replied. When he did he spoke like someone figuring things out as he went along.

"There is no excuse, nor are there any extenuating circumstances. Even as a child, Alison resembled her mother so closely that I began to feel that they were almost the same person. Later it was like taking up where I had left off, and if I had any doubts about her parentage, my subconscious suppressed them. I do not mean to offer that as an excuse. Not so very long ago I still believed that I was an important person with a crucial role in the drama of the universe and the salvation of the world. I was convinced that all the young women who had given themselves to me were helping me to fulfill my karma, not for me personally but for the future evolution of the human race. My consciousness was so fully engaged with the work I was trying to do that I thought that Alison's presence was something provided by the spiritual powers to replace Maria. I thought that the uncertainty about Alison's birth was their responsibility. My illusions began to slip away four years ago when Imre told me what he had found out about Phillip, but it was a long process. I confess with shame that the ambiguity of the situation had added to the excitement that I always felt in Alison's presence. I was deeply shocked when the ambiguity disappeared, but, being still full of spiritual pride, I was not shocked enough. I was no longer intimate with Alison, but I soon became involved with another young woman."

"OK, Klaus, that's enough about you for the time being. It's a revolting story and it makes me wonder whether I want to have anything more to do with Goerner. You'd better tell me about the rest of Phillip's letter."

"I think that Goerner would have been appalled at my behavior. As far as Phillip's letter is concerned, he said that having lost Maria and realized that he had no child of his own, and seeing no future for himself in the Archway Movement, he could see no point in living any longer. As long as Alison was unaware of the truth she might still regard him as her father and he might still be of some use to her, but now that possibility was gone. It was not a very warm or affectionate letter, and I think it will be best if Alison never sees it."

"What will you do now?"

"I shall return to Manhattan—perhaps Alison will be there by now. If not I shall try to find her."

"And what then? I can't believe she really wants to see you."

"I think it is in the nature of things that we shall find each other. In spite of everything there is a special kind of understanding between us . . . No, that is to give myself too much importance. It is just that I want to see her and I am afraid that she may kill herself."

He got to his feet, not with his accustomed sprightliness but with perceptible effort.

"I have begun to feel very old and tired, and I believe I understand why I have been allowed to live to such a great age. If I had died a year ago it would have been in a state of spiritual pride. Now that I have made the first steps in learning to see myself for what I am, perhaps I shall soon be permitted to go."

Virginia stood up with her usual vigor and took his arm.

"If we could see ourselves for what we really are it would probably kill us outright, so there's no need to tempt providence. It's getting dark and it's a four-hour drive to Manhattan, and I'm not sure you're going to make it. I don't believe you want to die yet, so you'd better come and stay the night in our funny household. In your present state I don't think you could hurt a fly. You're an old humbug, Klaus Hübel. If you get rid of your spiritual pride you'll still have an overdose of self-dramatization to deal with. Whether you die now or in ten years time isn't going to make much difference to the fate of mankind but, God help me, I don't hate you and if I'm not careful I might even begin to feel a little bit sorry you. But don't keep on about being old and tired."

Klaus sat down with a thump. He was past protesting.

Virginia hauled him to his feet.

"Listen Klaus, your sins may be worse than mine—I don't know how they grade these things—but I'm not the one to cast the first stone. I've been your confessor, so maybe one day you can be mine. Let's walk, it'll do us good."

(35)

Imre didn't wake up until eleven o'clock on Wednesday morning, and he would have slept longer if it hadn't been for the sounds of someone moving things around in the next room. The thought that it must be Alison had him sitting bolt upright in a flash, but getting up and seeing himself in his wardrobe mirror he realized that he looked as awful as he felt, and he remembered that Alison was the reason for his awfulness.

He stumbled to his door and opened it just in time to see a middle-aged woman emerging from Alison's room with a suitcase in one hand and a boom box in the other.

"Who are you?" Imre croaked.

The woman looked at him, appeared to register him as an unpleasant phenomenon and continued on her way down the stairs. At the front door she paused, looked back at Imre and said, "You should get something done about that mouth of yours."

Imre sat down on the top stair, fingered his lips and thought, "Yes, that's true, that's very true, that's goddamned exceptionally true."

After a minute it occurred to him to go down and see where the woman went, but by the time he reached the street she had disappeared.

*

Alison spent most of Wednesday afternoon with her boom box in the big living room of the doctors' apartment. There were a lot of set pieces for solo euphonists and plenty of scope for improvisation, which Alison liked best but wasn't usually allowed to do. She was still at it when Helen came to take her down to the office for an introduction to the duties of a receptionist. Alison was in the middle of a wild improvisation to the last movement of Debussy's string quartet, so Helen watched admiringly until it was over.

"Wow!" she said, "That's fantastic."

She looked at the collection of tapes.

"Bach, Corelli, Beethoven, Schumann—don't you ever do anything for fun?"

"It is fun—it's tremendous fun, but if you want something different you can lift up the top tray and look underneath."

"Motley Crue, Pink Floyd, the Stones. Can we put on one of these?"

So they put Pink Floyd on and Helen jiggled in the middle of the room while Alison circled her in crazy gyrations.

"Life's not so bad after all", Helen gasped when the music stopped, "but I'm a bit out of practice with this kind of thing. I think I'll sit the next one out. What's up, are we too loud?"

The question was addressed to Nick and Chris, who had come quietly into the room. They were looking very grave.

Alison switched off the boom box.

155

"What's the matter?" she asked.

"You'd better sit down", Chris said gently.

Alison sat on the couch, with Helen beside her.

"What is it?" she asked again. She had almost been able to relax, but now everything was tightening and twisting again.

Nick spoke.

"I tried several times to call Phillip Johnson and got no reply, so I tried calling the Archway School in Pittstown. No one knew where he was, but I left my number and someone called back a little later. Phillip died this morning."

Nick looked at Chris and Chris nodded.

"They think he committed suicide."

There was a long silence before Alison burst out, "Why? Why should he do that? No one ever did anything to him!"

Chris said, "You've had very little contact with him since you went to Ulm, so you don't know what he may have been through."

"I know that he ought to have told me something and he didn't."

Alison's body rocked back and forth as she spoke, and Helen put her arms around her.

"This isn't just a coincidence, is it?"

"It seems unlikely, but if it isn't a coincidence someone must have been in communication with him. The woman who called me said that I was the second person who had tried to contact Phillip in the past two days, and she wanted to know who I was. I told her it was a medical matter that I couldn't discuss, and then she told me what had happened. She said this other visitor had arrived while Phillip was still alive, but he had taken a huge number of aspirins and they couldn't revive him. I asked who the visitor was and she said if I wasn't going to tell her anything why should she tell me anything. Then she laughed and said, 'If you must know, it was his son-in-law.' And then she hung up on me."

"Klaus was there? I don't believe it."

"I don't know why not. My guess is that when Klaus discovered that you had left Glastonbury, he figured out where you were going and came after you as fast as he could. And if you hadn't lost your keys and fainted on Monday night, he might have found you in the brownstone on Tuesday. But you weren't there, so he went up to Pittstown early this morning and when he got there Phillip was dying."

"Yes", said Helen. "Klaus must have called him before leaving and . . ."

"You might as well say it." Alison squeezed the words out. "Klaus told him what had happened and he couldn't face the prospect of seeing me."

She carefully disengaged herself from Helen and kissed her on the top of her head. "Thanks, Helen. I'd like to go to my room for a little while. I promise I won't do anything bad."

"OK, Alison", Chris said, "But officially you are Phillip's next of kin and I'm afraid you'll find that the police and his lawyer will want to talk to you."

"Do I have to do anything now?"

"I think it can wait until the morning, and even then I don't believe you'll be under any compulsion to see them. It's just that it might be better to get it over with."

Alone in her room, Alison thought about Klaus, Imre, Phillip, Halcyon and Tom. She wondered how badly Klaus's massive self-esteem had been damaged, but he still had money and position and was an unlikely object for pity. Imre seemed like an actor who had played his part and faded into obscurity. It didn't occur to her that he might reappear in future scenes, since she wasn't planning any. Phillip she couldn't weigh up at all. The situation he had landed in wasn't his fault, but there had been a point at which he should have done something about it and he didn't. She felt guilty about the fact that the only strong feeling his death had aroused in her was that she was to blame for it. Otherwise she didn't seem to care very much. Tom caused her a lot of confusion. She wanted him very much, but she wondered if it was just the feel of his gorgeous body after a long period with the aged Klaus and then several years of nothing much at all? He was certainly a nice guy, smart, humorous, and free from the stock responses that she found so irritating among the CW's. He seemed clean or unspoilt or something that she couldn't define, that reminded her of the little love affairs she had had before she went to Ulm. Whatever it was, it was the opposite of how she felt about herself, although she couldn't define that, either. Dirty, damaged, defiled, abused—none of these words really seemed to fit. She decided that it would be better not think about Tom until she was feeling a bit more like her old self, if that ever happened. So what about Halcyon? Halcyon was one of a kind—well, Halcyon and her Mum. It struck Alison that if Halcyon's Mum had been there she could have sorted everything out with no trouble at all. Halcyon on her own would have been a great comfort.

Meanwhile Alison's ugly feelings of betrayal, violation, disorientation, guilt and dirt, were being supplemented by something much more straightforward; the anger that she already felt was turning into something so huge and concrete that it began to deaden the pain of all these other feelings. Mostly she was angry with Klaus and Phillip. Klaus had known the situation when he married her. She had made a fine substitute for her missing mother, and maybe he got a little extra excitement from the possibility that he was taking his own daughter's virginity. Phillip, for the second time in her life, had dodged his responsibilities, and had done so while Nick, Chris and Helen were busily trying to stop her from doing the same thing. Imre seemed more like something nasty that had escaped from the zoo—no use being angry with a rattlesnake, but if it didn't crawl back into its hole, you might have to do something about it.

Well, she would keep suicide as an option, but how about exploring some of the possibilities she had never considered before? There was nothing she could do about Phillip but there must be some way of getting back at Klaus. Apart from the fact that she was still legally married to him, she was free to do whatever she wanted. She could check out of CW, put euphonics on the back burner and try living the life of a selfish, attractive young woman in her mid-twenties, the real clincher being that if she played her cards right she might be able to get Klaus to finance her adventure; and if it went wrong she could go back to her original idea and kill herself. With that as her fail-safe option, there was no reason why she shouldn't go out and try a life of self-indulgence with some ordinary, everyday dirt.

For the moment she would behave herself and try to be grateful to her hosts, so she packed as many of her things as she could into her suitcase and joined Nick and Chris for a scratch meal of Chinese leftovers. She told them that she didn't feel like talking any more and would like to go to bed, which she did, but only after writing a note to the two doctors and Helen. Next morning, which was Thursday, she got up at five o'clock, took her suitcase, tiptoed out of the apartment, walked around the corner and very quietly let herself into the brownstone. Part of her plan involved a visit to Halcyon's room, which was on the third floor, next to Klaus's room. She soon found what she was looking for, and finding pen and paper in her friend's desk, left her a brief note. After that, she went halfway down the stairs to the second floor, sat down and let her mind go blank.

*

Klaus drove back to Manhattan early on Thursday morning, and this gave him plenty of time for thinking—more than he really wanted. What an odd woman Virginia Reddick was. First she had consigned him to the devil, then she had become quite sympathetic and understanding, and then she had invited him to her house and started confiding her guilty secrets. Certainly the girl Anna was extremely beautiful, but Klaus had finally reached the stage where the weakness of the flesh is a serious drag on the willingness of the spirit, or if not the spirit, at least the libido. Such as Anna were not for him any more. Or for Virginia, who had fallen in love with the girl when she was thirteen, had partnered with her mother so as to be near Anna, and had been living this lie for four years. Now that Anna was going off on a long trip with some friends, and after that to college, Virginia felt that she couldn't keep it up. Why did she tell all this to Klaus? Well, Anna was not the first and it was just a relief to meet someone who was working with a similar kind of guilt. Virginia didn't mind pointing out that Klaus's guilt was much worse than hers, but at least it was the same kind of thing, and she thought maybe it would help him to know that he wasn't the only one. Actually it didn't help in the least; all Klaus had got out of it was an uneasy night in an uncomfortable bed.

Virginia, however, was merely a diversion. Klaus knew that there was very little he could do about his own problems, which he felt would have to be worked out over several incarnations. He wanted to find a way of helping Alison to survive the crisis of this incarnation and return to some kind of relatively normal life, but any optimism he might have felt a couple of days previously had vanished along with large parts of his old self-image. He returned the car at the 97th Street garage and walked back to the brownstone. When he got there, just after ten o'clock, the first thing he did was to go to Imre's room on the second floor. There was no one there, but the unmade bed, the open suitcase and oddments of clothing strewn around the room told the story. Klaus went to Alison's room and saw that things had been rearranged and there was a suitcase just inside the door. This was hard to figure out, and he was just turning away when he heard Alison's voice.

"Good morning, Klaus. How are you?"

"Alison! I have been looking for you."

"Have you, Klaus? Why?"

"I thought I could help you . . ."

Alison, who had still been sitting halfway down the stairs when Klaus arrived, descended to the second floor landing.

"How could you possibly do that? With prayer and meditation? Or something about my karma?"

"So I believed, but I am not that person any more."

"Maybe you never were."

"Perhaps I never was. You are right, Alison. It is you who are guiltless and I who have sinned. I need your prayers more than you need mine."

If Alison had been in full command of herself she might have been able to consider this thought as a possible key to her inner turmoil, but she wasn't. It just seemed that this old man who had wronged her irremediably was now trying to shift some kind of responsibility to her, so she went on as if she hadn't heard his last remark.

"There is something you can do for me. I need some money—after all, you are my husband. I need $10,000. And please don't ask me what it's for."

Klaus sat down rather hurriedly on the nearest available object, which happened to be the floor. Alison looked down at him without much pity.

"You're not having a heart attack, are you?"

"No. It may seem strange to you, but my heart is remarkably strong. I am, however, extremely tired. Since you ask me to provide you with this money in my capacity as your husband, I believe I have a right to expect that, in your capacity as my wife, you should tell me what you have in mind."

"OK Klaus—I'm going away. And I shall go away whether you give me the money or not. But I won't be earning much and I'd like to be able to rent an apartment so I don't have to live in an SRO."

"SRO? What is an SRO?"

"Single room occupancy, usually full of criminals and cockroaches."

"And you are not intending to go to Pittstown?"

"Why should I go to Pittstown?"

"Because your father . . ."

"Don't put any more guilt on me, Klaus. Remember what you said a minute ago. I am not the guilty one and he was not my father."

The barely controlled fury in Alison's voice amazed Klaus.

"All right, Alison. In the circumstances it would be hard for me to refuse you anything, and this is very small compared with what I shall have to pay later. But it will take a little while to arrange. How would you like the money?"

"I'd like three thousand in cash and the rest as a cashier's check. Please. I'll wait in my room."

As Alison sat down on the edge of her bed she was wondering if this could possibly be real.

*

While Alison and Klaus were talking, Imre was on his way home from the dentist. Dr. Axelrod had spoken to him about bridges and implants. It was going to be very expensive, but his lips were beginning to heal and he was feeling more comfortable. He opened the front door of the brownstone just as Alison was disappearing into her room and her aged husband was getting to his feet. Klaus was chastened and humbled by recent events, but there was a great deal of the old Adam left in him and $10,000 was a lot of money. He remembered the enormous, slightly guilty feeling of satisfaction he had experienced when he hit Imre three days ago. The guilt seemed to have disappeared but the knuckles of his right hand were still sore, so as Imre reached the top of the stairs Klaus stepped in front of him and hit him again, this time with a straight left to the nose. Alison heard an almighty crash and ran out of her room just in time to see her husband stepping over the prostrate Imre on his way out. Imre sat up with his hand to his streaming nose. Klaus closed and locked the front door. He was feeling just a little better. Alison went back to her room.

Klaus returned an hour later, avoided the bloodstains on the hall floor and handed a bulky envelope to Alison.

"Here it is, exactly as you asked. May I ask what this ill-paid occupation is that you are expecting to take up? An Archway School, perhaps?"

Alison laughed.

"No, not an Archway School."

She whispered conspiratorially in his ear.

"MacDonald's"

As she turned away, Klaus said, "You do understand, don't you, that it is as my wife that you have asked for this money. Therefore, in accepting it, you certify that you still hold that position."

Alison dropped the envelope on the floor, picked up her suitcase and set off down the stairs.

"Wait, Alison. Please take the money. I owe it to you and will not expect anything in return."

When Alison got to the bottom she called back up to Klaus.

"You'd better get Imre to come and clean up his mess."

This was too much for Klaus. He picked up the envelope and hurled it at his wife. After a moment's thought, she retrieved it and took it with her.

In order to get to the subway station at Central Park West and 86th Street, Alison would have had to pass right in front of the building where she had spent the last two nights, so, in spite of the weight of her suitcase she walked all the way up to 96th Street.

(36)

Life was very busy at 287 Central Park West. Nick had to leave early for the hospital and Chris and Helen had a lot of paper work to catch up with before the morning's first appointment, so it wasn't until ten o'clock that Helen went to Alison's room and found her note, in which she thanked Nick and Chris for their extreme kindness and their professional services, and assured them that she would be in touch about fees. She explained that she simply needed to get right away and see if she could find some kind of a life among people who knew nothing about her past. She thanked Helen for the walk in the park and for dancing with her, but the whole note conveyed the chill of impersonal resolution that Alison had felt as she was writing it. There was a P. S. that gave Klaus's phone number and suggested that they ask him to come by and pick up the things that she had not been able to take with her.

"Stupid, stupid girl", Helen muttered. She had unbounded faith in Chris's therapeutic powers. "If she'd stayed a few more days we'd have figured her out and put her on the right track."

Chris was busy with a patient, so Helen couldn't tell him what had happened until an hour later.

"We must try to find her husband", Chris said. "He may be back on 88th Street by now, and if not we may be able to locate him in Pittstown. It might be a good idea to contact the police in Pittstown anyway. Presumably they have her father's body in the morgue, and in the absence of the heir someone's going to have to decide about funeral arrangements. I wonder where she's gone."

"She said something about Peoria when we were in the park."

"Good God! She talked about working for McDonald's in Peoria, but I didn't take her seriously."

"I don't know—she's a funny kid."

Chris had a patient waiting for him, so Helen made another trip to the brownstone and might well have bumped into Alison if she hadn't decided to go the other way. She had to ring the bell several times before Klaus appeared, and when he did she became uncharacteristically flustered. He helped her out.

"You have some news of my wife? I should very much like to hear it, but I should tell you that I have just seen her and she has gone away again. Do please come in."

In his deteriorating old age, Klaus still projected a powerful and distinguished masculinity, and Helen, feeling a little like the fly entering the spider's parlor, thought she could understand how he had been able to attract several generations of young women. They went into the workroom at the back of the ground floor, where Klaus had arranged all the furniture around the perimeter so as to leave a space in the middle big enough to work on euphonics movements. Sitting on a hard chair next to an upright piano, Helen told him all she knew of Alison's appearance and disappearance. Klaus sat on the keyboard lid and listened intently.

"So you know the reason for her distress", he said.

"All we know is what she told us."

"I believe that everything she said is true. She asked me for money, which I gave to her, and she left half an hour ago. I do not know where she is going, but I believe she may be safe for the time being."

"What makes you think that?"

"She asked for $10,000. She was in a very strange mood, most unlike her usual self, and I suspect that she wishes to try out a different mode of living. In the circumstances I could hardly refuse."

"You gave her $10,000?"

"Yes."

Both were silent for a minute.

Helen asked, "What will you do now?"

"I shall look for her, although I do not know where to begin."

"Did she say anything about Peoria?"

"Peoria? No, the only thing she said was 'MacDonald's'. I thought it was a joke."

"She said something to us about working at MacDonald's in Peoria. We didn't take it seriously."

Klaus was silent and Helen said, "May I ask whose blood it is on the hall floor?"

Klaus laughed bitterly.

"You need not worry. It is not that of my wife. It belongs, or used to belong, to my former secretary, Imre Takacs."

"Did anything bad happen?"

"No, I merely punched him on the nose."

"Oh", said Helen.

*

After Helen had left, Klaus sat down at his desk and wrote a brief note.

> "Dear Mr. Takacs,
>
> This is to inform you that I no longer require your secretarial services. As of nine o'clock on Monday morning, you will no longer be regarded as a resident of this house. By that time I shall expect you to have removed all your belongings and returned your keys.
>
> Yours truly,
> Klaus Hübel"

Klaus put the note into an envelope, addressed it and slipped it under his former secretary's door. Imre, who had taken a shower and was lying on his bed in his bathrobe, got painfully to his feet and picked up the note. He had been expecting something like this, but it was still a nasty shock. He had spent a lot of money over the past few days. He faced a formidable dentist's bill and was in trouble with the police, and now he was being thrown out onto the street with nowhere to go. He had got past the stage of blaming himself for the mess he had made, and his anger was directed at everyone else who was in any way involved—Halcyon, who had not hidden her contempt, and Alison, who had treated his advances as a joke; Tom Dexter, who had carried Alison off in front of his very eyes and, most of all, Klaus, with whom Imre had imagined there was an unwritten agreement. Imre believed that Klaus could have coerced Alison into a marriage that would have given him the access that he ardently desired. In so doing he aligned himself with the many people who had overestimated the old euphonist's powers, including the old euphonist himself. It seemed to him that if Klaus had performed as he could and should have, none of this bad stuff would have happened and Alison would have realized that marriage to Imre was a great improvement on her previous situation. He fingered his lips and his nose. It would be several days before he could appear presentably to the outside world and if Klaus wanted him out of there by Monday, he'd have to throw him out personally. Imre put aside the thought that the old man might be quite capable of doing this.

A major complication was that he was expected at the Manhattan Archway School next Wednesday to begin a science course for budding teachers. It was important to do this no matter what the state of his physiognomy, even at the risk of encountering Klaus again. It seemed highly unlikely that Klaus would appear, however, so he would stay in the brownstone as long as he could. After that there were one or two acquaintances who would be at the school on Wednesday and might be willing to take him in for a time. While he was thinking of this it struck him that there were other uses to which his circle of acquaintances could be put. He could tell them all the dirt about Klaus, put in terms that would reflect no discredit on himself, and explain that that was why he was leaving Klaus's employment. No one could continue to work for a man whose lifetime of lechery had culminated in an incestuous marriage. To ensure that the resulting rumors gained their maximum currency he would emphasize that this was all in strict confidence. Feeling a little happier, he sat at his desk and began to sketch a letter.

*

Dr. Ginsburg telephoned the police station at Pittstown and asked for the officer in charge of the Johnson case. On getting through to Sergeant Gerstman he described the sequence of events that had placed Alison in his care, and was surprised to hear that the sergeant knew all about the paternity issue.

"Well, Dr. Ginsburg, you could say that the old man let it all hang out. And we're keeping an eye open for Mrs. Hübel because after what he told us we were afraid she might be suicidal. In any case, she seems to be Mr. Johnson's only relative, so it would be helpful to have her here to clear things up. And you say she just walked out without any indication of where she was going?"

"Yes, except for something we thought was a joke. She talked about getting a job at McDonald's in Peoria, but we didn't take it seriously. I suppose it wouldn't do any good to alert the police there."

"Not really—they would need something a bit more definite and there must be hundreds of McDonaldses in the area."

"Yes, that's what I thought. There's one thing you might be able to do for me, however. Could you find out what Mr. Johnson's blood group was?"

"I think so. The police doctor is Dr. Frazer and he happens to have been Mr. Johnson's own physician. If you'll hold on a minute I may be able to get through to him."

It wasn't long before the sergeant was back on the line.

"He was group O, rhesus positive."

Chris groaned.

"I take it that's not very helpful, Sir."

"Not in the least, but thanks anyway. Would you be kind enough to give me Dr. Frazer's phone number?"

Now that Phillip was dead there was no reason why Frazer would be unwilling to talk about his possibilities as a potential father, just as one physician to another.

VI

Alison and Billy

(37)

A C-train took Alison down to the Port Authority Bus Terminal. While she was looking for the Greyhound counter she saw a bookstore, and it seemed like a good idea to find out something about Peoria before buying her ticket. It had been the first name that popped into her head, but all she knew about it was that it was supposed to be the archetypal small town and that it was somewhere in Illinois. The atlas that she examined was not very forthcoming—population 120,000, or 300,000 if you count the suburbs. Somehow she associated the place with theatrical ventures, but that was probably just a saying. She put the atlas back and went into the coffee shop next door to consider the position. Here she was at one of the great transportation hubs of the world with $10,000 in her pocket and JFK, LaGuardia and Grand Central all within easy reach, and all she could think of was a bus to Peoria? And, come to think of it, why had she put herself to all the trouble of taking the subway when she could easily have hailed a cab? Alison began a serious examination of the proposition that having $10,000 in your pocket radically alters your outlook on life.

*

While Alison was looking up Peoria, Klaus was in his workshop, doing the same thing and feeling rather stupid about it. In all probability it was just a caprice on Alison's part, but it was the only thing he had to go on. It looked as if it would be about a thousand miles from New York City, so how long would it take her to get there? With all that money in her pocket she could fly, but even if she went by bus it would only take a couple of days. However, if she did go to Peoria it would presumably be with the intention of staying for some time, so Klaus decided that he would make careful preparations before setting out on this forlorn hope. Taking a spare copy of Alison's passport photograph, he set off for the Westside Photo Shop at 88th and Broadway.

*

Alison decided to stick to her plan, but she could see no reason why she should sit in a Greyhound bus all day and all night, so she took a taxi to LaGuardia Airport. She knew that Delta flew to Chicago, and for once she was in luck, so by three o'clock she was on a flight to O'Hare with a connection to Peoria. This encouraged her to try thinking of some more blessings to count, but the only thing she could come up with was that the plane didn't smell of curry. "I seem to have lost my sense of humor", she thought, and, just for a moment, of all the things that had happened to her, that seemed the worst.

While changing planes in Chicago, she stopped at a newsstand and bought a copy of the *Peoria Free Press*. This would give her something to read on the second leg of her flight and it might be worthwhile to look at the job opportunities, but the second leg was so short that she hardly got past the A's before it was time to prepare for touchdown.

*

With the help of a friendly taxi-driver, Alison found the Radington Hotel in West Peoria and, after checking in at six o'clock, spent the next twelve hours in bed. It really seemed to be true—in this place, where she could be quite sure that no one had the slightest idea who she was, she felt more like an attractive young woman and less like a matricidal, suicidal, incestuous bastard. It was an illusion, of course. She could have walked the streets of New York City for days without ever meeting anyone who knew her. But it was an illusion that worked, at least up to a point.

She was quite hungry when she woke up, so she called room service, ate a modest breakfast and promptly fell asleep again. Later on, after eating lunch in the hotel dining room, she had another shot at the local papers. Finding no indication of McDonald's even existing, let alone needing new workers, she thought of another plan. She had had good luck with her first taxi driver, so she went outside, picked up a cab and told the driver she was an investigative reporter doing an article on McDonald's. The first thing she wanted to do was to drive around the city and get an idea of what the restaurants looked like from the outside and how they seemed to relate to the kinds of areas they were in. Did smart areas have smart McDonald's and seedy areas have seedy McDonald's and that kind of thing? The driver was tempted to say, "Lady, smart areas don't have McDonald's", but the $50 bill Alison gave him for starters helped him to keep his scepticism to himself.

After looking at dozens of McDonaldses, a few of which had signs about employment opportunities, Alison began to have second thoughts. The thing that worried her was that in order to get a job at McDonald's she would have to give her personal details, including name and social security number. It was possible that this might somehow enable someone to track her down. You never knew with people like Imre and Klaus, and she had visions of being trailed by private detectives. But at one point in her travels she saw something else—a traditional diner opposite a bus stop on the southern fringe of the city. On the door of the diner there was a big sign, so she stopped her cab and took a closer look.

*

The next morning, still feeling blessedly anonymous, Alison got off the bus and was relieved to find that the "Help Wanted" sign was still there. Freddie's Diner had the traditional railroad car look and stood back a little from the road. She walked up to the door, went in and looked around. It appeared that she had arrived in the lull between the end of the breakfast rush and the beginning of the lunch period. A couple of people were eating at the counter, and at one table orders were being taken by a young waitress wearing a bright green mini and a white blouse that didn't disguise the details of her underwear. A man in his early forties, chunky, red-faced and balding, was behind the counter, talking to a magnificent young man who was wearing a green apron over his white shirt and jeans. He was about the same height as Tom, but there the resemblance ended, since his nose was straight, his hair was dark and wavy, and he lacked freckles. Alison was so struck by his appearance that she stopped and stared for a full ten seconds, while her inner eye involuntarily created a vision of a young, exquisitely proportioned Greek athlete, naked as the day he was born, except for the javelin he was carrying. The face was that of the young man, and the body seemed to be exactly what one would expect to see if only he would obligingly remove his clothes. Alison pulled herself together and told the counter man that she would like to speak to the manager.

"I am the manager. What can I do for you? You want a job?"

"Yes. I'm an experienced waitress and I've just arrived in Peoria. Are you Freddie?"

"Freddie died twenty years ago. I'm his grandson Pete."

Pete looked at Alison speculatively.

"Where are you from?" he asked.

"New York."

"Couldn't you get work there?"

"Yes, but I'm not there now, am I?"

Job applicants didn't usually talk like that, but this one looked interesting.

"Well, you'll have to fill out a form. Come over to the office."

Turning to the young man he said, "Billy, take the counter for five minutes."

"OK, Dad, whatever you say."

His voice was surprisingly gentle.

The office was a small alcove at the end of the diner, with a desk and two chairs. Alison sat at the desk while Pete rummaged through several drawers before passing her a form, which she immediately passed back to him.

"Listen, Pete. I'm a writer and I'm working on a book about a young woman who leaves her family and goes to live in town more or less like this one. I want to get the atmosphere and I want to do it incognito. So here's my idea. I want to work here for a month and I don't need to be paid, so you won't need that form."

"It doesn't work like that—what's your name?"

"You can call me Anne."

"OK then, Anne, the point is that having you here for a month would just be a nuisance. You may be experienced but it takes a while to get the hang of things. Then when you're just getting useful you'll be leaving."

"I can understand that, but I learn very fast and I really want to do this, so I'm willing to pay for the opportunity."

Pete's eyes opened wide.

"How much?"

"Two hundred dollars."

"Make it three hundred and you're on."

"Two-twenty-five", Alison said firmly.

"You're hired."

"Great! Can I start now?"

"Wow, you are in a rush. Well, there aren't many days when somebody doesn't call in with some excuse for not working. I may be short a couple today, so if you're as smart as you seem you can probably be helpful. OK, but you have to fill out this damn form anyway—just make something up, it doesn't matter, and I'll sign it. Then you can go through the staff only door at the end of the counter. The changing room and the bathroom are on the left and the storage rooms and Candy's office are on the right."

"Who's Candy?"

"My wife. While you're on the way I'll talk to her on the intercom. Give her the form and she'll find you a uniform and show you the ropes. You look kind of standard size—well, maybe a bit small up top, but it should be OK. Where are you staying?"

"I'm in a hotel right now but I'll be looking for something nearby. You don't get the atmosphere in a hotel."

"Well, maybe we can help you with that. You married?"

"Sort of."

"Oh, I see."

Alison wasn't sure what it was that Pete had seen, and she didn't want to ask, so she picked up a pen and started on the form, amusing herself by filling it out in the name of Anne Weston and giving the address of the Manhattan Archway School. Just to confuse things she gave her age as twenty-two and her marital status as single. While she was doing this, Pete was on the phone to Candy. He was still talking when she reached the door and the last thing she heard was something about Billy.

*

Candy was a female version of Pete, except that she still had a full head of hair.

Her office was much bigger and better organized than Pete's, which was just as well, since she was responsible for managing the payroll and all the ordering. Along one wall there were racks of blouses and miniskirts, all looking spotlessly clean and fresh, and arranged according to size. Candy looked at the form and grunted.

"How'd you manage this so fast?"

"I don't know. How long does it usually take?"

"A couple of days, except when Pete takes a fancy to someone."

"Does that happen very often?"

Candy seemed to regret her last remark.

"Not too often—don't worry about it, he's perfectly safe. You OK with a mini? You can wear pantyhose if you like but nobody does. We have dark green pants for the older women but you wouldn't want to disappoint Pete and, to be honest, a lot of our customers are older men and they really like to have something to look at. The young guys seem to be able to get all they want anyway, but for an old guy . . . Well, you understand. The blouses are kind of semi-see-through, which might be a problem if you happen to be wearing black underwear."

Alison was thinking of an old guy who had always got whatever he wanted. With an effort she brought herself back to the present.

"Well, there is a problem", she said. "I'm not wearing a bra."

"I dunno—you're pretty small, so maybe it doesn't matter. The guys'll love it and you'll be a sensation if you're up for it. Want to try?"

"Sure!"

"OK, let's see what size you are."

They soon found a skirt that was the right size but they had to choose between a blouse that was slightly too big and one that was slightly too small.

"You can try them both but probably you better wear the loose one", Candy said. "The other might be a bit too revealing."

"Can you tell me one thing", Alison asked. "It's only curiosity, but why do you and Pete have separate offices? You could easily take care of everything here."

"Would you be surprised if I told you to mind your own business?"

"No—I'm sorry, I only wondered."

"That's OK. Reason one: Pete is completely disorganized and I won't allow him in here except under close supervision. Reason two: he likes to get a good look at the girls before I do. But, like I said, don't worry about it—he means well. Here's the key for your locker. The number's on it. Go and change and come back here so I can take a look at you."

(38)

The sign on the changing room door said, "WOMEN ONLY—PLEASE KNOCK BEFORE ENTRY." Alison obeyed the instructions and entered a room with a row of twelve lockers along the wall on the right and benches along all the other walls. Opposite the door there were high windows facing south, so that in the middle of a summer day the room was brightly lit. Sitting below the windows and next to a full-length mirror was a frizzy-haired middle-aged woman pulling on a pair of dark green pants.

"Hello, dear", she said. "You're new, aren't you? My name's Bess."

"And I'm Jackie", said the muffled voice of a young woman with her back to Alison and her head in one of the lockers. She was wearing a bra, panties and one shoe. "Where the hell is my other shoe?"

"Hello. Yes, I'm new and I'm Anne, and there's a shoe on top of your locker, Jackie."

"Oh. Hi Anne, you've only been here one minute and you've done something useful already."

Jackie turned out to be a nineteen-year-old brunette with a cheeky smile and an excellent figure. She and Alison sized each other up and each concluded that the other was not a waitress by trade.

"What do you do when you're not waitressing", Jackie asked.

"I'm a writer."

"Oh, are you going to put us in a book?" Bess asked.

"Maybe. What about you, Jackie?"

"I'm just a college kid earning a few bucks."

"Nobody ever asks me that question", said Bess plaintively.

"Bess has a husband and four gorgeous kids", Jackie explained. "They come here to eat sometimes."

While this conversation was going on, Alison opened her locker and started to change. As a euphonist she was used to changing in small rooms full of women, so she was surprised to find herself feeling quite self-conscious and hoping that the others wouldn't notice the absence of a bra, or if they did they wouldn't say anything. So she changed as quickly as possible, putting the miniskirt on before swapping her shirt for the blouse.

When she turned she saw that Bess and Jackie were both staring at her. Bess whistled and said, "You look sensational. With those legs and a little bit of tit showing, the guys'll be drooling into their fries, not to mention their underpants. Has Candy seen you?"

Alison looked in the mirror. She could see the outline and coloring of her breasts but the impression was fairly vague. "What the hell", she thought, "Who cares anyway."

"I don't know", she said. "I don't have a bra and I think I look quite nice. Candy liked the idea."

"Well, well, well", said Bess. "Peoria is looking up."

Candy seemed happy enough, and she gave Alison the spare blouse and strict instructions about laundering.

*

Alison's experience as a waitress consisted only of a few weeks at a diner before she went to Ulm nine years previously, but the work at Pete's was very simple, and what with the mini, the braless-ness and the graceful, euphonic ease with which she passed from table to table, she soon had everyone's attention. The male clientele couldn't decide which part of her to look at, and Billy couldn't take his eyes off her, a phenomenon which did not go unnoticed by his father.

"I think he likes her", Pete said to Candy on one of her rare appearances in the front of the diner.

"Well, it's something if he's even noticed her."

"How about her? Do you think she's noticed him?"

"Well, she's female, isn't she?"

*

"I don't know how she does it", Jackie said as she and Bess were picking up orders from the hatch. "I've been trying to get Billie's attention for weeks and she's got him eating out of her hand in five minutes."

"Maybe it's the bra—or the no-bra."

"You don't think she's got something I haven't got?"

"No, you've got something she hasn't got—on.

*

At nine o'clock last orders had been served and Alison began to worry about getting back to her hotel.

"I don't know when the last bus is, but I probably ought to leave soon", Alison said to Pete. "I don't want to get stuck over here with no way of getting back."

"You know what? You should come and stay with us. We have plenty of room and it's only for a month."

Alison's automatic response would have been to decline the offer with thanks, but she had made a lot of progress in switching off the auto-response system.

"All my things are at the hotel."

"I can drive you over there and get everything and bring you home."

"What about Candy?"

"Oh, she won't mind."

"You already asked her, didn't you?"

Pete was slightly embarrassed.

"OK, I did and I know what you're thinking, and it's nothing like that. We're very respectable folks."

Alison wasn't quite sure what she had been thinking, but Pete's offer fitted in very well with her need to stay out of sight, and it spared her the tedious job of looking around for somewhere to live.

"OK", she said, "Let's give it a whirl. How many other waitresses are staying with you?"

Pete looked shocked.

"None", he said. "The others are all local girls."

Alison changed back into her jeans and shirt, did her share of the clean-up, and went to the front door, where she found Billy waiting for her in a shiny black car that looked like something out of an old movie.

"Dad says I have to drive you to your hotel and then back home. Are you going to live with us?"

"Yes, Billy. I hope you don't mind."

"No . . . Anne", Billy said with a shy smile. "I don't mind. I . . . I think you're very nice."

"Thanks, Billy. I think you are, too."

Billy got the car moving and seemed to have something on his mind.

"Is that real? I mean, do you really think I'm nice? Or are you just being nice to me?"

"Why would you think that?"

"Oh, it's too hard to explain. Mom says I'm very good-looking and I ought to have lots of girl-friends, but I never seem to be able to get a girl-friend the way the other kids do. I think there must be something the matter with me."

"There's nothing wrong that I can see. You're kind of shy, aren't you?"

"That's what Mom says."

"I'm sorry. I didn't mean to sound like your Mom."

"That's all right. My Mom's OK and so is my Dad."

Billy pulled the car into the hotel courtyard.

"Anyway, Billy, I really do think you're nice. Let's get my things and you can tell me about it on the way back. If you want to, that is."

Alison paid her bill and Billy carried her suitcase and tote bag out to the car. Even in the lamp light she could see that it was in wonderful condition.

"It's a great car, Billy. What is it?"

"A '57 Ford V-8"

"You must spend a lot of time on it."

"Yeah, well, it kind of keeps me happy."

"But you'd rather have a girlfriend?"

"If I had a girlfriend I'd still need the car."

Alison looked at the spacious back seat. It made her think vividly of Tom's tiny Morris Minor, and she had to remind herself that she had decided not to think about Tom.

They drove in silence to Pete's house, which was south of the city, a mile or two beyond the last street lights. When they pulled up in the driveway, Billy said, "The trouble is I don't know what to do."

"What do you mean, Billy?"

"Well, other kids know when it's OK to kiss a girl and touch her, and I'm kind of scared. I mean, how do they know?"

"You just have to take a chance on it—after a while you get to know. You're not scared of me, are you?"

"I don't know. You mean . . ."

Alison leaned a little closer.

"Come on, Billy. Give it a try. First you put your arm round me, like this. Then you pull me a little closer and then you kiss me. It's easy."

Billy did as he was told and Alison realized that it was really true. Billy had never kissed a girl before.

"Thank you", he said, and Alison chuckled.

"You're not making fun of me, are you?"

"No, Billy. I think you're adorable. It's just that people don't usually say 'Thank you' at that point."

"Oh. Can I do it again?"

"Of course, and this time I'll show you how."

Billy soon got the idea. The kiss went on for a long time and when they broke Billy said, "I didn't know about that. It makes me feel . . . I don't know, I can't say it."

"I know—it makes me feel like that too. No, Billy—no more tonight."

"Tomorrow then?"

"Maybe. We'll see."

"Please?" Billy said, like a child fearing disappointment.

"OK, Billy, but we mustn't go too fast. People get hurt sometimes."

"But I wouldn't hurt you."

"I know you wouldn't. I wasn't thinking about me."

It took some time for Billy to figure this out.

"You're quite a bit older than I am, aren't you?"

"I don't know. How old are you?"

"Nineteen."

"Well, let's just say I'm quite a bit younger than your car."

Pete's voice came from the front porch. "Oh, there you are. I wondered what was keeping you. Come on in, Anne, and I'll show you your room. Then you can come down and have drink with us."

Apart from the porch light Alison couldn't see much of the house, but it seemed to be white clapboard with roses around the windows. She followed Pete up the stairs to a big room in the back of the house.

"The bathroom's right next to you and Billy sleeps in the front room. Candy and I sleep up on the next floor—we like it there."

The first thing that caught Alison's eye was a big double bed. She was beginning to have a faint suspicion about what Pete was up to, and why he liked to get a good look at the girls.

*

Alison looked at her face in the dressing table mirror. There was a trace of darkness under her eyes but, all things considered, she didn't think she looked too bad. She was a little worried about Billy. Billy might be a problem. Then again, he might be the kind of problem she would welcome, but she would have to be careful with him. She went downstairs and followed the sound of voices to the living room, where Candy was sitting at one end of a couch in front of a fire screen, Billy was stretched out on his back on the rug in front of her and Pete was dispensing drinks.

"What would you like? We have a bit of everything."

"I'd like a beer, please. I'm a bit dry."

"That's right", Candy said. "You can get very dehydrated at that job. I'm surprised you're still on your feet, though. Most girls are flat out after their first day. How do you do it?"

"Well, you see, I trained as a kind of dancer—that is, before I took up writing as a career."

"What do you mean—a kind of dancer? Night clubs and such?"

Alison laughed.

"No, not that kind of dancer. You probably won't believe this, but I'm really a very respectable young woman."

Alison sat next to Candy and started explaining about euphonics. "It's not exactly dancing or ballet, but you have to practice a lot and wear all kinds of funny costumes and you learn to feel the spaces all around you. Being a waitress is easy by comparison."

"I could see that. You really like it, don't you? I mean euphonics—and that's a daft-sounding name."

"Yes, I love it."

"So why did you give it up?"

This brought Alison up with a jolt.

"Well, I didn't exactly give it up."

"It gave you up?" Pete asked.

"Not really . . . Do you mind if we don't talk about it?"

"OK, so tell us how you got into the writing business."

But Alison had run out of adrenalin. She wanted to make up another story but her mind refused to cooperate. She was very annoyed to find that tears were rolling down her cheeks. Candy put her arm around her.

"Listen, honey, you're not a very good liar, are you? But maybe it doesn't matter. You don't have to talk about it if you don't want to."

Billy sat bolt upright.

"Mom! Don't call Anne a liar. She's the nicest person I ever met."

"Now then, Billy, you take it easy. I said maybe it doesn't matter. There are good lies and bad lies. If you want to know what I think, I think Anne hasn't had much practice at lying, so she's not very good at it. The trouble with us is we ask too many questions."

"I think I'd like to go to bed now", Alison said. "I'm not a writer, but please don't kick me out."

"Don't worry, sweetheart", said Candy, "you can stay as long as you like."

*

Alison looked at the contents of her suitcase and thought that if she was really going to stay for four weeks she'd have to do some shopping. One nightgown and one change of underwear wouldn't see her through, and maybe she ought to break down and buy a couple of bras. When she had agreed to come and live in Pete's house she hadn't realized that it would be out in the country. Presumably she would be dependent on Pete or Billy for transportation. Well, obviously, Billy would do whatever she wanted, but it might still be awkward. Sometimes you need to get away on your own, and she had a feeling that Billy might have a tendency to cling. He was an unknown quantity of a kind that Alison hadn't met before—physically grown up to his full age of nineteen but socially more like a kid of thirteen. Not that Alison was an authority—married to an old man at the age of seventeen, discarded as a lover at twenty-two, with a few brief encounters since then and, finally, Tom. Well, maybe it was different with women; obviously it was Eve who showed Adam what to do, and not the other way around. When she fell asleep she was thinking about Billy, not Tom. When he was fully clothed there was a degree of purely masculine beauty about his body that she had never encountered before. Now she made no attempt to dismiss the pictures of his naked body that her imagination had been producing ever since she first saw him, and she had forgotten to worry about hurting him.

*

"Billy seems to like Anne", Pete said to Candy as he was getting into bed.

"That's the understatement of the year. He's totally nuts about her."

"Why her and not all the others? Is it just the tits?"

"That's part of it, but she is kind of different. Did you say she'd been married?"

"She said 'kind of married'. I think she's pretty experienced."

"Yeah, she put twenty-two on the form but she's got to be twenty-five or twenty-six. Do you think we should ask her?"

"What—how old she is?"

"No, stupid—whether she'd be willing to give Billy some education."

"I knew what you meant and we might not need to. They were going at it pretty good in the car when I looked out."

"You don't say! Well, I'll be darned!"

Candy wriggled luxuriously down under the comforter, realized it was much too warm and threw it off.

"It makes me feel quite raunchy", she said.

"Me too", said Pete.

Some time later, Candy said, "You know, I think I'll have a little word with her, if I can find the right moment."

But Pete was already snoring.

*

Billy gradually came down from his high. Anne had let him kiss her—*really* kiss her—so now he knew what kissing meant and a switch had been moved into the 'on' position. The sexual experience that he had been longing for—vaguely idealistic in one part of his consciousness and hotly physical in another—now seemed real and tangible. He wanted it with Anne, but when he really thought about it seemed as if Anne had been more like a teacher than a lover—well, except at the end, just before Pete came out. *I'm in love with Anne, but I don't think she's in love with me. And she's only going to be here four weeks, so what's going to happen then?*

The only recourse was to indulge in some imaginary love-making, which was OK as far as his inexperienced imagination would take him.

(39)

Billy was disappointed to find, next morning, that he had to drive Pete to the diner early, so that they could work on a problem with one of the refrigerators. This struck him as odd, since he hadn't known about it yesterday, but he was used to doing as he was told. Candy, who would follow later with Alison, spent most of her days figuring out orders for the diner and refused to have anything to do with food in the home, beyond making sure that there were adequate supplies of coffee, milk, bread and cereal.

"We all fend for ourselves", she told Alison. "Just make yourself at home with the toast and cereal and you can make more coffee if you need it."

Billy and Pete set off on their imaginary task at six o'clock. Candy and Alison were to follow an hour later.

"Let's have another cup of coffee", said Candy. "I'm still not properly awake. Did you sleep OK?"

Alison was slightly surprised as she had already answered this question a couple of times.

"Yes, thank you. I was very comfortable."

After an awkward pause, Candy plunged in.

"Billy likes you very much, you know."

Now what was coming? Was she going to be warned or encouraged? Alison tried to think of something to say, but Candy didn't give her much chance.

"We worry a bit about Billy—he's never really quite grown up, you see. He has his car, which he adores, his weights and that sensational body, and he's not dumb, but he's always been scared stiff of girls. Do you think he's attractive?"

"Well, yes, of course, but . . ."

"Anyone can see he's fallen for you, but he might be too nervous to do anything about it. So Pete and I were wondering if you could . . . Er . . ."

Candy was floundering, but Alison could see what was coming.

"If I could?"

"Well, if you could show him the ropes, sort of. You know, how things work. Get him over the hump and give him some confidence."

"You mean you want me to seduce him?"

Candy was shocked.

"I didn't mean seduce. Well, I don't know. Maybe I did, now you put it that way. But Pete says the two of you were pretty close in the car last night, so at least you don't think he's repulsive. I suppose all I can say is, if you made out together I'd be very happy and you wouldn't have to worry about Pete coming after you with a shotgun."

"Is this why Pete likes to look at the girls first? And why I'm staying here?"

"OK, yes it is. I guess I didn't do a very good job of explaining this. If you want to leave, we'll help you find somewhere else."

For a moment Alison was off in some region where Tom Dexter seemed to be calling to her from a great distance, but this only took her back into the whole complex of agonizing experiences that she was trying to forget. She had made a decision about Tom and she resolutely kept it. Billy was clean, objective and totally separate from her past, and when she thought of him it was with that little pulse of excitement that she had not expected ever to feel again.

"What makes you think I want to leave? If this is really what you and Pete want—well, Billy's very attractive and I'm not sure what's going to happen, but . . ."

"What Pete and I want most is for Billy to find a nice woman and get himself settled, but the way things are, he'll just go on living with us and his car until he's too old to be any use to anyone. And if we could choose a daughter-in-law it would be you. But I suppose . . ."

"I'm married, Candy, and I'm quite a bit older than Billy. My husband likes young girls, so he found himself a replacement, but we're not divorced. If you want to know the truth, Billy's a real turn-on and a sweetheart at the same time, which is rare. Last night he started telling me his troubles and I had the impression that he'd never kissed a girl before. I like him very much but I don't want to get him into a messy situation. I mean, he's only nineteen."

"Did you teach him anything?"

"A bit, and he's a quick learner."

"Well, the diner's closed tomorrow, and Pete and I are going to be out most of the day. How about we just see what happens?"

The result of this suggestion was that the little pulse of excitement became much stronger and drowned out the little voice of conscience.

"OK, Candy, we'll see what happens."

"Great! Time to go to work, I guess."

Alison was thinking that Candy and Pete must be almost as innocent as Billy, but if that was what they wanted, it suited her and it seemed as if it would suit Billy.

*

When Alison went into the changing room it was almost a repeat of the previous day. Bess was sitting in the same place and Jackie was looking for something in her locker. The difference was that Jackie was wearing two shoes, a miniskirt and a blouse.

"I think you've started a fashion among waitresses", said Bess. "Turn around, Jackie, and let's see what she thinks."

Jackie did as she was told.

"I don't think I stick out any more than you do", she said to Alison, "and I want to do it, but I'm scared. It makes me feel very sexy."

"Well, dear, you *are* very sexy", said Bess. "What d'you think, Anne?"

"I think she looks sensational. It's funny because I was thinking I ought to go out and buy a couple of bras."

"Don't do that", said Jackie. "Think how disappointed most of our customers would be, and now that I've taken mine off I don't want to have to put it back on again. Just give me a little encouragement."

Bess grinned approvingly.

"That's right, go for it. You look even prettier when you blush, but just don't try encouraging me. I'm the wrong shape."

Jackie went out and Bess said, "Mostly she's just trying to level the playing field."

This remark gave Alison an idea—a kind of plan B that might be useful later on.

*

It was a long, hot day and a very warm evening, and Alison gave this as an excuse for not changing back into her jeans and shirt.

"It's not fair", Billy said, as they got into the car. "You can go around all day with your legs bare and I have to wear long pants."

"What's the matter, Billy, don't you like my legs?"

Billy didn't say anything but, greatly to Alison's surprise, he leaned across and kissed her thigh.

"Billy, what's come over you?"

Billy was immediately contrite.

"I'm sorry, I just wanted to show you how much I like your legs."

"It's all right—I liked it. Just take me somewhere quiet where we won't be interrupted. Do you know how to drive with one hand?"

"Yes, except when I have to change gear."

After all, Alison was thinking, why wait till tomorrow? Tonight could be a dress rehearsal, or maybe an undress rehearsal. When the car had picked up speed she snuggled up against Billy, took his hand and placed it on the inside of her thigh. The car showed some signs of directional instability, but Billy managed to get it under control. He drove for ten minutes in silence before backing into a narrow entrance.

"It's my grandfather's old house", he said. "It's going to be demolished and nobody ever comes here. Are we going to go in the back seat?"

"You're really coming along, Billy", Alison said as she opened her door. "Do you remember how to kiss?"

"Don't tease me, Anne. I'm not really stupid."

"I'm sorry. I want you to kiss me a lot and you can touch me wherever you like."

She unbuttoned Billy's shirt.

"Come on", she said.

She expected him to be clumsy, but he wasn't and soon he was kissing her breasts while she started on his belt.

When he came up for air he said, "Don't you ever wear a bra?"

Alison froze. It was a different car, a driveway instead of field and the question was asked in complete innocence instead of carrying a hint of mockery; but it was the same question that had been asked exactly seven days ago and it knocked a big hole in her defenses.

"What's the matter, Anne? Did I do something wrong?"

"No, dear sweet Billy, you didn't do anything wrong. You just reminded me of something I was trying to forget."

Well, now it seemed that she wouldn't be able to forget, but she might be able to fight her way through.

"Take me home and we can take our showers and then you can come to my room. It'll be much nicer and we can be quite sure that no one will interrupt us."

"What about Mom and Dad?"

"Don't worry. Trust me, and I won't be silly again."

"Silly?"

"Yes, Billy. Everything was so nice and I spoiled it. I won't do it again."

When they pulled into Pete's driveway the house was in total darkness.

"Don't bother about lights, Billy. I can find my way in the dark."
"OK, I'll shower downstairs. Shall I just come up when I'm ready?"
"Yes, and don't bother to get dressed."

*

Alison didn't want to keep Billy waiting, so she showered quickly and put the tight blouse on while she was still a little damp. It gave a very graphic impression of her nipples and could be interpreted as a mini-dress since it would just about have covered her panties if she had been wearing them. She had left the bedside lamp on in her room and Billy was sitting in the armchair, wearing a towel around his middle. She stood in front of him and said, "Do you like my dress? You should see how easily it comes off."

When he stood up, the towel slipped and would have fallen to the floor if it hadn't caught on a large projection that had appeared somewhere around the level of his hips. They both looked down and Alison laughed.

"Come on, Billy, you have to see the funny side of things. You do know what it's for, don't you?"

Billy laughed.

"I'll show you", he said and picked Alison up and carried her to the bed. "I think I can manage without any more lessons."

It all seemed exactly as Alison had hoped—very clean, purely physical, no strings attached—and now she wanted it very badly.

*

Candy looked at Billy when he came down for breakfast the next morning and thought, "My God, she's done it already!"

"What are you going to do today, Billy?" she asked.

"We're going to clean and polish the car and go for a drive."

Candy was still savoring the "we" when Alison came in, looking faintly self-conscious, and Billy became extremely attentive, helping her to coffee, cornflakes and milk.

"Yep", Candy thought, and had her first misgivings. These were dispelled to some extent when they both showed hearty appetites, but Billy's proprietorial air still made her anxious, as she realized that her little scheme might have consequences that she ought to have considered more seriously.

"Time to go, Candy", Pete said.

Yes, it looked as if she might have to have another talk with Pete.

(40)

The house face north and Billy had driven the car to the back so that it stood in full sun on a square of concrete in front of a garage and next to a wide lawn. It was another hot day and Alison put on her running shorts and yellow shirt for the car-cleaning session. Billy was wearing old blue jeans and a work shirt but when he saw Alison he sprinted back upstairs and reappeared shirtless and in his running shorts—three-quarter split with a half-inch inseam.

"I do a bit of road-racing", he explained.

"I'll bet people come from miles around just to get a look at your legs. I don't race but I like running."

"OK, let's go for a run after we finish the car. And then . . . You know what I want."

"First things first?"

Billy looked puzzled for a moment and then smiled.

"I don't get things quite as quick as you do, Anne."

"I think you get them plenty fast enough. OK, the car looks spotless and shiny already, but give me a bucket and sponge and I'll see what I can do."

It was hot sweaty work and after half an hour of it she remarked, "You're really lucky, not having to wear a shirt."

"Well, you don't have to wear one. The nearest house is a quarter of a mile away and nobody's going to see you here, except me, and I don't mind."

Alison looked around. The lawn was protected by a projecting wing of the house on one side and the car and the garage on the other. The lot went back two hundred feet to a line of trees.

"OK", she said, pulling her shirt over her head. "I'll do this side of the car."

It was Alison's opinion that after a good wash and a coating of turtle wax the car looked exactly the same as it did before, but she agreed that it was really important to preserve the paintwork. She lay down on the grass while Billy finished up and put things away. When he returned his shorts were dangling over his arm and he was carrying an air mattress.

Alison had to take a moment to dismiss the memory of Tom's old raincoat. Doing it in a meadow at night was one thing, but on someone's back lawn in the afternoon sunshine it was something else. The thought of it was very exciting and apparently Billy had the same idea.

"Let's skip the running."

"OK, only we better hose each other down first."

Billy picked up the hose and a jet of cold water hit her in the midriff. "Whew! That's kicky! All over and all around, please. OK, now it's your turn."

They laughed uproariously as Alison took careful aim at Billy's genitals. Then they lay side by side on their backs while the sun dried them off and warmed them up.

Alison raised herself on her elbows and thought once again how beautiful Billy was, everything in proportion and muscled exquisitely, not grossly.

"Good Lord", she murmured, "I think he's fallen asleep."

"No I haven't. It's just so nice lying here and thinking about what's going to happen next."

"Yes, I can see you're thinking about it."

"Is it OK if it shows? It doesn't mean I'm bad or anything?"

"No, Billy, it's very beautiful."

*

Afterwards, lying naked in the sun, she felt relaxed and satisfied. The bogeys had not been destroyed and would still have to be dealt with, but at least she had achieved a temporary sense of peacefulness. She wasn't sure if this was what was known as sex therapy, but it seemed to be working for both of them.

"Alison, when can we get married?"

She was so shocked by the question that she didn't at first realize that Billy had called her by her real name. She was about to say, "Billy, you know I'm already married", when she realized that Pete and Candy knew, but no one had told Billy. She was faced with another repeat of something that had happened with Tom. No one had told him, either. This was awful.

Temporizing, she said, "How did you know my name?", although she knew the answer.

"It was on your suitcase. Alison Hübel. It's a German name isn't it? I learned a little German in High School, so I know how to pronounce it. You're not German, though."

"No, Billy, I'm American."

The was no way of getting around it—she would have to tell him.

"It's my husband's name."

"But . . ."

Billy sat up, his face flushed with dismay that was rapidly turning to anger.

"I'm married, Billy. I ought to have told you. I'm sorry."

"How could you do this, you . . . slut?"

Billy picked up his shorts and ran into the house.

Crying uncontrollably, Alison mechanically took her things and followed. She heard the sound of the downstairs shower and, knowing what it meant to feel dirty, she knew that Billy was trying to feel clean. He had learnt sex—pure, ideal, simple and wonderful, something for two young people exclusively in love with each other. Now he was learning the ways of the world.

Fifteen minutes later he went to his room and Alison, still sitting on the edge of her bed, heard the sound of his door being locked.

*

Candy and Pete brought home a couple of pizza pies and a big bowl of salad and found the house apparently empty and dead quiet.

"I wonder where they can be", Candy said. "The car's here and the air mattress is out on the back lawn. Maybe they went for a walk."

Alison heard them and came quietly down the stairs. She was wearing the long purple dress. It was a bit creased and crumpled, but it achieved her intention of hiding everything.

"I need to talk to you. I've done something very bad."

They went into the living room and she told them everything that had happened since the first night in the car with Billy.

"I used to be idealistic", she said, "but I'd forgotten what it was like until Billy reminded me."

"What did he say?" Pete asked.

"He called me a slut."

Candy tried to comfort her.

"It's all my fault, darling. I wanted you to do it, and so did Pete, didn't you honey."

"Yes, I did. If you want to know the truth, I was scared he might be . . ."

Pete couldn't say it so Candy finished his sentence for him.

"Queer. That's what you thought, isn't it. We never discussed it, but I knew that was what Pete was worrying about. I've seen him looking at Jackie and I never thought he was . . . Well, you know what. I just thought he was terminally shy."

"It's not your fault", Alison said. "I started on him before you spoke to me. I think Pete saw us."

"Yes, and I cussed myself for interrupting."

"You shouldn't worry so much" said Candy. "He's young and he'll soon get over it."

Alison was afraid that because he was young and this was his first experience, he might never get over it, but this was too hard to explain.

"Listen, the real truth is this—you wanted me to give him some sex education, and I'd already begun and it was a pleasure because Billy is lovely and sweet and a quick learner. I needed it more than he did and it was really sex therapy for me, because I'm totally screwed up. And it was just beginning to work only now I'm a slut as well."

"What do you mean, screwed up?"

The last time Alison had told the story of her betrayal by Klaus, Imre and Phillip, it had been as a patient to a doctor in a quiet, soothing atmosphere. Now it was an act of self-justification, an attempt to excuse herself for what she had done to Billy. It was very painful to do so, but twisting the knife in her old wounds somehow made her present guilt a little easier to bear. When she had finished, she said:

"Do you think that if Billy knew about this he might be able to forgive me? You see, it's not just that I'm married."

"I know", said Candy. "You mean you wouldn't have married him anyway. Well I never thought you would, but I was too stupid to see what it might do to Billy."

A movement by the door caught her attention.

"Billy! How long have you been standing there?"

"I heard Alison coming downstairs and I followed her. I want to talk to her alone."

"You won't hurt her, will you?"

"It doesn't matter if he does", Alison said. "I deserve it."

"I would never hurt you, Alison. Go on, Mom."

"OK, but God help you if you lay a finger on her. Pete and I can go in the kitchen and Alison, shout if you need us."

"I already laid more than a finger on her and it was the most wonderful thing that ever happened to me."

"It's weird", Billy said after they had gone. "I love you and it hurts very much and I'm very angry with you. I'm glad you taught me about sex, and I still want to marry you. You hardly know me, and if you knew me better you might change your mind."

"Billy, I can't marry you. It's not because of my husband and it's not because there's anything wrong with you. I can't explain it."

"Is it because there's someone else? No, it couldn't be that because you wouldn't have . . ."

"Billy, you heard the story. I didn't know it myself until a week ago, and I'm still in shock. Being with you made me feel better . . . And if I divorced my husband he'd still be my father . . . And there was someone else but I don't know . . ."

"I thought you loved me, and I thought if people had sex together it meant that they would get married. You should have taught me about that first. And now I can't have you, I want you so much I don't know what's going to happen. Yes, I'm still angry and I don't understand anything. And maybe I do want to hurt you so no one else can have you."

Candy had been listening at the door and she burst back into the room.

"Billy, if you're going to talk like that we'll have to take Anne—Alison—right back to her hotel, where she'll be safe. Things like this happen to people all the time and they get over it—it just takes a while. Look what's happened to Alison. If you want to hurt anyone it ought to be her husband, or father or whatever he is."

Billy collapsed onto the sofa.

"I won't hurt her" he said through his tears. "I think I still love her, but I want to kill her husband."

He looked up at Alison.

"Where is he?"

"I don't know."

"I don't believe you. You must know where he is."

Candy was terrified.

"Don't you talk like that, Billy. I didn't really mean you should do anything to him. He's a very old man and he didn't know what he was doing. And now you're calling Alison a liar."

Alison tried to think of something that would slow Billy down.

"Truly, Billy. The last time I saw him he was in England."

"Where in England?"

"Don't tell him any more, Alison."

Billy got up, pushed past Pete, who was standing in the doorway and went out. A minute later they heard his car start up and roar away into the distance.

Candy looked anxiously at Pete.

"Nothing we can do except pray", he said, and it didn't sound like a merely conventional remark.

"Where is your husband really", Candy asked. "I guess there's no chance of Billy ever finding him."

"In New York, and he doesn't know where I am. I was just beginning to feel a little bit clean, and now I'm all dirty again. And I feel so guilty about Billy I'd let him do whatever he wants—if he killed me it might be a good thing."

"Alison!" Candy said sharply. "You're all grown up and experienced, but Billy's just a kid. Listen, darling, this is a terrible, terrible situation and you feel responsible, but you're only a part of it. You might get rid of your guilt by sacrificing yourself, but it wouldn't help Billy and it wouldn't solve anything for the rest of us. Pete and I feel just as guilty as you do."

So there it was again. Phillip had taken the easy way out, but she was being held to a higher standard.

"OK", she said miserably. "What do you want me to do? Maybe it's best if I leave right now."

"One of us would have to drive you and I think Pete and I should both be here when he gets back. He's doing a hundred down the interstate right now and maybe if he takes it out on the car it'll make him feel a bit better. And depending on how he is, it might be better if you're still around too."

"All right, I'll do whatever you say. What about tomorrow?"

"Let's see what happens tonight first."

(41)

When Billy returned shortly before midnight, Candy and Pete were waiting in the living room and Alison had gone upstairs. He looked calm, but it was the calm of rigid control, not of relaxation.

"Where's Alison?"

Candy answered him.

"She's in her room, but . . ."

"I want to see her."

"Billy, I don't think . . ."

"You can come up, and if she doesn't want to see me I'll go away again."

They went upstairs. Billy knocked on the door and said, "Alison, please may I come in?"

Alison came to the door. She was still wearing the purple dress.

"Yes, Billy, you can come in."

"Are you sure?" Candy asked.

"Yes, I'm sure."

They went in and closed the door. Candy stood outside for a moment and then went downstairs. Alison sat on the bed and Billy stood in front of her.

"Alison, I'm sorry I called you a slut."

"It's all right, Billy, I deserved it."

"No, you were just doing what grown-ups do, only I didn't understand it. Will you do something for me?"

"I'll do anything that would make you happy, except marry you."

"Then look at me."

He undressed and stood naked in front of her.

"Can you see anything wrong with me?"

"No, Billy. There's nothing at all wrong with you."

"Am I attractive?"

"Yes, you're very, very attractive."

"Then why won't you marry me? It's my mind, isn't it? I don't have the right kind of mind."

"It doesn't work like that. Nobody knows how it works. People fall in love and marry and no one can understand why, and sometimes they don't when you think they ought to. It doesn't mean anything bad about you.

And I don't want to get married any more—I'm too badly damaged and some of it's my own fault."

"How is it your fault?"

"Because I was stupid to marry an old man, and stupid not to leave when he found himself a new girl. And stupid because I still don't want anything bad to happen to him."

"I do", said Billy. "I don't know what would happen if I met him."

"Sit next to me, Billy. So far I've got everything wrong, so I'm going to let you decide. Do you want me to stay or would you rather I left."

"If you stay, will you still let me love you?"

"Yes, Billy. I like it when you love me and it makes me feel better. And I do love you in a way, only not in a marrying kind of way."

"I think one day something will happen and you will leave."

"Yes, I think so too. That's why it might be better if I left now."

"Nobody really knows what's going to happen, do they?"

"No, not for sure."

"That first night when you let me kiss you, that was before Mom talked to you about me, wasn't it?

"Yes. You don't have to worry about that—I already wanted you."

"Then I want you to stay, and I'll take a chance on it."

Alison was surprised to find that she felt very relieved. She stood up and took off the purple dress. It didn't occur to either of them that it might be a good idea to go down and tell Candy and Pete that the crisis was over, so an hour later Candy came up and knocked on the door.

"Are you OK, Alison?"

Alison hastily put on her bathrobe and came out.

"Yes, I'm fine."

"Well, you might have let us know. Is Billy still with you?"

"I'm sorry, Candy. He's here and we got kind of carried away."

"Then I guess Pete and I can go to bed. Just be careful with him."

"I'm doing my best, Candy."

"OK, darling—if he's going to get hurt he might as well enjoy himself in the process."

*

Tuesday was a good day at the diner. Jackie had made quite an impression on Sunday and word seemed to have got around that there were now two translucently bra-less waitresses. Business was very brisk and Pete knew that Alison might decide to leave at any moment, so he kept the help wanted sign on the door. Some of the applicants, seeing Jackie and Alison making their rounds, asked nervously whether they would be allowed to keep their bras on, while others had the opposite reaction. Billy, who was usually the general factotum, giving a hand wherever it was needed, spent most of the day helping Pete behind the counter. There was a bit of a lull in the middle of the afternoon but by five o'clock the place was jammed and Candy had to emerge from her den and give a hand. It was exhausting work and around eight o'clock, when there were only a couple of customers left, Jackie and Alison sat down for a moment at a table near the entrance. Billy came and joined them, and Jackie said, with a mischievous twinkle, "Billy, I have a question for you. I was here for weeks before Anne came and you never even looked at me, but the minute she arrived you couldn't take your eyes off her. Don't you think I'm attractive too?"

Bill went red with embarrassment.

"I think you're very pretty and I looked at you as much as I could, but I tried not to let anyone know."

"But you didn't mind everyone knowing that you liked Anne."

"Well, I couldn't help it."

"I think it was just the way she was dressed. Do you like the way I'm dressed now?"

"I like it very much but . . ."

"But you like Anne better. Uh oh, customers."

She got up to wait on two men who had just come in.

"Is she really upset with me?" Billy asked.

"No, she's just teasing you. But she likes you very much."

"How do you know?"

"Oh, I just know."

"I wonder if she's married."

"I don't think so."

Alison was shocked to find that she was feeling jealous. Billy seemed to pick up on it.

"I didn't mean anything, Alison. You're my girl."

"But if I weren't here, you'd know what to do."

"I suppose so."

"Couple of off-duty cops", Jackie said as she went by, "and they want to take us out afterwards."

"What did you say?" Alison asked.

"Told them I didn't want to get into trouble with the police."

*

Alison fell asleep in the car on the way home, and when they got there all she wanted to do was to crawl straight into bed. Billy found it hard to accept that she wanted to sleep by herself.

"It doesn't mean anything bad—I just need to be on my own sometimes. Do you know we made love five times in two days?"

"Six", Billy said. There was a little bit of pride in his voice.

"Billy, I believe you've been keeping score. Anyway, I need to take a night off and then it'll be better next time."

"I was scared it meant you didn't want me any more."

"Don't be scared—I still want you. And just remember, if anything happens and I have to go away, Jackie wants you too. And you would know what to do, wouldn't you?"

"Yes, but right now I want you, not Jackie."

"Tomorrow, Billy. I'm so tired, I just need to sleep."

*

Sleep came quickly and heavily but it was punctuated by strange dreams in which she was looking for someone and not quite sure who it was. It seemed to be a continuation of the dream she had had a few days earlier, for now she was climbing a steep hill towards a tower. As she struggled up the last few yards she saw someone lying at the foot of the tower and in the dim light she saw that it was Klaus. She tried to awaken him and he said, "Leave me alone now, Alison. I'm leaving, but don't worry. I'll see you again, next time around."

She woke up and looked at her clock. She had been asleep for less than an hour. The dream came back to her and the meaning was obvious; Klaus had died and he was assuring her that they would meet again in their next incarnations. It gave her just a little satisfaction to think that if things went the way they were supposed to, he would be a woman and she would be a man. It didn't occur to her that the dream might merely be a transformation of her last conversation with Billy.

She waited restlessly for sleep to overtake her again, but it wouldn't. Perhaps Klaus needed help and she should try to find him. During this whole orgy of guilt and sex she had scarcely thought of the philosophy of life to which she had committed herself at the tender age of seventeen, but the dream and the implications she had seen in it had brought back to her mind the central theme of Cosmic Wisdom, the idea that the only keys to understanding the trials and tribulations of the human race were reincarnation and karma. She and Klaus were inextricably bound together and whatever they didn't manage to sort out in this incarnation would be waiting to confront them in the next. Now she had deliberately involved Billy in this unhappy skein of fate, so he would be there too. In simple earthly terms she bore no blame for her incestuous union with Klaus, but in her heart she believed that it must have been the consequence of something bad that she had done in a previous life. Klaus might have given up on prayer and meditation, and she had tried to use sex to repair the damage to her own psyche, but they were both wrong. Prayer and meditation might give her the strength to do the right thing if only she could figure out what it was. It came to her that the right thing was pretty obvious. Klaus wanted to help her and she ought to want to help him. Together they might be able to change the course of their future lives. Then she thought again of the innocent Billy, dragged into her karmic mess because she hadn't got the right answer in the first place, and the contrast with Klaus; Billy, the naïf whom she had led into an enchanted world, and Klaus who, in the name of Cosmic Wisdom, had done the same for her and an unknown number of other *ingénues*.

Her anger returned and now it was as much with herself as with Klaus. And then, again, there was Goerner, who had given a whole history of the human race that was quite different from anything that Charles Darwin had ever dreamed of. According to Goerner we were the products of aeons of patient work on the part of powerful spiritual beings. They were responsible for the way things worked, and at this moment it seemed to Alison that they had created the ultimate snafu. It was not just that we had to live with it. We had to die with it as well, and then go on living and dying and living and dying until we got it right. And what was the prospect of that ever happening?

Finally, in the small hours, she got up and went to Billy's room. In all this time there had been one person who had not passed through her thoughts, but later on, when she woke up in Billy's arms, the first thing she said was, "Tom?"

Fortunately Billy was asleep and didn't hear her

*

Wednesday was a repeat of Tuesday except that the diner was even more crowded. The word seemed to have spread among prospective waitresses as well as among clients, so Pete and Candy had to turn away quite a number of high school girls who had no job experience but wanted the opportunity of showing that they had something to hide.

The two off-duty policemen from the previous night reappeared at half past eight, and this time they really seemed intent on making it with Alison and Jackie, so much so that they began to make a nuisance of themselves. One of them grabbed Alison by the waist as she went by and, not realizing that they were cops, Billy came over to help. At that moment, the door opened and a tall, elderly, white-haired man came in. As he was making his way to the counter, he looked around and, in a tone that mixed great wonder and incredulity, said, "Alison?"

(42)

Klaus had arrived at Peoria International Airport at midday on Saturday with a pocketful of photographs of Alison. He had admitted to himself that he no longer had any faith in his ability to help her, and she had made it clear that she would be best pleased if she never saw him again, so he wasn't quite sure why he was there. As always, in times of stress, he alternated between philosophical abstraction and anxiety to take action, but on this occasion philosophy didn't get him anywhere, while the action he was taking seemed patently absurd. He wanted Alison, and it wasn't for sex; sex seemed to be over as far as he was concerned. It wasn't even because she was his daughter, and the elevated purposes of reincarnation and karma demanded it. He wanted Alison because he wanted her, like a distressed child wanting its mother.

In the course of Sunday and Monday, Klaus spent hundreds of dollars on taxis and visited every McDonald's he could find. He talked to managers, distributed photographs, left the phone number of his hotel room and kept a careful record of each address and the time of his visit.

On Tuesday and Wednesday he did it all again, choosing his times so that he would meet a different set of employees. This was all of no avail. By eight thirty on Wednesday evening he had made his last call and was thinking of starting all over again the next day with Burger King. He had eaten very little for several days and was feeling very faint, but he was sick and tired of McDonald's and couldn't bear the idea of eating there. As his taxi passed along a street in the southern outskirts of the city he saw a sign—Freddie's Diner—and three stone steps leading up to a doorway that looked bright and inviting in the gathering dusk. The driver, who had been paid well in advance, was willing to wait while Klaus went in to buy himself a coffee and a sandwich. On his way to the counter he saw a waitress wearing a very short green miniskirt and a translucent blouse. For a moment he thought he was hallucinating.

"Alison?"

Alison wriggled out of the policeman's grasp.

"Who the hell is he", he demanded.

"It's my husband", she said, "and he's come to rescue me."

She began to laugh hysterically and Klaus tried to take her arm.

Billy got between them.

"You're Alison's husband?"

"Yes, I am, but . . ."

Billy punched him in the stomach. Klaus crumpled and Billy picked him up, carried him to the door and threw him down the steps. For a moment the whole interior of the diner was as stationary as a waxworks. Then there was frantic activity. One of the cops called in for reinforcements and an ambulance, while the other ran out to help Klaus. The taxi driver was already bending over him.

"I think he's dead", he said.

The policeman knelt and tried to find a pulse.

"He's still alive but I think he's pretty bad."

Inside the diner, Candy was screaming at Billy, Pete was trying to tell the other cop that Billy was really a good boy, and Billy was trying to say something to Alison, anything that might get her to speak. Alison alone stood as if made of stone. The cop pushed Billy into a chair and told him to shut up and keep still. Outside, an ambulance and a patrol car appeared. Billy was handcuffed and taken to the car, and Klaus was carefully lifted onto a stretcher. Finally Alison began to move, as slowly and painfully as she had on the day when she fled from Glastonbury. By the time she got outside they were about to load Klaus into the ambulance. He was still unconscious and she just caught a glimpse of his face.

"Klaus, oh Klaus, I'm so sorry."

It was said in a whisper that no one heard. The ambulance moved off, and as she turned away she saw Candy and Pete talking to the cops, pleading with them, trying to explain.

"It wasn't his fault", she heard them say.

"Oh, my poor darling Billy—no it wasn't your fault." First there was Klaus and then there was Billy, and in between there was Tom.

The patrol car moved off.

Alison started walking.

*

It was a long street and eventually it came to a T-junction. A left turn would lead back towards the city center, a right further into the outskirts, but it was only a minor road with very little traffic. Alison turned right and walked for a long time, unable either to think or to dismiss the hideous pictures that filled her mind; Klaus, in his impregnable self-satisfaction, teaching her his version of the art of love; Imre transformed into a sneering gargoyle; Tom frantically searching for her; Klaus again, now a distorted heap lying outside the diner; Billy shackled in a prison cell; Candy and Pete desperately pleading for him; herself exhibiting her body as a come-on in a diner. Gradually some vestige of the ability to think coherently returned to her, and with it the same old unanswerable question: why was all this happening? What had she and Klaus and Imre and Tom and Billy done in their past incarnations to bring about these dreadful consequences, and what terrible things would happen in her next one? It would be easy to lay the blame for everything on Klaus, but his treatment of her was no excuse for what she had done to Tom and Billy. Did it all start with Klaus and Maria and continue with Klaus and Alison, or did it go back further than that? If Goerner was right it went back much further, but what if he was wrong and this life was all there was? Tom and Halcyon were pure and unpretentious and ought to go straight to heaven, but she and Klaus had blundered along, wrecking people's lives, and now they were caught in a threefold tangle between the hope that things would turn out better next time, the fear that they would be much worse and the desire to have no further dealings with Goerner and his cosmic revelations. She wished ardently that she had never heard of Cosmic Wisdom and could find a priest to take her confession and grant her absolution. Goerner had said that Christ was now the Lord of Karma, and the bible said that Christ had given his disciples the power to forgive sins. Was it possible at this extreme point just to stop, and to confess and ask for forgiveness? Surely her sins were far too great to be simply erased like that.

She stopped walking, paralyzed by the thought. It had become very dark. Houses and street lights were few and far between. The sidewalk had come to an end and she was on the shoulder of the road. A car came towards her and in its bright lights she felt very exposed in her mini and her see-through blouse. Another vehicle passed in the same direction, but this time she heard it slow down and do a K-turn. She was very frightened but there was nowhere to go. The vehicle, a big delivery van, came up behind her, and a man yelled through the passenger window.

"Hey, honey, you're not gonna get many customers out here."

She started to say, "I'm not . . .", but someone grabbed her from behind and a big hand was clapped over her mouth. She struggled furiously until something hit her on the head and she passed out. When she came to she was in the back of the van, spread out like a starfish on a mattress and secured by her hair, her wrists and her ankles. There was no light and the van seemed to be going very fast. Eventually it slowed down, ran over rough ground for a few minutes and stopped. A dim light came on and two men in ski masks looked down at her.

"Well, if this isn't too good to be true! I know where you're from. Everybody wanted you and we got you."

He pulled out a knife and said, "Sorry about the uniform. When you're tied up like that we can't undress you the usual way."

The driver joined the party and there were hands all over her, feeling, squeezing, groping and fondling. Then the man with the knife was on top of her.

*

The assaults went on intermittently for several hours. With each episode the pain grew worse and was only mitigated by the gradual loss of consciousness. She woke up to find that the light had been turned off and the van was moving again. She had been untied and the men were holding her by her arms. The van stopped, the double doors at the back opened and she was thrown out onto the grass verge at the side of the road. Someone threw a handful of rags on her and said, "Say Hi to Pete." The doors slammed and the van sped off.

She lay semi-conscious and unable to move until dawn began to break. A car stopped beside her, and a voice that she dimly recognized said, "Oh my God, it's Alison."

VII

Tom and Halcyon in America

(43)

After arriving at the Ibex Hotel, a stone's throw from the perimeter of
Heathrow airport, the first thing Tom did was to call the Palmerston Hotel
in New York City. Halcyon's room in Klaus's brownstone would still be
available, but she and Tom had no intention of staying under the same roof
as Imre and Klaus. Just off the Avenue of the Americas, the Palmerston was
small, elite, tasteful, expensive and likely to be full. The mention of Tom's
title and the fact that his father was currently in the city precipitated a
short flurry of activity and the news that Lord Leyford and his friend could
be accommodated if they didn't mind a small, but extremely comfortable
suite in the top storey. Having stayed at the Palmerston as a boy, Tom
knew that one of its oddities was that the elevator stopped on the fifth
floor, and the sixth floor suite could be reached by either of two narrow
staircases with 180-degree turns at their midpoints. Halcyon, still in her
Graveney-induced adventurous mood, thought it sounded enchanting,
and Tom had the forethought to leave a message for Jack Peterson, telling
where he could get in touch.

The Ibex was very big and impersonal, and its air-conditioned
atmosphere had a vaguely chemical smell. Neither Halcyon nor Tom liked
it, but they were too excited to care very much, and if it occurred to them
that their homes were only a few miles away, with the welcoming arms of
Fortescue in one case and Halcyon's Mum in the other, neither mentioned
it. They had made their decisions, and the one remaining question on
Tom's mind was whether he ought to give Halcyon one more opportunity
to withdraw.

A double bed took up most of the space in their room so they sat side by side on it under the blank eye of a huge TV set. After a minute of slightly uncomfortable silence Tom said:

"Listen, Halcyon, I just want you to know . . ."

"Shut up, Tom. I'm coming with you and I'm staying with you. You got that?"

*

At two o'clock on Saturday afternoon, while Alison was spending her first day at Freddie's Diner, Halcyon and Tom stood at the corner of West 88th Street and Central Park West. They had left their luggage at the Palmerston and, tired and dusty as they were, had taken a cab uptown immediately. Tom was feeling more nervous than Halcyon.

"Come on", she said. "I've got a perfect right to go and get things from my room if I want to, but I'd be even more nervous than you are if I thought Alison was going to be there. But she isn't, you can take it from me. I saw her when she left and you didn't. And as far as Klaus and Imre are concerned, I don't care a monkey's left testicle."

"OK, but let's go very quietly and keep our voices down—something tells me that Imre might be here."

Halcyon had tiptoed halfway up the stairs, with Tom close behind her, when Imre came out of his room. He was wearing a tee shirt, shorts and sneakers, and he was checking the addresses on a pile of letters. As he started down the stairs, Halcyon called out, "Hi, Imre, what happened to your face?"

There was a convulsive gasp of astonishment and Imre had to grab the banister rail to avoid another undignified descent. The letters flew up in the air, some sailing downstairs, others flying over the banister and landing in the passage below, and one ending up in Tom's hand. He glanced at it, saw that it was addressed to someone in Pittstown and, needing a quick place of concealment, stuffed it down the back of Halcyon's jeans.

They all scurried around, picking up letters and when they had finished, Halcyon said, "We tried to figure out whether he hit you on the nose or in the mouth but it looks as if he got you in both places."

"Fuck you", said Imre and slammed the front door behind him.

Now the brownstone was quiet and apparently deserted. They went up to Halcyon's room, which was on the third floor, above Imre's and next to Klaus's bedroom. Tom tried to imagine what it must have been like for Halcyon, going out every morning as a schoolgirl and coming home every evening as the mistress of the movement's most venerable personality.

"I don't understand how it worked", he said, "or what was supposed to happen when you all got back. I mean, you've finished school, Imre didn't have anything much to do, and Klaus was more or less retired. Only Alison really had a job—so what would everybody do all day?"

"Beats me! Klaus talked about writing his memoirs and setting up a new Euphonics Group in New York. And I suppose Imre would have been helping Klaus—he's a good typist and he knows German and English. But it was all a bit vague and none of it's going to happen after this bust-up. I'll just get a bag of things to take to the hotel and then we can poke around a bit and see if anyone else has been here."

Klaus's room was locked but Halcyon's key fitted and she had no compunction about using it.

"He arranged things so that his key would open my lock, so naturally mine opens his. I know—that would have been funny a few days ago, specially since I never lock my door—but now it isn't."

It was all very neat and tidy, and there was nothing to show whether Klaus had been home. Halcyon opened the big old-fashioned wardrobe.

"Look, here's the suit he was wearing for his lecture. So he's been here and now he's somewhere out in the blue, looking for Alison. Let's go down and look in her room. It's the one next to Imre's."

Alison hadn't bothered to lock her door. Halcyon thought that she had been there, although probably not for long.

"I think she just came here, got whatever she needed and left."

"What's that?" Tom asked, pointing to a cardboard box.

"That's her boombox and tapes. I don't get it. Look, there's a note—'Property of Alison Hübel.' It's on a page from a memo pad but whoever ripped it off only got half the address. All you can see is NYC, NY 10025. Damn!"

"So she didn't stay here. She stayed with someone else . . ."

"Not far from here, it's the same zip code".

"And left some things behind which they returned later. She may have gone to Pittstown before that or she may be there now."

"Or she may not have gone there at all."

"That's true. Let's look at that letter."

"What letter?"

"The one in the back of your panties."

"Oh, that's what it was. I thought it was a funny time to start feeling me up."

Halcyon produce the letter, which was very warm and only slightly wrinkled.

"That was smart work. Are we going to read it?"

"Yes. He's obviously up to something and I want to know what it is."

The letter was addressed to Virginia Reddick.

"She's the chemistry teacher at Pittstown", Halcyon said.

"Do you know her?"

"I met her a couple of times when we did some euphonics up there and when she came down and talked to us about careers in chemistry. She's middle-aged and frumpy, but she seemed to know what she was talking about."

"Well, let's steam it open so we can reseal it and send it on—unless . . ."

"Unless what?"

"Unless we decide not to."

The electric kettle in the kitchen kept switching itself off when it reached boiling point, but eventually they got the letter open. Halcyon spread it out on the counter and they stood side by side to read it.

"Dear Virginia,

I hope you have had a good year at Pittstown, and finished all your faculty meetings and reports in time to enjoy the summer months. I attended the conference at Glastonbury, where I was engaged to lead workshops and speak about the metals and their planetary properties. Unfortunately certain events made it necessary for me to return early. Since there will undoubtedly be a great deal of gossip about these happenings, I decided to let some of my friends know what really transpired.

As you know, in addition to teaching and lecturing, I have been Klaus Hübel's secretary for several years and have lived as part of his household, along with his wife Alison and the young girl Halcyon, whom I can only describe as his concubine. I have always thought of Klaus as a great spiritual leader, possibly a true initiate, and one whose destiny necessitated behavior that would be regarded as reprehensible among lesser mortals. It was with some concern, however, that I learned from an unimpeachable source that there was some doubt about Alison's parentage. It seems highly probable that Phillip Johnson is incapable of fatherhood. It is also known that there was a deep attachment between Klaus and Phillip's wife, Maria, and that they were together around the time of Alison's conception. None of this is in any way conclusive but certain other facts came to my attention which made me feel that it was imperative to raise the matter with Klaus. His response was laughter. "So my little Hungarian secretary has finally discovered my guilty secret. And what does he propose to do about it?" I said that even for the greatest initiate in the world such a relationship was totally inappropriate unless, possibly, both parties knew about it. And I said that it was clear that Alison was unaware of the situation. Klaus laughed again and said, "Well, you know that I have moved on, don't you? Now that Halcyon is comforting my old age perhaps it doesn't matter so very much."

At that moment Alison came into the room and Klaus said, "Hello, my dear. Imre thinks you should know that I am your father and that our delightful relationship was incestuous." Alison seemed almost to faint and asked me if it was true. I said that it seemed so and she asked Klaus. He nodded and said, "Yes, my dear. I'm afraid Phillip arrived on the scene a little too late. Does it really matter now?" Alison screamed and ran from the room. I got up to follow her and Klaus, for no reason at all, assaulted me.

By the time I had recovered, Alison had already packed and left. Fearing for her welfare and assuming that she would go straight to Pittstown, I followed as quickly as I could. When I reached New York I encountered Klaus, who must have left Glastonbury soon after I did, and he assaulted me again, so I have been unable to make the journey.

The sudden departure of Alison, myself and Klaus must have completely disrupted the conference. Knowing the power of rumor and the ease with which misinformation can be circulated, I decided to let a few of my closest friends know exactly what has happened, trusting that the information will be regarded as strictly confidential. Obviously this is the kind of situation that might have serious repercussions for the Archway Movement and the Society. We must all do our best to keep the damage to a minimum. It seems to me that Klaus will have to be asked to end his public activities and that Alison will need a great deal of care and consideration if she is to make any kind of recovery. Out of your great friendship with Phillip you may be able to help.

I should mention that these events have made it necessary for me to resign my position as Klaus's secretary.

With all good wishes,

Imre"

"I don't believe it", Tom said, his heart pounding. "You were there. How much of this is true? Any of it?"

"He's a bloody lying little bastard. It didn't happen like that at all. Alison was in the kitchen with Klaus before Imre went in and started talking. Klaus tried to shut him up but he wouldn't stop. So that part's all lies. I don't know about the rest, but I do know about Klaus. I guess it could be true."

They were both at a loss for words.

Finally Tom said, "No wonder Alison was wiped out. She told me that her mother had been staying with Klaus just before she met Phillip, and that Klaus was in love with her but she wasn't having any. Maybe she was—it would explain why she didn't want Alison to go to Ulm."

"But Phillip let her go. Maybe it's true and Phillip didn't know."

"Maybe he still doesn't know for sure. Anyway, Alison must have gone to see him, so if we want to find her we'll have to go to Pittstown. I doubt whether she stayed there very long, but Phillip may know where she's gone."

"Then we'd better go and ask him. What do you think we should do with this stupid letter? Tear it up and flush it? Or maybe we take it to Virginia and tell her the real story. That way we could make sure there's one person who knows what a bunch of crap it is."

"OK, only I think I need to not do anything for a little while. I feel a bit shaken up."

"So do I", said Halcyon truthfully, although the cause of her shaken-up-ness was not quite the same as Tom's. "Let's go and take a nap in my room—or I could go in Klaus's room if you want me to leave you alone."

"I don't want you to leave me alone. You keep the demons away—if there are such things."

Tom was silent for a long time, and Halcyon understood the reason for his silence.

At last, as they were getting into bed, Tom said, "Halcyon—what do you think it would be like?"

Halcyon shook her head.

"I don't know, Tom. I can't bear to think about it."

(44)

Tom sat up, looked over the edge of Halcyon's bed and saw his clothes lying in a disgusting pile on the floor. He had been wearing them for more than thirty-six hours and was revolted by the idea of putting them on again. Halcyon was still asleep, so he got up, went to the door and looked out. There was no one about and he remembered that they hadn't locked Klaus's door. A minute later he was rummaging through the old man's clothing drawers and finding some underwear and a shirt that fitted him quite well.

"Where have you been?" Halcyon asked as he returned, "And where did you get that shirt?"

"Klaus lent it to me."

"Klaus?"

"Don't worry—he doesn't know about it."

"You mean you've been wandering about the house with nothing on?"

"Well, only as far as the next room. I want to go straight to Pittstown and I needed something clean to put on. You have some clothes here, haven't you?"

"Yes, but if we're going to do that I need a shower. You can come too and we can scrub each other's backs. How are we going to get there?"

"We can look for somewhere to rent a car."

"No need—Klaus gave me a set of car keys for my birthday. That was last October when he still thought he was full of what it takes. And I have a card so I can get it from the garage."

"What happens if he's got it out already?"

"Then we can just walk over to West End and rent one there."

"OK. I guess we can get Phillip's address out of the phone book."

"It's probably in Klaus's address book by his phone."

Halcyon was right

"It looks as if it's next door to Virginia Reddick's house. There's a phone number too, so let's give him a call and find out if he's there."

But the only information they got was that Phillip's phone had been disconnected and the number was no longer in use. Halcyon was very concerned.

"Something bad's happened—I know it."

"Yes, let's make it a quick shower and get on the road."

It was only when they were back in Halcyon's room after showering that she found Alison's note.

"Dear Halcyon,

IOU 15 pills.

Love, Alison"

"I kept a spare supply in the bottom drawer of my desk and she knew where they were."

"Well, that's that, I suppose."

"What do you mean, that's that? You never know what's going to happen and some guys are not very considerate, so you have to be prepared. Come on, Tom, you're not really in a position to complain, are you."

Tom was still looking at her, and she went on:

"No, I'm not as promiscuous at that sounded. If you could just decide that you really want me you'd have absolutely nothing to worry about."

"I really do want you. It's just that . . ."

"You really want Alison as well. Come on, let's go and get that car."

*

Imre had no desire to meet Halcyon and Tom again, so after mailing his letters he waited at the street corner in the hope of seeing them leave. After fifteen minutes he gave up and returned to his room. When he got there, there was nothing much to do except sit around, waiting for something to happen and listening to random noises coming from the room above. Eventually it got very quiet and he dozed off, only to be awakened a little later by the sound of water running in the bathroom and Halcyon's voice saying, "Hurry up Tom, I don't want fatso to see us." Finally there were footsteps on the stairs, and the front door closed softly. Imre thought idly of following them but could see no point in it. That part of his life, he reminded himself, was over, and it was best not to think about it.

*

Klaus's taste in cars was rather like his taste in women; he preferred the newest model and he never kept one for more than two or three years. His latest acquisition was a 1988 BMW, which Halcyon, who had been unable to cope with Mrs. Barrington-Smythe's old wagon, drove fluently. Tom was very impressed by her ability to weave her way though the traffic on 96th Street and the Westside Highway.

"It's euphonics", she explained. "It trains you to feel the spaces moving all around you and anticipate where they're going."

"God Almighty", Tom exclaimed, "you ought to have been a physicist, talking about spaces moving, instead of objects. Anybody would think they were positive holes moving through a p-conductor."

"Well, I have no idea what that means, but Klaus used to say it's a bit like the bubble in a spirit level, only we're making the spaces swirl around instead of going in a straight line. Will you teach me physics one day?"

"I will if you teach me euphonics."

*

By the time they reached their destination, the sun was setting and the lower half of Phillip's cottage was in deep shade. There was no light within and no reply to Tom's repeated knocking.

"I'm afraid Phillip isn't here any more."

The voice in the dusk quite close behind them was startling and the implication clear; Phillip hadn't just moved out of town

Halcyon was the first to recover.

"What's happened and who are you?"

"I'm Michele Weiss and I live next door. Are you friends or relations?"

"No", said Halcyon, "We're friends of his daughter and we're trying to find her."

"Phillip died three days ago—he committed suicide. My partner could tell you more about it, only now she's my ex.

"Is your ex Virginia Reddick?" Tom asked. "Please forgive the question—it's not just curiosity."

"Yes, she drove off in a U-haul this morning but she'll be back tomorrow afternoon to pick up some more of her things. You'd better come in for a minute."

The house that Virginia, Michele and Amy had lived in for four years was not looking its best. The hall was littered with suitcases and tote bags and there were obvious gaps where Virginia's furniture had stood. The lampshades had evidently belonged to her, and Michele looked pale and drawn under the bare bulbs.

"I'm terribly sorry", Halcyon said. "Are you very . . . I mean . . ."

"Upset? Yes, it was right out of the blue and it wasn't just that we split up—it seems she's been living with me under false pretences for all these years. Well, you look like nice people and it would be a relief to talk about it, but you really want to know about Phillip, don't you."

Tom felt out of his depth and left the conversation to Halcyon.

"Yes, but if there's any way we could help you . . ."

"Thanks—I guess I'll get over it. We'd better go in the kitchen. Most of the furniture was Virginia's but there are still some chairs there and I was just opening a bottle of wine."

Michele had been at work all day on Wednesday. She didn't hear about Phillip's death until she came home in the evening to find Virginia ensconced in the living room with a strange German called Klaus, to whom she was apparently telling her life story.

"She broke off long enough to tell me what had happened to Phillip. I was terribly shocked, but she seemed to be in a funny mood and didn't want to talk about it, so I left them and went and found my daughter Amy in the kitchen. She usually makes a sandwich and some coffee for me when I get home. Amy didn't know much about it—just that Klaus had found Phillip when he was still alive and the police and the ambulance came, but he died and they took him away. I found out later that he had taken a huge number of aspirins. Klaus and Virginia went on talking for a long time and I went up and helped Amy with her packing. She was leaving on a trip the next morning and not expecting to get back until just before it's time to start school in September, so there was a lot to do. When I went downstairs they were still talking, and Virginia told me that Klaus would be staying the night. So I said OK and went to bed.

"Next day Klaus left very early. I went to work, and some time in the middle of the day Virginia called me and said she was really sorry but something had happened and she was leaving. I asked her when she would be back and she said she wasn't coming back. I tried to get her to say what it was all about but she wouldn't, so I got in the car and rushed home as quick as I could. She was just trying to leave but I wouldn't let her out of the driveway so she had to talk to me."

Michele took another drink.

"OK, Virginia never cared for me. Well, maybe she did at one time and I think she still kind of likes me, but all the time I thought she was in love with me it was really Amy she wanted, and now that Amy's leaving she can't bear to be here any more. She said I could keep any of the furniture I wanted and she would keep on paying her share of the rent. I told her I couldn't stand the sight of her things and I'd pay my own rent. So she left and came back this morning with the U-haul and one of her pals from school. I've no idea where she's living, but I guess it's somewhere around here—unless she's leaving the school, too. She has to do it again tomorrow, so if you want, you can come over and wait for her. Amy called me later to say she had arrived and she told me that Virginia had made some kind of pass at her and been very insistent, so she locked herself in her room till her friends got here."

On the way to their motel on route 7, Halcyon said, "Everybody in this whole mess seems to be totally screwed up, including you and me."

(45)

Virginia kept her personal difficulties to herself and gave a succinct account of Phillip's suicide and Klaus's confession. Halcyon listened with considerable scepticism.

"It may be true that he's Alison's father, but I just can't see him as a groveling penitent. He'll find some way of proving that everything he did was cosmically necessary."

"I think you're wrong", Virginia said. "And maybe I'm in a better position to understand."

"OK, I get you, but now there's something else. Maybe you know enough about Imre Takacs to understand what a nasty piece of work he is. This letter is for you—he dropped it and we picked it up. Before you read it I want to tell you something."

Halcyon described the scene in Mrs. Barrington-Smythe's kitchen and she and Tom watched while Virginia read the letter.

"Nasty piece of work is putting it mildly", she said. "I take it you read this."

"Well", Tom started, in an embarrassed voice.

"That's OK. You're not the first person who ever steamed a letter open, and I'm sure I'd have done the same. Lying his ass off to cover his rear end—that's our Imre. Did you know he was blackmailing Klaus?"

"No", said Tom, "but we thought he must have some kind of hold over him."

"Yes, I heard the whole story from Klaus, and most of it fit with what Phillip told me. And I guess I should tell you old Frazer had given Phillip a fertility test and told him that he couldn't possibly be anybody's father. I know something about human biology and in my opinion none of those tests are definitive, but he believed it and it completely demoralized him. We were great friends you know, and he didn't seem to talk to anyone else."

"You said most of Klaus's story fitted. What was the difference?"

"Klaus made it sound much more likely that he was Alison's father. Maria told Phillip that she had never been serious about Klaus and that she had just taken pity on him when she was leaving. Klaus made out that she was passionately in love with him, and they got a bit careless in their final fling."

Halcyon was shocked.

"So when he married Alison he knew she was probably his daughter!"

"Only if he's telling the truth now", said Tom. "And even if he is, we still don't know for certain whose daughter she is. There's one consolation, though. Part of Imre's story is true. Klaus hit him in the mouth in Glastonbury and on the nose in New York."

"Excellent", said Virginia.

*

When Sergeant Gerstman arrived at the station on Monday morning he found Tom and Halcyon waiting for him. He listened to their story politely, but there was very little they could tell him that he didn't know already, and he was puzzled about their standing in the case.

"I understand that you are friends of the deceased's daughter and that you are very concerned about her welfare, but I really don't know what I can do for you."

"We're extremely worried about Alison", Tom said, "and we're really clutching at straws, so we wondered if there's anything you know that might help us find her or give any kind of clue about her paternity. Do you think Phillip Johnson's doctor might be willing to talk to us?"

"That's difficult—physicians are very reluctant to provide information about their patients even to the police and even when the patients are dead. May I ask what you want to talk to him about?"

"Well this whole mess hinges on a fertility test. The doctor might be willing to give us his opinion of its reliability even if he can't talk about the individual patient."

"All right, I'll give you Dr. Frazer's phone number, but I doubt whether you'll have much luck with him. I mean, you're not even relatives."

Halcyon, who had been listening with growing impatience, decided it was time to stick her oar in.

"Listen, Mr. Policeman, relatives are not always much help—I shouldn't really say that 'cause my Mum's the best—but Alison had a husband and a father and they're the ones who caused all the trouble, along with that slug Imre. Tom and Alison were going to be married as soon as she could get away from Klaus, so can you imagine how he feels? And Alison and I were like sisters. We lived in the same house and I was the one who helped her when she needed to leave. So have a heart and try and think of something helpful."

When Halcyon talked like this it wasn't just a case of eyelashes and sex appeal. She was so sincere and convincing that even the very proper Sergeant Gerstman was moved.

"Well, there is one possibility. I had a call from a Doctor Ginsburg in Manhattan. Apparently Alison Hübel stayed with him for a couple of days and he was treating her, but then she just walked out with no explanation. He talked to Dr. Frazer and may have learned something useful. I don't have his address, but here's his phone number."

The sergeant handed Halcyon a page from his memo pad.

"Dr. Christopher Ginsburg. 212-873-2935"

"Good Lord", Halcyon exclaimed. "So that's where she was. I know him—well not exactly—I mean one of my friends at school used to go to him. He lives just round the corner on Central Park West and he's a shrink."

*

They got back to Manhattan in the early afternoon, found Dr. Ginsburg's office and talked to Helen. She didn't have much time but she was touched by their concern for Alison and gave them a brief rundown of the story. Alison had talked about suicide, had left abruptly on Thursday morning and had given only the vaguest indication of where she might go. Describing her encounters with Klaus and Imre, Helen mentioned that Klaus was in a very strange mood, and said that she wouldn't be at all surprised if he had dashed off to Peoria.

"Do you think that's where Alison went?" Tom asked.

"No, I think she was just talking. If you ask me, she's still in Manhattan, having a good time with her ten thousand bucks."

"What?" Tom and Halcyon asked in an incredulous unison.

"Yeah, I forgot to tell you. She made Klaus give her $10,000."

"How?"

"I guess it's his guilty conscience."

"Well, that proves something", Tom said. "He really does think he's her father, so he wasn't just bragging about him and Maria, and he must have known what the probabilities were when he married Alison."

And then it struck him that it might equally well prove the opposite.

"That Imre person seems like a real slime-ball", Helen said, "but Klaus seems like a decent guy. It's hard to imagine him pulling a trick like that."

"That's because you don't know him", said Halcyon. "I don't find it hard to imagine at all. When he wants someone he just says it's his karma. Do you know whether Dr. Ginsburg talked to Dr. Frazer in Pittstown about Phillip being infertile?"

"Yes, he did . . ."

Helen wasn't sure whether or how to continue.

"It's not just curiosity, you know", Tom said.

"All right, I'll tell you, but it mustn't go any further or I'll get it in the neck. Phillip Johnson had Klinefelter's Syndrome."

Halcyon and Tom were totally unenlightened, so Helen explained.

"It's an extra X chromosome and it almost always causes infertility. There are often noticeable physiological effects, like enlarged breasts and small genitals, but apparently Phillip seemed quite normal. That's all I can really tell you."

"I think it's enough", Tom said.

Helen produced some business cards.

"Dr. Ginsburg may still be able to help her, so you'd better take a couple of these, just in case you find her."

*

"So what do we do now?" Halcyon asked when they were out on the sidewalk.

"You get whatever you need from your room and we go to the Palmerston and give ourselves a little holiday. How about dinner and a show?"

"Oh, goody!" Halcyon exclaimed, without a trace of irony. "But you haven't got anything to wear."

"Don't worry, there's a place just round the corner where I can get something decent off the hook."

"Oh, and you have pots of money. I keep forgetting. OK, here we go."

Imre heard them open the front door of the brownstone and, fearing that it might be Klaus, he locked his door. But Klaus's room remained empty and undisturbed.

"I'll bet you the old bugger's gone to Peoria", Halcyon said. "Either that or he's gone back to Ulm."

"What about Alison?"

"I don't know. Helen may be right—there's a lot you can do in Manhattan with $10,000 in you pocket. But if you want to know the truth, I think she's in Peoria. It's the kind of thing she would do—she has impulses, you know. But then, she probably got there on Friday and she may have had another one by now."

Halcyon wasn't being guileful when she said this—it was just what she honestly thought, having momentarily forgotten that Tom might have been one of her friend's impulses and that another might be to kill herself. Tom hadn't forgotten; he knew that he had already experienced Alison's impulsiveness without quite being aware of it at the time.

"Well", he said, "I'm not dragging you round all the McDonaldses in Peoria on the off chance. Tonight and tomorrow we'll do the town, and then I'm going to the training session at the Archway School to see if Klaus or Imre shows up and if anyone there knows anything."

Halcyon vaguely felt that this was encouraging, but her mind was elsewhere.

"It's Monday", she said, "So we can go to a movie tonight and a show tomorrow."

(46)

On Monday evening, Halcyon and Tom saw *A Fish Called Wanda*. It didn't quite dispel the background of anxiety that was always with them, but it helped, and so did the extremely comfortable double bed at the Palmerston. It was the simple fact of Halcyon's presence that was most deeply comforting to Tom, and it seemed to her that the easy give and take of affection that had developed between them was a better sign than the continual dependence on sex that had marked the first days of their relationship.

Their plan to take Tuesday off was modified to the extent that they decided to visit the Archway School, ostensibly to get some information about the schedule for the forthcoming training sessions, but in reality to see if anyone had heard anything from Klaus or Alison.

The school on West 90th Street, between Central Park West and Columbus Avenue, had originally been a couple of fairly fancy town houses, and in spite of all the alterations that had been made, that's what it still looked like. No. 29 was wider than No. 27 and had an imposing entrance and a fine marble staircase, at the foot of which they saw Anne Weston talking to Imre Takacs. Imre looked very put out and kept an uneasy silence, but Anne made a good pretence of being delighted to see them.

"Well, thank God someone else has made it back from England! Imre is here, but I haven't heard a word from Klaus or Alison. And Thomas, I'm astounded—I wasn't expecting you to be here for at least another month."

"Oh, I just went ahead and arranged it. And, by the way, my name is Tom."

"I ought to have explained this before. We believe it's important to call people by their real names, not by abbreviations or nicknames. It helps in forming a relationship to the real being of the person in front of you."

This struck Tom as hifalutin nonsense.

"First of all", he said, "If you want to talk to my real being, you'll have to call me 'Tom'. It's what I was christened. Secondly, parents don't always get it right. Thirdly and consequently, the nickname often fits the person much better than the given name."

"And fourthly", Halcyon added, "I don't believe Goerner ever said a word about it."

Anne was quite taken aback. She wasn't used to being spoken to like this, especially by a teenager who had been a student in this very school only a few months previously. But Halcyon had occupied a privileged position, and Anne was pretty sure that she would soon be needing her services as a euphonist, while Tom was in her cross-hairs as a future physics teacher; so it seemed wise to keep on the right side of both of them.

"Well, Tom, if that's your given name I suppose I'll have to use it—as you say, parents don't always get it right. Goerner died fifty years ago, and since than we have developed many new insights, as I'm sure you will too, if you follow the path that he indicated. Now Halcyon, if I'd known where you were, I'd have contacted you sooner. Would you be willing to teach the euphonics sessions? Tomorrow is just registration and the opening meeting, which Klaus was going to address, so you wouldn't have to start until Thursday."

"But I've never done any teaching."

"I know, but you are one of the world's finest euphonists, and perhaps you can lead by example. None of these people have much experience of euphonics—it's really a matter of giving them some exercises in space and movement."

Not knowing what Tom had in mind for the next few days, Halcyon was in a quandary.

"I can't tell you right now", she said. "I need to think about it a bit. Can I call you this evening?"

"It's good of you to be willing to think about it at all. Only not too late, please."

There were obvious reasons for Imre's surliness and for the note of anxiety in Anne's voice. Halcyon put two and two together without having to think about it.

"OK. And did you say you hadn't heard anything from Klaus and Alison."

"Not a word."

"But you must have seen this letter that's been going around about them?"

Imre, shuffling his feet impatiently, had scarcely been listening to all this stuff about euphonics, so he was taken completely off guard.

"Who told you about that?" he demanded.

"Virginia Reddick. You left hers lying around, so we delivered it for you. So now there are three of us who know that the whole thing is a big fat lie."

Halcyon turned back to Anne.

"Have you seen it? He sent out at least twenty of them."

"Yes, I've seen it, but I really don't think this is the time or the place to discuss it."

"I don't want to discuss it. I just want you to know that I was standing right outside the door when this conversation between him and Klaus and Alison is supposed to have taken place. You can take it from me, that bit of the letter is 100% fiction, which doesn't say much for the rest, does it?"

Imre recovered quickly and spoke to Anne before she could reply.

"You have to understand that Halcyon is a close friend of Alison's and is naturally very anxious to protect her. As you know, the purpose of my letter was to make a few important people aware of Klaus's er . . . problem, and to try to protect the movement from the damage that it might cause."

"And to conceal your own dirty tactics."

Halcyon turned back to Anne.

"The real truth of the matter is that this fat slob wanted Alison, and he was blackmailing Klaus to help him get her. And when it came right down to it, Klaus wouldn't play ball, so Mr. bloody Takacs let the whole thing out in spite of Klaus's efforts to stop him, and Alison couldn't stand it. I helped her pack and catch the bus, and nobody has the faintest idea where she is now. Klaus is out there somewhere looking for her and so are we, and maybe you don't know that her father killed himself when he heard what was going on and *he* says . . ." Halcyon pointed at Imre. "*He* says he was just trying to be helpful. And if you want another opinion about him you should ask Virginia. *And* I'll tell you one more thing, if he's taking part in this training course you can include me out."

Tom had to suppress an impulse to hug Halcyon. Now he merely added, "It seems very unlikely that anyone will ever know the truth about Alison's paternity, and the only reason for pursuing the matter would be to settle something in her own mind. Apart from that it really isn't anyone else's business. Klaus came back to New York last week and went to see Phillip Johnson, but by the time he got there Phillip was dying and it was obvious that this man's activities helped drive him to suicide. Virginia Reddick had a long talk with Klaus. From what she says I doubt whether he will ever want to appear in public again. So the effect of this letter is only to spread gossip with malicious intent and to divert attention from its author's shameful conduct. You can add my name to the list of people who would prefer never to be under the same roof as this apology for a human being."

Halcyon hadn't quite finished.

"And do you know how his face got this way? Klaus punched him in the mouth in Glastonbury and on the nose in New York. Doesn't that show that Klaus is improving? And don't forget what Klaus said about him that night in Bill Graveney's house. Come on, Tom, let's get out of here."

"Wait", Anne implored, "I heard the news of Phillip's death while I was still in England, but there were no details. These are very serious charges that you have brought against Imre, and I shall have to make some decisions about this training course. I'd like to hear what he has to say in your presence."

"All right", said Tom. "But I hope he'll be brief. He makes me sick."

Imre decided to brazen it out.

"Everything I said is true. Everything I have ever done has been for the good of the Movement, and this is the reward I get. These people are just trying to protect their friends, and you may be interested to know that Mr. Tom Dexter, who presents himself as a paragon of virtue, committed adultery and fornication in the same week. What do you say to that, Halcyon?"

"That you have a lurid imagination and, wow, aren't you jealous?"

Tom handed Anne a card and said, "If you need to get in touch, that's where we're staying. Meanwhile, it would be a good idea to give Virginia Reddick a call. She got the whole story straight from Klaus."

Anne looked at the card and received the first intimation that Tom wasn't quite the impecunious school teacher that she had imagined. The Palmerston was not for the penurious.

"I feel sick, too", said Halcyon as they rounded the corner onto Central park West.

*

Halcyon didn't call Anne Weston, and an evening spent with "Cats" did something to improve her mood. When they got back to the Palmerston there was a message asking Halcyon to call Anne, however late it was.

"I suppose I really have to", she said. "Well, here goes. Hello Anne, this is Halcyon."

She listened for a minute, covered the receiver and told Tom, "She's talked to Virginia and Imre is out. Whoopee! Oh, sorry, Anne, you weren't supposed to hear that."

A few more minutes of listening and then, "OK, I need to talk to Tom and we'll get back to you in a few minutes."

"She wants me to start euphonics on Thursday and, wait for it, tomorrow she wants you to give a shortened version of the talk you gave last week."

"She must be out of her mind!"

"Well, maybe, but she can't find anyone to take Klaus's place, so instead of having one long boring speech . . ."

"She's going to have two short boring speeches."

"No, three. Jane Malone is going to talk about art, Anne's going to do administration, and she asked Carolina Ende to talk about science, but Carolina doesn't like making speeches in English, so she suggested asking you. What I want to know is what happens if we start on this and then hear something about Alison. Do we just say ta-ta for now and vamoose?"

"Yes, if you're willing. There's bound to be a lot of talk about Phillip Johnson and Imre's letter and why Klaus, Alison and Imre aren't there. If there's any news to be heard, we'll hear it. And there's something else, and this is only for your ears. I have a feeling that somewhere in Archway or Cosmic Wisdom there's something I want to get into even if it means clearing away a mountain of nonsense to find it. If we do hear something and need to leave, I think Anne will understand. I know she seems like a cold fish, but that's what happens to administrators."

"Yeah, I've heard that she used to be quite human before they made her Faculty Chair. OK, I'll do it. And you know what? I'm basically just an ignorant schoolgirl, but I have the same feeling about CW."

"Darling Halcyon, you're not a schoolgirl any more."

It sounded quite natural—just an ordinary thing to say. Halcyon was transfixed and seemed for a moment to hear the sound of trumpets. Then she reached for the telephone.

"I'll tell her and then you'd better talk to her."

(47)

The next morning Tom spent an hour looking up references at the main branch of the New York Public Library. Democritus had said it, Galen had said it, J. B. S Haldane had said it and Carolina Ende, presumably inspired by Wolfgang Goerner, had said it at the Glastonbury conference. Tom liked Haldane's version best.

"If my mental processes are determined wholly by the motions of atoms in my brain, I have no reason to suppose that my beliefs are true . . . and hence I have no reason for supposing my brain to be composed of atoms."

That would be one in the eye for Elwyn if he ever saw him again.

Carolina's version was more succinct but less transparent.

"A science that denies the validity of sense impressions must ultimately contradict itself."

And Heisenberg had wanted to discard all mental images of what went on among the atoms and just stick to the equations.

Well, that was a lot to get into the forty minutes he had been promised, so he would ask questions and not try to provide any answers. Is science as objective as some people make out? Not according to Eddington, who maintained that the objective things were consciousness, life and spirit. That would give the trainees something to think about.

*

The audience was very different from the one Tom had faced in Glastonbury. Apart from a sprinkling of well-dressed CW's, the average age was under thirty and the dress was mostly average unisex undergraduate style, with tie-dyes, batiks, sawn-off blue-jeans and hair styles ranging from extreme shaves and Mohawks to Afros and Godiva-length tresses. Most of them looked extremely serious and there didn't seem to be a whole lot of laughing and joking going on.

Being the junior member of the trio of speakers, Tom went third. Anne kept strictly to the fifteen minutes she had allotted herself, but Jane overshot her forty minute allowance by half an hour and everyone wanted to ask questions about art. By the time Tom rose to speak a third of the audience had slipped downstairs to the cafeteria and many of the rest were yawning. Ten minutes into his talk, Tom recognized the kind of glazed expression that he often saw on the faces of his Glastonbury C-streamers halfway through a physics double period. He had not yet realized that to many CW people the word "science" was a turn-off, especially among the New-Agers who thought that Cosmic Wisdom would provide them with a nice warm bath of easy spirituality. He did, however, see that he had to make a decision. He could keep talking to the people who were still taking an interest, whom he judged to make up about a quarter of the remaining audience, and let the rest drowse uncomfortably for another twenty minutes; he could fudge some kind of quick ending and let everyone go; or he could pause, comment on the lateness of the hour and say that although he had only used a third of his allotted time, he would understand perfectly if people felt that they couldn't take any more. He decided on the third possibility, adding that while science might not be everybody's cup of tea, the things he was talking about were of great general interest, especially to anyone who wanted to understand Goerner's philosophy. This last comment was really a shot in the dark, but he had intuitively grasped something of this from Carolina Ende's comments in Glastonbury.

After an awkward pause a few people picked up their handbags and coffee cups, but Carolina, sitting at the end of the front row, was the first to stand.

"It is perfectly correct what Thomas has said. Dr. Goerner has himself stated that without inventing the atomic substrate, to find the necessary connections it is with the sense perceptions that we must work. And it is an example of the attitude of mind that in all our study of nature, whether we are scientists, artists or teachers, we must cultivate. Dr. Goerner has shown that the basic approach to knowledge must for all of us be the same. So, let everyone take a deep breath and Thomas will continue." The handbags and coffee cups were put back on the floor, but most of the glazed looks remained.

*

"Carolina's in love with you", Halcyon said as she and Tom stood in the cafeteria with teacups in their hands. "I'm glad she's an old married lady."

"Yes, and Anne Weston has been fawning round me, and she's not so old and not so married."

"She's not the fawning sort, so she must want something."

"She wants me to teach a course and stay and teach here next year, that's what she wants."

"What did you say?"

"I told her I'd be willing to meet anyone who was interested tomorrow and we could take it from there. I just feel that I have nothing in common with most of these people, but maybe there are a few who could convince me otherwise. What time is your euphonics class?"

"Eleven o'clock. Are you coming?"

"Of course, even though I'll probably look a complete fool. My meeting is after lunch at one o'clock."

"OK, I'll be there and I won't look a fool. All I have to do is keep my mouth shut. Can we go to the movies again tonight?"

*

When Tom and Halcyon went downstairs the next morning there was a surprise waiting for them in the Palmerston's breakfast room.

"Good Lord", Tom exclaimed, "There's my father. Hello, Dad. This is my friend Halcyon. Halcyon, my father."

Lord Otterill stood up to greet Halcyon. Since making the transition from Duke of Brueland and Street to Baron of Fleet Street, he had cultivated a more popular image than was commonly associated with the high aristocracy, so instead of a formal "How d'you do?", Halcyon was greeted with a frank stare.

"Well, my son really does pick 'em. I'm very glad to meet you, Halcyon. Sit down and have a cuppa and tell me how on earth you got that name?"

Before Halcyon could reply, a waiter approached and murmured discreetly to Lord Otterill, "There's a telephone call for Your Grace and the manager would be pleased if you would take it in his office."

"My Grace will certainly do so, and in future "Sir" will be good enough for me."

"Manager's strict instructions, Your Grace, Sir."

"Well, tell him the customer is always right."

The waiter lead the way, and Halcyon and Tom plainly heard him announcing, "His Grace the Duke of Brueland and Street."

"Tom!" Halcyon said, and was then speechless.

"I'm sorry—I really was going to tell you but somehow . . ."

"You forgot? I might have known that was pure BS about your Grandpa's investments. Are you sure he's real?"

"Now, where were we?" Lord Otterill asked as he resumed his seat. "Yes, Halcyon was just going to tell me how she got that extraordinary name."

Halcyon replied in her poshest accent.

"Well, your Lordship or Grace or whatever, if you would kindly inform me as to the correct form of address for your exalted rank, I may consent to answer your question."

"Tom, I want you to marry this girl. OK, you can call me Jim. Now then!"

"OK, Jim", Halcyon continued, reverting to pure Stepney, "Me Mum and Dad, that's Mr. and Mrs. Bert Tompkins, called me Doreen, and Doreens are as common as muck, and 'oo ever 'eard of anyone famous called Tompkins, so me theatrical manager told me to call meself 'alcyon when I went on the stage."

Tom would have enjoyed letting the badinage run on if he hadn't had the feeling that there was a serious purpose behind his father's presence.

"Excuse me for butting in, but I thought you were staying with Ted Murdoch. How did you know we were here?"

"I have a message for you from Jack Peterson. He thought you were in New York but he didn't know where—apparently some fool mislaid a message—but I thought I might find you here. It's about those Hübels you were asking about, and I'm afraid it's bad news. Apparently Jack had someone on the lookout for references and something seems to have turned up in Peoria of all places—unless there's more than one Klaus Hübel."

"No", said Tom. "He talked about going to Peoria."

"Well. It seems that Klaus got involved in a brawl in a diner and ended up in hospital with severe head injuries."

Halcyon was incredulous.

"Klaus in a brawl? In a diner? That's impossible."

"I'm afraid it's true. I talked to our man in Peoria half an hour ago and the story's still fresh, but they say that Klaus went into a place called Freddie's Diner in the south of the city and claimed that one of the waitresses was his wife. Apparently there was a young fellow there who took violent exception to this and threw him out. They say that Klaus will probably recover but it may be a long job. The waitress in question was a new employee and she was staying with the owners of the diner. She gave her name as Anne Weston but the other waitresses think it might not have been her real name. She disappeared immediately after the incident and no one knew where she was."

"Anne Weston—that settles it", Tom said. "It's Alison and she really is Klaus's wife—well, sort of."

Halcyon looked forlornly at Tom. It looked as if their little holiday was over.

He took her hand and said, "I know, darling."

"And that telephone call was another bit of news. It's still pretty fragmentary and it's bad. The young man who assaulted Klaus is the son of the owners of the diner. They spent most of the night with the police and lawyers, trying to get him out of jail. When they got home very early this morning they found Anne or Alison lying naked at the side of the road. She was incoherent, and by the time they got her to hospital she was delirious. From what they could piece together she just walked away from the diner and was abducted and raped by some men in a van. They dumped her outside the house where she was staying, so they must have known something about her."

"Where is she now?" Tom asked. From what was happening inside him he thought he must still be in love with Alison, but for Halcyon's sake he tried to appear calm.

"In the same hospital as Klaus, and all they can get out of her is that she wants to see Halcyon. Do I take it you'll be going to Peoria?"

"Yes", said Tom, "As soon as we can get a flight."

"OK, leave it to me. I'll have a car here in half an hour. Off you go."

Lord Otterill moved quickly. By the time Tom and Halcyon were downstairs again he had booked their flight and made hotel reservations as close as possible to the hospital. As he was seeing them to the car he said, "Well, it would have been nice to have a little chat, but I suppose that will have to wait until this episode is over. I guess there's no chance of a good story coming out of this."

"No, Dad, only a very bad story, and I don't think we'll ever want to tell it."

"Thanks for helping us, Jim", Halcyon said. "Tom never told me that you were a Grace or a Lordship." Then she added her highest commendation. "I think my Mum would like you."

"Thanks, 'alcyon. I 'ope we'll 'ave the chance to meet some time. And Tom, you'd better keep in touch. One thing leads to another, you know, and I don't run the only show in town. I'll be here until Sunday."

*

Anne Weston had already left her apartment when Tom tried to call her, so when she got to school there was an unwelcome message waiting for her at the receptionist's desk. Tom had been unwilling to give any details to the unknown young woman who answered the phone, so the message simply said, "We have had to leave the city on the business that we discussed with you. Will telephone this evening."

It was a quarter to nine, people were already assembling for the opening session, and Anne was sick and tired of filling in holes and dealing with emergencies. She said nothing, went to her office, closed her door, sat down and let her mind go blank. Someone knocked. Anne didn't answer. The door opened a crack, revealing the anxious face of Carolina Ende. Anne had to stifle the impulse to yell, "Go to hell." Here was a chance to fill a hole, even though the peg might not be a very good fit.

"Is it true", Carolina asked, "Thomas will not be here today?"

"Yes, it's true and his name's Tom."

It was almost a snarl.

"Oh, I am sorry. Is there something I can do?"

"Yes, you can take his Goddamn seminar."

"Oh. Oh. I see . . . Well . . ."

(48)

Peoria General Medical Center lies just off Route 74 in the southeast corner of the city, and is only a fifteen minute drive from the point where Alison was found. When Halcyon and Tom got there in the middle of the afternoon, ten hours after Pete had called 911, she was still in intensive care. They explained who they were and after they had waited for a long time a young doctor walked in and asked if there was someone there called Halcyon.

"I'm Dr. Painter", she said, after Halcyon had identified herself. "Your friend is under heavy sedation at the moment and we're not really sure who she is. Apparently the people who found her weren't very coherent, and nobody knows whether or not the old gentleman who was brought in a few hours earlier is really her husband. So anything you can tell us would be very helpful."

"Her name is Alison Hübel and her husband's name is Klaus. We heard that he is here too. Is there any news of him?"

"He took a severe blow to the abdomen and a nasty crack on the skull. He's badly concussed and there may be brain damage."

"Do you think he'll get better?"

"It's hard to say, but there's a good chance. Do you know if either of them has any other relatives?"

"I don't think so. Alison's father committed suicide a few days ago and we were afraid she would kill herself."

"And she had left her husband."

"Yes. She . . ."

"Well, I see there's a whole story here, but maybe that's enough for now. Does she have a permanent address?"

"Well, she did—in Manhattan. I live there too. Will I be able to see her? And I'd like to see Klaus too."

"Alison should wake up in an hour or so and then we'll have to see. If she still wants to see you it might be a good thing. Klaus is another matter—he may be out for quite a while yet. Meanwhile I'm afraid you'll have to talk to the police. They asked us to let them know if anyone showed up. I think that's a policeman coming in now."

*

It was going to be a sensational case, but it hadn't hit the headlines yet, so the first thing Inspector Krebs wanted to know was how Tom and Halcyon had made it there so fast. This led to Tom's having to explain who he was and how he had heard the news, which in turn led to a certain degree of caution on the inspector's part. Was this young man the son of one of the most influential business men in the world, or was he a crook or delusional? If genuine, he would have to be treated with a little extra care and respect. In circumstances like this it was important not to screw up.

Sensing what was running through the inspector's mind, Tom said, "I'm afraid I haven't got anything that identifies me as Lord Otterill's son. I just travel as plain Tom Dexter, and I hope it can stay that way, but you could probably get confirmation by calling the Palmerston in Manhattan or Ted Murdoch's home."

"I expect we'll do that, Sir, just for the record, but just for now we'll proceed on the assumption that you are who you say you are. And your friend?"

Halcyon pulled out her New York State driver's license and handed it over.

"Doreen Tompkins—thank you. Now I'd like you both to tell me about Anne or Alison—we're not even sure what her name is—exactly who she is, where she comes from and anything else that may be helpful."

Halcyon looked questioningly at Tom, who said, "There's a very difficult and unpleasant background to this and I don't know how much of it will interest the police. Her name is Alison Hübel and her husband, Klaus, is here too."

"OK, that settles one thing then. He's got to be at least fifty years older than she is and it sounds like a typical run-away wife story."

"Actually it's nearer sixty and he wanted to help her. I can explain why, if you want to know, but to put it very briefly, she had run away because she had received a terrible shock, in the shape of a piece of past history about her parents. Halcyon and I . . ."

"Halcyon?"

"Doreen is a performing artist and that's her stage name. It's what everybody calls her. Anyway she's Alison's best friend and we're trying to find Alison because she may be suicidal and we thought we might be able to help. Klaus has been trying to find her for the same reason."

"That's helpful to some extent, but it doesn't explain why this kid Billy attacked him. We have an idea but maybe you know something."

"No, I'm afraid not. You see, the last thing we know is that Klaus gave Alison some money and she just disappeared into the blue. It seems that Klaus followed her here because she said something about Peoria which nobody else took seriously."

"Does she have some connections here?"

"None that I know of", said Halcyon. "I don't know of any relations at all except Klaus. She's an only child and her mother died ten years ago and I don't know of any aunts or uncles."

"Well then, let me explain the situation a bit further. We have two separate crimes here, the assault on Klaus Hübel and the abduction and rape of Alison Hübel. We have some leads on the second one, and we're hoping that Alison will soon recover enough to tell us something. That's where you may be able to help us, Miss . . ."

"You can call me Halcyon."

"It's often very hard for the victim to talk in cases like this, and maybe she'll tell you things that she wouldn't be able to tell us."

"I'll try", she said, "but I don't want to ask her a lot of questions."

"I understand. The first thing is to see if she can talk about it at all. We don't want to make things harder for her than they already are, but we have to remember that Alison wasn't the first and unless we can catch these men she won't be the last."

"All right, I'll do my best."

"Thanks. Now let's get back to Klaus. We have a story from Billy Bigley's parents that may offer some extenuation, and I'm afraid I'm going to have to ask you for the whole background that you mentioned. Candy Bigley gave us a story, but she was in a terrible state about her son and I'd like to hear it from you."

"You tell it, Tom", said Halcyon.

"All right, but I warn you, Inspector, it's not short."

*

"That's a horrible story", the Inspector commented. "Mrs. Bigley got the bare bones of your part of it right as far as she knew it, but I see there's a lot more. There she is now."

Candy had entered the waiting room and was walking towards them. A night at the police station and a morning spent coping with the shock of finding Alison had robbed her of her color and taken all the vigor out of her step.

"I'm sorry to interrupt. I just wanted to know if there's any news of Alison and Klaus. They wouldn't tell me anything but then I saw you."

"I'm sorry, Mrs. Bigley, but as far as I know there's no change. Klaus is still unconscious and Alison is under sedation."

"Klaus won't die, will he? Oh my poor Billy . . ."

Thirty years of police work had inured Krebs to the horrors of physical violence without robbing him of his humanity, and he was thinking that Billy might be almost as much of a victim as Alison and Klaus.

"Candy", he said, "This is Tom Dexter and his friend Halcyon. They're friends of Alison and Klaus. I think it would be good if you would tell them about Alison and Billy while I see if I can get the latest on Klaus."

This was not merely a humanitarian gesture. He had the impression that he was dealing with three essentially honest people and that leaving them to talk might eventually help him to get a clear picture of the whole story. Candy pulled herself together and gave a vivid account of Alison's performance as a waitress and as much as she knew about her affair with Billy.

"And I don't blame her a bit", she said, "specially as we egged her on. She needed Billy and we thought it would be good for him, and we were dead wrong."

Tom was thinking many things, the chief of which was how strange it was that Alison needed Billy and apparently didn't need him. His feelings about her were more confused than ever, but at least there was a kind of symmetry about the situation. She had found Billy and he had found Halcyon. Perhaps it would have all worked out quite neatly if Klaus hadn't shown up.

*

Inspector Krebs had left and Candy had gone to see her lawyer, but Tom and Halcyon still waited.

"I don't know why it seems so weird", Halcyon said. "I mean, she never wore a bra anyway and there are topless waitresses all over the place. And meeting a nice boy and having it off with him—there's nothing unusual about it."

Halcyon looked at Tom and added, "Well, you know what I mean."

231

Tom talked as lightly as he could.

"Yes, I know exactly what you mean. In fact Alison and I did just about the same thing. We promised each other eternal love and then got into steamy affairs with the first eligible person we met."

Halcyon didn't care for this description of her romance with Tom, and he saw that he had hurt her feelings.

"I'm sorry, darling. Our steamy affair is wonderful and I never want to have one with anyone else. But now these horrible things have happened to her I think I have to see her before I move on. I just don't want to send her over the edge again."

Halcyon wondered if Tom really understood what he had just said. It sounded hopeful—but why did he have to be so damn cautious?

"But she's been over the edge all this time and she's still there, and I don't think she was really herself even before Imre let the cat out of the bag. And if she really wanted you, why didn't she go to you instead of just vanishing like that?"

"Because she wanted to get away from everybody who knew her."

"Maybe. I think part of her problem was that she never had any serious affairs before, except for meeting Klaus in his bloody ideal realm, and maybe it would have been better if she had. I mean, running around in those tiny shorts with her nipples sticking out all over the place. I'm not being catty—I'd have liked to do the same thing but I never had the nerve. It never occurred to me that I was her best friend until you said it, and now maybe I think she didn't have any other real friends."

"So you think she went for me out of frustration? And the same for Billy?"

"No, dammit, I didn't mean that. Any girl would go for you, in spite of your funny face—look at me for instance."

"Well, you've been a little frustrated too, haven't you?"

Now Halcyon was really alarmed.

"Didn't we have this conversation before? Can't you tell I'm in love with you?"

"Yes, and I'm in love with you. But maybe Alison was really in love with me too."

"And you with her?"

"I don't know."

But Tom did know and Halcyon knew that he knew. The trumpets that had sounded a few hours previously had gone silent.

"What will you do when she can talk again?"

"It's you she wants to see, not me. Maybe she won't talk to me."

"But if she does?"

"Halcyon?"

It was the doctor they had seen before.

"Alison is sitting up in bed and has been able to take a little nourishment. She still wants to see you, so just try to be a good listener."

Halcyon followed the doctor along the corridor to the private room to which Alison had been moved at the request of the police. She was feeling very nervous and had no idea what she was going to say, but when she saw her friend, propped up against the pillows and looking deathly pale except for the dark smudges around her eyes, all she could feel was enormous compassion. She kissed Alison, took her hand and sat by the bed without saying anything. Alison seemed to have fallen asleep, but after a few minutes she spoke without opening her eyes.

"What do you think of Cosmic Wisdom now?"

The question took Halcyon completely by surprise. As she had told Tom a few days earlier, she hadn't really thought about it; it had just grown on her.

"It's important", Alison said. "I need to know."

"The trouble is I've never thought of it that way. I love euphonics and it's partly that I'm really good at it and I don't seem to be much good at anything else."

Alison opened her eyes and squeezed Halcyon's hand.

"That's not true. You're really good at people—much better than I am."

"I'm not sure about that. Why is CW so important?"

Alison didn't answer the question but asked Halcyon if she knew about Klaus.

"Yes. They say he's still unconscious."

"They just told me that he woke up and wants to see me. I think I ought to see him, but the doctor said I should wait. I don't think he's sure about Goerner any more. It must be terrible for him."

"What about you?" Halcyon asked.

"It's odd. You wouldn't think so, but I've been lying here thinking about it and it all seems very clear. It makes a pattern and now this part of it is nearly complete. Goerner and Klaus, Klaus and my mother, my mother and Phillip, my mother and me, me and Klaus, Klaus and you, and then the catastrophe when Imre spoiled the pattern and in my selfishness and stupidity I made Billy the sacrificial lamb. And now Klaus and I are lying in the same hospital. First we must do something for Billy and after that I think we shall go together and then some time we'll return together and try again."

Halcyon understood that when Alison spoke of leaving together, she wasn't talking about the hospital. It frightened her and she didn't know what to say.

"Don't worry. I shall be fine. Klaus said that if I didn't do as he asked there would be terrible consequences. He was right—I ought to have stayed with him and if I had, none of this would have happened."

Halcyon's buoyancy wasn't gone long.

"And you'd have ended up as Mrs. Imre bloody Takacs. Talk about a fate worse than death. And what's all this about you and Klaus going together?"

Alison's eyes had closed and she seemed to be sleeping. After a minute she squeezed Halcyon's hand again and said, "I love you very much and I never knew it before."

"Then listen to me. You're talking as if this was all your fault and you're going to take all the blame. You're a good sort, Alison, and maybe all this stuff is karma, but you don't have to just take it on the chin and die duck-hearted."

Alison smiled.

"Is that what your Mum says?"

"Yes, it is and she's right. She has a placard that says, "Fight Back", and when she feels bad she hangs it up in the kitchen."

"I don't believe your Mum ever feels bad."

"Yes she does—only it isn't anything like this. It's things like never having quite enough money, and Dad being so bloody idle."

Alison had perked up a little, but now her eyes closed and she whispered, "Come back and see me again."

This time she was really asleep and Halcyon, deeply disturbed, went back to Tom.

How was he going to feel when she told him that Alison was adrift somewhere between heaven and earth and seemed to have forgotten him? Perhaps he would stop dithering. Or perhaps Alison had another reason for not mentioning Tom.

(49)

Tom was still having a hard time keeping his thoughts in order. All those old analogies from physics kept intruding. The three-body problem was just as insoluble as it had been a few days previously, and now Heisenberg kept sticking his oar in on the matter of uncertainty. Well Heisenberg was safely dead and buried, and there was no real analogy between his kind of uncertainty and Tom's, but Tom was disjointedly wondering whether the great physicist had been buried or cremated. If he had been buried, the position of his remains must be fairly well known and presumably they would have the same velocity as anything else on the surface of the earth, whereas if he had been cremated, his location would depend on whether his ashes had been scattered or kept in an urn. In the former case his location would be very indeterminate, especially if some of them were still floating around in the air.

It was all nonsense, of course; it was just Tom's mind's way of avoiding the real problem. So he tried it another way. *Suppose I had no moral obligations either way—which one would I choose?* This produced the abhorrent picture of the two women being exhibited by a salesman, with himself as the potential purchaser weighing up their respective assets and liabilities, and this was nonsense too. They were all asset and the only liability was being female and therefore incalculable. More nonsense—to be human is to be incalculable. *For God's sake, Tom, why do you have to think so much? Do you really not know what you want? No, I really do know—I want Halcyon and I can't let Alison go.* Well, maybe Alison didn't want him any more, but what if she did and, on top of everything else, had to accept that he had committed himself to Halcyon? He was so preoccupied that when Halcyon returned, she had to say his name three times. He looked up, saw the extreme anxiety on her face and misinterpreted it. This didn't clarify anything in the slightest, but it produced a surge of feeling, so that what he said came straight out of his gut.

"Halcyon, will you marry me?"

If this had happened under any other circumstances, Halcyon would have given an ecstatic assent, but her brief encounter with Alison had left her with the feeling that everything was still in a state of flux. She sat down and put her arms around Tom.

"I love you very much and I want to marry you, but I won't say 'Yes' until you've seen Alison. It's got to be fair and square. I've seen her and talked to her and it's done things to me, and I'm afraid of what it might do to you. I don't think she's really here. She's very sweet and otherworldly, and blames herself for what's happened to Klaus and the boy. She never mentioned the rape and she didn't say anything about you. She's deep in Goerner and CW. Being with Klaus is her karma and she said they'll go together and come back together. The thing is, I don't know if it's really her speaking or if she's temporarily lost it. I mean, after all she's been through . . ."

Tom was silent and Halcyon looked at him anxiously.

"I do love you, Tom, and I want you and I want to have a house and make babies with you, but I'm kind of ordinary compared with Alison."

"It's funny—Alison said something like that."

"You mean about being ordinary or making babies?"

"She said she'd like to be ordinary—she thought her life had been weird and she wanted something sort of normal."

"Well the thing is I really am ordinary and she isn't. She had all this CW in her blood before she ever met Klaus and it's absolutely real to her, but I'm only a working girl from Stepney and I just don't think about things that way. I don't mean it isn't true—it's just a bit too abstract for me. Anyway, it's not just CW. She's kind of quirky and you never know how she might react to anything."

While she was saying this, Halcyon realized something that had been staring her in the face ever since she heard who Tom's father was.

"You like being ordinary, too, or you wouldn't be teaching in that grammar school. You'd be living it up in London and helping your dad with his newspapers."

"That's true up to a point but, damn it, you're NOT ordinary. Look at the life we've been living for the last ten days. And if we were together we'd think up all kinds of funny things to do . . . Anyway, what happens if Alison doesn't want to see me?"

"I don't know. I guess I ought to have asked her but she just fell asleep on me. Do you really want to marry me?"

"Yes", Tom said, and he said it unhesitatingly because he knew that any hesitation would seem like a lack of complete conviction and, due to a disagreement between his mind and his gut, complete conviction was exactly what he lacked. And Halcyon was right—when he saw Alison his gut might change its mind.

"Let's go and get something to eat", said Halcyon. "I'm starving."

236

On the way out they asked where Klaus was and were told that he was still in the intensive care unit at the opposite end of the corridor from Alison's room, and that he wouldn't be able to see anyone except his wife for at least another day.

*

Consciousness gradually returned to Klaus as a confused mixture of sleeping and waking that generated a random succession of pictures; the Archway in Ulm, Freddie's Diner, Maria saying goodbye, Glastonbury Tor and King Arthur, Alison in her waitress's uniform, Maria as a little girl, Alison on stage, winking at someone in the audience. He stirred, and all the pictures disappeared without a trace. Someone said, "Hello, are you awake?"

He waved a hand feebly and it took him several attempts before he could speak.

"Where is Alison?"

"Alison?" the nurse said.

"Yes, my wife. I should like to see her."

He fell into another deep sleep and dreamed so vividly of Maria that he when he awoke again he thought she was standing in front of him.

"Maria!"

"No, Klaus, it's Alison. I'm sorry."

"Why are you sorry?"

"Because you loved her and I killed her."

This was too much for Klaus to take in.

"Why are you dressed like that?"

Alison hesitated.

"I had an accident and we're in the same hospital."

"Have I had an accident? I don't remember."

"Yes, you fell down some steps."

"And what happened to you?"

"I'm not sure. I was on the street and something hit me."

"Do you know where we are?"

"Yes, we're in Peoria."

The name had the faintest resonance in Klaus's mind.

"Peoria—why did I come here?"

"I think you were looking for me."

"Why was I looking for you? Had something happened?"

Klaus was becoming agitated, and the nurse shook her head at Alison.

"Don't worry about it, Klaus. See if you can sleep some more. I'm just at the other end of the corridor, so when you wake up you can see me again if you want to."

"It is so odd", Klaus said. "I truly thought that you were Maria."

"Perhaps I am, in a way."

Alison went back to her room, where she found Inspector Krebs waiting for her.

*

"I can tell you as far as when the van came along. After that I can't talk about it."

"OK, just tell me what you can and then I'll leave you in peace."

Alison described her long walk and as much as she had seen of the van and its interior. She tried to recall the voices and whether the men had any particular accents, but it didn't amount to much.

"The light was so dim I'm not even sure what color the van was—just a very dark color or black. It seemed kind of old and the men were all wearing ski masks. They sounded just ordinary, not old and not very young either. The only particular thing I remember is that they had seen me at the diner and they said something about Pete."

"And they evidently knew where he lives. That may be helpful. Well, you have my card and you can call me if you remember anything else or feel that you can talk more about the assault. We need to catch these people and put them away for a very long stretch."

"They thought I was a prostitute—it's just come back to me. I think they were looking for prostitutes, and my uniform . . ."

"That's what we thought. These guys think that kidnapping, murder and rape are OK, but they object to prostitution. They thought it would be a neat joke to leave you on Pete's doorstep—otherwise you might not be alive now. Maybe that's how we'll get them. One other thing—we think we know why Billy attacked your husband, and it may be helpful in getting him treated more leniently if you can confirm Mrs. Bigley's story."

This was almost as hard as talking about the rape, but Alison wanted to do her best for Billy, so she started with the evening before her talk with Candy, and told the whole story. The inspector listened without comment except to say, "Thank you, I think that may be helpful. With any luck this will never come to trial, and we won't need to bother you any more about it. The rape is another matter. If we catch the perpetrators your testimony will be needed, so when you leave here we'll need to know how to get in touch with you."

Alison felt completely exhausted, but talking about the rape brought the whole scene back to her, including the despairing thoughts about absolution that had passed through her mind just before it happened, and it kept her awake. She tried to think about Tom and couldn't understand why she hadn't gone straight to him instead of running away. Tom was the one good thing that had happened to her, so why had she left him out of the pattern that she had recited to Halcyon. Well, that was because he *wasn't* part of it. He was the odd piece from a different jigsaw puzzle, an alien from another world, a stranger within the gates of the CW community. Had she felt that she was inescapably part of the whole karmic sweep that went all the way back from Imre, Klaus, her mother and Phillip Johnson to her grandfather, Goerner himself and further and further back to the beginning of ordinary time, and that Tom was merely a distraction from a tangle that had to be worked out in order to create a tolerable future? She would have enjoyed being the wife of an obscure schoolmaster in rural England, but it would have meant leaving all her karmic business unfinished, so that something worse would ensue next time around. The last thing she was thinking as she drifted into sleep was that although this might all be true, it wasn't the real answer. She had run away out of sheer horror and disgust, and one inescapable fact about the present was that she wished she were with Tom again. Another was that Klaus was still her husband and he was lying in the same hospital, injured in his body and troubled in his spirit. This brought back the image of Klaus lying in a heap outside the diner and then, inevitably, the memory of Billy, handcuffed and being pushed into a police car.

Alison sat up with a surge of panic. This was what she had done, and the punishment had come very quickly, without in the slightest degree alleviating her sense of guilt. Now she wanted to see Candy and Pete and find out if there was anything she could do for Billy. Perhaps if she devoted herself to helping Billy and taking care of Klaus it would count as some form of atonement. She wanted to hurt herself as much as possible by telling every detail of the rape to Inspector Krebs. She wanted to see Tom and ask him if they could just cancel the past week, and take up where they had left off. The thought of absolution returned again, and the idea that she could shed her karmic load just by confessing to a priest seemed ludicrous in the extreme. If only Halcyon would come and hold her hand again. Her heart was beating so violently that it scared her and she realized in a detached way that she didn't want to die, not yet at any rate. She didn't want to think any more either, so she pressed the button at the side of her bed.

The nurse was very kind and two little pills did the trick.

*

After Tom and Halcyon had had a scratch meal in the hospital cafeteria, Halcyon looked in on Alison again, but she was fast asleep and likely to remain so for several hours. It was nearly eight o'clock, the end of normal visiting hours, so they took a taxi back to their hotel.

"I'm exhausted", Halcyon said. "Let's just go to bed and not talk about things any more—just hold on to each other a little bit until we fall asleep."

Halcyon still had the ability to calm Tom down and relax his tense mind and body, even though she was deeply involved in his tension. He thought this was extraordinary, and as she fell asleep in his arms he realized that in spite of everything he must have the same effect on her. This seemed to be a pretty good reason for them to get married.

Neither of them had given Anne Weston another thought.

(50)

It was Friday morning and Halcyon and Tom were sitting in bed sipping their coffee.

"Why are we here, Tom? Is it just so you can find out if you're still in love with Alison? Or if she's in love with you?"

Tom didn't answer, so Halcyon went on.

"In the first place something happened to Alison and you took a long time making up your mind whether to stay or go. Klaus and Imre didn't hang around thinking about it, but you wanted to wait and see what happened. Maybe she would write to you or you'd hear something. Well, she didn't and you didn't. So then we came over here and we had to find her before she killed herself. And then we had to hang around in New York while Klaus was actually chasing her down here. And now we've found her and maybe she doesn't want to kill herself just yet, and you still can't make up your mind whether you want her or me."

"But, damn it, I already asked you to marry me."

"Yes, but you're still not really sure, are you?"

"I'm sure that I want you."

"All right, but you can't quite pull the trigger, can you. You feel sorry for Alison and maybe when you see her it'll be back to square one. But let me tell you something—if I'd been in her position and something like that happened I'd have come straight to you, not just disappeared without a word. Just think what she did. First it didn't occur to her to check up on their story, so she didn't go and see Phillip and pretty soon it was too late. Then she gets some money from Klaus, comes to Peoria, of all places, gets a job as a waitress and has a wild affair with a young kid. If you ask me, she thought if she had a lot of sex it would make the hangover from the stuff with Klaus easier to bear. That's why she took my pills. And now I think she wants to go back to Klaus. As far as I can get it, you're feeling sorry for her, she's feeling sorry for Klaus and Klaus is feeling sorry for himself. And don't think I'm trying to make you feel sorry for me—my Mum says it's apt to be insulting when people feel sorry for you. I just want you to stop dithering."

Tom was having a moment of enlightenment about himself—something about why he was teaching in an obscure grammar school when he could have been well into an exciting career in the newspaper business—but he didn't waste time thinking about it, since it had also dawned on him that he was in danger of losing Halcyon.

"I think I'm going to like my mother-in-law", he said. "Please will you marry me, Halcyon?"

"No ifs, ands or buts?"

"Absolutely none!"

"You're sure?"

"Yes, and stop teasing me."

"All right, I don't mind if I do", said Halcyon, reverting again to Stepney. "Can we go out and buy a ring?"

"Of course! But just put down that coffee cup for a few minutes."

"OK", said Halcyon.

*

Halcyon's ring was simple and tasteful, plain gold with single diamond, and as they were entering the hospital it occurred to her that it might cause a problem.

"Do you think I should wear it when I go to see Alison?"

Tom had a good reason for saying, "Yes", and an equally good one for saying "No." He didn't want Halcyon to think he was shilly-shallying again and he didn't know what kind of a shock it might be to Alison.

"I don't want you ever to take it off", he said, "but I think I'd better go in first and explain things to her."

Halcyon's heart sank. She had a picture of Tom going into Alison's room and coming out five minutes later with the news that he had changed his mind.

Tom saw the look on her face and said, "Darling, if you don't trust me now you never will."

"It's not like that. It's just Alison—there's something kind of supernatural about her—well, maybe not supernatural, but . . . I don't know."

"Fey?"

"Yes, except I don't really know what that means. Couldn't we go in together?"

By now they were standing a few feet from Alison's door and the decision was taken out of their hands. Alison was on her way to see Klaus, but she stood for a moment in the doorway, transfixed at the sight of Tom and scarcely noticing Halcyon. Then she burst into tears, ran to Tom and threw her arms around his neck.

"Please take me away, Tom, anywhere. I've been so bad and I'm so sorry."

In this moment of complete confusion, it took some time for Tom to regain his equilibrium, gently detach her and turn to Halcyon. But Halcyon was nowhere to be seen. Tom felt as if everything in his body had turned into stale dishwater.

"I'm sorry, Alison", he said. "I have to find Halcyon."

No one in the waiting room had seen her and the security man at the entrance swore that nobody resembling her had gone out. Tom remembered something and, clutching at a straw, ran back to the corridor where he had left Alison. She was still standing in a daze by her door, and Tom saw Halcyon coming along the corridor towards him from the direction of Klaus's room. He ran to her and held her so tightly that she could scarcely breathe.

"What's up?" she gasped.

"I thought . . ." Tom began, relaxing his grip just a little.

"You thought I'd run away? After I've stuck to you all this time?"

"I'm sorry—it was just that Alison . . ."

Tom seemed unable to complete a sentence, so Halcyon tried to help him out.

"I know. You thought I would think . . ."

"Yes. I thought I had lost you and it felt like the worst thing that could ever possibly happen to me."

"Well I'm not going to tell you what I thought. Anyway, all I did was to go and see if Klaus was awake and he wasn't."

She released herself a little and smiled her best perky smile.

"Now we don't have to think any of those things, do we?"

"Never again!"

Looking over Tom's shoulder, Halcyon saw Alison walking towards them.

"Here she comes."

They thought that she was going to speak to them but with the gait of a sleepwalker she passed by and disappeared at the other end of the corridor.

*

Alison sat by Klaus's bed for a long time. When he woke up he knew where he was and who she was, although everything else still seemed confused.

"How are you, my dear? It is kind of you to take pity on a wicked old man."

"You may be wicked, but you are my husband and there is no one else left in the world for me to take pity on."

"So you are not here out of affection?"

"I'm not sure whether I believe in affection any more."

"Then why are you here?"

"Do you still believe in karma?"

Klaus paused for a long time. He knew that he had been worrying about something and perhaps this was it. Maria, Alison, Goerner, karma, Glastonbury, the mystery of the Grail—it was all very muddled in his mind.

"I am not able to think very well. Perhaps if you would tell me why you are asking . . ."

"You are not any more wicked than I am. If two wicked people stay together can something be solved?"

"I do not know why you call yourself wicked, but supposing that you are so, you still know very well that no one is wholly wicked. Even I am not wholly wicked. And I still feel affection for you even though you feel none for me."

"I think perhaps I do feel some affection for you, Klaus, but I also think that love and affection may be illusions and that it may be better to try to ignore them. You told me that you wanted me to take care of you in your old age. Because you had abandoned me and I wanted to live a different kind of life, I chose not to. You know some of the consequences, and when you are better I shall tell you the rest if you want to know them. What I really mean is, if we try to live now as we ought to have lived before, will it help to wipe out some of the guilt?"

"My dear, I don't know. I thought I was someone special and now I am just an old man with a broken head. I think the only way in which we can find out is by trying. But this is only if it is what you wish. I have no right to expect anything of you."

"And I am just a young woman with a broken heart for which I have no one to blame but myself. When you are well enough, if you wish, I'll take you back to New York, and do my best to take care of you."

"You are very kind. It would ease my mind if I could know that you do not consider me utterly detestable."

"No, Klaus. Look at me. I killed my mother and married my father. I have lost the man who wanted to marry me, I have ruined the life of the young man who assaulted you because of me, and I have been raped repeatedly. Now I don't seem to have any feelings of any sort about anyone, and if I did, why should anyone care?"

Alison left while Klaus was still trying to grasp what she had said.

*

"Darling", Tom said as Alison disappeared into Klaus's room, "don't let it spoil anything."

Halcyon tried to pull herself together.

"What the hell do we do now?" she asked.

"What would your Mum do now? I'm serious. What would she do?"

"She'd put the kettle on and make a nice hot cup of tea. And she'd say, before you go about trying to solve everyone else's problems you'd better try and solve your own."

"That's better. So what are our problems?"

Halcyon thought for a moment.

"We have to decide when we're going to get married, where we're going to get married and where we're going to live."

"Ten out of ten! And all this stuff is going to go on hurting and we'll have to learn to live with it, even though it's out of our hands now. But there's one other problem that you didn't mention."

"What's that?" Halcyon asked nervously.

"You can't get a decent cup of tea in Peoria."

"Then let's go back to New York—they actually make real tea with boiling water at the Palmerston."

(51)

With a flight booked for the next morning, Tom and Halcyon returned to the hospital later in the afternoon. This was mostly on Halcyon's initiative.

"I don't know why or what good it'll do, but I want to see both of them before we leave."

"I think I'll just stay in the waiting room", Tom said. "I can't imagine that Alison will want to see me."

Alison looked more like her old self but seemed very far away, and this time there was no hand-holding or kissing.

"Thank you for coming, Halcyon. I feel much better, but they want to keep me under observation for another day or two. Then they're going to throw me out."

"What will you do then?"

"Why do you want to know? I mean, does it really matter?"

"But I thought we were friends."

"So did I. Can't you imagine what it was like for me to see you with Tom? Not everything that's happened is my fault. I didn't ask to be married to my father and to be raped twenty times. I thought Tom had come to take me away."

"I know that, but if you had really wanted Tom he was there for you. He loved you and he wouldn't have cared if your father was the man in the moon. He'd have given you as much sex as you wanted and you wouldn't have had to get involved with Billy the Kid. And . . ."

"And I wouldn't have been raped, Billy wouldn't be in jail and Klaus wouldn't be lying here with concussion and God knows what else. Go ahead pile it on. Don't you understand that I couldn't bear to be with anyone who knew me before? No, I don't suppose you can—like everyone could see that there was something sick and dirty about me."

"OK, I can believe that's what it felt like, but I don't think it's true. You saw yourself that way but that doesn't mean everyone else would. If you had sent Tom any kind of message he'd have been over here like a shot, but you didn't, so something else happened."

"But I thought he would see it like everyone else. And when I saw him it seemed like a miracle—only he did see it."

"I don't think that was what he saw, and anyway, what about Billy? He didn't see anything wrong with you."

"That was what was so wonderful. It all seemed very clean and bright and he thought I was perfect."

"Well, you didn't ask him to assault Klaus. You don't have to blame yourself for that."

"You're doing your best, Halcyon, but I was wrong and stupid and deserved what happened to me, and Billy and Klaus were trying to help me and didn't deserve what happened to them. If Klaus agrees I shall give Pete and Candy the money that he gave me, and when Klaus is well enough I'll take him back to New York and devote the rest of my life to taking care of him. Apart from Klaus I'd rather not see anyone."

"What do you mean, the rest of your life? He's sixty years older than you."

"It's with the Gods. When they take him I think they'll take me too."

"Maybe they'll have other ideas."

*

Klaus was amazed.

"Halcyon! How did you find me?"

"It's a long story, Klaus. We were really looking for Alison. Anyway I just wanted to say Hi and I hope you're feeling better."

"We?"

"Tom and me. You remember Tom? You said he would be my best friend and he is. Are you feeling any better?"

"Yes. I hope to be released in a few days and to return to New York. Alison has promised to take care of me. Have you seen her? She said things that I did not understand. Is it true that she was raped?"

"Yes, it's true and I was wondering if you had ever thought that you should take care of her"

"But she seemed quite well when I saw her."

"Well, she isn't, and you'd better get it into your cracked skull that she needs more help than you do. Only I can't explain it—somehow you'll have to get her to."

"I am not quite as self-centered as you think. I only meant that she seemed quite well in her physical being. Am I to assume that you know the whole story?"

"Yes, you are—and I know some things that you don't, things that Alison will probably never tell you and that I certainly can't. All I can say is that she's been hurt worse than you can possibly imagine, and she thinks she's the worst person who ever lived. She'll take care of you for the rest of her life and then I think she'll kill herself."

Halcyon took a card from her purse.

"When you get to New York, call Dr. Ginsburg's office and tell him or Helen that you and Alison are there. They know her and she stayed in his apartment when she first got back from England. See if you can make Alison go and see them."

"Yes, I talked with Helen one day. She is an excellent person and I shall do as you say. Are you and Tom to be married?"

Halcyon looked at her ring.

"Yes and it's very hard on Alison, but it's not the worst thing."

"I wish you would tell me more of what has happened to Alison."

"I'm sorry, Klaus, I can't. Just be kind to her and make her see Dr. Ginsburg. Now I'd better go or Tom will think I've got lost."

Halcyon thought of kissing him, but decided she didn't want to, so she just waved her hand and went back to the waiting room, where she found Tom talking to Inspector Krebs.

"He has no idea why Billy assaulted him", the inspector was saying, "and I didn't think it was a good idea to tell him."

"No", said Halcyon, joining the conversation, "and he doesn't know anything about the rape either, except that it happened."

"Inspector Krebs is going to talk to Klaus again. He was just waiting until you had finished. If Billy comes to trial we may be needed for the defence, but there's no reason why we can't go back to New York now."

"That's correct", the inspector said, "and with any luck there'll be a deal with a fairly short prison sentence. The background information that you've given will be helpful and I think Alison will be anxious to speak on his behalf."

"I'm very worried about Alison", Halcyon said. "She was already feeling pretty bad before the rape and now . . ."

"Yes, we'll keep an eye on her as much as we can, and make sure she sees someone. We have a rape victims' support system, and we'll need her to stay here a bit longer. Do you know what she intends to do when she leaves?"

"She told me she's going to look after Klaus, so I guess she'll be here as long as he is. Then I expect they'll go back to New York."

"OK, well, thank you both very much and good luck!"

*

Back in the hotel, Halcyon looked at her husband-to-be, who was busy packing.

"I'll be glad to get away from here. It probably means I'm a bad person, but sometimes I feel like a little girl and I don't want to be mixed up in all this complicated adult stuff any more. I'd just like to see my Mum."

"Nah ven, dearie, don't die duck-hearted."

Tom's imitation-Stepney wasn't very good, but Halcyon got the point.

"Will you take care of me, Tom? Sometimes I just need to be taken care of."

"I'll always take care of you—and we can just hop on a plane and go and see your Mum, and you can tell her you've brought home a young man."

"Oh, let's do that. She'll be so excited, even if she doesn't know who you are. Only . . ."

"Only what?"

"Well, before we leave I'd just like to find out what's happening at the Archway School."

"Well, there's a phone next to your elbow. You could give Anne a call and find out now."

"I s'pose I could, but then she'd probably say, 'Halcyon, come straight back and start teaching euphonics and bring that Tom character with you.' And besides, I don't know how much I should tell her about us or Alison and Klaus. Oh shit, that scared me!"

This last comment was caused by a loud ring from the phone.

"You take it, Tom—it makes me too nervous."

The caller was Inspector Krebs, who spoke very apologetically to Tom.

"Someone is going to get fired for this. We did a routine check, like I told you, to make sure of your identity. Evidently someone let it out and the press and local TV are all over it. Lord Otterill is a big name and anything to do with the aristocracy goes over big in the tabloids. We have reporters here already and you'll be getting them over there any moment now. I guess hotel security will keep them away from you, but it'll be on the six o'clock news and on the front page of the *Planet* in the morning. What time is your flight?"

"Half past ten."

"Well, I have a suggestion. Have you booked a car for the morning?"

"Yes, it's supposed to be here at eight."

"OK then. I'll have an unmarked car at the back entrance pick you up at 7:45. Don't cancel your car—I'll make that end of it OK. The news boys will certainly have found out about it and they'll be waiting for you at the front of the hotel."

"This is extremely kind of you, Inspector."

"Well, we screwed up at this end, so it's the least we could do. I suggest that you get the driver to take you to Chicago, because when they miss you at the hotel they'll make a dash for the airport and try to catch you there. There are plenty of flights out of O'Hare and you can probably book something this evening. Bon voyage!"

Tom had good luck in finding a flight that would land them at La Guardia in the early afternoon, and was equally lucky in catching his father at Ted Murdoch's house. There was, as he told Lord Otterill, good news and bad news.

"The bad news is that the local media have made the connection between you and me. The assault and rape were sensational enough already, as far as the local outlets are concerned, but now it looks like being something really major."

"'It certainly does. I've been getting the news and we'll figure out the best way to cover it. Now let me guess the good news—you're intending to marry this Halcyon girl."

"Yes, Dad. I hope you don't mind."

"Well, I'd marry her myself if she'd have me, but I guess having her for a daughter-in-law is the next best thing. Where and when is this going to happen?"

"We don't know. As soon as possible and somewhere in England"

"Well, for goodness sake keep me informed. Now, what I want to know is whether there's anything in the background of all this that's going to cause serious embarrassment."

"OK, Dad. As far as I'm concerned the only thing is that I had a one night stand with Alison just before I met Halcyon, and I think the only people who know anything about it are my old landlady, Mrs. Trathgannon, and my friend Elwyn Davies. Mrs. T also knows that I took Halcyon home the next night and Halcyon told her we were going to get married, so I guess there's a story there. Halcyon lived with Klaus, the old man who was assaulted, for a couple of years and they'll probably make hay out of that, but the real dirt, if it ever comes out, is about Alison, Klaus and the young man she met in Peoria."

"OK, you'd better give me the whole works."

Which Tom did, and it was a very long call that ended with an agreement to talk again over dinner the next day at the Palmerston.

*

Klaus was still quite weak in his physical body, but his mind seemed to be working a little better. On the whole he would have preferred the situation to be the other way around, since his mind could produce nothing for his comfort. The transition from spiritual pride to abject penitence still had some way to go, and there was a big obstacle in the way, something that he could still scarcely admit to himself, let alone reveal to anyone else. He had lied about his last night with Maria, and he knew the lie for what it was—a statement of what ought to have happened, something that would have been so right, proper and inevitable if it had happened, something that he had so desperately needed to happen that it was still almost impossible to admit that it hadn't. Well, his unregenerate self pointed out in a determined rearguard action, it isn't really a lie, just an exaggeration. But it had had the same effect as a lie. Maria ought to have passionately thrown caution to the winds and told him that he was her one destined lover for all eternity. But she didn't do either of those things. Instead, on her final appearance, after absenting herself from his bed for several weeks, she had chuckled and told him he was a romantic old thing and she liked him very much, but she needed to change direction and find someone nearer her own age.

"You spoke in a very different way when you first came here", Klaus said.

"Well, you know the old line—I was young and foolish then. Do you realize that when I'm thirty-seven you'll be sixty and when I'm forty-seven you'll be seventy? I want to change the course of my karma."

Klaus's sense of stupefied amazement came back to him over the years. He had thought that he and Maria were united for this life and for all future lives, so it was not only her rejection of him as a lover that wounded him so deeply, but also her jocular reference to karma.

"Come on, old sweetheart, you're still pretty good and you'll soon find someone else. Besides, don't forget you have a perfectly good wife."

So they slept together for the last time but there was no wild abandon and it was only a moderate success. When Maria returned to Ulm after meeting Phillip, Klaus was cold and distant.

"Hurt in his pride", she thought, but that wasn't the whole story. Pride certainly came into it, but so did Klaus's love for her, which she had underestimated, and his faith in the Goernerian structure of the universe. This seemed him to be a break in the pattern of destiny, a break that he would eventually find a way of repairing. And so, after many years, it turned out. It had been a great tragedy that Alison had been responsible for her mother's death, but Klaus saw the hand of fate at work. Alison became the new Maria, the Maria who ought to have been. And if by some remote chance he was her father, so be it, for it made the whole web of destiny so much tighter and lent an additional thrill to the sexual union. In his spiritual presumptuousness he felt himself to be like the great Germanic God Wotan, who sowed his seed wherever and whenever the spirit moved him, above and beyond the petty anxieties that ordinary mortals feel about such things as incest and infidelity. Wotan's twin son and daughter had united to produce Siegfried, and Siegfried would have married his Aunt Brunnhilde if he hadn't been diverted by a magic potion. Alison's ready acceptance of Klaus's courtship and her willingness to go a step further than her mother and actually marry him had convinced him that he was absolutely right. After a while, however, he began to wonder. Maria had certainly had a sense of humor, but there was something unpredictable, almost capricious, about Alison, and Klaus himself had begun to change. He thought less about karma and, as his body sent him more frequent signals about age and incapacity, he became more preoccupied with sex. If Imre's innuendos had come a year or two earlier he might have simply told him to go to hell, but the need to assert his virility and, so to speak, proprietorship of Alison made Imre's claim such an ego-booster that the regenerate side of his personality had no chance of putting the situation in its proper perspective. It was a piece of news that he wanted to hug to himself and not to be broadcast through the CW community, so he went along with Imre's demands. As his status as Alison's father changed in his imagination from fantasy to plausibility, he stopped sleeping with her, not so much out of moral considerations as because something was happening to his desire. His subsequent infatuation with Halcyon became part of the chain of events that eventually led to a more objective appraisal of himself, starting with the recognition that he had really always needed young girls to stoke the fire and that he had been living a kind of Hübelized version of Cosmic Wisdom which surrounded his sexual desires with a beautiful spiritual aura. It took him a long time to recognize the degree to which he had perverted Goerner's philosophy. As his sexual relationship with Alison disintegrated, his genuine affection for her increased and he began to feel more like the father that he wanted to be. He still couldn't face the fact that the only woman who had ever continued to turn him on when she was past the age of about twenty-two had tired of him and happily gone to test the waters elsewhere; but that was long ago and now, lying helpless in his hospital bed, he was nearly ready to make a final renunciation of his old self-image. He wanted to be forgiven, to feel genuine contrition, to be merely a humble student of Goerner's philosophy and somehow to be absolved. Since his last encounter with Alison, full repentance seemed to be within his powers.

To be absolved, however, he would have to tell Alison the whole truth, which was very confusing. He wasn't convinced that Phillip's medical condition really proved anything, so maybe the probabilities were about 50/50; or maybe not. He relived his last night with Maria and concluded that his share of the probability was much less than 50%. But he had let Alison believe that she was certainly his daughter, and had repeated his self-serving version of the story to Virginia Reddick and the Pittstown police. The consequences of his actions were incalculable. He knew that, karmically speaking, he was in for a beating and that the longer he delayed his efforts to change course, the worse it would be. He must see Alison again as soon as possible. Having made this resolution, he fell asleep, only to realize when he woke up, that things were not so simple. How would Alison react to the knowledge that all the terrible things that had happened were the results of his prevarication? Her present appearance of calm was clearly maintained only at tremendous personal cost; the truth would almost certainly send her right over the edge again.

And then, looking at things in the cold light of a Saturday morning, he began to wonder what Maria had been doing in those several weeks when she had withdrawn from him before leaving, and in the two months she had stayed in Ulm after the conference. If he probably wasn't Alison's father, and Phillip probably couldn't have been, who was?

(52)

Inspector Krebs's plan worked perfectly. While reporters and camera crews milled around the main entrance of the hotel, Halcyon and Tom left by the back door and were soon on the interstate to Chicago. But although they had avoided harassment in person, they had not escaped totally unscathed. The local papers carried reports of the assault on Klaus and the rape of Alison and these were given extra prominence because there appeared to be some connection to Lord Otterill. "Press Baron's Son linked to Rape Victim", the headline blared. Reporters had found people who had seen Tom and Halcyon together, and since no one had any idea who his companion was, there was an open field for juicy speculation. The reports made much of the fact that Tom had managed to remain in obscurity for several years, suggested that he might be on some special mission for one of his father's papers, and hinted that there was an engagement in the offing. One rather surprising thing was that although Billy's name was given as the person charged with the assault on Klaus, there was hardly any information about him, which was because Candy, Pete, Jackie and Bess had decided not to talk to the press.

"You see what you've let yourself in for", Tom said as they sat in the plane waiting for take-off. "We won't be able to keep it quiet much longer. There'll be your picture in the papers and reporters interviewing your Mum to get all the family details. Her picture will be there too."

"My Mum will be very proud and she'll know how to deal with them. And, you know what, I don't care—I'm proud too, and excited, and maybe your Dad can help keep the lid on a bit."

"He can do that with his own papers, but it will only make the opposition wilder. My guess is he'll tell his editors to give us the full treatment, only it will be done with a certain amount of dignity."

"Do you think it's OK with him?"

"He's delighted—he took a liking to you straight away. There's nothing snobbish about my father and as far as the papers are concerned you have one enormous advantage."

"What's that?"

"Well, I don't know whether I mentioned this before, but you're very, very beautiful. He's going to enjoy putting you on the front page."

"Well, tell him not to do it before I tell my Mum about it. She might die of shock!"

"How about giving her a call?"

"She hasn't got a phone. She says if people want to talk to her they can come round. I told her she should have one so I could call her when I needed advice, and she said that was another good reason for not having one. I s'pose we could send her a telegram, but it might scare the life out of her before she got it open."

"Well, we could get there almost as soon as a telegram. Dinner tonight with my father at the Palmerston and then a red-eye to Heathrow—are you up for it?"

"Sure!" said Halcyon.

*

"What this son of mine needs", Lord Otterill proclaimed between sips of antique brandy, "is someone to stir him up a bit. Here he is, the heir to a dusty old title and, more to the point, to my vast empire", this last said with a twinkle, "and all he wants to do is moulder among the buttercups and daisies of rural Somerset. Can't you do something about him, Halcyon? Next thing I'll hear is that he wants to buy back the ancestral home and set you up as the local Duchess who's very handy for opening annual church bazaars and raising funds to repair the church organ."

Halcyon had also imbibed considerably.

"Listen, Jim, first of all you have to admit that if you don't like the way he's turned out you only have yourself to blame."

Her future father-in-law chuckled.

"Secondly, the only organ I'm interested in works just fine."

Tom was faintly embarrassed, but Lord Otterill's guffaw was heard all over the room.

"And thirdly, there's not much I can do until after we're married. Then I can really get to work."

Tom sat up and took notice.

"Hey, wait a minute. What was all that you said about being ordinary?"

"Well, I only said I *was* ordinary, not that I wanted to stay ordinary."

"Anyway", Lord Otterill pointed out, "to all intents and purposes you're married already—all we have to do is make it official. Now look here, Tom, Andrew Davy—that's my senior science correspondent—has been making noises about retiring, and I want you to think about coming on board. He'll talk to you about it and you could learn the ropes under him for a year or two. You could still live in your blasted rural paradise and go on teaching for a while if you want to . . ."

"And if they'll have me back . . ."

Tom looked at Halcyon.

"What do you think?"

"I'm a little bit drunk", she said, "but it sounds exciting to me."

"You see, Jim", she added, "I was only kidding. I'm really an old-fashioned kind of a girl, and whatever he decides to do is OK by me."

"'Stand by your man'", the duke intoned in a loud, unmodulated baritone.

"I'll think about it, Dad", Tom said. "First I want to find out if they've already replaced me at the grammar school. I'd like to leave them with the idea that I'm not totally irresponsible. I'd also like to talk to Andrew and find out if it would be practical to work with him while I'm still teaching at Glastonbury. And I'll tell you something else—you probably don't know what a euphonist is, but Halcyon is probably the greatest one in the world, and I want her to be able to keep it up."

"You know, it's a funny thing", Halcyon said, "but I'd sort of forgotten about euphonics."

"You'll have to tell me about it another time", said Lord Otterill, looking at his watch. "Take care of yourselves and I'll see you in London in a couple of days."

As Tom and Halcyon sat in their taxi on the way to Kennedy Airport, everything seemed set for the best possible future, but Halcyon said, "I feel bad about leaving Alison all alone to cope with Klaus after all that's happened to her."

"So do I", said Tom. "But she didn't want us."

"I know. But maybe she'll want us later."

*

A quick trip on the Heathrow express to Paddington Station, a ride on the London Underground to Stepney Green, a slightly hazardous crossing of the Mile End Road, and soon they were standing on Mrs. Tompkins's doorstep.

Tom was feeling nervous.

"It's half past six on a Sunday morning—do you think she'll be awake?"

At that moment the door opened and Tom had the impression that he was looking at Halcyon's older sister—ten years older, perhaps, although that was impossible, and with the same blond hair, blue eyes and impish grin.

"Well, look what the cat brought home", she said.

"Hello, Mum. It's brought home a young man."

"Well, don't just stand there. Bring him inside, tell me his name and let me look at him."

Her accent was identifiably but not oppressively East End, and the light dressing-gown that she had put on over her night-dress was belted around a waist almost as slender as her daughter's. Tom, who had been expecting a lively and humorous version of Mrs. Trathgannon, stood there with his mouth open.

"His name's Tom and he'll be able to speak once he's stopped gawping at you. He just wasn't expecting anything quite so glamorous."

"Come on, Tom. I'm perfectly safe and I expect you've got used to the way Doreen talks—I'm afraid she gets it from me."

"What I'm wondering is where *you* got it from."

"Ah now, that would be telling. First I have to find out all about you."

"I thought the first thing was to put the kettle on—that's what Halcyon told me."

"All right, you got me there. And I suppose I'll have to get used to calling her Halcyon."

"Look, Mum", Halcyon said, holding up her left hand.

"Oo-er, so it's really serious. I don't know what your Dad's going to say."

"Oh, I forgot about Dad."

"Well, I know he's easy to forget about. He's still in bed, of course."

"Well, just leave him there for the time being—we can tell him all about it later, when he gets up."

"'If', not 'when'. Now I'm going to sit you both down in the kitchen and while the kettle boils you can tell me all about it. Come on, Tom, give your future mum-in-law a kiss."

After a full-body hug and an enthusiastic kiss Tom began to realize that it wasn't just her way of talking that Halcyon had got from her mother.

"You'd better call me Iris—I'm not old enough to be your Mum. In fact I wasn't really old enough to be Doreen's Mum, but you know how these things happen. Something tells me that she hasn't told you much about her parents."

"No, well . . ."

"But you mustn't let me run on—I want to know all about you and how you met and when you're getting married. Doreen's a naughty girl—she doesn't write much but I love her anyway."

"She talks about you all the time, so I almost thought I knew you already but . . ."

"You thought I would be an old lady with a Cockney accent who said things like 'firty-free fevvers on a frush's froat.'"

"Well, not exactly . . ."

"Mum, I think the kettle's boiling."

"Oh, yes. I don't know whether you've realized it, Tom, but 'The kettle's boiling' means 'Shut up, Mum, you're talking too much.'"

"Milk but no sugar", Tom said.

"OK, you win. But first . . ."

"Mum! Get on with the tea and then we'll tell you the story."

Halcyon was good at telling a story, keeping as close as possible to the truth and editing carefully as she went along, so Tom left it to her. After a few minutes, Iris knew that he and Halcyon had met in Glastonbury at the Archway conference, and that they had gone to New York to help Alison out of some kind of trouble. Iris had talked with Klaus on a couple of occasions when it was being arranged for Halcyon to go to Ulm, and she was very concerned to hear that he had met with an accident, which Halcyon gave as the explanation for the trip to Peoria, a city Iris had never heard of. Halcyon was quite open about the fact that she and Tom had been sleeping together and Iris remarked, "Well, much better him than Klaus—I mean he's a nice old bloke but . . ."

"Mum!" said Halcyon.

"Oh Lor', does Tom know about this or have I wrecked everything?"

Tom was sitting next to Halcyon at the kitchen table.

"Don't worry, Iris, I've heard all about it and Halcyon thinks I'm a great improvement."

"OK, Tom", Halcyon gasped, "you don't have to squeeze the life out of me. Mum, Tom is . . . Well I don't know how to say it . . . I love him so much . . ."

There were tears running down her cheeks and Iris said, "My dear, you really have got it bad, haven't you. So tell me all about yourself, Tom, and later on Doreen can tell me all the bits you left out."

"You tell her", said Tom, "I'm too embarrassed."

"OK, Mum. You'd better sit down."

"Why, is it something really bad?"

"Yes, his father's Lord Otterill."

Iris laughed heartily.

"Oh, I thought maybe he was the Emperor of Siam."

"No, Mum, I'm serious. How do you think we were able to do all this flying about and staying in hotels?"

Halcyon's Mum was uncharacteristically speechless.

"I'm afraid it's true, Iris", Tom said. "Halcyon's going to be a duchess one day unless my father outlives us, which he's quite capable of doing. And you're going to see yourself on the front page of one of his papers. That's why we came back in such a hurry. We wanted to tell you before it was all over the press."

"And Mum, you'd better tell Tom about Dad."

"Wait a minute! One father at a time, please! Tom is the honorable something-or-other . . ."

"He's already Lord Something-or-other—that's 'cause his father's a superior kind of Duke."

"O my God—what are the neighbors going to say?"

"Come on, Mum, you don't care two hoots what the neighbors say. You're gonna be news, so you'd better get used to it. Tell him about Dad, or I will."

"All right, all right. Doreen's father—I'll never get used to 'Halcyon'—seemed like a dashing young fellow when I met him. I was sixteen . . . Listen, Doreen, this means I've got to tell him about your grandma."

"The lot, Mum, tell him the lot."

"OK, I was living with my mum in the back bedroom of *her* mum's house. When I was little they told me that my father had gone away and it wasn't till later that I found out he'd only been there long enough to put a bun in mum's oven. They used to say he was a film star but nobody really knew—just someone she met one night when she was working at the Horse."

It took Tom a moment to realize that the Horse had a capital letter and its full name was "The Black Horse", the local pub.

"Anyway, Doreen and I didn't get our looks from my mum, so maybe there was something in it, and she was run over by a bus on the Mile End Road a year after Doreen was born, so we'll never know now. Anyway, as I was saying, when I met my husband he was what they call tall, dark and handsome, which he certainly is not now, and I didn't realize he was more than twenty years older than me. So it all sort of runs in the family if you see what I mean. You aren't pregnant, are you, love?"

"No, Mum, at least I shouldn't be."

An awful thought struck Tom and his face showed it.

"No, Tom, you mustn't worry about that. I don't have to explain, do I? And anyway, the poor old sod hasn't been able to get it up properly for months."

Tom's grip on Halcyon tightened a little. When she talked like this it was apt to precipitate certain physiological processes and cause an almost unmanageable escalation of his desire to carry her off to the nearest place where they could be horizontal together, or if not that, to proceed in whatever position was currently available. Halcyon responded, her complexion taking on a visibly pinker hue, which was not due to embarrassment, and Iris said, "Would you like me to leave you two alone for a little while?"

"No, Mum, we'll try and save it up for later. Go on about Dad."

"Well, I will say this for him, when he found out that I was up the spout he did the gentlemanly thing, and it was then that I discovered that he was nearly forty. He'd been working at Hartley's—you know, the fancy car show room—and they doll them up in smart suits and give them that smooth look, so—well, anyway, we came to live here and then a car fell on him and . . ."

"What?" Tom asked involuntarily.

"Well, not just out of the sky. They have these ramp things at the back of the show room and he was looking at the car when some fool pressed the wrong button. It did something to his back and he couldn't work any more, or so he said. He got a lawyer and tried to sue the company, only the company sued the people who made the ramp and it was a mess and in the end the company agreed to pay Albert his wages as long as he couldn't work. Well, he never liked work very much so every year he goes to the company doctor and puts on an act and always gets away with it. What he likes is staying in bed and watching the telly between naps. He gets up now and again and then he complains about his back and goes back to bed. The money's not much but it comes in regularly and I . . . Well, I s'pose I have to say it—I have a friend. Only we're very discreet."

"Come on, Mum. That's not quite all, is it? You'd better tell Tom who your friend is."

"All right, if I have to. He's the company doctor."

Tom laughed uncontrollably and after a while Halcyon joined in. Iris looked at them with a slightly puzzled expression, but soon a big grin spread over her face and she began to laugh too.

(53)

For once in his life Fortescue was unsure of himself. There was no difficulty in greeting Tom as "Your Lordship", but the question of how he should greet His Lordship's fiancée did not occur to him until Tom and Halcyon appeared on his doorstep. Tom saved the situation, addressing the butler exactly as any self-respecting butler would have wished.

"Good morning, Fortescue. This is my intended. Everyone except her Mum calls her Halcyon and she'll eventually get used to it. You'd better call her 'Miss Halcyon' unless you want to be a real stickler and call her 'Miss Tompkins'."

"Thank you, your Lordship, 'Miss Halcyon' will do very well for me and, if I may venture to say so, Miss Halcyon will do very well for you, too."

"Well", said Halcyon, while Tom was recovering from his surprise at Fortescue's unwonted pertness, "it's a funny world, isn't it? Your boss tells me to call him 'Jim' but I have to call his butler 'Fortescue.'"

She pronounced the butler's name in exaggerated stage English and added, "Don't worry, old dear, I'll try to behave nicely."

Fortescue allowed himself a discreet smile.

"Yes, Miss Halcyon, thank you very much. Allow me to show you to your room. His Grace is expecting to see you and His Lordship as soon as you are ready."

*

"Will Your Lordship be sleeping in the den tonight?"

Tom was momentarily confused. The den was the room he had claimed as an eleven-year-old, where he had his old desk, books, other survivals from his youth, and a rather narrow bed that pulled out from the wall. This was where he still habitually slept when he visited his father, but now he thought the butler had found a discreet way of asking whether he was intending to sleep with Halcyon.

Sensing Tom's train of thought, Fortescue added, "I merely wondered whether a bedroom more suited to Your Lordship's position might be considered appropriate."

"Oh, I see. 'Or convenient', you might as well say, you old rascal. Well, since you ask, I'm all for convenience."

"Miss Halcyon is in Adventure, Your Lordship."

"That does seem appropriate. Well then, put me in Sentinel and I'll keep an eye on her."

"Very good, Your Lordship, unless you would prefer to be in Opportunity. If I may say so, His Grace's decision to base his system of nomenclature upon the names of his major publications seems finally to have justified itself."

"I've always wondered, Fortescue—did someone teach you to talk like that or does it come naturally?"

"It comes from having read the appropriate literature, Your Lordship."

Fortescue disappeared before Tom could make any further enquiries, so he went up to see how his young lady was getting on with Adventure.

*

"Is it OK if we sleep together?" Halcyon asked. "I have this great big gorgeous room and it's a bit scary—like family ghosts or something. I mean, Mr. Fortescue and Alice are bound to notice."

"Oh, so you met Alice. She's really the housekeeper and socially almost on a par with Fortescue, but it seems that she doesn't trust Elspeth to look after you properly, so she's decided to do some house-maiding herself. She doesn't look it but she has a romantic heart. She'll get quite a kick out of it if she finds us in bed together, and Fortescue's paid a large salary not to notice things. And you'd better get used to leaving out the 'mister'—I tried to get him to soften up once and it doesn't work. After we're married you'll be 'Your Ladyship' to him and 'Lady Tom', which sounds excessively stupid, to the slightly higher-ups. Anyway, all we have to do is decide which room. Traditionally I wait till everyone else is asleep and then I come to you, but Dad is usually up till the small hours so we might as well be brazen about it."

"Either way is OK by me. I'll expect you when I see you. Does Alice bring tea in the morning?"

"Yes, unless you tell her not to. And being a well-bred servant she's apt to come in without knocking."

"Oh Lord! What happens if I get something wrong?"

"Well, as I said, it will be just as if nothing whatever had happened. That's what servants are for. But I'd better clear out before she arrives so that we can all keep up the pretence that nobody knows what's going on."

*

Looking across a pile of newspapers at Tom and Halcyon, Lord Otterill tried to summon up a stern expression but couldn't quite manage it.

"Well, you have put my foot in it, haven't you? And this is only a little bit of the story! So far it's only on the front pages of what my high-class colleagues call the gutter press, and there's nothing in any of my rags. You see, Halcyon, with a bit of low cunning, a certain amount of luck and a little help from my friends, we've managed to keep your fiancé's doings quiet ever since he left Cambridge, but that's all over. Now we have to cook up a story for tomorrow—I can't just pretend nothing has happened. Well, we'll deal with it. Have you decided where and when you're going to get married?"

"We don't know where", Tom said, "but soon and small. I wish it could be in Glastonbury but I suppose that would be asking for trouble."

"Yes, by now they'll have got the Somerset connection. Am I right in assuming that you want a church wedding?"

"Yes, although I'm not sure I could explain exactly why."

Tom looked questioningly at Halcyon.

"I wouldn't feel happy with just an old J. P.—somehow it wouldn't feel like really being married. And Mum would be terribly disappointed."

"Well, that brings me to another point—I gather that you have your head screwed on the right way, but can your mother be trusted? I mean not to gossip the thing all over Stepney."

Halcyon was slightly offended.

"Listen, Jim. My Mum talks nineteen to the dozen in her own kitchen but she's very wise for such a young woman, and she has her own little secrets which she knows how to keep."

"Young?"

"Well, if you want to know, she's thirty-five and she's very beautiful."

"I can't wait to meet her. Tell me about these secrets—it's not that I really want to know about your Mum's private life, but I do need to be prepared for what's going to turn up in tomorrow's papers."

"You tell him, Tom."

Tom told his father about Iris's husband and the company doctor.

"Well, there's nothing we can do about that except hope for the best. If they've been really discreet we may possibly get away with it. I gather the neighbors haven't twigged any of this."

"I don't think so. I'm sure we'd have heard about it if they had."

"OK, well just tell her to be extra careful until the buzz dies down a bit. Now, I have the beginning of an idea. My so-called friend, Ted Murdoch, has a so-called cottage, which means ten bedrooms, eight bathrooms, two ballrooms and at least six so-called reception rooms, in Haverhill. You remember Haverhill, Tom?"

"Yes, a couple of miles outside Cambridge."

"Well he's mostly in New York so the place is shut up a lot of the time, and he told me that since I haven't got a country house of my own, I'd be welcome to have the use of his whenever I feel like getting away from London. It's really just a bit of one-upmanship on his part, but I think it would be a real joke to make use of it. We can decide on a date, get a special license as late as possible, and I'll let it be known that I'm planning a gathering of my business associates and bringing my own servants. I expect the local Vicar can be kept quiet with a nice donation. Ted will be furious, but he may just possibly see the funny side of it."

"Frankly, Dad, I think they'll sniff it out. Couldn't we keep the wedding separate from the joke?"

"Hmmm, well maybe you're right. Let's see if old Fortescue has any bright ideas."

He pressed a button on his desk and after hearing the details of the problem, the old butler remarked, "I believe we may find the answer in the pages of Miss Sayers—with variations, of course."

Lord Otterill thought for a moment before banging the desk with his fist.

"'Busman's Honeymoon'!"

"Precisely, your Grace."

"So that's the appropriate literature you mentioned", Tom commented. "Bunter would be proud of you."

"Thank you, your Lordship. I am sure that a sufficiently eminent and dignified personage can be found to address the multitude."

"Excellent", said Lord Otterill. "I know the very man."

"Who's Bunter?", Halcyon wanted to know.

"Lord Peter Wimsey's man", Tom explained. "So indispensable that he even accompanied the Wimseys on their honeymoon."

Turning to Fortescue, he added, "Don't even think about it."

"Certainly not, your Lordship."

*

The Headmaster of Glastonbury Grammar School was very surprised to receive a call from his former physics master.

"Well, I must say, Dexter, you have a nerve."

"Yes, Sir", said Tom.

Slightly nonplussed at not receiving the expected explanation and apology, Mr. Pryce-Jones spluttered a little and continued, "Well, it's true that we have not yet found a replacement for you. But surely you can't expect me just to say, 'All is forgiven and welcome back to the fold.' Some of your colleagues—your former colleagues, I should say—have expressed considerable displeasure at your behavior. Can you give me some guarantee that another such episode will not occur?"

"All I can say is that I certainly don't anticipate anything of that nature. I wasn't expecting an immediate decision, and there are things that I'd rather not discuss over the telephone. What I need to know now is whether you would be willing to see me on Tuesday, with a view to my possibly returning to the school."

The headmaster agreed that this was a reasonable proposition. He was still trying to guess what it was that Tom couldn't discuss over the phone when it rang again. This time it was his secretary, Flossie Howe, and she came straight to the point without even a "Good morning."

"Have you seen today's *Strumpet*? Well, I don't suppose you have, seeing you only read highbrow papers."

The *Strumpet* was Flossie's name for the *Trumpet*, one of Ted Murdoch's more sensational publications.

Mr. Pryce-Jones didn't want to admit that he was an avid reader of the *Strumpet* and that at that very moment the Sunday edition was concealed beneath his copy of the *Observer*.

"Well, I believe we have a copy here—the boy must have left it by mistake."

He picked up the *Observer* and was surprised to find his former physics master staring at him from the front page of the *Strumpet*.

"Well, bugger me", he muttered as he replaced the *Observer*.

"I beg your pardon."

"Hrrm, just clearing my throat. Thank you for bringing this to my attention, Mrs. Howe. I'm sure I shall find it most interesting."

Obviously her boss didn't want to discuss the matter, so Flossie hung up, murmuring something about a blasted old hypocrite. Her timing was a little off, so the headmaster thought he heard her saying something about a hypocrite, but he was already entertaining visions of the future and it never entered his mind that she might be referring to him. There might be certain advantages in having Lord Leyford, son of the Duke of Brueland and Street, on his faculty, but would the advantages outweigh the potential problems? On the whole, he thought so, but first it might be a good idea to find out what all the fuss was about. He pushed the *Observer* firmly aside and picked up the *Trumpet.*

*

At eight o'clock the next morning, when Alice came in with the tea tray, Tom and Halcyon were still fast asleep. The housekeeper's performance was a minor *tour de force* and, for once, Halcyon was slightly flustered

"Good morning, Miss Halcyon", Alice said as if Tom were not in the room. "Would you like the curtains open?"

"Yes please, Alice. I er . . . we er . . ."

Halcyon petered out as the curtains swished, and Alice said, "It's a lovely morning. Would there be anything else, Miss Halcyon?"

"Oh, no thank you, Alice."

"Thank you, Miss Halcyon."

Alice departed and Tom said, "Now do you understand about servants? Of course, there aren't many like Alice."

The door opened again and without a word, Alice placed a tray on the bedside table next to Tom. Tom caught her eye and she almost smiled.

*

An hour later, Lord Otterill was laying down the law over breakfast.

"Fortescue and I have worked out the details of our end of the deal and we need you to make up your sweet little minds about yours. If you want your wedding quiet and secret you'd better make it pretty small and pretty soon, and get right off the scene for a few weeks. I've put them off the scent for a while, and they still haven't got Halcyon figured out, but it won't last long. They already tracked Tom down to his lair in Glastonbury and interviewed his landlady, and you only have to look out of the window to see that this place is under siege. That's a remarkable old woman, that landlady of yours, Tom."

He imitated Mrs. Trathgannon's raspy contralto.

"'Mr. Dexter's private affairs are none of your business, or mine either, and if he is Lord Leyford, all the more reason for giving him some respect.' Slam! It made lovely TV, but I'm a little surprised they showed it—reporters standing there like lemons with their chins hanging down. Anyway, how about a place and a date? Are you still sure you want a church wedding?"

"I don't know", Tom said. "It's complicated, isn't it, with residency requirements and banns. I don't see how we can get away with it. Maybe we should just announce the wedding and let the media do their worst."

"I'd be scared out of my wits", Halcyon objected. "Maybe we should do what I told Mrs. T. and just have a J. P. for now and do the job properly later on."

"Good girl!" said Lord Otterill. "The main thing is to get the two of you spliced and off on your honeymoon while the bloodhounds are still waiting for the happy event at Haverhill. If you do it that way you'll escape an enormous amount of unpleasantness. After you get the special license, the public notice of your marriage only has to be up for one day, and since this place counts as a stately home within the meaning of the act, we can have the wedding here. I'll telephone Fred Brookings and get things moving, and then you can tie the knot almost any day you please."

"Who's Fred Brookings?" Halcyon wanted to know.

"He's the Superintendent Registrar for this district and he owes me a favor. He'll come at four in the morning if I ask him, and we'll get Fortescue and Alice out of bed and have a little party. I'll let the cat out of the bag when we have our little do at Haverhill, and later on when you have your real wedding it won't be so much of a sensation. And, by the way, I suppose you haven't thought of such a small detail as where you're going to live when you get back from your honeymoon."

"Well, I do have an idea, only it's not exactly what you might expect."

"I know", said Halcyon. "You want to go back to your old lady."

"Well, just for a few months, while we look around. What do you think?"

"It would be ever so romantic", Halcyon intoned with the stickiest sentimentality she could manage. "No, really, I like the old duck, and she would know that I've made an honest man of you."

VIII

Alison and Klaus, with Interruptions

(54)

The staff at the Medical Center were amazed at the speed of Klaus's recovery.

"I've never seen anything like it", Nurse O'Halloran said to Alison on Saturday morning. "Here he is, eighty-five or something, with injuries that somebody half his age would take weeks to recover from, and after three days he's walking around as if there's nothing the matter with him. And so polite and charming."

"How soon do you think he can leave the hospital?"

"Well, you'll have to ask Dr. Painter, but I think he'll be well enough to travel in a couple of days, as long as you're looking after him. If you want to know the truth, I think the doctor's more concerned about you than she is about him."

"Don't worry about me, I'll be OK", Alison said, adding absent-mindedly, "I've decided not to kill myself for the time being."

The nurse looked at her for a moment, trying to decide whether or not this was supposed to be a joke, and Alison said, "I'm sorry—I didn't mean to scare you. Anyway, I expect they'll be discharging me soon so you won't have to worry any more."

"But you'll be visiting your husband, won't you?"

"Yes, so I'm afraid you won't have seen the last of me after all."

Nurse O'Halloran went to look for Dr. Painter and while she was gone, Candy Bigley knocked on Alison's door. Alison was sitting on the edge of her bed and Candy sat down beside her.

"I brought your suitcase. I just wanted to see you, and now I'm here I don't know what to say. That night when Billy was arrested and I realized what had happened, I tried to blame you for everything. Pete said it was his fault, he started it, and then we found you on the road and we were afraid Klaus would die. It was all too hard."

"Don't say anything, Candy, just put your arms around me. I'm so cold inside. We both got it wrong, but I was much more wrong than you were. What's going to happen to Billy?"

"They're working on a deal. Billy will have to go to prison, but maybe only for a couple of years. They want to have another talk with Klaus when he's well enough."

"Do you have enough money? I want to help pay for Billy's defence, but it's really Klaus's money and I haven't asked him yet. He doesn't know about Billy, you see."

"We're OK for the moment, but the fact is, the diner hasn't been doing real well, well, not until you came. We could probably use a little help, specially if there has to be a trial."

"All right, Candy, I'll talk to Klaus and as soon as I can get to the bank I'll arrange something. Do you think I could go and see Billy?"

"I don't know. I mean, you could, but . . ."

"He might not want to see me?"

"Well, like I said, I don't know. You see, Jackie goes to see him every day and she's—well, I think she's in love with him. You see what I mean?"

"Yes, I do."

Alison examined the pang of jealousy that she was experiencing, and realized that it wasn't caused so much by sexual desire for Billy as by the fact that these two people might develop a nice uncomplicated relationship. Well, maybe it wasn't a fact . . .

"Are you OK?"

"Oh, sorry, I was just thinking. How is Jackie doing?"

"Well, she's really upset about what happened to you—she likes you very much and she'd like to see you, only between working at the diner and going to see Billy whenever she can—well, you know. We were closed the day after the . . . incident, but we opened the next day and the place was crowded out for a couple of days. Jackie asked me if I thought she should put her bra back on and I said it was up to her and she said she liked not wearing one and it made her feel sexy. But she's a good girl and now she's taken a fancy to Billy I don't think anyone else is going to get very far with her. And she brought a friend along and she's very pretty and doesn't wear one either, so you really started something there."

Alison had tuned out about halfway through this last paragraph, but the last phrase caught her attention. So that was her legacy to Peoria, she thought; *sic transit.*

She gave Candy a hug.

"Thanks for bringing my case. I'll call you on Monday when I've sorted out the money thing. Now I want to talk to Klaus."

*

As Klaus's physical body repaired itself, he found it harder to maintain his attitude of contrition and self-abasement. After several days of extreme weakness, the sensation of feeling a little stronger had a tendency to go to his head, and he was less inclined to admit the possibility that his expansion of Goerner's philosophy was simply a way of justifying his sexual propensities. What he had striven for was in accordance with the esoteric indications of some well known spiritual authorities. It was unfortunate that from their point of view his explorations had not met with much success, but a little voice that he could not entirely suppress kept hinting that he had, after all, given those young women a lot of enjoyment, and not many men of his age . . . No, he shouldn't be thinking like that. He ought to be thinking about Alison. She had said that she would look after him, but, as Halcyon had said, she needed more care than he did, so it should really be the other way around. He didn't know exactly what had happened to her, but it seemed to have been a terrible experience, and she was in a state of deep shock. Well, he was still her husband, and Halcyon was now otherwise engaged, so the obvious course would be for them to return to Manhattan and resume their married life. Maybe they could form the nucleus for the new euphonics group that he had considered founding, and go on a world euphonics tour . . .

At this point in his cogitations, Alison walked into his room. He thought she was looking a little better.

"Good morning, my dear, how are you."

Alison ignored the greeting.

"There's something I have to talk to you about."

She wanted to give him a full account of all that she had done and everything that had happened to her since she left Glastonbury, but when she came to her involvement with Billy she found that she couldn't put it into words without making it sound sordid, at least to Klaus's ears, so she simply said that she and Billy had become extremely close friends. Apart from that her report was plain and unvarnished, starting with her rescue by Dr. Perlman and ending with a generalized account of the rape. It was delivered with an astonishing lack of emotion, as if it had all happened to somebody else. Finally, Alison described Billy's plight and asked:

"I want to give most of the money to Billy's parents—is that all right with you?"

Klaus was horrified by the story.

"Yes, of course, the money is yours. You may do whatever you wish with it. I see that you are more in need of care than I am and that it is I who should be caring for you. Now that I know the full extent of your suffering I beg you to allow me to live up to my responsibilities as your husband."

Klaus tried to continue with a statement of what he thought those responsibilities would be, but Alison was already laughing, and it was the kind of uncontrollable, mirthless laughter that moves inevitably towards hysteria. Nurse O'Halloran came into the room, looked reproachfully at Klaus, and put her arm around Alison's shoulders.

"Come on, darling. We'll put you back to bed and give you something."

"He wants to live up to his responsibilities as my husband!"

Alison's words were punctuated by violent cackles which soon turned to gusty sobbing.

"Couldn't you euthanize him or something?"

Klaus heard this last remark and, for a second, saw himself though Alison's eyes.

*

By the time Nurse O'Halloran had shepherded Alison back to her room, Dr. Painter was on the scene. Alison was still sobbing and it was only with difficulty that they managed to get her attention long enough for her to swallow the little white pills and a mouthful of water. Ten minutes later she was asleep, and she didn't wake up until eleven o'clock the next morning.

It was rather like the day at Heathrow when she had run away from Glastonbury and everything hurt, but, still drowsy from the drug, she couldn't understand why. Gradually the details of her last encounter with

Klaus returned to her. She forced her aching body into a sitting position on the edge of her bed. A new nurse came into the room and asked her how she was feeling.

"I must see my husband", she said.

"Your husband?"

"Yes."

It was too hard to explain, so Alison pointed towards the other end of the corridor.

"Oh, the old gentleman in 914? He's gone—checked himself out early this morning. He's not really your husband is he? I mean . . . ."

After the nurse had gone, Alison stood up unsteadily and found the suitcase that Candy had brought. The old purple dress would do. It would cover everything up, and they couldn't stop her from leaving if that was what she decided. Klaus had checked out so she must do the same. She had made a decision to take care of him, and this was something that she might be able to do without hurting anyone or making a mess of it. She'd made a bit of a mess yesterday, but if only Klaus knew how ridiculous he sounded . . . Well, not merely ridiculous—not *chastened* enough, not aware enough of the excess of his self-importance and the depth of his moral failure, unable to see the people around him as anything other than adjuncts to his high-flown mission. *That's not my job*, she thought. *He'll get chastened enough after he dies, and so will I. But if there's any justice, his will be worse than mine.*

Alison assumed that Klaus had gone back to Manhattan and might have decided that he didn't need her or didn't want her. Well, that would make things easy—it would mean that there was no one left to worry whether she was alive or dead. Apart from sending some money to Candy, she would be entirely without responsibilities, would owe nothing to anybody, and if she left, no one would notice that she wasn't around anymore. This was an enormously comforting idea.

She decided not to say anything. She would rest a little and eat her lunch, and by that time she would feel strong enough to dress, pick up her case and leave. She still had plenty of cash and she ought to be able to get back to New York soon after Klaus. She would find out if he needed her, and if not—well, then she could make up her mind. Her feelings about death were still very confused, but at that moment it seemed less scary than life, which included not only the dreadful realities of incest, rape and assault but also trivial impossibilities like talking to anyone. It was usually pretty quiet after lunch, so she would just put on the purple dress, and walk out as if she had been visiting someone. The thing that would make her conspicuous was the suitcase, but there was very little in it that she really needed, and Candy had brought her handbag.

After eating a little lunch she pretended to fall asleep. Once the bustle of clearing things away had died down, she slipped the purple dress over her hospital things, combed her hair, put on some shoes and packed whatever she could squeeze into her handbag. The corridor seemed to be deserted, but a loud altercation was coming from Klaus's room. She thought she recognized Inspector Krebs's voice.

Thinking that the inspector was furious because Klaus had gone, and fearing that she was the next item on his agenda, she ran to the waiting room, passed though it as decorously as she could and made her way to the main entrance. There was a constant stream of taxis arriving and leaving, and in a few minutes she was on her way to the airport.

(55)

When Klaus had arrived in Peoria he had been looking for someone. He had found her and lost her, and for the first time in his life he felt utterly alone. He thought with no pleasure of the several ex-wives who were dotted around Europe, and with a certain amount of regret about Halcyon; but it was Alison that he really wanted and needed, and now she had finally rejected him. Her words still echoed in his ears.

"Couldn't you euthanize him or something?"

Imre was probably still hanging around the brownstone, and Klaus was realistic enough to know that his former secretary was unlikely to leave unless someone actually threw him out. But Imre was not exactly company. As Klaus understood him, he was a nonentity, a physical body with no spiritual content, a creature of reflexes, a vacant space in the soul life of humanity. There were such people—Goerner had spoken of them—and it was their very vacuity that made them so vulnerable to demonic beings, and therefore so dangerous to real people. What brought this image so vividly to Klaus was the sensation of his own inner emptiness. In his life of meditation he had tried to create a free space in his soul, so that the good influences of the cosmos could pour in; a carefully maintained, loved and guarded space, like the seed beds that Goerner used to talk about, not a desolation created by the withdrawal of all those who had loved him. He tried to remember exactly what he had said that had precipitated Alison's outburst, and saw again the cycle that he had recognized before; some kind of shock would lead to a period of deep self-abasement, but this would not be proof against the resurgence of the old Klaus, who would turn out to be not such a bad fellow after all, full of hot air and plans for putting the world to rights.

Never again, he thought, but it seemed to him that the thought had arrived too late to be of any use.

By the time he reached the brownstone it was early afternoon. Exhausted and acutely depressed, he left his suitcase in the front hall, slowly and painfully climbed the stairs to his room and fell on his bed. When he woke up, the room was lit only by the rays of a street lamp. He groaned and reached for his bedside lamp, but a voice said, "Don't turn the light on, Klaus. Let's sit in the dark and talk."

"Alison—I don't understand. I thought you wished me to be dead."

"Perhaps I did, but if so it was only for a moment. I really wish to be dead myself but we are so tied to each other that I think when the time comes we shall go together. There must be a reason for all this, and I don't have the faintest idea what it is, but I think I must do my best to love you and see you through to the end."

This was not exactly a comforting message, but Klaus was so moved by the thought that Alison would be with him for the final leg of his journey that he almost wept. He still knew that at some point he must tell her that she was probably not as closely tied to him as she believed, but that action would have to be postponed until he felt a little stronger.

"I want to go to Glastonbury", he said. "Will you come with me?"

As far as Alison was concerned, it was all one whether she was in New York, Glastonbury or Timbuktu.

"All right, Klaus."

"But don't you want to know why?"

"Only if you need to tell me."

"I wish to climb the Tor to the tower of St. Michael. When I was there on the day when you left, I was granted a vision, and in my arrogance I neither grasped it correctly nor took it into my soul as strongly as I should. I wish to return and implore those who gave me that vision to speak more clearly and give me the strength to follow whatever guidance they may give."

Even as he spoke, Klaus knew in his heart that this was the old Klaus, the Klaus who would hold high converse with the spiritual beings who control the destinies of the human race, the Klaus-Moses who would bring great spiritual truths to lesser mortals.

He groaned again.

"Oh my dear, once more I am being foolish. I only felt that somehow on the Tor I might feel forgiveness coming from above. Will you come with me?"

"Yes—I have said that I will. Maybe I shall find forgiveness too."

"Why should you be in need of forgiveness?"

Alison thought of Billy, thought of explaining the whole thing in words of one syllable; but she was too weary and couldn't imagine what good it would do.

"I'm going to bed now, Klaus. I have a couple of things to take care of in the morning and then we can talk about going to England."

"All right, my dear. But there is one thing that I do not understand. Why did that young man attack me? I can see that as your friend he would be angry, but there was hatred there and extreme violence . . ."

"Not now, Klaus. Perhaps it's something that you don't need to know."

"Do you know?"

"Yes, I do."

"Then why . . ."

But Alison had gone. As she lay down on her bed she was thinking of Halcyon's mother. What was that rhyme that Halcyon had passed along? Something about Timbuktu?

"Once I was a cassowary,
On the plains of Timbuktu.
There I ate a missionary,
Arms and legs and hymnbook too."

What if the Pythagorean version of reincarnation was right and Goerner's was wrong? Maybe she could reincarnate as an animal. There wouldn't be so much responsibility. Maybe she could be an owl and Klaus could be a mouse—Klaus the Mouse. She started thinking of other rhymes for Klaus—Klaus the Spouse, Klaus the Souse, Klaus the Louse. She giggled weakly and had to work hard to avoid another descent into hysteria.

*

Klaus was right in some respects about his former secretary, but not in others. Imre was still occupying his room in the brownstone, and there was certainly a great deal of empty space in his inner world. In this space there were many objects that might well have been placed there by the evil beings that Klaus regarded as obvious components of the cosmos, but there was also the residue of his long admiration for Klaus, and there was his intense physical desire for Alison, which carried a tincture of genuine affection.

Inseparable from his feelings about Alison was the great pain arising from his acknowledgement that he had burnt his boats very thoroughly and made a complete mess of his efforts to make a new beginning. He had taken a certain pleasure in the fabrication of his schemes, and it had come as a shock to realize that as a plotter he was a dismal failure. When he heard Alison moving about in the next room he felt the slightest twinge of remorse. He had had the impression that Halcyon had detached Tom from her, but he had very little hope of being able to move into the vacated spot. And what would she think of his letter, which she was bound to see at some point. Knowing that the action was foolish and hopeless he got up, went into the dark hall and knocked on Alison's door. There was no response, so he knocked again. Alison opened the door and said, "What is it, Klaus?"

Imre began to say, "It isn't Klaus."

Alison gasped and slammed the door. Imre backed away and spoke into the darkness.

"I'm sorry, Alison. I just wanted to talk for a moment."

Alison didn't reply, but a voice came from the darkness of the upper floor.

"Come here, Imre."

This was Klaus, consciously acting the part of his old self and hoping that the assumption of an authority that he no longer felt would be convincing. It didn't occur to Imre to disobey, so he felt his way up the stairs and waited for his master to speak again.

"I see that you have not yet removed yourself. Since that is the case, it is possible that you may still be of some service to me."

Imre still didn't say anything, so Klaus continued.

"My wife and I will be going to England, and I am not sure when we shall return."

He was canny enough to omit the information that he was not expecting to return at all.

"If you wish, you may continue to occupy your room and your role will be simply that of a caretaker. You may live here rent-free and I shall pay you three months in advance at half the salary of your former secretarial position."

Imre was overwhelmed. This offer would solve his immediate problems and allow him to use the house as a base for reviving his career. It was such a welcome surprise that he even forgot to haggle. When he was half way down the stairs he heard Klaus speak again.

"And you must not, under any circumstances, attempt to communicate with my wife."

*

Klaus was hoping to find a small cottage that he could rent in the Glastonbury area, so he spent most of Monday morning on the phone, and it wasn't until the middle of the day that he remembered that he had Dr. Ginsburg's card in his wallet. Meanwhile, Alison opened a new account, deposited her check and sent $6,000 to Candy. That left her with an emergency fund of $1,000 for which she had no immediate use, but having given up trying to foresee the future, she felt that a little caution wouldn't be a bad thing. When she got back to the brownstone, Klaus gave her the card and told her where it came from.

"I don't want to see them", she said. "I don't want to see anybody."

The next morning, as if impelled against her will by something she didn't understand, she walked around the corner. Chris Ginsburg would probably be busy all day and she wouldn't have to talk to him, but she would be able to see Helen and give a proper apology. When she entered the waiting room, however, Helen wasn't there and Chris was explaining something a young temp. Alison started to turn away but Chris had already seen her.

"Hello, Alison. Let's see, what were we just saying?"

Alison couldn't help smiling.

"I'm sorry, Chris. If I hadn't run away, things wouldn't be so bad now. That's what I really came for—just to apologize."

"Well, come inside for a moment. There's something you may want to know. My next victim is already fifteen minutes late so if I keep her waiting she can't very well complain. Zelda, if Mrs. Schumann shows up, give me a buzz and tell her I'll be with her in a few minutes and don't give any reason for the delay."

"It's Mrs. Mendelssohn, Doctor."

"Whatever."

"Now look, Alison", Chris said as he closed the door, "I don't have time to beat about the bush or lead up to something gently. I have some information relating to the question of your parentage. Do you want to hear it?"

Alison wasn't sure that she did, but she knew that she couldn't possibly leave without hearing what Chris had to say.

"OK", she said. "I probably don't want to, but go on anyway."

Chris explained about Klinefelter's syndrome.

"I can't say it's impossible that Phillip Johnson could have fathered a child, especially as to outward appearances he seemed quite normal, but it's very unlikely. And it seems that he knew about this four years ago. I'm sorry."

Something on Chris's desk buzzed twice but the doctor was in no hurry.

"You'd better sit down for a moment."

"I'm OK", Alison said. "I really knew it already but I suppose it's good to be sure of something. I think I'll go now. Thank you for seeing me."

"Where are you going?"

"Back to the brownstone. Klaus is there and he wants me to go to England with him."

Chris started to speak, but Alison interrupted.

"Don't worry. I think you've done all you can for me and I'm really grateful. I don't want to keep Mrs. Beethoven waiting any longer."

*

After two discouraging days of telephoning, Klaus gave up on the idea of a rental in the vicinity of Glastonbury and decided to book a flight and a hotel room, and hope for the best. Neither he nor Alison had any further interest in current events, so their first inkling of the media sensation swirling about Tom and Halcyon came at Kennedy airport on Friday

Screwing Upward

morning. They had missed the initial splash in the dailies but they couldn't fail to see Tom staring at them from the lurid front pages of the tabloids. There was nothing to say, however. They already knew how things were between Tom and Halcyon, and they digested the information about Tom's aristocratic status in silence. What difference did anything make now? Nothing could make them more sick at heart than they already were.

(56)

Alice Murrell, Lord Otterill's housekeeper, was elderly, sharp-featured and quite short—"five foot and a tater", as they say in Somerset. She looked rather scary and didn't smile much, but her face was completely transfigured when she did. She was usually as formal as Fortescue, but somehow this didn't seem to work with Halcyon.

"Well, you're not exactly what we expected, Miss Halcyon", she said as she cleared away the breakfast things on Tuesday morning.

Tom had driven down to Glastonbury very early while Lord Otterill busied himself with arrangements for the wedding and hatching fresh plots in the newspaper world, so the two women had time for a cozy chat.

"But then, I'm not sure we expected anything in particular. Master Tom had his own ideas and he never seemed to care much for the aristocracy. From what I've seen I can't say I blame him."

Alice characterized the aristocracy with a loud sniff, but seeing an apprehensive look on Halcyon's face, she added, "Now don't misunderstand me, dear, His Grace is one of the best and anyone can see that he thinks you're the bee's knees—and as for Master Tom, he can hardly take his eyes off you. And then there's Mr. Fortescue."

"Yes, Mrs. Murrell?"

There was a note of reprimand in the old butler's voice but he was smiling.

"Oh, Mr. Fortescue", said Alice meekly. "I'm sorry—I didn't know you were there."

"I have been here for some minutes, Mrs. Murrell, and although your sentiments have been expressed in an uncustomary way, I must say that I find myself in total agreement with them. His young Lordship is very lucky to have found someone of such superior quality and, if I may say so, extreme beauty."

He was about to add, "among the working classes", but, biting it off just in time, he paused, apparently expecting some comment from Halcyon, who was standing there with a scarlet face and an open mouth.

"Now you've embarrassed the poor girl", Alice said reproachfully.

When Halcyon finally found her voice it was half mocking and half serious.

"Coo, I wish my Mum was 'ere."

Fortescue smiled.

"His Grace has asked me to speak to you on a practical matter, Miss Halcyon. Not wishing you to be a prisoner of the press corps, he suggests that we should equip you with a maid's uniform so that you may make one or two unobtrusive forays from the servants' entrance. He understands that you wish to visit your mother today, and Alice will take you to Elspeth's room for that purpose. Elspeth is of approximately your stature, Miss Halcyon, and will be honored to provide you with suitable attire."

"In fact", he added, "she's all of a doo-dah about it."

Halcyon already suspected that Fortescue's usual style was part of an act that he enjoyed putting on, and this final remark, in addition to the twinkle that was never far away, confirmed her suspicion. She felt so happy that she wanted to run around hugging people.

*

Wearing Elspeth's uniform, and not realizing how sensationally sexy she looked in it, Halcyon set off with Alice as if they were making for the underground station, but after a few minutes' walk Williams, Lord Otterill's chauffeur, drew up beside them and whisked the pseudo-maid off to Stepney.

This was just about the moment when Tom arrived at Glastonbury grammar School. Flossie was delighted to see him.

"You can't go in yet", she said, pointing in the general direction of the headmaster's office. "He's got someone else in there."

At that moment, Mr. Pryce-Jones's door opened and Elwyn Davies emerged. He looked in through Flossie's open door, saw Tom, started to speak, changed his mind and kept on walking.

Tom said, "Hey, wait a minute", but Elwyn ignored him.

"It's all over the whole school", Flossie said. "And somehow it got around that you want to come back. It's the most sensational thing to happen in Glastonbury since Lancelot laid Guinevere."

"I don't think that was in Glastonbury."

"Well, wherever it was. Anyway, you'd better go in."

But the headmaster was already at Flossie's door.

"Good morning, Dexter, or should I say, "Lord Leyford"?

"Good morning, Sir, and thank you for seeing me. My name is still 'Dexter', whatever the reporters may think."

"Well, come in and have a seat and let us talk things over."

The headmaster was quite jovial.

"They seem to be quite confused about the real reasons for your trip to America and, of course, it's none of our business here."

He paused in the hope that some enlightenment might be forthcoming but, getting no response, he continued.

"You are an excellent teacher, Dexter, and you have always been a good influence on the boys and girls under your tutelage. I should very much like to have you back if we can iron out one or two complications, the foremost of which is that Davies has just this minute told me that he intends to resign if you return. I find this very extraordinary and I should be glad of any light that you can shed on the situation."

"Elwyn was very angry with me for suddenly deciding to disappear and, from what I saw a moment ago, he is still very angry. I'd have to talk to him before saying anything further, but I'm not sure whether he will be willing to see me."

"I see that there is more in this than I thought. I shall ask Davies to see me at lunch time and tell him that before I take any further action it will be necessary for him to speak with you. Will you be on hand at that time in case he should agree?"

"Absolutely. And if he refuses to change his mind I shall withdraw my application to return."

"Hmmm, yes. Well, whatever else you are, Dexter, you certainly aren't wishy-washy."

Recovering from his mild surprise at the headmaster's use of such a plebeian expression, Tom found himself wondering whether Halcyon would agree. She had more or less accused him of wishy-washiness.

*

"It's not you, Tom" Elwyn said. "You've been a damned nuisance, but that doesn't amount to much. It's the girl. I can't get her out of my mind. If she's going to be in Glastonbury and married to you of all people, I'll have to go a long way away."

"Does Diana know about this?"

"Sort of. Well, she knows something's up and I think she thinks I'm having an affair with someone."

"Listen, Elwyn, it's only been about two weeks since you first saw her and you're talking as if this is going to be a permanent condition. And there's no need for you ever to see her."

"You don't understand how painful this is. I keep trying to make it go away and it won't. And you know as well as I do, the way things are with chemistry teachers I could get a job anywhere in the British Isles."

"OK, I grant everything you say, but remember there's another seven weeks before school starts again in September, and although something like this can be utterly intolerable, it always goes away and leaves you feeling like a damn fool, knowing that you took some stupid job in Inverness because of an infatuation amounting to temporary insanity. And how are you going to explain it to Diana? She loves it here."

Elwyn tried to object to "infatuation", but Tom overrode him.

"It *is* an infatuation and it just goes to show that all that stuff you're always saying about people being just conglomerations of electrons and such is partly true. Your wavelengths happen to chime and off you go, and you have no idea what the other person is really like."

Elwyn wasn't at all convinced.

"Well, what about you. Aren't you suffering from temporary insanity too?"

"Maybe, but there's a big difference."

"Oh, really? Tell me about it."

"I'm not married and I haven't got a small son."

There was a moment of silence while this sank in. Elwyn seemed to have run out of ammunition, so Tom went on.

"I don't know where we're going to be for the next seven weeks and I think it would be a good idea if you could be somewhere where you knew there was no chance of seeing Halcyon for a while. I have a suggestion but I'm not sure if I dare make it."

"Does it involve money?"

"Yes."

"Well, try me."

"OK, you have three more days of school, and then I think the best way for you to get over this is to take Diana and Mickey and spend several weeks at some exotic place where you have no idea what's going on in the rest of the world and you won't have to see stupid headlines in the tabloids about what Lord Leyford is up to. You know what I'm going to say next, so you can just tell me to shut up if you don't like the idea."

"I'm all ears—the only problem is how to explain it to Diana."

"Well, you'll have to figure that out for yourself. I'm sure you'll think of something. I suppose you wouldn't consider telling her the truth."

"You mean about the girl or about the money?"

"Or both."

"I don't think I can tell her about Halcyon but . . ."

"Well, you can explain it any way you like, but just get it into your temporarily unbalanced brain that this is not compassion or sentimentality. I want to come back here, and if this makes it possible it's worth the money. Then, when you've got over it we can be friends on the old basis."

"Well, bugger that", said Elwyn, "but I'll take the money anyway."

*

After settling things with Mr. Pryce-Jones, Tom drove out along the A361 to Ashwell Lane. He didn't know whether he and Halcyon would return to Mrs. Trathgannon's establishment but he thought it would be a good idea to let the lady know what the situation was. As he approached the house along the narrow lane he saw several parked cars, people milling about, and a van marked QTV AVON NEWS. Evidently they were having another go at his intrepid landlady and this wasn't such a good time to call, but the van left barely enough room to get by and he had to slow to a crawl. When he was almost by he heard a woman scream, "That's him!" and almost immediately an engine started. He put his foot down and drove as fast as he dared along the lane until he came to the sharp right bend that led back down to the main road, where he squeezed into a small gap between two trucks. Soon he was well on his way back to London, feeling that he had successfully eluded the news hounds and learnt an important lesson at the same time. There was no hope of keeping them permanently at bay, but a proper degree of caution would certainly pay dividends.

*

While Tom was attending to business in the West Country and Halcyon was communing with her Mum, Lord Otterill wasn't idle. The next morning the fruits of his labors appeared on the front pages of his rivals' papers, but not on his own. There was nothing official yet, but an unaccountable leak from the Otterill camp had resulted in several papers running "exclusive" stories to the effect that Lord Leyford was engaged and that his wedding would take place with a big splash in Haverhill, near Cambridge, where Lord Otterill had been given the use of Ted Murdoch's country cottage for the reception. In view of the great rivalry between the two press lords this was presented as an extremely magnanimous gesture on Murdoch's part. No date had yet been announced and officially the event was billed as a business conference, but the Murdoch press knew better and everything pointed to a wedding on the first Saturday in August. There was frustratingly little information about Lord Leyford's fiancée and not even a picture, but it was speculated that she was the extremely attractive young blonde with whom he had visited a rape victim in Peoria, Illinois, and who had been seen with him at the Palmerston Hotel in Manhattan.

"That should distract them for a few days while we get things organized", Lord Otterill remarked to his butler, pointing to the front page of the *Trumpet*. "Murdoch's going to be very upset when he discovers he's missed the wedding, but it serves him right. He shouldn't crow so much about his posh country house."

*

Lord Otterill was right. Once the rumors of his son's impending wedding in Haverhill had appeared in the media, surveillance of his house decreased considerably and the emphasis was placed on the Murdoch estate and the identity of the bride. On the day the story broke, which was Wednesday, Halcyon's Mum was smuggled into the house via the servants' entrance. Later on, the observers who saw her coming and going thought that she was the same young servant who had been seen on one occasion leaving with Alice. Bert Tompkins preferred to spend the day at home in bed, so Iris set him up with a big plate of sandwiches and a supply of beer, enabling him to spend a glorious day in front of the TV, free from any kind of female interruption.

"I'm glad you're here to hold my hand", Iris said to Halcyon. "You've been round the world a bit, but I'd be terrified on my own."

"Don't worry, Mum, they're all sweethearts, even Fortescue when you get to know him."

Iris was further intimidated by being placed next to her host at lunch, which was spent discussing the very simple arrangements for the wedding. It was set for five o'clock on Friday morning. Mr. and Mrs. Bert Tompkins would arrive on the previous evening and Williams would deliver Fred Brookings at 4:30 a. m. After the ceremony, which would take only a few minutes, the chauffeur would whisk the couple away to an obscure garage in the eastern suburbs of London, where the Morris Minor was being checked for every possible mechanical defect.

"I think your Dad likes my Mum", Halcyon whispered to Tom. "Maybe Dr. What-his-name is going to get some competition."

"I dunno, it's a bit complicated, isn't it, with my Dad being on the scene as well. I mean, if the doctor gets his nose put out of joint, Dad might have to go back to work."

*

Thanks to Lord Otterill's excellent staff work, the myth of the August wedding of Lord Leyford at the Murdoch estate became an accepted fact and speculation intensified over the identity of his bride. There were various people who had some information. Bill Graveney was pretty sure he knew which way the wind was blowing, while, in America, Candy Bigley and Inspector Krebs had been introduced to Halcyon; but none of these people had any desire to communicate with the media. Anne Weston didn't bother much with newspapers and television, and Imre was out of circulation for the first few days of the brouhaha, remaining in his room most of the time until Klaus and Alison left on Friday. His deep depression was partially alleviated by the knowledge that he was secure for the next three months and by the pleasure it gave him to have the house to himself, with the freedom to come and go without the fear of running into Klaus. It was on the day of Tom's and Halcyon's wedding that he finally took a good look at a paper. It took him some time to digest all the news, after which he went into a huddle with himself and conceived another of his little schemes. A few hours later Ted Murdoch learned of the offer of an exclusive interview from a man who claimed to know exactly who Lord

Leyford was marrying and to have actually lived in the same house as the young woman in question.

*

Cosmic Wisdom people are not usually avid TV watchers, but those who did happen to tune in to their morning shows on Saturday were astonished to see Imre's countenance confronting them. He had been heavily coached by the staff at Wolf News, part of the Murdoch empire, and the interview was carefully edited, but he was hesitant and appeared ill-at-ease. This was not only because of the unaccustomed presence of lights, cameras, technicians, make-up artists and an interviewer notorious for his obnoxiously overbearing manner, but also because he had qualms about what he was doing. In addition to the handsome under-the-table payment for his participation there were prospects for remunerative articles in magazines and newspapers, but as far as the CW community was concerned he feared that he was cooking his own goose pretty thoroughly. At a more personal level he had almost certainly destroyed the possibility of any further relationship with the parties most deeply involved. As far as Tom and Halcyon were concerned this didn't make any difference, but Klaus and Alison also came into the story in a big way, and the knowledge that what he was doing could only add to Alison's distress made him deeply uneasy. He comforted himself with the thought that Alison was a lost cause and the money would be very handy, but he knew in his heart that his real motivation was to get back at the people who had assaulted and scorned him.

"What the hell is euphonics and who's this Hooble?" Bob Reilly had demanded while the interview was being prepared.

Imre had embarked on an explanation about Goerner and CW, but Reilly soon shut him up.

"Just tell them it's modern dance and leave Gonner out. Tell them Hooble was her teacher and make sure everyone realizes he was screwing her, without actually saying so."

This took a lot of coaching but eventually Imre got it right.

"Now, what about this Alison—Hooble's wife? She's the one who got raped in Peoria, the same day he got damaged at the diner, right?"

This was all news to Imre and at first he couldn't take it in. Alison's name had been kept out of the papers but Reilly knew all about it. After he had explained it, Imre said, "I don't want to do this."

One of the executives said, "Listen, Mr. Takacs, we've got all this stuff from you and we'll use it whether you like it or not. The only difference is if you pull out now you won't get paid, and there's nothing you can do about it."

So Imre reluctantly continued and the juicier details of Klaus's ménage emerged. The Wolf News staff thought that some of the statements were definitely actionable, but the general opinion was that the chances of Klaus or Alison taking the network to court were negligible.

The interview wasn't completed until the small hours of Saturday morning, New York time, and it began airing at 7 a.m. there and simultaneously in England at midday.

Meanwhile, the news hounds were busy investigating Klaus and Alison, and tracking down Mr. and Mrs. Bert Tompkins in Stepney. What they didn't find out was that by that time Tom and Halcyon were already married and the rumored event at Haverhill was an elaborate hoax.

(57)

Driving out of Glastonbury on the A361 towards Shepton Mallett, one passes along several intriguingly named thoroughfares—Bere Lane, Chilcote Street and Coursing Batch. Just opposite the left turn into Ashwell Lane, where the redoubtable Mrs. Trathgannon lived, stands the New Avalon Hotel. The hotel, which was new in the reign of Queen Victoria, is a respectable three-storey structure with a nice view of Glastonbury Tor from the top floor, which is why Klaus settled on it as a temporary residence. On Saturday morning he and Alison took the train from Paddington to Castle Cary and completed their journey by taxi. When they checked in at the hotel at half past eleven they were too preoccupied with their own miseries to be at all conscious of what was going on in the world around them, so they failed to notice the large TV screen in the lounge, which was promising startling revelations in the twelve o'clock news.

"You understand, Klaus, that I shall do everything for you that a wife should do, except sleep with you", Alison had said, and Klaus had reluctantly agreed. So although they signed in as Mr. and Mrs. Klaus Hübel, they went immediately to rest in their separate rooms.

"May I knock on your door in one hour?" Klaus asked diffidently. "I should very much like to climb the Tor this afternoon."

Alison's immediate inner response was that her husband must be crazy. Eighty-four years old, severely injured only ten days ago and at the end of an exhausting journey—how could he possibly contemplate the five-hundred-foot climb at this moment?

"I see that you hesitate", Klaus said. "Perhaps after two hours?"

Alison smiled in spite of her depression.

"All right, Klaus, let's say half past one, and if I wake up sooner I'll come and knock on your door.

Alison was feeling desperately weary and intolerably rattled. She collapsed onto her bed, fell into a brief doze and woke up with a spasm of acute anxiety that flashed through her whole body and set her heart racing. The hotel was very quiet but traffic was still flowing and the sun was still shining, so evidently the world had not yet come to an end. Something must be happening, she thought, so she picked up the TV remote control and switched on. It was just one minute past midday.

*

Klaus sat at his bedroom window looking out at the Tor. Things were turning out as well as he could have hoped in the circumstances, and he was feeling much better and not at all sleepy. Alison seemed to him to have accepted her role as wife/daughter and would be with him as long as he needed her. There was still the awkward fact that she was probably not his daughter, and he was moved to consider the category of awkward facts. At one time it had been an awkward fact that she was probably his daughter; now it was an awkward fact that she probably wasn't. Well, perhaps after all, he need never tell her. Their relationship might become quite comfortable and amicable, and there was no real need for him to contemplate the approach of death. They might go on in this relatively pleasant manner for years. Having persuaded himself into a tolerably peaceful frame of mind and a more positive relationship to the world, he thought it would be salutary to find out what the world was doing, so he reached for the remote control. It was just a minute after midday.

*

Most of the people in the hotel lounge were thinking about lunch when the twelve o'clock news started, but the promise of a big story involving Lord Otterill and his son had everyone glued to the screen. The introductory comments produced a sudden hush, and at one minute past twelve, Imre and Bob Reilly were seen facing each other across a shiny mahogany table. Most of the people in the room thought they were seeing a live interview and wondered where this acquaintance of Lord Leyford had popped up from. The make-up artists had cut his hair and contrived to make him appear less chubby and more youthful. He seemed to be an earnest and sincere young man who was concerned about his friend's welfare. No details were given about how long Imre and Leyford had known each other or under what circumstances, but there was a strong implication that they had been pals for years. Reilly's intention was to bring out as many juicy details of Leyford's and Halcyon's lives and recent activities as he could, and the more embarrassment it caused in the Otterill camp the better. Imre's program was slightly different; Halcyon had treated him with contempt and he wanted to get his own back. So had Tom, of course, and Klaus had punched him in the mouth and on the nose; but Halcyon's derisive dismissal was by far the most galling. Alison had rejected him too, but he didn't want to talk about her and did his best to keep her out of the conversation. Anyway, Halcyon was the main object of everybody's curiosity so it wasn't hard to keep the focus on her.

"Although there has been no official announcement, Wolf News has learned that Lord Leyford is to be married in a few weeks' time. The wedding party will gather at Ted Murdoch's estate near Cambridge, England and the one thing that everyone wants to know is who is the bride. Wolf News has found the man who can answer that question—Imre Takacs, who is a friend of bride and groom and has consented to fill in the details for us."

That's what Imre did. Yes, he had known the bride for several years and had twice met her in the company of Lord Leyford, who was better known to his friends as Tom Dexter. Dexter was a teacher at the Glastonbury County Grammar School, and lived in an apartment on Ashwell Lane. ("Just round the corner", someone said in the lounge, with a gasp of satisfaction.) Imre hadn't known about the apartment—the last piece of information had been supplied by Wolf's investigators. Imre explained that he was private secretary to Klaus Hübel, who was very prominent in the Archway School Movement and was a pioneer in the development of a kind of modern dance called euphonics. The young lady in question had become a member of Hübel's household at the age of sixteen and she was now nearly nineteen. She had studied euphonics with Klaus and performed under the name of Halcyon. She and Tom had met in Glastonbury only a couple of weeks ago. Imre had been with the two of them in Glastonbury, at Klaus Hübel's house in Manhattan, and again at the Manhattan Archway School. As far as he knew, they had known each other for less than two weeks.

"Why are you so sure that Halcyon is the bride to be?"

"Because they were behaving as if they were already married."

"Can you be more specific?"

"Well, they went to bed together and showered together."

"And generally behaved like an item?"

"Yes."

"Can you tell the viewers more about Halcyon's position in the Hübel household? You said she was sixteen when she moved in?"

"Yes. Klaus was supposed to be her teacher, but he was obviously in love with her. After a couple of months they gave up trying to disguise the fact that they were sleeping together."

"So she was sixteen, and how old was Klaus?"

"Eighty-one."

(Another gasp.)

"And what about Klaus's wife? I suppose an elderly woman would find it very hard to accept a situation like that."

"She isn't elderly—she was twenty-three when this happened."

(More gasps.)

"You are describing a very unusual situation."

"Yes, but it wasn't unusual for Klaus. He's been married at least four times, always to a woman much younger than himself, and on each occasion his wife has been displaced by an even younger woman."

"Don't you feel any compunction about betraying your employer's secrets?"

"I might if they *were* secrets, but Klaus feels that these—activities have been part of his spiritual mission and he has never made any attempt to be discreet about them."

"Well, well, well. So the future Lady Leyford and, perhaps Duchess of Brueland and Street, has been an old man's mistress for several years. Can you tell the viewers more about her? Surely Halcyon isn't her real name."

"No, her real name is Doreen Tompkins. She comes from somewhere in the East End of London and she talks a lot about her Mum."

The interview went on for several more minutes, and Imre had to answer some awkward questions about Cosmic Wisdom and the Archway Schools—awkward because his involvement in these movements was as close to being sincere as anything he was ever likely to achieve. He could see no future for himself outside them, and it was difficult to talk briefly about them without making them sound cultish or ridiculous. As far as the viewers were concerned, the message was clear; Lord Leyford had been bowled over by a girl of eighteen whom he had known for less than a couple of weeks, and who at the age of sixteen had become mistress of the octogenarian leader of a dubious movement for so-called spiritual renewal. She performed weird dance routines under the fancy name of Halcyon, but she was really a Tompkins and spoke with a Cockney accent. Wolf's researchers had dug up a picture of Klaus from the program of one of his American tours, but as yet there were no pictures of Halcyon.

Finally Reilly thanked Imre and faced the audience solo.

"You may have been startled by some of these revelations, but you can be sure that there's more to come and Wolf News will keep you informed."

*

It was a general principle among the more devout and less self-aware CW's that anger was always a negative and deplorable reaction. Many of these people sincerely believed that they never grew angry or raised their voices, and deeply resented charges of humbug and hypocrisy. Alison had no such illusions, and it was anger that roused her from the paralysis and torpor to which she was increasingly subject. At first she simply couldn't take in what she was seeing, but after a while the reality of the situation sank in and she cursed Imre with every execration she could think of. When it was over she decided that she and Klaus must talk immediately and get out of the hotel as soon as possible. They had signed in under their real names and it wouldn't be long before someone would make the connection and the news would spread.

*

291

Klaus was stupefied, and when he got his mind working again his first thought was to regret having already paid Imre three months' salary. Klaus had always maintained that anger was a perfectly appropriate response to certain kinds of provocation. People should be made to realize that their actions have consequences. Imre would certainly suffer for this, but in the meantime Klaus would have to do his best to see that Alison didn't become a victim of the press, who would surely be only to happy to grill the displaced wife. Obviously the first thing was to get out of the hotel and find more unobtrusive lodgings. He opened his door and his wife walked in.

"I think I know where we can go", she said. "It's worth a try, anyway, and it's only a couple of minutes' walk from here."

Klaus held her in his arms and for a moment she allowed it.

(58)

"It's wicked, what these television reporters get up to", Mrs. Trathgannon said to her husband. "Harassing an old woman like me, just to make up a whole rigmarole of lies. You can't believe a word they say."

"Well then", Mr. Trathgannon said quite reasonably, "I don't know why you watch them. Usually you'd be out in the garden on a day like this and I'd be watching cricket."

But Mrs. Trathgannon ignored these comments and retained control of the remote, watching Imre's performance in silence.

"Disgusting", she said when it was over. Her husband knew that she was referring to the behavior of those who had delivered the story, most of which she undoubtedly thought was pure invention. "Mr. Dexter may have been a naughty boy, but he wouldn't be involved an anything as sordid as that. And that girl of his—the second one, I mean—she's probably been naughty too, and she may be a Cockney, but there was something about her . . . Oh, well, I hope they just leave us alone now."

She went to put on her gardening shoes, and her husband was just changing the channel when there was a knock on the front door.

"Go and see who it is and don't open the door till you're sure it's not a reporter."

Peering through the bay window, Mr. Trathgannon saw a tall, elderly, white-haired man and an attractive young woman wearing a long purple dress. They looked eminently respectable.

"Probably Jehovah's Witnesses", he thought, so he opened the door.

"My name is Klaus Hübel and this is my wife, Alison."

Mr. Trathgannon's recognized the name and his mouth fell open. A voice behind him commanded, "Don't just stand there—ask them in."

*

Lord Otterill watched the program with mixed feelings. It was galling to have to listen to Ted Murdoch's minions letting so many cats out of so many bags, but it was some consolation to dwell on the fact that his son was already married to an excellent young woman and that they were now safely on the other side of the English Channel. He would allow Wolf News to continue in blissful ignorance for a few more days, and then it would give him great pleasure to announce to all those who showed up at Haverhill that his son had been married more than a week ago.

*

Like Mr. Trathgannon, Bill Graveney preferred cricket to scandal, but he had got wind of some advance publicity and wanted to find out what was up. Much as he was revolted by Imre's willingness to wash other people's dirty linen in public, he was delighted to hear that Halcyon had achieved her purpose.

"Good girl!" he thought. "I hope she remembers that I gave her some good advice."

Bill was essentially pure in heart but, as Tom had surmised, he really liked Halcyon's legs, and he could still recall the sensation of her hug and kiss. It gave him a lot of pleasure. He had just switched back to cricket when the phone rang. After a certain amount of incoherent spluttering it became clear that the caller was Harry Grainger. The spluttering represented his outrage at what he had just seen and his determination that something should be done about it.

"Yes, I agree", said Bill patiently, "quite disgusting. Your feelings do you great credit. And you want to bring a suit for slander against Takacs, QTV and Wolf? Who exactly would the plaintiffs be?"

"Well, of course, Klaus ought to sue them, but I believe the Society could bring an action and young Dexter or whatever his name really is might be persuaded to join."

"Unfortunately, it seems that most of what Takacs said is true."

"But don't forget, the greater the truth the greater the libel."

"Again, unfortunately, the rules were changed in 1843. And if you're going to admit in court that his stories are true, it's going to make marvelous publicity for the Movement."

"So what do you suggest?"

"Ignore it."

*

Bert Tompkins had fallen asleep and forgotten to switch the channel. He was still dozing in front of his TV when the name Tompkins penetrated his mental fog. By that time the interview was more than half over and he was very puzzled as to what the fuss was all about, so he achieved the extraordinary feat of getting off his bed and going downstairs. At the sight of his striped pajamas Iris remarked, "Well, I'll go to sea in a bucket—look who's here! What was it—an earthquake or a stick of dynamite?"

"What are they saying about our Doreen?"

"Nothing you don't know already—or would know if you ever paid any attention. You know she went off to study with that old man, and if you didn't put one and one together there's something wrong with the space between your ears. And you were too lazy ever to go and see her doing euphonics, even though she's gorgeously beautiful and dances like an angel. And you were at the wedding, so you know that bit and she's Lady Tom Dexter. What's the matter—scared the reporters might come after you?"

"My back hurts—I'd better go back to bed."

"Do you think you can manage it, or do you want me to carry you upstairs?"

There was a loud knock at the front door. While Bert propelled himself up the stairs with remarkable speed, Iris ran to the front room to peer through a chink between the curtains. A television van was standing at the curb, people were messing with cameras and two perspiring suits were standing at the door.

The knock was repeated. Iris, after giving the situation a moment's thought, loudly shot the bolts on the front door and pulled down all the blinds on the front windows.

"If that doesn't give them the idea, they're stupider than I thought."

*

On the other side of the Atlantic, Imre's revelations were eagerly received by the tabloid-loving part of the population and ignored or greeted with a big yawn by most of the rest. The exceptions were the CW and Archway people, who were neither eager nor bored. Over a leisurely breakfast, Carolina Ende and Anne Weston were discussing the fate of the summer training program. Klaus and Alison had disappeared without a trace, Imre had been dismissed and there had been no word from Halcyon and Tom Dexter. The program had staggered along for another week, but there was growing dissatisfaction among the participants. Saturday's sessions had been cancelled and a full meeting scheduled for Monday morning, when an announcement would be made. Carolina was enjoying herself in New York, and cancelation of the program would mean that her funding would stop and she would have to return to Germany immediately. She was in the middle of a list of all the good things that could still be done when Anne made an impatient gesture.

"For God's sake, Carolina, stop. We've been improvising and muddling through ever since the second day of the Glastonbury conference and I can't stand it any more—always apologizing and never delivering. I'm going to stop thinking about it and spend a day at the beach."

She switched on the radio for the weather forecast and a voice said, ". . . revelations about newspaper magnate Lord Otterill's son, who goes under the name of Tom Dexter, heard and seen this morning on the Wolf News Channel. Apparently no footage or audio is yet available. All we can tell you is that he seems to be engaged to a young woman called Halcyon who is said to be a professional dancer with an allegedly murky past. The whole interview will be repeated at ten o'clock, so you'll be able to see for yourselves. In sixty seconds we'll have the traffic report . . ."

Carolina sat with her mouth open while Anne tried to bring her thoughts out of orbit. She looked at her watch—it was 9:51. Well, the beach would have to wait a little while. She switched on the TV and waited impatiently until Imre's face appeared.

"I might have known who was at the bottom of this", she said.

Tom Dexter—Lord Otterill's son—Halcyon an eighteen-year-old dancer with a murky past, mistress of the elderly leader of two dubious cult-like institutions—CW and Archway made to sound ridiculous.

"Come on, Carolina, time to go."

"Where are we going?"

"To the beach, of course. What's the use of going anywhere else?"

*

Tom and Halcyon were blissfully unaware of the Wolf-Takacs show until the next morning. Since the Spanish papers didn't regard it as a matter of any great importance, the couple would have missed it entirely if an officious hotel-manager hadn't brought it to Tom's attention, with many apologies, over the breakfast table. Tom's understanding of Spanish was based only on the four years of Latin that he had absorbed as a schoolboy, but the names Otterill, Takacs and Halcyon were unmistakable.

"Don't bother", he said when the manager offered to translate. "I get the general idea."

"It's our lovely friend Imre, blowing the whole gaff on TV", he told Halcyon.

"Obnoxious little bastard", Halcyon said. "What are we going to do today?"

"I'm going to get a crew cut and a pair of dark glasses and start growing a beard."

Halcyon vetoed the crew cut.

*

While Tom and Halcyon were discussing how to spend their Sunday in Madrid, a telephone rang in Fortescue's room in London.

"A call for you, your Grace", Fortescue murmured via the intercom. "On the general line."

The general line was the one used by tradespeople to communicate with Lord Otterill's staff on domestic matters.

"Who the hell is it?"

"A Mrs. Tabitha Trathgannon, your Grace."

"Trathgannon? Trathgannon! Well, for God's sake put her through."

"Certainly, your Grace."

Lord Otterill was suddenly at his most charming.

"Good morning, Mrs. Trathgannon. This is Jim Dexter, alias Lord Otterill. How are you?"

Mrs. T. had not put herself though all the agonies of finding a phone number for His Lordship in order to discuss her health or the weather, so she ignored the niceties and came straight to the point.

"I really wanted to talk to Mr. Tom Dexter or whatever we're supposed to call him now, but they tell me he's away, so I thought you might be able to help."

"I'll be happy to try—what's up?"

"Well, to cut a long story short, I have a Mr. and Mrs. Hübel in my house—Klaus and Alison Hübel, that is—and they're looking for somewhere to stay where they won't be hounded by all these horrible reporters and TV people. They stayed in my spare bedroom last night, but there's Mr. Dexter's little flat upstairs that would be perfect now that they've stopped harassing me. Only Mr. Dexter has paid the rent for the next four months and perhaps he'll want to come back, so I wanted to ask him if it would be all right for the Hübels to stay for a little while. Naturally I would refund the rent for the period to Mr. Dexter."

"Mrs. Trathgannon, I think you are a splendid person and I can't tell you how much I admired the way you dealt with that TV gang the other day. I'm sure Tom would be delighted. I'll let him know that I told you so, and if he has any complaints he can direct them at me. But I'm sure he will be only too happy to help out. He won't be back until the end of August, so there'll be time to work something out."

"Well that's a relief. Mr. and Mrs. Hübel seem to be very nice people and I don't believe a word of what that awful man said on television."

"Good for you", Lord Otterill said heartily. The capacity for disbelief, he was thinking, must be very useful, although if more people had it it might be a bit of a nuisance to the media world.

*

Sleeping with Klaus in Mrs. Trathgannon's spare room had been agony for Alison and she looked forward to sleeping on the sofa in Tom's living room. This would be agony too, in a different way, as she relived the last day and night she had spent with Tom. But she thought it probably wouldn't be for long.

*

Imre returned to the brownstone in the early hours of Saturday morning and spent most of the day dozing fitfully on his bed. His mind was full of images of the TV studio and the leering face of Bob Reilly, and empty of any coherent thought about what he had done and what lay ahead for him. The one positive thing was that he had a check from Klaus and a check from Wolf TV and a place to live. If he wanted to he could stay in his room and no one could do anything to him. He still had to eat, however, and since there was no food in the house he dragged himself outside and as far as the corner of 88th and Columbus, where there was a small family restaurant. Unfortunately, there was a television set over the take-out counter. The sound was off but the captioning was on, so the first things Imre saw as he walked in were his own face and the words he was saying in cold print.

"... *he was obviously in love with her and after a couple of months they gave up trying to disguise the fact that they were sleeping together.*"

"*So she was sixteen and how old was Klaus?*"

"*Eighty-one.*"

"*And what about Klaus's wife? I suppose an elderly woman would find it very hard to accept a situation like that.*"

"*She isn't elderly—she was twenty-three when this happened.*"

Imre stood in the doorway with his mouth open. Someone behind him said, "Excuse me, please" and he took a couple of steps further into the room. Then he saw someone pointing and he realized that people were staring at him. He turned blindly and left, squeezing awkwardly past the people who were entering.

"Did you see that? I'm sure it was him", he heard as he reached the sidewalk. He ran back to the brownstone. Perhaps he could risk going to the deli a little later, but for now he didn't want to see anyone. He threw himself on his bed and wept copious tears, not of contrition but of self-pity. Unlike Judas, he kept the money and didn't go and hang himself.

*

It was nine o'clock and getting dark when Imre crept out again. The deli man stared at him but didn't say anything, and he made it safely back home with his sandwich and coffee. On the way in he noticed that there was something in his mailbox. It turned out to be a letter from Germany. The postmark was Ulm but the writing was not his father's. It couldn't have anything to do with his TV appearance, so he opened it. It was from a German lawyer who regretted to inform Imre that his father had died suddenly, apparently of a stroke.

"We have tried repeatedly and unsuccessfully to contact you by telephone. By the time you receive this, your father's body will have been cremated in accordance with his express instructions. His will names you as his sole beneficiary, and it will be of the utmost importance for you to come to Ulm and deal with his assets and personal effects."

As far as Imre's father was concerned, the news had little resonance—they had been estranged for so long—but the letter went on at some length and the point that burnt itself into Imre's fevered brain was that the total value of the estate appeared to be in the region of $250,000. The letter, which was dated July 20th, had probably been lying there in the mailbox for two or three days. If he had known about it he almost certainly wouldn't have had anything to do with Wolf TV. Well, the first thing to do in the morning would be to book a flight to Germany, and Imre wondered whether when he got there he would still find people staring at him and whispering behind his back.

(59)

Klaus and Alison had arrived at the Trathgannons' on a Saturday afternoon. On Sunday night Klaus slept in Tom's bed and Alison on the living room couch, and they both had the feeling that this might be their last lodging on earth. In some ways it suited their situation ideally, but once the relief at escaping from the curiosity of the hotel residents and the attentions of the media had died down, they realized that there were certain practical disadvantages, one of which was that their landlady had become very attentive. In her gruff and grumpy way she had been quite attached to Tom, and she had taken a liking to Halcyon in their brief acquaintance. She wasn't quite so sure about Alison, who had sassed her on the only previous occasion when they met, but the tall, white-haired old German gentleman with impeccable manners had gone straight to her heart. So it looked as if she was developing the habit of popping in to see if they were all right, and, if possible, to chat. This happened on Sunday afternoon, and while she discoursed about the iniquities of Wolf TV and the awful man who told all those wicked stories that she knew couldn't possibly be true, there was a gleam in her eye that suggested a slight lack of conviction in this verdict and a desire to be more fully informed. It would not have been totally unwelcome news if, in addition to all his other admirable qualities, the old gentleman had turned out to be a bit of a rake. But Klaus remained politely uninformative and Alison silent, except when startled into speech by Mrs. Trathgannon's remark that she was glad to hear that Halcyon and Tom would soon be getting properly married.

"What do you mean, 'properly married'?"

"Oh, didn't you know? They said they were getting a special license so they could get married before they went to America. Then she said they were going to do the job properly when they got back."

Alison was stunned. Tom had promised eternal devotion to her, and a few days later he had married Halcyon.

She stood up and went into the bedroom. Mrs. Trathgannon, sensing that in some way she had put her foot in it, said something about her husband's tea and left the room. Realizing that his wife would rather be left alone, Klaus stretched himself out on the sofa. It was much too short for him, but he suddenly felt very tired and soon he was asleep.

*

Early on Monday morning, the first day of August, Klaus and Alison set off for the Tor. It was a bright, sparkling day but they were too preoccupied with their thoughts to enjoy the walk along the narrow hedgerow-bounded lanes.

As they climbed the steep path Klaus, who had always been quietly proud of his stamina and athletic ability, was alarmed to find that things were not as they had been only a few weeks ago. He stopped and sat down on a grassy bank.

"I'm sorry. I do not know what is the matter with me, but I need to rest."

Alison sat beside him.

"Perhaps it would be better not to go any further."

"No, my dear, I shall be all right in a moment."

And it seemed that he was. They made it to the tower and looked at the panorama of fields and little hills spread out all around them. It was as lovely as ever, but Klaus was not looking for natural beauty. He sat in front of the tower, as he had sat on that rainy night three weeks previously.

"They are silent", he said, and Alison knew exactly what he meant. At one time she might have made a facetious remark, such as, "Well perhaps it's the wrong time of day. They're probably still in bed." Now there was no facetiousness left in her. If the Gods wanted to ignore Klaus, that was their business. Something was speaking to Alison, however. She wasn't quite sure what it was, and it certainly wasn't the Gods, but it seemed to be saying, "You're still young and strong and beautiful. Why do you want to kill yourself?"

"Because I don't want to be old, weak and ugly", she murmured, but she knew she was only playing with words. The real reason—well, the real reason was that in spite of everything that Goerner had said, the thought of being dead was the only thing that gave her any comfort.

*

At the beginning of August, Wolf TV and the Murdoch press were puzzled by the fact that, apart from what he had read in the papers, the Rector of Haverhill Parish Church had no knowledge whatsoever of a forthcoming wedding involving the Otterill clan. The information that they had received, however, seemed to be very reliable, so the only possible conclusion was that the event would take place with an imported clergyman at Murdoch's mansion instead of the church. On the afternoon of Friday, August 5th, the Wolf team, accompanied by representatives of the BBC, ITV and other less august bodies, began stationing themselves as close as possible to the main gate and the smaller entrance to the surrounding parkland. All the gates were locked, however, and it did not go unnoticed that there appeared to be quite a number of rather mean-looking individuals patrolling the grounds. Nothing happened until eight o'clock in the evening, when the watchers were rewarded by the sound of a helicopter landing behind a distant clump of trees. There was nothing they could do about it, so the more important members of the press squad retired to their hotels, while the rest dozed uncomfortably in cars and vans. They were all in place again by seven in the morning, gazing along the tree-lined avenue that led to the house, but there were no signs of activity until ten o'clock, when a burly young man on a motorbike appeared at the foot of the broad stairway below the main entrance to the house. At the same moment Fortescue emerged from the front door, descended in a most leisurely fashion and mounted the pillion of the motorbike, which then proceeded along the two hundred yards of avenue to the main gate. Meanwhile, several more burly young men had taken up positions on the stairway and along the drive. Fortescue dismounted and produced a large megaphone, while the motorcyclist turned his machine.

"Lord Otterill", Fortescue announced, "is pleased to invite the ladies and gentlemen of the press to meet him in the small ballroom ten minutes from now. The room is set up for a press conference and, as you see, ushers are ready to assist you in finding seats."

The old butler remounted and was driven away, while one of the "ushers" approached the entrance with a key that opened only a small wicket gate at the side of the main entrance. The reporters had time to reflect that these particular ushers looked as if they would have been more at home in a bar-room than in a ballroom, but they allowed themselves to be led on foot in a meek procession along the avenue, up the stairs and into the small ballroom, where Lord Otterill stood on the dais with an elderly man of obviously immense importance and distinction. Some of the press corps had assumed that the reason for meeting in the small ballroom was that the large one was all set up for the wedding. Others had already begun to feel deeply suspicious, and at the sight of His Excellency the British Ambassador to the Soviet Union, all became aware of the aroma of rat. Under such circumstances, however, it's hard just to get up and leave.

"The workings of the media world are quite remarkable", Lord Otterill said cheerfully. "I organized this conference on the future of the Soviet Union and the Eastern Bloc because it seemed to me that major developments are soon to take place and that it would be extremely helpful to all if there was a good working relationship between the press and the government. I must confess that I had not expected the media in general to take such an avid interest in the proceedings. Naturally there are things that the government cannot share . . ."

He went on for several minutes before introducing Lord Battishill. The ambassador praised the media for their keen interest in foreign affairs and gave a forty-five minute address on the state of Anglo-Soviet relations in which it was noticeable that he didn't tell his audience anything that they didn't know already. At the end there was desultory applause and Lord Otterill rose to ask if there were any questions. After an awkward silence a young woman rather apologetically mentioned that she knew it didn't have anything to do with the Soviet Union, but she had heard that there had been some talk of a wedding.

"A wedding?" Lord Otterill exclaimed in a surprised tone.

"Yes", said a loud male voice, "we heard that your son was to be married."

"Oh, *that* wedding. Good gracious, I thought everyone knew about that."

After a moment of concentrated silence, the original small voice said, "I'm afraid I don't know about it."

"Well, I am surprised. My son was married, let's see, eight days ago, and he's now enjoying his honeymoon somewhere or other in Europe. Well, I hope he's enjoying it!"

"Lord Otterill, could you tell us his wife's name?"

"Yes, of course. Her name is Lady Tom Dexter. Thank you all for your attention."

The burly ushers, who had been seated around the room, all stood up while Lord Otterill escorted the ambassador through a small door behind the dais.

"I think we've all earnt a drink", he said to Fortescue, who had been lurking in the background. You'd better join us."

"If your Grace so desires—I don't mind if I do."

IX

Alison and Imre

(60)

After a few days sunning themselves on a quiet Spanish beach, Halcyon and Tom went on a grand tour of Europe. Tom could have travelled as much as he liked, but he had always been too much in love with the English countryside to want to spend much time elsewhere, so Milan, Rome, Dubrovnik, Athens, Venice, Prague, Vienna and Salzburg were just as new and wondrous to him as they were to Halcyon. The news that Klaus and Alison were now living in Tom's apartment took a few days to catch up with them, and the minor furore over Imre's revelations touched them hardly at all.

"I don't know", Halcyon said, "I was kind of looking forward to going back there, but I s'pose if it makes life easier for Alison we could find somewhere else. How about buying back your old castle, like your Dad said, only he didn't mean it?"

"I vote we don't worry about it till we get there. As far as the ancestral home is concerned, it's true, I've thought about it. But we'd have to find the school another place, and I'm not sure I want a house with a big auditorium in the front, although I am sure that crowds of people would come to see you perform."

"Will you mind if I still want to be a euphonist?"

"Of course not—only we'll have to find some way of keeping Elwyn out of the building."

Nearing the end of their trip, they were driving into Germany from Salzburg with the intention of travelling through the Black Forest into Switzerland. They were looking at the familiar names on the road signs—Munich, Stuttgart, Nuremberg—when Halcyon spotted Ulm.

"Can we go there?" she asked. "I want to show you where we used to live and the school."

Tom wasn't particularly anxious to see the house where Halcyon had received her sex education from Klaus, but after three weeks of marriage he was still in that state of bliss in which it is virtually impossible to say, "No." So, after passing by Munich, they took a turn to the north, entered the city of Ulm and crossed the Bahnhoffstrasse, where Einstein was born, and the Danube, which they had last seen in Vienna. Tom insisted on taking a look at the Minster, and soon they were standing in the Münsterplatz, staring up at the tallest church tower in the world. As they returned their gaze to ground level, the first object that caught their attention was Imre Takacs.

Imre, dressed with unusual elegance and looking very pleased with himself, was sauntering along as if he had nowhere in particular to go; just a man of means, out for an early afternoon stroll.

"What the hell is he doing here?" Halcyon muttered.

At that moment Imre turned and saw them. His air of self-satisfaction disappeared instantaneously, and he stood irresolute for a moment before dashing off almost at a run.

"I bet he's staying in the old house—Klaus still owns it, I think—or maybe he's visiting his father. Tom, is it OK if I change my mind? Now I'm here and now I've seen him, I'd really rather be somewhere else."

*

Imre was very annoyed with himself for having turned tail and bolted when he ought to have greeted those people with a careless air of enormous *bonhomie*, as a man-about-town possessed of considerable wealth should, or simply stuck his nose in the air and walked past them as if they didn't exist. He had been very pleased to find that the good citizens of Ulm had very little enthusiasm or respect for tittle-tattle coming from the other side of the Atlantic or even from the other side of what they regarded as the German Sea. The lawyers had acted is if they were very pleased to see him. His legacy, which included a considerable amount of ready cash, would soon be available, so he could blue the money from Klaus and Wolf TV as freely as he pleased. He had never had any significant money before, and it was a heady sensation.

He had decided to continue renting his father's old apartment for the time being, while he sorted out the mass of papers and personal possessions that had been left behind, but he was enjoying himself and there was no hurry. So why had the sight of Tom and Halcyon put him so very much out of countenance? Well, for one thing, they had treated him with derision and humiliated him in front of Anne Weston. For another, they reminded him of Alison, whom he was very anxious to forget. Furthermore, they forced him to remember the ill-judged behavior that had more or less finished him as a participant in anything to do with CW or Archway, at least in America and England. And, finally, they were two people who had found great happiness in each other, while Imre was learning that although money acted as a magnet, the kind of objects that it attracted were usually worn on the surface and hollow inside.

He decided that the best way to regain his equilibrium would be to go back to the apartment and get down to some serious work on his father's papers. It was there that he received another shock, in the form of a shoebox full of letters from Maria Schmidt, later Maria Johnson. The sheer quantity of the letters and the beginning of the first one he looked at—"My Darling Bela"—shed a new and very disquieting light on a question to which he thought he knew the answer. After spending several hours on the letters, he was sure that he had been wrong, that everyone had been wrong. Maria had had a steamy affair with his father, and it had settled down into the sort of casual sexual give and take that could go on unhindered by other relationships, including marriage. In a letter mailed from Glastonbury in July 1961 she had given an amusing description of her last encounter with Klaus, and Imre was slightly shocked to discover that after humoring her old lover she had spent the rest of the night with Bela. "The old boy was so preoccupied with making his final fling a good one that he could hardly perform at all. Anyway, it isn't that he can't, it's just that he doesn't turn me on the way he did when I didn't know so much about sex, so it was a relief to get back into bed with you."

A few days later she gave an intimate comparison of Phillip's technique with Bela's. Phillip, apparently, wasn't bad but she couldn't wait to get back to Ulm for a few more weeks, and she was sure they'd be able to arrange something when Bela came to New York. She found it very amusing that neither Klaus nor Phillip had the slightest idea of what was going on. The final revelation came a few months later in a letter from New York. "Guess what! I'm pregnant!! I'm sure it wasn't Klaus and from the timing I don't think it can have been Phillip—I don't have to explain, do I? I just hope he won't figure it out. So congratulations!!!"

Now everything fell into place. Imre understood why his family had moved to New York in 1962. Evidently the affair had been much more serious for Bela than for Maria, and it had gone on under Phillip's idealistic nose until 1979, when Maria died and Bela returned to Ulm, perhaps to be near Alison. Imre became quite certain that Alison was his half-sister and, examining his feelings towards her in this new light, he found them too complex to grasp. The physical attraction was undiminished, perhaps even heightened, and there was very little sense of the emotional abhorrence or moral inhibition that he would have expected to feel at the idea of having sex with her. It was too difficult to think about, so he focused on Klaus instead. How could he have failed to know what was going on between Maria and Bela? Judging by Maria's letter, he hadn't been able to perform on that last night; so why had he let Alison go on thinking he was her father? This was something that Imre could get his teeth into and he mentally rubbed his hands together at the thought of a new way of making life miserable for his old boss. In spite of all his animosities and resentments, the perception that Klaus was virile, indestructible and spiritually superior continually pulled Imre back to his old discipleship mode; but at the same time it made the prospect of taking him down another peg even more enticing. It would have come as an immense shock to Imre to learn that his former master was now a feeble old man lying in a hospital bed in Glastonbury.

*

During the first few days after their venture up the Tor, Alison and Klaus were able to settle into a routine. There was a small general store within easy walking distance, where Alison could do their basic grocery shopping. Mr. and Mrs. Trathgannon made weekly visits to the supermarket in Glastonbury and were happy to pick up a few items for the Hübels. Klaus had talked about buying a car, but he now seemed to be chronically fatigued, and lacked the vitality for such a venture. He and Alison stayed at home most of the time, making extensive use of Tom's personal library, which contained many books on the history and philosophy of science as well as a lot of miscellaneous fiction and volumes of Somerset lore.

In her precipitate flight from the hospital in Peoria, Alison had left her book on reincarnation and karma behind, but with Klaus at hand, books on Cosmic Wisdom were not necessary. His ability to quote freely from almost any of Goerner's dozens of books and thousands of lectures was both a blessing and a curse. It gave them plenty to talk about, but now, wherever they started, they always seemed to come back to the prospect of an agonizing passage through the spiritual world and succeeding incarnations in which they had to pay for their present follies. The big item on Alison's mind was her contemplated suicide, which was the greatest karmic no-no that could possibly be imagined. Her spirit would be bound to the earth for the foreseeable future and she would undergo suffering far beyond what she was now experiencing.

"Once I am gone", Klaus tried to reassure her, "you will no longer feel the need to end your life", but Alison didn't believe it. In order to justify herself she finally made up her mind to tell Klaus the whole story of her relationship to Billy and all the details of her abduction and rape.

Klaus listened in silence while his inner voice screamed, "No, this cannot be!"

But it could be, and it was, and it was all because he had been too proud and besotted to admit that his last session with Maria had been a flop. If Alison was worried about her karma, what could he say about his own?

Well, maybe Goerner was wrong. If only the higher powers would speak to him again as they had on that rainy night that now seemed so long ago. In spite of his weakness he knew that he must somehow climb the Tor again, so one morning at the end of August he announced this intention to his wife.

"You can't do that", Alison said. "It might kill you."

And then she thought perhaps that was what Klaus wanted, and if it did she would then have to make her own decision about life or death.

"I must go", he said, "but it is not necessary that you accompany me."

"Don't be silly, Klaus."

*

It was a chilly day of low cloud and thin mist, with a taste of autumn in the air. Everything was dripping gently, and the Tor was almost invisible as they made their way slowly between the hedgerows. By the time they reached the wicket gate from Stone Down Lane into the fields below the Tor, the mist had thickened into a steady drizzle. They had taken only a few steps into the meadow when Klaus gave a little gasp and sank to his knees.

"What is it, Klaus?"

"I do not know. I feel . . ."

He slumped sideways and lay on the wet grass, apparently unconscious and breathing noisily. Alison couldn't think of anything to do but to protect her husband from the rain, and hope that some help would come along. After covering him with the raincoat that she had borrowed from Mrs. Trathgannon, she removed her sweater and made a pillow of it.

Klaus made an effort to speak.

"Why are you being so kind to me?"

Alison was wondering the same thing.

"I don't know, Klaus—I truly don't know."

A feeling of the imminence of death prompted Klaus to speak again.

"Alison, there is something I have to tell you. I have not been entirely frank with you . . ."

"Is anything wrong?"

A man on a bicycle was looking over the gate.

"My husband—he's been taken ill."

"Oh dear", said the cyclist as he dismounted and approached, "and you with nothing to keep the rain off you. Oh, and he's an old man. You should get him into hospital."

"Yes", said Alison, feeling that she must be dealing with the village idiot. "Could you go and find a telephone?"

"A telephone? Me? I don't know. I have to . . ."

Klaus spoke. It wasn't much more than a whisper.

"Please do not bother. I have no wish to cause further trouble to anyone."

The man gaped.

"Well, I don't know, I'm sure. In that case I'll be getting along."

Which he did.

Klaus was unconscious now. Alison knelt by him for long time, feeling that she couldn't leave him and that the best chance was that someone else would come along. Eventually she heard the sound of hooves, and two people on horseback appeared in the lane. Alison, soaked to the skin and shivering, called to them and they quickly sized up the situation.

One galloped back up the lane, while the other tied her horse and joined Alison.

"My brother's gone back to the farm to telephone 999", she said.

*

"Are you Mrs. Hübel?" the doctor asked in open amazement. "I beg your pardon, but he's well over eighty, isn't he?"

Alison, wearing a blanket over a hospital gown, was sitting in the hospital waiting room. "Yes, I'm Mrs. Hübel", she answered wearily, "and he's eighty-four."

"Is there any history of heart trouble?"

"Not that I know of. He's always been very proud of his heart, but he's been very tired recently."

"Well, I can't tell you any details now—we'll have to do some more tests—but there's certainly a problem there. He's awake and talking and you can see him now, but he's quite weak and we'll have to keep him here for a day or two. And then I think he's going to have to take things very easy."

Alison was still wondering what it was that her husband hadn't been frank about, but at the sight of him, his eyes dull and his skin pale and sagging, she knew this wasn't the time for questions. She felt very sorry for him, not in a connubial way, but simply as one distressed human being to another. She held his hand and, with odd formality, he said, "Thank you for coming."

*

Klaus was in the hospital for a week, during which time the medical staff learned of his former escapade on the Tor, when Halcyon and Tom rescued him, and of the assault in Peoria. It seemed that there was some valve damage and possibly the onset of congestive heart disease. In any case, when the patient is eighty-four the tendency is to deal with the problem and not spend a lot of time hunting for the causes, so Klaus was sent home in an ambulance with several boxes of pills and the admonition that his days of mountain climbing and other strenuous physical activities were over. Mrs. Trathgannon fussed over him like an anxious hen, and it became even more difficult to keep her out of the upstairs apartment.

With rest and medication, Klaus grew a little stronger. As the immediate prospect of death receded, his determination to tell Alison everything ebbed with it, so when she asked him what he had started to say while they waited in the rain, he told her that he couldn't remember.

There was something else on Alison's mind. She was worried about Billy Bigley, so she sat down and wrote to Candy.

(61)

The comforts of Imre's life in Ulm were some compensation for his lack of desirable female companionship. He was sensible enough to realize that although the possession of a quarter of a million dollars was a pleasant thing, he would still have to find some form of regular income. This could be postponed for a while, however—one never knew what might turn up. He decided to keep his hair short, lose a little weight and see if he could enjoy himself among the gold-diggers without excessive expenditure. Meanwhile, he finished dealing with his father's papers and possessions and pondered his relationship with Alison. After years of fantasizing about her, it was hard for him to think of her as anything except a sexual partner; but the thought of her as a sister had its attractions, and a new kind of fantasy emerged. Perhaps they would live near each other and meet from time to time. They might have lunch and discuss Cosmic Wisdom. There might be embraces when they met and who knows . . . Better try not to think about that.

There were several hurdles that would have to be got over before this could happen. One was that Alison would have to know that she was his sister—well, half-sister—and another was that there was a lot that she would have to forgive. This led him to look at his behavior though Alison's eyes, which made him feel very uncomfortable, and to relieve his feelings by blaming Klaus for everything. It was Klaus who had really screwed things up by not telling the truth when he had the chance. Well, it might be possible to achieve Alison's enlightenment and Klaus's discomfiture at the same time. Imre began to think about writing another letter. The big problem was that he didn't know where Klaus and Alison were, but he consoled himself with the thought that there was no hurry; thanks to his legacy he could afford to take his time.

There was, of course, another hurdle, which pre-empted all the others; Alison had found him quite repulsive long before the present situation developed. But he conveniently forgot this.

311

*

The problem of Klaus's and Alison's whereabouts also afflicted Inspector Krebs and Candy Bigley. With the help of Alison's money, the Bigleys had raised bail for Billy, but although his case had been considered by lawyers, Assistant District Attorneys, police officials and judges, it was still in limbo. Although Klaus and Alison had recorded their testimony with the utmost care, they were required to appear in person, and the result of their efforts to avoid the media was that the police had no idea where they were. The Inspector had a bigger item on his mind, however. Thanks to the efforts of some intrepid policewomen, the rapists had been trapped, and now Alison was needed so that they could be charged with their assault on her. As far as the police were concerned, dealing with Billy was a minor matter in comparison to the task of putting these creatures away for the maximum possible time, but by the time the sub poenas and the letters from Candy started arriving at the brownstone on West 88th Street, the place was deserted.

*

Tom and Halcyon had managed to stay out of sight by such manoeuvres as never booking anything in advance. This is possible when you have plenty of money. If the car ferry is full when you arrive at Ostend, you simply spend a pleasant evening doing the town, and stay the night at a convenient hotel. So there were no fanfares when they arrived in Dover early on the day of Klaus's heart attack, and the old Morris Minor attracted no attention at all.

This was a Monday, and Glastonbury Grammar School was due to open for the Michaelmas Term on the Tuesday of the following week. Since they were going to have to find somewhere to live, they drove straight to Glastonbury. It would have been nice to see Halcyon's Mum and Tom's Dad, but those pleasures had to be shelved for the time being. Still trying to avoid the media as long as possible, they found a small bed-and-breakfast a mile or so out on the road to Street and only a few minutes' drive from Ashwell Lane. Tom's dark glasses and incipient beard seemed to be quite effective, and they remained unrecognized for the time being. Tom telephoned his father and received a blow-by-blow account of the fake wedding.

"And", Lord Otterill added at the end of the story, "I want you to come up and talk to Andrew Davy at the earliest opportunity.

Tom was beginning to feel excited about working as a science correspondent, but there were more immediate things to deal with.

"I have to go to my old apartment to sort things out with Mrs. T and pick up some books", he told Halcyon over breakfast the next morning, "and then I want to see what's up with Elwyn."

"I s'pose that means you have to talk to Klaus and Alison. Do you want me to come with you?"

"Yes—you always seem to know the right thing to say and, to be honest, I'm scared about seeing Alison."

"I know—so am I. OK, but I better not go near Elwyn. Do you know who I'd like to see?"

"Wait—let me guess—Bill Graveney, right?"

"Right."

"OK—then you'd better wear one of your minis."

"I was just thinking the same thing."

But when Halcyon joined Tom in the car, she was wearing jeans and a dark blue shirt.

"I don't want any more old men getting interested", she said. "One was enough."

*

As was to be expected on a bright day in late August, Mrs. Trathgannon was weeding the flower beds in her front garden. She looked up as Halcyon and Tom emerged from the car, and for once she was tongue-tied.

Seeing the problem, and half afraid that the old lady might start curtseying, Tom said, "Don't worry about it. We're still the same people and you can still call me Mr. Dexter or Tom, if you feel like it. Anyway, it's nice to see you, and I'd just like to collect a few of my books. And considering all the trouble you've taken, there's really no need for you to return any of the rent."

"That's very kind, Mr. Dexter, but I like everything to be right and proper. I'm very glad to see you and the young lady properly married. Goodness me, you are a handsome couple and I'm sure you'll be a credit to the nobility, especially when the beard grows a little more. But I have some news for you about Mr. Hübel, so you'd better come in and have a cup of tea."

"They went out for a walk early yesterday morning", she said while the kettle was boiling, "and didn't come back all day. Mrs. Hübel came in about ten o'clock at night and I went to see if she was all right. She said her husband had had a heart attack and he was in hospital. He's pretty bad, it seems, and they say he'll have to be very careful for the rest of his life. She went to see him again this morning and she didn't say when she was coming back."

Mrs. Trathgannon seemed to think that the right thing for them to do would be to visit the hospital immediately and pay their respects to the distressed Hübels. She also thought it would be quite all right for Tom to go up and collect whatever he needed, and Halcyon went with him.

"All as clean as a new pin", Tom said as they got back into the car. "Not a speck of dust anywhere—do you think that's Mrs. T?"

"Maybe, but Klaus was always a neat-freak. I don't know about Alison, though."

What they didn't know about Alison was that to cope with her inner disgust she needed her outer world to be utterly clean and totally ordered.

"Do you agree that we're not going to the hospital", Tom asked.

"Yes! The last thing Alison would need would be to have us poking around."

*

Tom drove Halcyon to Bill Graveney's house and escorted her to the front door.

"Well, congratulations, your Lord-and-Ladyship", Bill said, with a broad grin and no trace of deference.

"You can cut that out, Bill", Halcyon replied, giving the old gentleman a hearty hug. "Tom has to go and see someone, and I just wanted you to know I've taken all the advice you gave and some that you didn't. Only I'm already full of Mrs. T's tea so don't bother with the kettle."

Tom wasn't gone long. There was no one at home at Elwyn's house, and the disheveled appearance of the garden suggested that the place had been deserted for some time. Something had obviously gone badly wrong with his scheme for solving Elwyn's heart problem. Tom made his way thoughtfully back to Graveney's house, and he was still looking concerned when Halcyon met him at the door.

"Oh Lor'", she said. "Something bad's happened, hasn't it?"

"They've all gone and it looks as though nobody's been there for weeks. If you ask me, Diana's moved out with Mickey, and Elwyn can't stand being there on his own."

"Well, come on in. Bill's getting drinks ready and we can worry about Diana later."

"It's Elwyn I'm worried about. I might have to take his classes."

Tom spoke lightly, but he was concerned about his friend and felt irrationally responsible.

"Anyway, has Bill made a pass at you yet?"

Halcyon made a fake moue.

"Not even one."

"I told you you should have worn a mini."

Bill wondered why Tom was back so soon. When Tom simply said that there was no one home at Elwyn's house, Halcyon said, "Come on, Tom, tell Bill the story. He's very smart and he'll probably think of something."

With occasional help from his wife, Tom gave a brief version of the story. When they had finished, they both looked expectantly at Bill, who was amused by the idea that he might have a cure for Elwyn's condition.

"You remind me of the story of the two old soldiers, both in their eighties, reminiscing about their early days in the army. The first one says, 'You remember those pills, George?' And George replies, 'What pills, Arthur?' And Arthur says, 'Those pills they gave us so we wouldn't keep thinking about gals.' Well the conversation goes on and eventually George says, 'Well, what about those pills?' And Arthur says, 'Well, I think mine are beginning to work.'"

After the polite chuckles had died down, Halcyon said, "I don't know about pills, but can't it also be done with surgery?"

"That might be rather hard on Diana", Bill said.

"In other words", Tom concluded, "I ought to have left it to them to sort it out for themselves if they could."

"Maybe, but I'm sure you didn't do any harm. Anyway, if you need a chemistry master, there's always Mr. Takacs. I suspect he may be unemployed at the moment."

This last was said with a sly grin, but Tom was not amused.

"Imre! He can't tell the difference between an anion and an onion."

"What's an anion?" asked Halcyon.

(62)

Like most English headmasters, Mr. Pryce-Jones had no particular liking for faculty meetings. Assignments and schedules had been mailed out towards the end of August, and there would be only a brief gathering at five o'clock on the day before school opened. While Elwyn's house remained deserted, this would be the earliest that Tom could expect to see his old friend. A visit to the school and a couple of hours spent checking the labs revealed that everything was in order, but Tom doubted very much whether Elwyn would be back for opening day. There was nothing to be done about it, however, so he took Halcyon on a house-hunting expedition.

Halcyon's picture of bliss was a little Tudor cottage with a thatched roof, timbered white walls, window boxes and roses, but the nearest they could find was an old redbrick farm cottage on Stone Down Lane, with roses in front and an extensive vegetable garden behind. Next to the cottage was a new-looking garage, and at the bottom of the back garden there was a shed. It was locked, but the window was clean and all the usual garden tools were to be seen neatly arranged on the walls.

"What's the rope for?" Halcyon asked.

"Probably a clothes line", Tom said, pointing at a post a few feet from the back fence. "You'll look very pretty hanging out the washing every Monday morning."

The "For Sale" sign gave the address of an agent on High Street.

"Two up, two down, fully modernized, h and c, upstairs bathroom and loo, garage and toolshed. Only a mile to the bus stop and convenient for the Tor if you like walking. Engineer's report."

While agent's clerk was doing his spiel, Halcyon was sitting at the coffee table, looking though the listings. Seeing something that she recognized, she exclaimed, "Look, Tom, it's the B-S house. I wonder if the poor old girl's kicked the bucket."

"No, Miss", said the clerk. "If you mean Mrs. Barrington-Smythe, she wants to go and live in Harrogate Spa, though why she'd want to do that when we're only a few miles from Bath, I can't imagine."

"She's probably in love with her doctor", Tom suggested.

"Beautiful, commodious residence", the clerk intoned like a child repeating a lesson, which he more or less was, "two recep, three bed, two bath, h and c up and down, garage, stands in nearly half an acre, wanna see it? The old lady put in a caretaker, so all you have to do is knock on the door."

He eyed his prospective customers. Tom, with his half-grown beard and sunglasses, had a slightly hippyish air, and Halcyon looked like not much more than a schoolgirl.

"Bit pricey, though", he added.

"Never mind about the price", Tom said. "What do you think, Halcyon? You actually stayed there."

"I think it would be a real lark—let's go and give it another look."

"OK, but first I want to pay a visit to Mirabelle. I'm hungry."

"Mirabelle?"

Halcyon was puzzled, and so was Tom until he remembered that it was not Halcyon that he had treated to fish and chips.

Blushing furiously, he said, "Oh, I'm sorry. I'd forgotten that you hadn't met my fish and chip lady."

Halcyon was very quick on the uptake.

"It was Alison, wasn't it."

"Yes, but . . ."

"It's all right, Tom, it's all right. Just hold me for a moment."

While the prolonged embrace was going on, the clerk was muttering to himself, "Halcyon—that rings a bell. And him—I'm sure I've seen him somewhere."

Emerging from Tom's arms and recovering her poise, Halcyon looked sternly at the clerk.

"It's really just two bed and a box you could almost swing a cat in. Come on, Tom, I want to meet Mirabelle."

Having handed over an order to view and wished his prospective clients a very good afternoon, the clerk thought for a moment and pulled a file from the cabinet behind the counter.

"Shit! The old girl's not on the phone."

After putting up the "Closed for Lunch" sign, he went and got his camera and his bicycle.

*

Mirabelle was unexpectedly tactful. She had seen Imre's exposé, and Tom's stubble and sunglasses were of no avail.

"He may be a Lordship", she said to Halcyon, "but he's a good one and he'll never let you down."

"How does she know?" Halcyon asked.

"She doesn't. She's just a romantic old soul trying to make things OK. But she's right. I'll never let you down."

*

"Look", said Halcyon as they pulled up outside the B-S residence, "the old wagon's still there."

"That's not surprising—we've only been away a few weeks. Maybe it goes with the house."

"Or maybe it doesn't go at all."

Preferring to stay in Harrogate for the rest of the summer, Mrs. B-S had left a caretaker in charge. Having been briefed by the perspiring clerk from the estate agent's office, this rheumy and rheumatic elderly gentleman was to pretend that he didn't know who the clients were and, in pointing out the assets of the property, to bear in mind that they had virtually unlimited wealth at their disposal. Unfortunately, the old boy had been brought up to respect the aristocracy. On opening the front door, he bowed with creaky ceremony and greeted them hoarsely with the words, "Welcome, your Lordship and Ladyship. My name is Alfred, and it would be a pleasure to show you round the premises."

"Please don't bother", said Halcyon kindly, "we know our way around."

But Alfred, not being allowed to lead, insisted on following, not because he thought they might get up to any mischief, but because they had such nice voices and seemed so young and beautiful to his tired old eyes. Everything looked exactly the same except that the box room had been fitted up as a temporary dwelling for Alfred. The do-over included the installation of a small television set, on which he had seen Imre's broadcast.

"Very nice", Halcyon said.

"Thank you, your Ladyship. Mrs. Barrington-Smythe has been very good to me. But, if I may say so, you should keep an eye on young Robby."

"Robby? Who's Robby?"

"The clerk at the estate agent's. He doesn't mean any harm, but he's as thick as three in a bed with Johnny Berry."

"Who's Johnny Berry?" Halcyon asked patiently.

"He works at the *Evening Star.*"

"That's the local paper", Tom put in.

"Yes, your lordship. They call it that because it's always late coming out." Alfred chuckled with antique merriment at his little joke.

"Well, bugger that!" Halcyon remarked, much to Alfred's surprise, before reverting to the question of buying the house. "What do you think, Tom? I kind of like the idea."

Tom wasn't so sure. It was true that he had never been there with Alison, but the place made him feel a little uncomfortable, and there was something to be said for making a clean break from old associations. So why, a disturbing little voice said, had he come back to Glastonbury?

"Let's sleep on it."

"That's what Klaus always used to say. Oops . . ."

Tom had thought that Halcyon's period as Klaus's mistress was not a problem for him, but now the image of the two of them in bed and probably not sleeping found him unexpectedly vulnerable. Halcyon saw the change in his face.

"Sorry, darling", he began, "I . . .", but he didn't know how to finish the sentence.

"Come on, Tom, let's get out of this silly old place. Take me home and I'll show you how much I love you."

So they did that, and the next day they signed a contract for the cottage on Stone Down Lane. The previous owner had left it clean but empty, so they took the precaution of measuring all the rooms. Then, being young, and one of them being impetuous, they piled into the Morris and drove to Stepney. One result of this was that they didn't see the headline in the *Evening Star.*

"Lord Leyford and Bride House-hunting in Glastonbury"

Below was a very clear picture of Tom and Halcyon leaving the B-S residence arm-in-arm. This was followed by an article detailing their visit to the estate agent and their interest in Mrs. Barrington-Smythe's house and the cottage on Stone Down Lane. Thanks to Imre, everyone in Glastonbury already knew that the pleasant and unassuming physics master at the Grammar School was really Lord Otterill's son, but he had been out of sight for several weeks and it was a tremendous scoop on the part of the local paper to bring him back. The tidings soon spread to QTV and the Murdoch media empire, so, for the first time, Halcyon's picture became available on both sides of the Atlantic to anyone who was interested.

(63)

Iris Tompkins was not feeling quite so happy. Her "friend", the company doctor, was getting very nervous about the fact that the woman with whom he was having his bit on the side was in danger of becoming a public figure. Ordinary discretion might not be enough if she was being followed about by reporters with highly developed noses for smutty little secrets.

"I haven't seen him for nearly a month", she said over the teacups to Tom and Halcyon. "And if he sees this"—she indicated the TV set on which the latest revelations were appearing—"it'll all be over. Not that I care that much—he's nice and he's good at what he does, but I'm not in love with him. It's just that it's so—well, convenient, and maybe Bert will have to go back to work, although that might be good for him."

"Maybe it would be good for you, Mum. I think you're in a bit of a rut. You'd be free all day and someone else might turn up. You made a real hit with Tom's Dad."

Iris smiled dreamily.

"Now that's a real man."

*

Fortescue was delighted to see Tom, and his dignity was not seriously damaged by the receipt of a fervent hug from her new Ladyship.

"If your Ladyship pleases, we are putting you and his Lordship in Fulfillment—*Fulfillment* is really a publication for the elderly, but the name seemed, if I may say so, quite appropriate."

"Excellent, Fortescue", Tom said. "Your humor, if I may say so, improves with age."

"Your Lordship is most kind. His Grace is in the study."

Lord Otterill rose to greet them and, having recognized Halcyon as a compulsive hugger, did a little jig round his desk to get within range. She looked at him and said coolly, "You know I only hug people I really like."

For once in his life, the Duke of Brueland and Street looked slightly crestfallen, so Halcyon put her arms round him and gave him a very tight squeeze.

"Golly", he said, "you really had me worried for a moment. Well, it didn't take long for you to get back into the news. That's a very nice picture. Is this stuff all true?"

"Sort of", said Tom, "and as a matter of fact, tomorrow's news will be that we bought the cottage on Stone Down Lane. We're going to call it Stone Down Cottage."

"Well, good for you. How's your Mum, Halcyon?"

When Halcyon explained about the company doctor's dilemma, Lord Otterill seemed very interested.

"Old Bert would hate to go back to work, wouldn't he?"

"I'm not sure he could even do it. He's been off such a long time."

"Hmmm . . ." said Lord Otterill.

*

The next morning, which was Saturday, Tom spent half an hour making a mysterious phone call before he and Halcyon set off for the West Country.

"What was that all about?" Halcyon wanted to know, but Tom merely smiled and said, "Just finishing off a bit of business."

"Well, it can't be anything bad or you wouldn't sit there looking like the cat that swallowed the canary."

Things got a little more mysterious when Tom stayed on the road to Bath instead of taking the turn to Glastonbury. Eventually they parked outside the show room of Langford's Motors and Tom said, "Come on!"

Standing in the yard next to the show room was a bright red Mini-Cooper.

"That's your wedding present. Here's Bob Langford—he'll show you how it works."

"Beautiful little car—ten years old but better than new, not a scratch or a dent anywhere . . ."

"OK, Bob", Tom interposed, "I've already bought it."

"I know, but I thought the young lady would like to know all about it."

Bob was refreshingly free from obsequiousness.

"Now the one thing you have to realize is that the steering is rack and pinion and it's very responsive and if you forget yourself you'll be in the ditch before you can say 'Lord 'elp us'."

Halcyon was too excited to pay much attention.

"But, Tom, I haven't given you anything", she said when she had calmed down a little.

"No, you've given me everything. And you're going to need a car of your own, so I thought I might as well make a present of it. Now listen to what Bob's telling you because I want you back in Glastonbury all in one piece. You'd better follow me because if I had to follow you, I'd never keep up in this old crate."

*

Back at the B and B, with a dull green Morris and a bright red mini-Cooper parked outside, Tom said, "We have an empty house to furnish and I start work next week so we'd better start figuring things out."

"I have an idea", Halcyon said. "I was wondering if your Dad would lend us Alice for a few days."

"Brilliant! Alice knows everything, and you could talk to her and maybe order some stuff from London. And I think there's a spare room here where she could stay while we get organized."

*

Tom spent most of Monday in the physics lab before going to the faculty meeting at five o'clock. Colleagues he bumped into congratulated him on his marriage but tactfully refrained from commenting on his aristocratic status. There was no sign of Elwyn all day, but about twenty minutes after the meeting started, when the teachers had finished getting their cups of tea and the headmaster had just begun his opening remarks, he slipped in and sat close to the door. He looked healthy and suntanned, but he obstinately refused to meet Tom's eye. After a graceful reference to the presence of blue blood in the room, Mr. Pryce-Jones spoke about the difficulty of maintaining the traditions of English Grammar School education in the present political climate, asked for greater economy in the use of materials, wished everyone good luck, and added in a stern afterthought that it was really a matter of good preparation and management rather than luck. Teachers yawned covertly. Flossie sat next to the headmaster and took notes, although what possible use they would be no one could imagine. At the end, everyone stood up and by the time Tom looked round, Elwyn had gone. Flossie touched his arm.

"Can I have a word with you, Tom?"

"Of course. What's up?"

"Come down to my office."

Sitting in the secretary's office, looking out over the playing fields, Tom heard a tale of woe.

"It's about Wendy", Flossie began.

A whole scenario flashed before Tom's mental eye.

"Elwyn?"

"Yes, Elwyn. Well, she's twenty and has a mind of her own, but going off to the Riviera for a month with a married man—I ask you. Where the hell did he get the money, and what's happened to poor Diana and the child?"

Tom explained about the money. He was feeling angry and stupid.

"Where are they living?" he asked.

"Somewhere in Bath, I think, but Wendy won't talk to me now. When I found out she was going away with him I told her what I thought, and she didn't like it. She said Diana henpecked him and shouldn't have got so fat, and a man needs someone attractive to come home to. I told her that if she takes after her mother, she'll be much fatter than Diana by the time she's thirty. She packed her bags and left without saying a word, and I haven't seen her since. Diana's gone away too, and nobody knows where. And how that man has the nerve to turn up here, I can't imagine. You saw how he slipped in and out without talking to anyone."

"It's a terrible situation", Tom agreed, "but I can't think of anything we can do about it."

"I can", said Flossie militantly. "I'm going to tell the HM and see if I can get him sacked. When the silly little besom realizes he has no job and no money she'll be back home like a shot."

"I doubt it", Tom thought, but he didn't say anything.

*

Tom arrived at school half an hour early the next day, and was soon surrounded by an excited crowd of students, including Janet and Marilyn. Some of them quite seriously wanted to know if they had to call him, "Your Lordship", while others thought that the whole story had been made up by the newspapers. The crowd broke up when the bell rang for assembly, and Janet shyly put a beautifully wrapped package in Tom's hand. It was about the size of a shoe box and quite heavy.

"It's your wedding present", Marilyn said, "from us. Don't open it till you get home. And we were wondering if . . ."

Marilyn looked at Janet, who helped her out.

". . . We could possibly meet . . . I mean, one day . . ."

". . . Lady Tom, only we don't know what to call her", Marilyn finished with a rush. "She's so lovely."

Tom smiled.

"I'm sure she'll be delighted and she'll tell you what to call her. I can't invite you or I'd have to do the same for everybody, but if you happened to be going by on your bicycles on Saturday afternoon . . ."

*

While Tom was at school a large furniture van drew up behind the little red car outside Stone Down Cottage and three people descended from the cab. Two of them were large and muscular, and the third was the diminutive figure of Alice. Carpets, beds, tables, chairs and a refrigerator appeared and disappeared like magic, while Alice directed the traffic and Halcyon stood by in an awed daze.

"We ought really to have scrubbed all the floors with disinfectant", Alice said, "but the previous owners seem to have made quite a good job of cleaning the place."

She looked at the mini.

"Is that vehicle safe?"

"Of course it's safe—Tom gave it to me."

"He also told me that you are an excellent driver. Well I suppose I'll have to take his word for it."

Alice had momentarily forgotten who the young girl was that she was talking to.

"Your Ladyship", she added.

"Do me a favor", Halcyon said. "Just call me Halcyon except when old Fortescue is about. Anyway, Tom's right, so where are we going?"

"To buy a few household necessities."

"Oh, I get it—toilet paper and soap and so on."

"Yes, Your Ladyship—Halcyon—and something for his Lordship's breakfast."

*

324

Tom arrived at Stone Down Cottage just in time to see the furniture van disappearing into the distance.

"Where's Alice?" he asked.

"She wouldn't stay", said Halcyon, pointing to the departing van. "She's crammed into the front with two enormous guys. Come in and see. It's not finished yet, but she said you were quite capable of doing the rest. We still have to unpack the crockery and there are no cabinets or shelves in the kitchen—just chairs, a table and a fridge. She thought the most important thing was to provide a bedroom fit for a lord and his lady."

Halcyon could walk and talk at the same time, so by now they were standing in the front bedroom, which looked across the narrow lane towards the Tor. Alice had dug up a beautiful old brass bedstead with the traditional knobs but, as Halcyon was quick to explain, the spring and the mattress were brand new and the latest design.

"I'm going to do the curtains", she said, "but Alice told me exactly what to get and how to do it. She was going to send somebody down, but I told her that anyone who can manage euphonics costumes shouldn't have any trouble with curtains. Then she said we at least ought to get blinds, and I had to promise not to stand at the window with nothing on. What do you think?"

"I think you should definitely wear shoes."

"What?"

"When you stand in front of the window."

*

They were still booked in at the B and B, but the new bed was much too enticing, so the next morning Tom woke up in his own home. Halcyon was already up and various noises in the kitchen indicated what she was up to. Tom put on his dressing gown and went down just in time to watch his gorgeous wife cracking eggs, cutting up tomatoes and putting bacon into the frying pan.

"Good morning, m'Lady", he said, "You look like a real expert. Did Iris teach you?"

"Yes, my Mum's a very good cook and anyway, plain cooking's easy if you put your mind to it. But we forgot to buy a toaster so you'll have to have fried bread like the working classes."

"That's OK and in any case you're not exactly a plain cook. And all this talk about cooking reminds of something I've been meaning to ask you."

"Let me guess", Halcyon said, putting a plate of bacon and eggs in front of him and her arms round his neck. "You want me to stop taking the pill?"

"Yes."

Halcyon sat down in front of her own plate but didn't start eating.

"Tom, I'm afraid you're going to be very angry with me."

"What have you done? Out with it, woman!"

"Well, I thought it didn't matter after we were married, so I already stopped."

Moments like this always sent Tom's hormones into overdrive, but it would soon be time to leave for school, so he merely kissed his wife and told her to eat her breakfast.

"You're probably going to need the extra nourishment", he said. "Oh, I almost forgot—we have a wedding present. It's still in the bottom of my backpack."

"Who from?"

"Well, you have two admirers at school—they think you're outrageously beautiful and they want to meet you."

He rummaged in his backpack and handed the present to Halcyon.

"It's a silver plated biscuit barrel", she said. "That's what people always give, only I think it's really chromium."

"I don't think Janet would have done anything so corny—let's see."

The wrappings concealed a box labeled "Glastonbury Treasures" and inside there was a scale model of the Tor, all done in exquisite detail.

"'To Lord and Lady Tom with love from Janet and Marilyn'", Halcyon read. "They must be in love with you."

"No, they fell in love with your picture and they want to come and see you in person. I told them we'd be at home on Saturday afternoon if they just happened to be passing."

"Oh Lor'! How old are these kids?"

"A few months younger than you."

"Well, you know what'll happen, don't you. They'll tell all their friends and the whole school will be here."

"Oh—I hadn't thought of that."

*

Halcyon had quite a gift for foretelling the future, but on this occasion she was wrong. Marilyn and Janet didn't want anyone else at their party, so they hugged the knowledge to themselves and arrived at Stone Down Cottage on their bicycles just in time for tea on Saturday afternoon. It was a chilly, drizzly day, even though it was technically still summer, so Tom had lit a fire. Halcyon, wearing jeans and an old sweater, and not looking in the least like a prospective duchess, gave each of the girls a hug.

"We don't know whether to all you Lady Leyford or Lady Tom", Janet said.

"For goodness sake just call me Halcyon. I know it's a funny name but you'll get used to it. But I don't know what you're going to call him."

Marilyn turned to Tom with the air of one who expects a hug, and Tom said, "I thought you didn't approve of men."

Marilyn said, "We don't, but we still like hugging."

So Tom hugged her and Janet, and Halcyon said, "Hey, what about me?" and Tom hugged her, too, after which she announced, "I'm sorry the butler's away so there's no cucumber sandwiches and we forgot to buy a toaster, but we can sit round the fire with hot chocolate and make toast."

And Tom said, "You can call me Tom, but only within these four walls. Got it?"

There was only one toasting fork but Tom had improvised another by wiring a steel skewer to an ordinary fork and they managed quite well. When they were full of hot chocolate and toast they stood and admired the model of the Tor, which had been arranged on the sideboard.

"It's lovely", Halcyon said. "When the weather's like this we can look at it and just imagine being up there."

"It's supposed to be very accurate", Janet said proudly. "All the circles and contours are exactly the way they are on the hill, so if you study it carefully you'll be able to find your way in the dark."

"Nice girls", Halcyon said, when she and Tom were alone again. "I don't know why you didn't marry one of them."

"I don't think the headmaster would have liked it."

"Well, the headmaster wouldn't have got it, would he."

*

The reason why Alice refused to stay overnight in Glastonbury was that she and the furniture van had a date in London. At precisely midnight they pulled up in front of Iris's house in Stepney, where they found Williams waiting with Lord Otterill's town car. There they packed the van with all the furniture and personal items that Iris and Bert wanted to take with them, and convinced Bert that he didn't need to take his TV, as there was a better one where he was going. Iris locked the front door and they set off for the Otterill residence.

(64)

While Tom was on his way home from his first day of teaching, his old landlady was delivering some groceries and a newspaper to the Hübels. Klaus was asleep, so Alison got the full benefit of Mrs. T's enthusiasm.

"Look", she said, exhibiting the front page of the *Evening Star*. "They've bought that cottage on Stone Down Lane, and it's only a mile or so up the road from here."

Alison remembered the redbrick cottage, which she and Klaus had passed several times on their way to and from the Tor. She had also passed that way with Tom only a couple of months previously, and the memory was grievous to her. She forced a smile and said something noncommittal. Her landlady, realizing that she had been a trifle tactless, bustled off on her daily round of cooking, cleaning and weeding.

Alison looked at Klaus, dozing on the sofa. She was still wondering what it was that Klaus had started to tell her, and she didn't believe that he had forgotten.

*

The next morning, which was Wednesday, Alison received three letters from America. One was from Candy, and the others were sub poenas to appear as a witness in the trials of Billy Bigley and three other men whose names she didn't recognize. Billy was charged with assault and the other three with a whole list of crimes in which the word "rape" appeared prominently. In Billy's case there was also a sub poena for Klaus. Candy apologized for having given Alison's address to the police, and pleaded with her to come and help Billy. Jackie was no longer seeing Billy, who had appreciated her kindness and affection but continued to proclaim his lifelong devotion to Alison. The worst of it was, Candy wrote, that he showed no remorse for his attack on Klaus, and said that if the opportunity ever arose he'd do the same again.

Alison was terrified at the thought of having to give evidence in a rape trial, but as an American citizen she was bound by the sub poenas, and in any case she wanted to help Billy. Klaus, however, had always maintained his German citizenship, and was obviously unfit to travel.

"I have to go", Alison told him, "and I'm going to ask Mrs. Trathgannon to look after you while I'm away."

Klaus wasn't convinced.

"I don't believe that they have the legal authority to force your return. And I do not wish to be in the position of relying on Mrs. Trathgannon for my daily needs."

"Klaus, I have to go. I owe it to Billy, and maybe some day I'll want to go back and live there—that is, if I don't . . . Well, you know what."

Klaus thought Alison merely meant somewhere in America, but she was actually thinking specifically of Peoria. She was thankful that she still had a nest egg in the bank in New York, and she regretted having to ask Klaus to finance her flight. Klaus, however, was too weak and guilt-ridden to make an issue of it. Mrs. Trathgannon, who was delighted at the thought of taking care of the old gentleman, told Alison that there was no need for her to hurry back.

Alison left the Bigleys' address and telephone number with her landlady and did all she could to prepare Klaus for her absence. On the following Monday she was on her way across the Atlantic again.

*

Mr. Pryce-Jones listened politely to Flossie's complaints about Elwyn, but he made it clear that as long as the chemistry master behaved himself in school there was nothing he could do about it. Elwyn made a habit of arriving at school at the last possible moment, leaving at the earliest, and confining himself to his lab as much as possible, all of which suited Tom very well, since he had no desire to continue their old friendship. The situation went on like this for several weeks, so Tom was very surprised early one morning in October to find Elwyn waiting for him in the physics lab.

"I brought you this", Elwyn said, handing Tom a check for £4,500.

"That's too much", Tom said.

"I added some interest. Wendy's gone home to her mother and I haven't got anyone to spend it on."

"I thought you'd already spent it."

"I have."

"So?"

"So I borrowed it. Some poor fool at the bank seems to think I'm a good risk."

"Why did Wendy leave?"

"She went to see her mother. When she came back she said she didn't want to live in sin any more. She said she would marry me if I got a divorce, but . . ."

"You're not so sure?"

"Right."

"Why not?"

"Well, she has a lovely body. You should have seen her on the beach at Menton."

"OK, don't bother to explain. You miss Diana's brains—so where is she?

"It's not only her brains. And she's somewhere between Boston and Los Angeles, but I have no idea what she's doing."

Odd how old Heisenberg keeps popping up, Tom thought, but he asked "So she just said, 'I'm going to America', and hopped it?"

"She sent me a note. The only other thing she said was that she would send me an address when she had one, so that we could start on the divorce proceedings. She thought it would be a cooperative divorce, only I haven't heard from her since."

"Maybe she can't make up her mind. Do you want her back?"

"Yes."

"Didn't she go to Tanglewood with her clarinet?"

"Yes, but that was years ago."

"Maybe she kept in touch with someone."

"Well, she gets a Christmas card every year . . ."

"Elwyn, for God's sake pull yourself together. If it's the only place in America where she's ever been, it's worth a chance. So go home and see if you can find one of those cards. And . . ."

Tom held up the check and tore it in several pieces.

"Get it?" he asked.

"Got it."

*

"You know what?" Halcyon said as she sat in front of her eggs and bacon the next morning. "I think I must be pregnant. I can't eat a thing and my period's ten days overdue. Is it OK if it's true?"

"Of course it's OK. I'll pick you up and dance round the room with you if you feel up to it."

He was already on his feet but instead of dancing he took Halcyon by the hand, led her to one of the armchairs in the living room, sat down and carefully placed her on his lap. His arms were around her but he was careful not to squeeze too hard.

"I don't know what to say except I'm very happy and I love you."

"So do I. I mean I love you and I'm happy. I s'pose I'll have to go and see the doctor and make sure it's not just an illusion. It doesn't feel like an illusion but you can still hold me tight if you want to."

*

Imre stayed in Ulm throughout September, trying to enjoy himself while working on new contacts in the German Archway movement, but the thought of Alison preyed on his mind. Now that she had emerged as his half-sister, and Klaus, grotesquely enough, as his half-brother-in-law, the new relationship was becoming an obsession, and his fantasy of sex with Alison swirled around with pictures of cozy little family gatherings. It would be a very small family, and how he could possibly work things out with Klaus he couldn't imagine. He still had the urge to take the old man down a peg, but he didn't see how he could do this and worm his way into Alison's confidence at the same time. One way or another, however, they had to be told the truth.

All Imre knew about Klaus and Alison was that they had gone to England for an extended stay, but when he really put his mind to it the answer seemed obvious. Klaus loved Glastonbury and seemed to regard the Tor as his spiritual home, so that was probably where they would go. Tom and Halcyon had been looking for Alison and might have some information, but Imre, who had avoided English or American newspapers since his arrival in Ulm, didn't know where they were, either. The first thing to do would be to go and ask Tom's old landlady if she knew where the newlyweds were living. They would probably refuse to talk to him, but it was worth trying. Imre put some of Maria's more explicit letters into a big envelope, booked a flight to Heathrow, and on Tuesday, October 11th, he arrived in Castle Cary. He rented a car and drove to Glastonbury, where he checked in at the New Avalon Hotel. Several members of the staff recognized him and there was a lot of whispering behind his back, but business was business.

(65)

On Wednesday morning, when Imre knocked on Mrs. Trathgannon's front door, she recognized him immediately.

"You! How dare you show your face here after all your shenanigans with that dreadful man on the television? Now I suppose you want to make more trouble for my poor old gentleman, as if he hadn't had enough trouble already."

"Your poor old gentleman? You mean Mr. Hübel?"

Realizing that she had made a mistake, Mrs. Trathgannon was silent for a moment.

"I've come a long way to see him", Imre said. "I want to apologize."

"Well, he's in bed and asleep and in very poor health. I'm certainly not going to wake him up on your account."

"Then maybe I could talk to Mrs. Hübel."

"Mrs. Hübel is away and I don't know when she will be back. Now be off with you—I can't stand the sight of you."

Imre retreated. He knew it was no use asking where Alison was, but he had achieved part of his object. He might not be able to see Klaus, and he wished he had asked what was the matter with him, but at least he could write. Finding that the New Avalon had entered the twentieth century sufficiently to install a photocopier in an alcove off the hotel lobby, Imre made copies of the two pages in which Maria Johnson described her last night with Klaus and compared him with Bela and Phillip, and of the page in which she congratulated Bela on his fatherhood.

Although his main motivation was the forlorn hope of repairing the past, it was impossible for him to maintain the apologetic tone that he had intended. It might have been different if Alison had been there, but as it was, his message was an odd mixture of repentance and righteous indignation.

"Dear Klaus,

I am writing to apologize for my behavior over the past two months—for speaking to Alison as I did on that awful day in Glastonbury, for the untruthful letters that I sent out when I was in New York, and for my ill-considered appearance on television. I have caused a lot of unhappiness for many people, but especially for you and Alison.

You may not be aware that my father died at the end of August. While going through his personal papers, I have found things that have profoundly altered my perception of the state of affairs between you, your wife and myself. If you read the enclosed pages, you will see that the truth about Alison's birth is quite different from anything that we had imagined, and that I am not the only one who has been at fault. For the past nine weeks you have allowed your wife to believe that you are her father, and you have seen the terrible consequences of your inability to tell the truth. Maria Johnson's letter makes it clear that you must have known that this was extremely improbable. I am in no position to cast any judgement on you, however, and I feel that the best thing would be for us to talk and decide how best we can help Alison, now that we know that she is my half-sister and you are my half-brother-in-law.

I'll call again in a couple of days and hope to be allowed to see you.

Sincerely,
Imre."

This was written on hotel notepaper and enclosed with the photocopies. After mailing it in time for the afternoon collection, Imre spent the evening and the next day wandering around Glastonbury with nothing much to do. Now he was not sure that he had done the best thing. Alison might find this piece of information even more devastating than anything that had happened up to now, and would not thank him for having broken the news to her ailing husband. He wished he could get the letter back, but that was impossible. He would have to go through with his plan. On Friday morning it was a much less confident Imre who approached the Trathgannon residence. Before he could knock, the door opened and an elderly man in a blue suit appeared before him. Apparently he was expected.

"I'd like to talk to . . ." he began, but the man interrupted him.

"I know who you are, you bastard. Mr. Hübel is in hospital again and if he dies they should hang you for murder. We have your filthy letter safely under lock and key in case it's wanted for evidence."

Imre was momentarily frightened.

"But . . . But what happened?"

"Mr. Hübel read your bit of scum and he had another heart attack. Not that we believe any of it—it's just a woman making things up—but it upset him so much that he's almost dead of it. Now bugger off before I call the police."

Mr. Trathgannon, as tall and skinny as his wife, but obviously frailer, took a step forward and Imre retreated hastily to his car. Now he had several more things to worry about. Would Klaus die and would he be responsible if he did? What would Alison's reaction be? And why had he simply assumed that everything Maria had written was true? It might be, but then again, it might not. Quite possibly Mr. Trathgannon was right and it was just a bit of make-believe. The only person left who knew any part of the truth was Klaus, and he was at the point of death.

*

At the time of Klaus's second heart attack, Alison had been in Peoria over a month. Billy's trial had been short and not very sweet. The policemen who had seen what happened asserted that the assault was brutal in the extreme and completely unprovoked, and the District Attorney, anxious to show his desire to crack down on violent crime, had refused a plea agreement. Billy was still out on bail when Alison arrived and, against her better judgement, she had stayed with the Bigleys. With the help of her testimony, the defence attorney had tried to show that Billy was an innocent caught up in a situation that was too difficult for him to handle. The unfortunate result was that the entire population of Peoria knew that this young woman was the wife of the elderly German victim, who was now too sick to travel, and that she had carried on a red-hot love affair with the defendant. The attempt to present Billy as the naïf that he actually was turned out to be a mistake, which the prosecutor used to great advantage, asking Alison if she was still sleeping with the defendant. Billy, they said, was simply trying to get rid of a rival, and he knew exactly what he was doing. The defence tried to use Billy's outrage at the way Klaus had treated Alison as a mitigating factor, but the prosecution pointed out that outrage didn't justify brutality and violence, and the defendant was lucky not to be charged with attempted murder. As far as the judge and the jury were concerned, the only things in Billy's favor were his youth and his clean record. He was found guilty and sentenced to three years.

The information that Billy's elderly victim had taken a sixteen-year-old girl as a lover, and that this girl was now married to Lord Otterill's son and heir, had not come out at the trial, but it was plastered all over the newspapers and TV screens. This, together with Alison's testimony at Billy's trial, meant that when the rape trial began it would have been impossible to find twelve jurors who didn't know all about Alison's past and her relationships with Billy and Klaus. There were several counts against the three men, but the evidence for the earlier ones was rather flimsy and in the case of the final one, in which a sting operation had been set up, the defence was arguing entrapment. So, Alison's evidence being crucial, the defence set out to destroy her. They said that her personal history indicated sexual depravity, and asked why a woman would walk the dark streets at night, wearing only the briefest possible miniskirt and a transparent blouse, if she wasn't looking for sex? The jury was asked to look at a young assistant from the DA's office wearing a uniform from Freddie's Diner. This created quite a stir, including wolf whistles from the back of the courtroom. A woman, the prosecution said, sees her husband assaulted by her young lover, and what does she do? She goes for a long late-night stroll, wearing next to nothing.

But it wasn't possible to destroy Alison. Everything in her that was capable of destruction had been destroyed already. Outwardly calm and inwardly numb to the point of death, she answered all the questions in the same flat tone. This didn't appeal to the jurors, but neither did the defence tactics. There was plenty of material evidence and deliberations were not expected to take very long. It was while the jury was out that Candy brought Alison the news about Klaus.

*

335

Klaus didn't die, but he lay in the hospital for a long time in a region between death, sleep and waking, where he met, or thought he met, the spiritual beings who hover over places like Glastonbury; not the beings of myth and legend, like Arthur and Gwyn Ap Nudd, but the real objective presences who sometimes appear when our teeming brains have been so disciplined or beaten into submission that we no longer resist them. There was no message or command, no "do this or do that and you will be forgiven", but only a feeling of profound sorrow, not in Klaus's heart but in all the surrounding regions of the cosmos. At the moment when he was closest to death it seemed to him that he was approached by a knight clad in shining golden armor, but bare-headed, with youthful features and hair to match his armor. In each hand the knight bore a chalice, and Klaus knew what was in them. The cup in the knight's left hand was filled with the fruits of Klaus's life, transformed into a bitter-sweet wine that might mingle forgetfulness with longing for the days of his youthful conquests and mature victories. He had been strong, vigorous and powerful. He had taken what he wanted, enjoyed it and never doubted that the good spirits were on his side. The only thing wrong with the past was that it was over. That was the bitter that went with the sweet, the reason why forgetfulness of things that could never come again was so much to be desired, why it would be so comforting to let go and drowse one's way into death.

The cup in the knight's right hand carried a different kind of wine. It would bring wakefulness, courage and the will to embrace the sword of truth and conscience, not to wield it but to be pierced by it. Which was it to be? Klaus stretched out a wavering hand towards the second cup, but as he did so the vision faded. His eyes opened and he saw that Alison was sitting at his bedside. He stretched out his hand and Alison took it.

(66)

Mrs. Trathgannon had given Imre's letter to Alison, but it was still in her handbag and she had not yet read it. She went home, lay down on the sofa in Tom's old living room and took it out.

Alison had thought that nothing worse could happen to her, but now something had. In the midst of her turmoil she had come to a kind of equilibrium in her feelings about Klaus. Guilty of selfishness, egotism and deceit, and quite ready not just to admit, but practically to claim that he had married his daughter, he was still thoughtful, gentle and considerate.

Some of his girls might have been under-age, but they had been more than willing. He had never forced himself on anyone. But now Maria's letter made it clear that he was perfectly aware that he was most unlikely to have been Alison's father, and the only reason for not saying so was that he couldn't admit to having been a failure with his old flame. Everything that had happened to Alison since the day she fled from Glastonbury was a direct result of Klaus's prevarication. Her rage was silent, cold and bitter. There were only two choices; to end her life or to endure the unendurable. She tried to imagine what it would be like to go on living—never a second without some vivid picture of what she had lost and what had been done to her—and not only to her. She had lost the man she wanted to marry, had been brutally raped, had been dragged through the police courts, branded as a prostitute and a trollop, and tacitly accused of egging Billy on in his assault on Klaus. And because of Klaus, Phillip Johnson was in his grave, Billy was in jail and Candy and Pete were in agony. Well, Klaus had had his punishment too. He undoubtedly owed his present condition at least partly to what Billy had done to him, but to Alison this was nowhere near enough. Merely to be lying in a comfortable hospital bed waiting for death was no punishment at all. He ought to be kept alive until he was so stricken with remorse that he would beg to die.

And then there was Imre—the parasitical Imre who had wanted to be her lover and was now claiming her as his sister, who had tried to blackmail Klaus and, having failed, had made a little money and cheap publicity by spreading his mixture of prejudicial truths and sly lies over the airwaves. Imre as a brother might be slightly less disgusting than Imre as a lover, and there was nothing much she could do about it except to avoid him. Now the question of truth and lies began to trouble her. Imre was a habitual liar but Klaus wasn't. Apparently he lied only when his emotions pushed him into it. But what about Maria?

This was the worst of all. Apparently she had deceived Klaus and had been quite happy to continue her habit of deception after marrying Phillip. It struck Alison, as it had struck Imre and Mr. Trathgannon, that maybe Maria was a liar too, and that the truth would never be known. Maria was dead, Phillip was dead, Bela was dead, and shortly Klaus would join them. Now her mother headed the list of characters whom she would never be able to think about without acute pain.

She came back to herself. She ought to have trusted Tom. Halcyon had said it. "He wouldn't have cared if your father was the man in the moon."

337

And Halcyon would have been a good friend instead of a successful rival. Alison tried to assemble the bits and pieces again.

Klaus didn't know about Bela. Maria may have lied to everyone about everything, in which case her last session with Klaus may have been responsible for her pregnancy; or Maria may have been telling the truth, in which case Klaus must have known that he wasn't Alison's father or, at least, that it was very unlikely. This might be what Klaus had started to tell her about and then conveniently forgotten, which would mean that Maria's story was probably true. And the verdict of medical science seemed to be that none of this totally ruled out Phillip as a possibility, although he had receded far into the background.

Alison's thoughts spiraled on and on. Why should she blame Klaus for everything, now that she knew the part that her own mother had played? Maria had apparently been totally amoral, fooling about with whoever pleased her, playing with Klaus and gulling Phillip, while getting her real kicks from Bela. And her story rang true; it was flip and matter-of-fact, and in her happy-go-lucky relationship to sex she showed no sign of needing an ego-booster. It may have been different for Bela. It was indecent to think that two people could share such an attitude, and maybe he had been deeply unhappy. How long, Alison wondered, did they carry on in New York? Right up to the time of Maria's death? Maybe that was why she killed her. Nothing happened without a reason—or so Goerner maintained. It was all karma, but that wasn't the end. Karma doesn't just stop and genes don't either. She was her mother's daughter, and resembled her in so many ways that she must have inherited her share of karmic entanglements and genetic propensities; but she had never had any desire to practice the kind of deception that her mother had indulged in. She and Tom would have lived together openly, and Klaus would have had to put up with it. Her later misadventures had resulted from circumstances over which she had no control, like being led to believe that she had married her father; in every case she had had a choice, but the powers that regulate karma had made it much too hard for her. She could have stayed in Glastonbury with Tom; she could have gone to see Phillip as soon as she arrived in America; and she could have avoided the entanglement with Billy; but, all that being admitted, she had made two decisions that must be judged right by any standard—to see Klaus though to the end and to do as much as she possibly could for Billy. As far as Klaus was concerned, she was surprised to find not only that it seemed right, but that it was what she actually wanted, like taking care of a wayward, incontinent, elderly pet animal or a criminal in the condemned cell. Billy was a different matter. He had never heard of Goerner, but he had the power to drive the evil spirits away, at least for a while. If only she could be with him now . . .

The daydream about Billy didn't last long. It was interrupted by pictures of Imre, sneering across Mrs. Barrington-Smythe's kitchen table, begging to talk to her in the brownstone, prying into everyone's affairs and brazenly trumpeting them over the air waves. The mystery of her birth was insoluble, and without Imre's intervention she would never have known about it. She couldn't bear to think about her mother, and she was bitterly angry with Klaus, but he, at least, had some redeeming features. Imre was a different matter. She had thought of him as an animal, but no animal could be so utterly detestable. Her anger with him was compounded with a profound hatred that was much harder to deal with. She thought, "If I don't do something, even if it's only a gesture, I shall go mad."

*

Imre was drinking a lot of coffee because he preferred the ambience of a small café to that of the hotel lounge. The only vision that came to him was of himself as an outcast from the movement to which he had devoted his life. He had to admit that this was entirely his own fault, and although the thought that it might be the result of moral incapacity crept stealthily into a corner of his mind, it was for a series of tactical blunders that he cursed himself as a total screw-up. His best course would obviously be to go back to Ulm, where he still had acquaintances, if not friends, and was not a pariah—well, not yet. But he couldn't tear himself away. Alison would presumably come back and he might find some way of meeting her. He had no idea what he would say, and he was overcome with confusion when he returned to the New Avalon one evening and found her waiting for him in the lobby.

"Hello, Imre. Order some coffee—I want to talk to you."

Alison led the way though the crowded lounge to a vacant spot in the far corner, where they sat next to each other on a leather settee.

"You seem surprised to see me", Alison said. "I'd have thought that now I'm your sister and Klaus is your brother-in-law you'd have made a point of visiting."

"Well, I did but . . ."

339

"You didn't feel exactly welcome? I'm sorry—I'll have to explain things to Mr. and Mrs. Trathgannon. After all, family ties are very important and it isn't every day that you acquire a new brother."

Imre looked at Alison in surprise. She was dressed so as to appear tastefully provocative. Her skirt was only a few inches above the knee when she was standing, but when she sat it exposed a good deal more. The top three buttons of her shirt were tantalizingly open, and Imre found that if he got his head into just the right position, he could see the curve of her breast. She gave no sign of being anything other than sincere, but he still couldn't believe what he was hearing.

"Well", he began, but Alison wouldn't let him speak. She told him that this new relationship changed everything and she was sure past misunderstandings could be forgotten.

"I think the three of us should get together and try to be friends. I'll talk to Klaus about it as soon as he feels a little better. I ought to get back to the hospital but I just wanted to make . . . contact with you."

She stood up and put her hand on his shoulder.

"I must say you're looking very handsome."

It seemed too good to be true, but Imre was ready to take it. As he stood up, Alison made a little movement towards him that seemed to invite a hug and a kiss, so he put his arms around her and moved in. At the precise moment when his lips were an inch from hers, she gave an exclamation of disgust, pulled away and slapped him as hard as she could on the cheek. There was a little burst of applause from some of the people who had been watching, so she turned and left the room exactly as if it were a stage and she had just finished a euphonics performance, except that she added a little pirouette at the end.

Once again, Imre felt as if everyone was staring at him. Alison hadn't drawn blood but there was a big red welt on the side of his face. He left with all the dignity he could muster and went up to his room.

Alison couldn't face seeing Klaus, so she went back to the Trathgannons', lay down on the couch and cried herself to sleep.

*

Imre was still sitting on his bed when the hotel manager knocked on his door. He remained there while that smoothly rotund specimen of elevated lackeyhood delivered his message.

"I'm sorry to disturb you, Sir, but I understand that there has been an incident in the lounge."

He understood this because several people had immediately gone to his office to complain about their fellow-guest's behavior.

"He grabbed her and tried to kiss her", one said while the others nodded their agreement, "and you can't blame her for dotting him one."

None of the complainers seemed to have noticed that the young lady had encouraged Imre or that she seemed to be delighted with the result.

The manager went on with his message.

"Now I understand that such things can happen in the heat of the moment, Sir, but all the same, hotel policies are very clear and I'm afraid I shall have to ask you to leave."

"Now?" Imre asked incredulously.

"No, Sir, we only ask you to leave by the normal time of eleven o'clock tomorrow morning, and to avoid the public areas in the meantime. You may have a meal served in your room if you wish."

This was too much. Imre, who had endured many indignities, and habitually preferred stealth and guile to physical retaliation, finally lost it.

"Well, screw that", he yelled as he hurled himself from his sitting position. The manager, who had been standing just inside the door, instinctively turned away so Imre got him from behind, propelled him along the corridor and heaved him down the stairs. Fortunately they began with a short flight that led to a right-angle turn, so, although he was badly shaken, the only part of him that was seriously injured was his dignity.

Imre went back to his room. Having let it all hang out and removed the self-satisfied smirk from the manager's face, he was feeling a little better. Instead of following his usual pattern of licking his wounds and slowly calculating his response, he wanted some immediate action. It seemed that a woman who slapped you instantly became even more sexually desirable, and he stopped worrying about whether he wanted Alison more as lover or as a sister. He just wanted her any way he could get her. He looked in the mirror and felt that she had been right about one thing; with his shorter hair and loss of weight, his appearance had certainly improved. He didn't want to spend another night at the New Avalon, so he packed his bags and went down to his car.

One of the B and B's with which Ashwell Lane was dotted was almost opposite the Trathgannons. Yes, the tourist season was over and they would be glad to take a paying guest by the week. Imre had the choice of several rooms, so he opted for a front room where he could keep an eye on what was happening on the other side of the lane.

(67)

Imre didn't like to think of himself as the worm that turned, but he did feel that he had scraped the bottom of the barrel and was on his way up. He still wanted what he wanted, and the fact that Alison had taken so much trouble to create the opportunity to slap him had restored his faith that he might somehow get it. The problem was to present Imre Takacs in a better light, both to himself and to the people across the street. He was still determined to take the offensive, but the adrenaline rush had died down enough for him to plot his next actions very carefully and even to think briefly about their moral implications. The decisions he took were self-serving, but he managed to give them a comforting appearance of moral rectitude. If they eventually led to something with Alison, it might even be regarded as the reward of virtue.

*

Unless her visit happened to coincide with one of the Trathgannons' supermarket trips, Alison had to walk the two miles from the Trathgannon's house to the hospital. A couple of days after her encounter with Imre, she was trudging through a steady drizzle when a car pulled up beside her and a voice said, "May I give you a lift?"

She stopped and saw that Imre was leaning across from the driver's seat, holding the passenger side door open for her. She instinctively recoiled, but the rain was getting harder and he said, "Come on—no strings attached. I'll just drop you there and leave."

"How do you know where I'm going?" she asked.

Imre shrugged.

"You're going to visit Klaus", he said. "Come in out of the rain."

Alison got in and Imre was as good as his word. He made no attempt at conversation, but when he left her at the hospital he said, "I can do this whenever you want me to—I live right opposite you. And I can pick you up and drive you home."

There was a lot of repugnance to overcome, but Alison was pretty sure that she could deal with anything that Imre tried to pull, so she said, "OK. If you could pick me up an hour and a half from now, it would be wonderful."

Klaus was very sleepy, so Alison spent most of the time reading *The Manifestations of Destiny—How Karma Works*, which she had found in the local library. Goerner had written about everything under the sun and a good deal that was beyond it, but Alison was still preoccupied with her karma and her future incarnations. Being quite sure that after facing up to things in the spiritual world she would be meeting all these people again next time around, it seemed like a very good idea to try and get some of it done ahead of time. She hoped that later on she would be able to square things with Billy and his parents, but in the meantime she would try to cope with Imre and Klaus.

Imre picked her up and drove her home, once again in silence.

As she got out of the car, Alison thanked Imre and asked, "Why are you doing this?"

"I don't really know. Does it matter? Same time tomorrow?"

"All right. Thank you very much."

Imre drove to his favorite coffee shop. It was absurd and humiliating, but the fact was that just being in the car with Alison made a feeling of warmth spread through his body and soul, even though he knew that she despised him. So he really did know why he was doing it, and perhaps one day he would be able to tell her.

*

For the next two weeks Imre drove Alison to and from the hospital almost every day. When Klaus was finally released, conditions were very strict. There was no prospect of any real recovery and he would require constant nursing, but if he stuck to his regimen of pills and avoided any strenuous exertion, he might survive for a long time. Imre and Alison followed the ambulance back to Ashwell Lane and at last there was some conversation.

Told about Klaus's prognosis, Imre said, "I'd like to help, so you can have some time off occasionally. I could sit with him for a couple of hours sometimes."

"I don't know. Considering that your last letter gave him a heart attack, it might not be wise. I think Mrs. Trathgannon will help."

But for several days Klaus was scarcely conscious enough to know who was sitting with him, and one afternoon when Alison was finding the little apartment particularly claustrophobic and her landlady wasn't available, she ran across the lane and knocked on Imre's door.

"Klaus is asleep and I just need to get away for a little while", she said when her old enemy opened the door.

"You can take the car if you like", Imre said, very anxious to please.

This seemed such a delightful idea to Alison that she actually smiled.

*

Alison hadn't driven for a long time and had very little experience of driving on the left, so she decided not to go very far. Taking the A39 south out of Glastonbury, she branched off on a B road that passed through Street and a few miles later came to the village of Compton Dundon. The parking lot of the village inn was empty, so she left the car there and followed a sign leading to a footpath up to the ancient earthworks on Dundon Hill. Apparently no one was quite sure when it had all started, but according to an inscription below the sign, it might have been as long ago as 3,000 B.C. It was a short, sharp climb, rather like going up the Tor except that the slopes were heavily wooded. Quarrying had destroyed some of the old fortifications, and a casual visitor might have been forgiven for failing to notice the remains of any earthworks at all. The weather was what the English call "fine", meaning that it was grey and overcast but not actually raining, and the air was quite clear. There was a large, fairly flat, open space at the top, from which Alison could look through a small gap in the trees and see the Tor in the middle distance, looming ominously over the surrounding levels.

"Five thousand years ago", she thought. "I wonder what I was doing then. Something awful, I expect, but that's about ten incarnations for ordinary people. You'd think I could have gotten it right by now."

But she obviously hadn't, and when she tried to imagine what she could do to make things better next time around she met a blank wall. She knew what Goerner would have said—she must start on the road of self-purification, she must achieve selflessness through prayer and meditation, calling on the help of the good spirits who watch over the destiny of the human race, and if she could find someone to guide her along the road, so much the better. Well, Klaus, who was supposed to have been her guide, was probably the most spectacular screw-up in the whole history of such endeavors. You were supposed to silence all the inner turmoil, but her inner turmoil was so loud and insistent that the still, small voice was overwhelmed. She tried to think of something hopeful— "I'm taking care of Klaus and I've made a little progress with Imre"—but it didn't work. Her anger with them had not abated in the slightest; what she was doing for Klaus was no more than her duty, and she had merely overcome her detestation of Imre to the point of making a convenience of him. And what if, eventually, she went back to Peoria and gave herself up to Billy? It would be doing him no favors if it was just an act of atonement. It would have to be done out of love, and Alison felt that she would never love anyone again. If she didn't kill herself she might live with these knots in her soul for another fifty or sixty years before natural death threw her back into the endless cycles of karma. Suicide would make things even worse. Here she was in one of the holiest places on earth, where people through the ages had looked for God and thought they had found Him, and she felt utterly lost and forsaken. The words hammered themselves into her soul; "No escape. No escape. No escape." She collapsed onto the grass and beat on it with her fists in time to the rhythm that wouldn't stop: "No escape, no escape, no escape." Trying to get a grip on herself and finding that she couldn't, she got up and ran all the way down the hill to the car. The inn looked very inviting, and as she sat panting in front of the steering wheel it struck her that there would be a lot to be said for alcohol as a temporary solution. It would probably make things worse next time around, but it might help her get through this life without killing herself. She was sufficiently in control to realize that if she was going to start drinking, it would be safer to skip the village inn and visit the liquor store in Glastonbury instead.

*

By making himself available whenever he was needed, and keeping his mouth firmly shut most of the time, Imre achieved his initial objective of being tolerated in Mrs. Trathgannon's house. Alison seemed more relaxed and sometimes quite talkative. She borrowed Imre's car quite often and on more than one occasion he heard the clink of bottles when she reappeared with a large shopping bag.

345

(68)

Tom spent most of his spare time working on his father's suggestion about becoming a science correspondent and mixing some of Goerner's ideas on physics into his articles. The fact that although the quantum theory worked quite well, nobody really understood why, seemed to him to support his feeling that maybe Goerner had a point.

His marriage with Halcyon worked too; so well, in fact, that he was almost afraid to think about it. Her physical attractions were outstanding but what really did it for Tom was the quality of her mind. She understood things and saw them whole without having to do any calculating. Her responses were straight from the heart, but somehow they generally managed to agree with what the head might have come up with, given enough time. To know the right answers simply by seeing them seemed to be a divine gift, a rare ability that was not just a matter of feminine intuition. It also seemed to be what Goerner was driving at, but according to him it might take many years or lifetimes to reach that point. In the meantime one had to keep on trying to figure things out, and this was something Tom enjoyed—it was a very bracing activity. It just seemed better not to try to figure Halcyon out.

*

Halcyon's birthday was October 24th, which happened to be a Monday and to coincide with Tom's half-term holiday. Confirmation of her pregnancy came in on the Thursday before that, and after a certain amount of hugging and kissing, Halcyon said, "You know what, Tom? I have a feeling we don't need to get married again."

"You think we're married enough already?"

"Yes. I mean this kind of proves it, doesn't it? And it would save an awful lot of bother."

"My father would probably be very relieved, but what about your Mum?"

"Well, first we have to tell them the good news, and then we can see what they say about the wedding."

"OK, I'll give Dad a call and we can go up for the weekend."

A voice said, "Lord Otterill's residence" and a big smile spread over Tom's face as he handed the phone to Halcyon.

"Hello", Halcyon said.

"Doreen!"

"Mum! What are you doing there?"

"Well, I was going to tell you, but Jim wanted it to be a surprise. I work here now."

"What kind of work?" Halcyon asked suspiciously.

"She wants to know what kind of work", Iris said, not into the phone.

Lord Otterill picked up another phone, pressed a button and said, "Your Mum has a hard time realizing that as the mother of Lady Leyford she's now part of the Otterill establishment, so she thinks she ought to be an assistant housekeeper or something daft like that. Anyway her real job is just keeping me happy."

Halcyon laughed.

"Well, you old devil! Anyway, Mum, I'm not surprised. What happened to the company doctor?"

"I never heard from him until it was time for your dad's annual exam, and then he said Bert was fit to go back to work."

"What's dad doing now? Is he at work?"

"Good Lord, no! He's upstairs in his room, watching TV. He's in *Green Pastures*. It's a magazine for farmers. Mr. Fortescue said it was just right for someone who was being put out to graze."

"You mean to say you've both moved in there? When did this happen?"

"Well, if you want to know, it was the day you moved into your cottage, and don't complain that I never tell you anything—you're just as bad or worse."

"OK, Mum, I admit it. And what about you?"

"What do you mean, what about me?"

"I mean what did old Fortescue think up for your room?"

"Well, he hinted that Jim's thinking of starting a financial publication called *New Acquisitions* but just for now . . ."

"Shush!" said Lord Otterill. "Now, to what do we owe the honor of this call?"

Halcyon unexpectedly became shy and tongue-tied.

"Well, you see, Mum . . ."

"Don't tell me I'm going to be a grandma at thirty-five!"

"Yes, but I think you'll be thirty-six by the time it happens. We have a long weekend so we want to come and see you. And here's Tom—he wants to talk to his dad."

Tom wanted to know if he could spend a couple of hours with Andrew Davy, and Lord Otterill thought this would be easy to arrange. Tom didn't raise the question of another wedding, since he had a feeling that the next one might involve his father.

*

Tom and Halcyon returned from London to Glastonbury with a carload of presents and a great deal of good advice, most of it from Alice who, as far as Tom knew, had no personal experience of motherhood. Andrew Davy had been very encouraging and thought that while Tom ought first to establish himself in the mainstream, a series of articles on alternative approaches would be very interesting to many of the paper's readers. Tom was deep in thought when he arrived in the lab on Tuesday morning and found Flossie waiting for him.

"The Old Man wants to see you pronto", she said.

"Any idea what it's about?"

"Elwyn. You'd better hurry—there's only five minutes before assembly."

Mr. Pryce-Jones didn't give Tom the chance even to say, "Good morning."

"Dexter, how much chemistry do you know?"

"Enough to get by, Sir. Has something happened to Elwyn?"

"Yes—you set an unfortunate precedent and he has followed it."

Tom grinned internally but kept his face straight.

"You mean he's gone to America? Is he coming back?"

"I have no idea. I must admit that you were very honest and straightforward, whereas Davies merely telephoned Mrs. Howe on Saturday and told her that he was going to be away for a few days. She managed to keep him on the line long enough to worm out of him that he was going to the United States and had no idea whether or when he would be back. I gather that there has been some kind of domestic difficulty and his wife has left him."

This last sentence was intended as a question but Tom ignored it.

"I'm very sorry to hear it", he said. "Naturally I'll do whatever is necessary to cope with the situation until there's some resolution."

"The most important thing is to keep the O and A-level classes going full steam ahead. Ferguson can take over your elementary maths classes and . . ."

The headmaster went on with the details of substitutions and schedule changes. It was hard luck on Ferguson, but Tom had always liked chemistry and thought it would be fun to teach it.

(69)

November was a long month for everyone. Halcyon was still enchanted by the thought that she was carrying Tom's baby, but she felt nauseated a lot of the time and postponed her return to the euphonics scene. Officially there was no word from Elwyn, but Tom received an irate note to the effect that he and Diana were talking and that she had got involved with the Archway School in Pittstown, only a few miles from Tanglewood, for which Elwyn seemed to think that Tom was to blame. Tom and his colleagues soldiered on with their extra-heavy teaching loads while the headmaster searched for a replacement. Meanwhile, Tom Dexter was introduced to Lord Otterill's readers in the columns of his egghead Sunday paper, *The New Observer*, and his article on the latest developments in particle physics was well received. Alison's trips to the liquor store became more frequent, deadening her consciousness but doing little to ease her inner agony. Imre felt that although he had gained admittance, there was little hope of progressing any further towards intimacy, however one defined the word. Klaus didn't say much, but he deeply resented Imre's presence and the dependency that made it necessary. Alison seemed to have gone far away and no longer talked with him about the burning issues of life, death and eternity that consumed his soul.

In December things got better for Tom and Halcyon, but not for Alison. Mr. Pryce-Jones found a replacement for Elwyn, and Halcyon was feeling much better. Elwyn wrote to say that he and Diana were getting back together but that he refused to have anything to do with those damned CW people. The Grammar School was to close for the Christmas holidays on Friday, December 16th, and on the morning of the 15th snow began to fall. By the time Tom got home in the late afternoon, it was a couple of inches deep in the lanes.

"I want to stay here for Christmas", Halcyon said, continuing a conversation that had been going on for several days, "and I want to have a party. We can invite Bill Graveney and Flossie and a couple of your friends from school."

"Great", Tom said, "and we can go to London for the New Year. We can celebrate with lemonade."

"OK but you don't really have to lay off the alcohol."

"I know—I just don't want Junior to smell my breath. Anyway, I think I'll pick up a few bottles on my way home from school tomorrow—there's nothing like being prepared."

*

The liquor store was quite busy on Friday afternoon, and while Tom was waiting to complete his purchase, he saw Alison come in. He knew that it would be best to avoid her, but she had seen him and their eyes met. She stood just inside the door, so that it wasn't possible for him to leave without speaking.

"Hello, Alison", he said. There seemed to be something wrong with his voice.

"Can we talk, Tom, just for a minute? Please?"

"OK, just for a minute."

"Don't worry, it's pitch dark and no one's going to see us."

She followed him out to his car and he opened the passenger side door for her.

"Same old car", she said. "Why don't you get a new one? Is it because of the associations?"

"Alison . . ."

"I'm sorry—it's not your fault. How is Halcyon?"

"She's very well. How is Klaus?"

"He's very sick, but I think he'll last longer than I shall. Kiss me, Tom."

"Alison, please don't."

Her arms were around his neck and she laughed.

"You really do need a new car—this old gear lever is such a nuisance."

"Alison, don't do this. Halcyon is pregnant and I . . ."

"Halcyon is pregnant, so you can't kiss me. That's very funny."

Tom kissed her savagely and then leaned across her and opened the door.

"It's over", he said. "It would have been wonderful but it's over."

Alison went back to Imre's car and Tom drove off. He was so shaken that when he got home Halcyon asked him if anything was wrong.

"Just a difficult day at school", he said, which was a lie.

"Come here, Tom. Hold me tight and tell me what happened."

Tom told her, except that he didn't mention the kiss, and she did her best not to let him see how disturbed she was. It wasn't so much that she distrusted Tom as that Alison frightened her. She couldn't help wondering how much longer they would be living almost next door to each other, and how often Tom might bump into her in the future.

*

When Alison got home she realized that she had left the liquor store without buying anything and she was down to her last bottle of scotch. She desperately needed a drink, but she had returned Imre's car and dropped the keys through the letter box. After her encounter with Tom she felt like drinking the whole bottle and leaving tomorrow to take care of itself—like her next incarnation.

"It's hopeless, Klaus", she said that evening, not referring to the approaching alcohol shortage, and even in his feebleness her husband could smell the liquor on her breath. "Why even think about it? They're going to give us hell when we get to the other side. I'm having a little holiday from it now. Wouldn't you like to do the same?"

She disappeared into the living room and returned a moment later with the whisky bottle and two glasses, one of which was already full.

Klaus shook his head.

"Leave me", he whispered. "It is too distressing to see that you have been reduced to this."

"You don't want to be tempted by a fallen woman? It's not an apple I'm offering—just a glass of scotch. Think of it as medicine."

"No. You are not yourself. Please leave me."

This struck Alison as quite comical.

"Well, if I'm not myself I must be someone else. Who do you think I am? The butcher, the baker, the candle-stick maker . . . Someone without such a screwed up karma . . . That would be nice."

She began to laugh.

"That's funny—all screwed up! Goerner said we passed the bottom of the curve—you know, the great curve of human evolution—and now we're all ascending in a spiral—get it? We're all screwing upward!"

She put the full glass down on the bedside table, slopped some scotch into the empty one and when Klaus wouldn't take it, still shaking with laughter she took a big gulp of it. She choked momentarily, dropped the glass and the bottle and went off into even louder peals of merriment.

Realizing that something wasn't quite right, Mrs. Trathgannon climbed the stairs and peered nervously into the apartment in time to see Alison emerge from the bedroom with a full glass in her hand and sit down on the couch.

"Hello, Mrs. T", she said quite brightly as she worked on her drink. "You probably don't recognize me. Klaus says I'm not myself, but he won't tell me who I am. Do you know who I am?"

The smell of scotch was overpowering. Mrs. Trathgannon looked into the bedroom, saw that Klaus appeared to be all right and sat beside Alison.

"This won't do", she said, trying to take the glass from her hand.

"No you don't", Alison said, unexpectedly resisting and splashing half the drink on her landlady's dress. "Klaus is no good, so I was going to take a bottle of scotch to bed with me, and now that's gone and you're even trying to take away my last drink."

Feeling that the situation called for the presence of a man, Mrs. T ran downstairs and told her husband what was going on. He told her very firmly that if that was the way things were he wasn't having anything to do with it, and the Hübels could leave the next day. Without stopping to argue, Mrs. T hurried across the lane and knocked on Imre's front door. When she returned a few minutes later, with Imre at her heels, Alison had decided that it was bedtime and taken everything off except her T-shirt, and was lying on the couch with a full glass beside her.

"Look", she said, "there was still a little left in the bottle. Not like Klaus—there's nothing left in his bottle."

This struck Alison as extremely funny and it was some minutes before she could speak again.

"You know what? I've remembered who I am. I'm the fallen women, the bad, bad, bad fallen woman. I've done incest, seduction and prostitution. I'm a tart and a trollop, and a big guy with a funny face just told me to get lost. And you know what's nice? I've fallen so far there isn't any farther to go."

At that moment she saw Imre, who was standing just inside the door.

"I don't know though, maybe there is. Beggars can't be choosers. Klaus is no good, I can't have Tom and Billy's too far away . . ."

Imre touched Mrs. T's arm.

"You'd better leave this to me", he said.

Mrs. Trathgannon was reluctant to leave Imre alone with this intoxicated, half naked young woman, but she was disgusted by Alison's behavior and her remark about Klaus.

"Very well. Make sure Klaus is all right and tomorrow we'll have to make some new arrangements."

Imre looked into the bedroom, saw that Klaus was asleep, picked up the bottle and the glass and went back into the living room. Alison had taken off her shirt.

"Lock the door and come here", she said. "Isn't this what you always wanted?"

Imre had had the same idea, so he did as he was told.

(70)

Alison lay in a long stupor, not quite asleep and not fully aware of what she had done. In the small hours, needing to go to the bathroom and still only semi-conscious, she got off the couch. It took her some time to realize what it was that she had stepped on, and when she saw that it was Imre she screamed. Klaus woke up, got painfully to his feet, opened the bedroom door and turned the light on. Both occupants of the living room were naked, Imre sitting on the floor next to the couch and Alison standing by him. The three looked at one another for a long moment before Alison said to Imre, "You'd better go now, before he throws you out." She continued her journey to the bathroom, and by the time she got back the living room was empty.

*

Imre had gone back to his room across the street, where he lay on his bed for a long time, mentally re-enacting his session with Alison and realizing that there was not as much pleasure in the memory as he would have liked. He ought to have been gloating over his success and relishing the opportunity of replaying the scene, at least in his imagination if not in physical fact, but this was not quite the way it had turned out. He had always pictured himself getting Alison's consent after a long and exquisite process of seduction, but in the end she had pulled the strings and he had merely obeyed orders. It was not to be expected that there would be any love in the love-making, but there wasn't even much lust, since it had all seemed so mechanical. Passive at first, Alison had become more and more demanding, as if Imre were some kind of machine that wasn't functioning up to its purchaser's expectations. The worst of it was that he had run out of gas before she did, so that in the end she pushed him off the couch and said, "Get out of here, you're not much better than Klaus."

She had then fallen into what appeared to be a deep sleep, and Imre, remembering that there was an still some scotch in the glass on the table, had polished it off and dozed on the floor for a couple of hours, only to be rudely awakened when Alison stepped on him and screamed. Then, to be seen by Klaus in that farcical situation and ignominiously dismissed by Alison . . .

He got up and looked out of his window. It was almost daylight and snowing hard. He went back to bed and slept heavily for several hours. When he woke up again, he had already suppressed some of the awkward facts, and things didn't seem quite so bad. Alison had slapped him, relied on him for help with Klaus, and had even had sex with him. Now the memory of the sight and feel of her naked body excited him. "You never know", he thought. "Maybe she'll want me again."

*

Waking up in the early afternoon, Alison knew exactly where she was and what she had done. She certainly had a mild hangover, but apart from that she felt better than she had done for months, and that was hard to understand. She ought to have felt totally messed up, but instead she felt free, as if she had shed a huge load.

"It's true", she said to herself as she took her shower, unaware that she was echoing something Imre had said to himself several weeks earlier. "Now I really have hit bottom. I've done it on purpose, and Imre just happened to be convenient. I almost feel sorry for him—he can't seriously have believed that I wanted him for the pleasure of having sex with him, and he didn't seem to be having much fun. Tom's totally gone and Klaus won't want me any more—I can move out and Mrs. Trathgannon can look after him—she'd adore that. Or he can go into a nursing home—he has plenty of money. So that's another good resolution gone west."

Returning to the living room she saw a small off-white bundle at the end of the couch.

"Damn Imre—he's left his underpants here."

In her mood of the previous night this would have seemed hysterically funny, but now she just picked the bundle up with her thumb and forefinger, dropped it into the garbage can and went to wash her hands.

The next thing would be to talk to Klaus, but when she went into the bedroom, Klaus wasn't there. Old, frail and sick as he was, he had punctiliously tidied his room and left a note for Mrs. Trathgannon, apologizing for the spilt liquor, thanking her for her kindness, and telling her that he intended to return to the hotel and that someone would call for his luggage. Alison's mood changed instantaneously. She knew that if she gave herself time to think, her thoughts would be very bad, so she got dressed as quickly as she could and went downstairs to telephone, hoping against hope that she wouldn't bump into her landlady. The hotel staff had no news of Klaus.

Alison weighed the possibilities. Klaus might have set off for the hotel and not made it there, or he might have gone in the opposite direction, along the lanes to the Tor. Knowing Klaus as she did, she thought the latter possibility was more likely. It looked like another situation where Imre's help would be needed, so she put on her overcoat and went outside.

*

The snow was heavier than ever when Imre looked out again, and having nothing better to do, he sat at the window and watched it for a long time. Eventually he saw Alison emerge from the Trathgannons front door. She saw him in the window and signaled to him, so he got dressed, put on his heavy jacket and went down.

"Klaus has gone", Alison told him. "I don't know when or where. He left a note saying he was going back to the hotel, but they haven't seen him. I think either he's gone up the Tor or he didn't make it to the hotel, and this is going to kill him if we can't find him soon. Maybe it already has and he's lying in the snow somewhere. Could you drive up the lane and see if you can find him, and I'll run down to the hotel."

Alison set off immediately. A few moments ago she had been glad not to be responsible for Klaus any more, and now she was anxiously looking for him. She felt like a pinball, bouncing from one projection to another and likely to fall down a hole at any moment.

Imre took a long look at the state of the lane, wondering whether it would be better to go on foot. The snow was at least six inches deep and might well be deeper where the lane narrowed and passed between banks and hedgerows. Feeling that it was important to find Klaus as soon as possible, Imre decided to take the car and try to get as far as the wicket gate at the foot of the Tor. It didn't occur to him that there might be some advantage in letting the old man die in the snow.

(71)

On Saturday morning Tom and Halcyon felt more or less normal. It was glorious to be together in their own warm cottage, singing snatches of old songs and stoking up the fire, while the snow piled up outside.

"Let it snow, let it snow, let it snow—we've got our love to keep us warm."

Later that day they stood side by side, looking out of the front window.

"That looks like Klaus", Halcyon said, as a heavily bundled up figure moved slowly along the lane.

"It can't be. He wouldn't be out in weather like this."

"I know, but it sure looks like Klaus."

"Do you think I ought to . . . ?"

"No, Tom."

There was a note of panic in Halcyon's voice.

"I don't want to be left alone on a day like this."

As it gradually got dark, the snow fell thicker and faster and the wind piled huge drifts against the hedges and the walls of the cottage. There was a knock at the front door, and Tom went to see who might be calling on them on such a day. The door opened inwards and a huge blast of wind sent an avalanche of snow over the doorstep.

"Imre! For God's sake come in so I can close this door."

It took two of them to close the door against the wind and the snow.

"Have you seen anyone go by", Imre asked. "Klaus or Alison?"

"Someone went by an hour or so ago. We thought it looked like Klaus but . . ."

"Klaus is missing and Alison has gone to the hotel to see if he's there. My car is stuck in a drift. You can only get by on foot and I wasted a lot of time trying to move it. Could you walk down and see if Alison's there while I go up and look on the Tor?"

Tom couldn't see what good this would do, and in this irresolute moment Halcyon called out, "No, Tom, no."

"I can't", Tom said.

Imre shrugged his shoulders and opened the door. The wind had dropped for a moment and in the little remaining light they all saw Alison. She was walking as fast as she could through the deep snow and was already some way up the lane approaching the wicket gate. Tom took an involuntary step forward and as the wind blew up again, Halcyon again gasped, "No!"

Imre turned and gave Tom a hard shove.

"Telephone the police and take care of your wife", he said, and with an enormous effort he closed the door behind him.

The police sergeant was the same one who had been unwilling or unable to help on the previous occasion when Klaus had been missing. He asked Tom whether he knew for certain that there was actually someone stranded on the Tor, and said that even if there was it would take some time to organize a search party.

Halcyon sat by the fire, weeping bitterly.

"You would have gone, wouldn't you?"

"Maybe—but I would have come back. I thought you trusted me."

"It's what you did before you had time to think. She's still there inside you."

"Damn it, Halcyon, everything that you ever do is still there inside you. You can't get rid of it. And yes, she's going after Klaus and now maybe she needs help. I don't want anyone to die out there, but I'm in love with you, not Alison. What are you doing?"

Halcyon was pulling on her boots.

"I'm sorry, Tom. It's not that I don't trust you—it's just that there's something about her that scares the hell out of me, and being pregnant makes me very nervous and I'm afraid you'll fall into a snowdrift. You don't want me to give birth to an orphan, do you?"

She stood up and went for her overcoat.

"Come on, Tom, we have to go together. Bring the big flashlight and don't argue."

Tom didn't argue, but he went out to the tool shed and returned a minute later with a shovel and a coil of rope.

"It may slow us down", he said, "but once we get to the path we're going to clear as we go so we have a better chance of getting back. And the rope will be handy if someone falls into a drift."

What he was thinking was that at the first sign of any significant danger he would pick Halcyon up and carry her home.

*

Klaus had come to the wicket gate while it was there was still some dim light.

"'Strait is the gate and narrow is the way'", he said aloud, "'and few there be that find it.'"

What was life all about if you could live for eighty-four years and realize at the point of death that you know nothing?

"'Wide is the gate and broad is the way that leadeth to destruction.'"

Irrelevant details sneaked into his mind.

Was that why the big street that snakes across Manhattan was called Broadway?

The path up the Tor was steep and narrow—strait but not straight.

In America young women of a certain type were often referred to as broads.

He had taken the broad way and had never given it up—it had given him up.

Maria had turned out to be a broad and so had Alison.

No, that wasn't fair—Alison had been driven to it.

He ought to have spent the last years of his life performing acts of contrition, but it was too late for that now. To repent and throw yourself on the mercy of God—to admit that you are a poor, helpless creature, totally unfit to enter the Kingdom of Heaven except through the grace of God, and even then only after aeons of purgatorial cleansing and self-abasement—such ideas found a place in Klaus's consciousness, but they were too foreign to his habitual way of thinking to make much headway.

If only he could make it to the top of the hill, just one more time, perhaps someone would take pity on him and tell him something.

*

The snow had obliterated most of the stone path that led to St. Michael's Tower and, in the gathering gloom, Klaus was in continual danger of slipping off onto the steep slopes of the hill. His heart was doing alarming things and he had to stop and rest every few minutes. He had reached a bend not far below the tower when he lost his footing, fell into a snow bank at the edge of the path, and found that he couldn't get up. He thought that if he stopped struggling, closed his eyes and rested for a while, he might be able to continue. When he opened his eyes again, the pain had gone, and it seemed to him that he had slept for a long time.

It was quite dark now, but when he looked up he saw that the sky was brightening and a great aureole was descending over the Tor. Soon the tower was bathed in golden light through which waves of lilac gently pulsed. The wind and snow had stopped and he could see the path. He felt as light as a feather as he walked up to the foot of the tower, stood in the midst of the glory, and gazed out over the transfigured countryside. He was no longer restricted to the little space of his body, but could fly out over the hills and farms, and dip down into the trees and hedges, where every leaf was tipped with gold. He thought perhaps there was music in the air, strange harmonies such as he had sometimes heard in dreams, but it was elusive and he couldn't quite catch it. His mind had become passive and his brain no longer generated irrelevancies. All was well—he was forgiven and going where no foul beasts or fiends of hell could hurt him. *Oh death, dear death, take me, for I am yours. Through you I shall* . . .

"Klaus! Klaus! Wake up! God damn you for a stupid old man, WAKE UP!"

"Alison?"

Klaus was still lying in the snow at the side of the path. He stirred and looked up. The tower was invisible, and the aureole, the trembling gold and lilac, and the music had all gone; but the feeling of his vision was still in him and it took him a long time to realize where he was. He spoke reproachfully.

"They came for me tonight and now you have brought me back."

"Come on, Klaus, let me help you get back on the path before you freeze to death."

"I am quite warm and comfortable. I shall stay here and wait for them to come again."

"Do you know what that means? I can't just go away and leave you here, so it means I'll have to stay and freeze to death with you."

Klaus was beaten. He had wished for a revelation, and was sure that he had received one. Death was coming to him without pain and with hope, and he had welcomed it, but now he had to give it up so that Alison could live. Perhaps this was the final act of contrition and selflessness that was demanded. With Alison's help he managed to get into a kneeling position, but as he tried to stand, a crushing pain smote him deep in his chest and he fell across the path. Alison took his head in her arms.

"Alison, forgive me", he whispered.

A multitude of thoughts passed through Alison's mind in the space of a few seconds.

"Yes, Klaus, I forgive you. Do you forgive me?"

But Klaus didn't reply.

*

"This is my husband", Alison thought. "He is dead and I must stay by his body."

No, not really—this was just a pretext for suicide. And as she knelt there in the snow and wind and bitter cold, in which it would be so easy just to lie down and let go, she was frightened because it seemed that she was about to die whether she wanted to or not, and she hadn't really made up her mind. It had been almost dark when she found her way up the path, and now all she could see was an immense field of uniform, glimmering whiteness. She stayed on her knees and tried to grope her way down, feeling for the stonework with her hands. It was extremely slow work, and the intense cold was sapping her vitality, so that she began again to wonder why she was still struggling when she could just cradle her body in the soft snow. She thought wryly that she might soon know whether Goerner was right, and then she wondered if, being dead, she would know that she knew. The wind and cold were no less intense, but they began to seem irrelevant. This brought a new wave of fear, because it meant that her physical body was irrelevant, and she was on the way out.

But the feeling passed and was replaced by disinterested curiosity; would she have the kind of out-of-the-body experience that she had read about. Would she float up into the air and look down on the Tor and the tower? Perhaps she would see Klaus's body.

None of this happened, but out of vast realms of space she heard someone calling her name. There was something earthly about it that brought her back a little, and she began to feel the wind and the snow again. It wasn't the angel of death. It sounded like . . . Imre! She almost giggled in her relief and weakness. She opened her eyes and saw a tiny light approaching. She heard her name again and now she was sure it was Imre, but when she tried to call back, she found that she could hardly speak.

"Imre, I'm here", she croaked, but her voice was lost in the rush of the wind. The light seemed to stop moving, and the thought that Imre might not find her gave her a little burst of energy. With great effort she got to her feet and tried to walk towards him, but in her eagerness she slipped off the path and a moment later she was half sliding, half rolling down the steep slope towards the hedge that marked the beginning of the meadows below. The snow held her less than fifty feet from the path, but her voice was feeble and Imre continued up the hill without hearing her.

The few moments of hope had changed Alison's mood again. Now she so violently didn't want to die that the thought that she was almost certainly going to became intolerable. She tried to get back to the path but among the ridges and channels where the depth of snow varied from a few inches to several feet she wasn't sure of the direction. After a few minutes of desperate effort, she hit a deep pocket and pitched forward. Struggling only seemed to make matters worse, so she lay there half submerged, barely able to breathe. This seemed to be the end, but it was unacceptable and it made her furiously angry. All this misery, abuse and struggle to reach the point where she actually might want to live, and now . . . Her anger boiled over.

"Damn Klaus, damn Imre, damn Tom, damn Halcyon!"

And then, "What a way to go, damning everybody, but I can't help it. It's not my fault. Damn them all! Damn, damn, damn . . ."

Her anger wasn't hot enough to melt the snow around her face, but it served to free her voice for a few seconds, so that in spite of the wind, her damns could be heard all over the hill.

*

Some of the tracks left by Imre were still visible in the strong beam of Tom's flashlight, and he and Halcyon had spent some time studying the model of the Tor, so they reached the beginning of the stone path without much difficulty. The object of the shovel was as much to locate the stonework and leave a visible track for the return as to clear the way ahead. Every ten paces Tom stopped and cleared several feet of pathway while Halcyon held the light. He was being extremely methodical and it took a very long time, but Halcyon, looking at her husband, thought, *He's right*, and then, *I hope my baby's not going to catch a cold*, and then, *He's not perfect but you can trust him. Yes, you can trust him.* The flashlight wavered and Tom said, "Are you OK?"

"Yes, I'm OK. I'm really OK. What was that?"

Tom paused over his shovel and heard a woman's voice.

"It's Alison."

For a moment the voice came to them clearly between gusts of wind.

"She's yelling, 'Damn'", Halcyon exclaimed, as she played the flashlight beam across the snow. My God, there she is!"

Alison had seen the light and was waving her arm, which was the only part of her body she could get above the level of the snow.

"Hang in there, Alison, we're coming", Halcyon yelled.

"We'd better go a bit further up the path", Tom said, "till we're level with her." He moved forward as quickly as he could, pushing the shovel in front of him. "Keep the light on Alison—we don't want to lose her. Now stay on the path and hold the end of the rope."

He left the path, shoveling as he went. There were some deep drifts to go through and by the time he reached Alison she was barely conscious. He fastened the rope under her arms and called up to Halcyon.

"Step off the path and brace yourself against it so you can keep the rope tight—just enough to stop her from slipping back."

While Halcyon held the rope, Tom dug footholds so that he could pull Alison up to relative safety. Once on the path he handed the shovel to his wife, took Alison by the wrists and heaved her up onto his back. In this way they reached the bottom of the stone path and came to the wider track through the field, where Alison was able to walk with Tom and Halcyon supporting her. She had been as limp as a rag doll, but now she began to wake up.

"Where is Imre?" she asked feebly. "He was looking for me."

"We didn't see him", Halcyon said. "He must have missed you."

"Then he must have found Klaus."
"Klaus?"
"Klaus is dead."

*

Klaus was not dead. When consciousness returned to him out of an immense pit of darkness, he whispered, "Yes, I forgive you"; but Alison was no longer there. The realization that she had followed him through this howling storm and must now be struggling for her own survival brought him at last to realize the full immensity of his folly. There had been no aureole, no pulsating waves of golden light and no celestial music—only the wish-fulfilling dream of an old man who had once thought himself important. He was not like John Bunyan's Mr. Valiant-for-Truth, for whom all the trumpets sounded when he reached the other side. The evil results of his mendacity weighed on him intolerably, and the effort to find something to give him a respite from this load of guilt brought to his mind the picture of heaven that he had cherished as a child—St. Peter, the Pearly Gates and the saints marching into the New Jerusalem. It seemed to him that his judicious mixture of truth and lies qualified him at best to be allowed to crawl in through the back door and face an eternity of painful cleansing. None of this had anything to do with Goerner's message, but now Klaus was deep in his childhood, and for a few moments it was almost as if he had never heard of Goerner. Alison had forgiven him, so perhaps God would too. He began to say the prayers that he had learnt long ago, and as he did so he saw a small light approaching.

*

Imre was overweight, self-centered and self-indulgent, but the innate toughness of body and soul that had enabled him long ago to survive the manhandling and taunts of his classmates was still with him. He had climbed the steep hill as fast as he could and as he came closer to the tower he looked back and saw a light moving on the lower slopes beyond the beginning of the stone path. So Tom had decided to help after all. Imre's little flashlight had enabled him to follow the fast-vanishing trail of different footprints, but he had missed Alison. As he made his way further up the hill, he saw a dark, kneeling figure at the side of the path and thought for a moment that he had found her; but it was the voice of Klaus that he heard.

"Alison?"

"No, it's Imre. Where is Alison?"

Klaus's voice was so faint that Imre had to kneel close beside him to hear.

"I do not know. I came here alone and did not want her to follow me, but she found me and I believe she may have gone for help."

Klaus would certainly die if he stayed there much longer, but Alison was somewhere on the hill and she probably needed help too. Well, Tom was on the way up—perhaps between them they could get Klaus to safety and find Alison. He looked back but now Tom's light was going in the opposite direction. It seemed that he had failed the test and Imre would have to cope. Since he hadn't seen Alison he thought perhaps she had gone down the other side of the Tor to look for a telephone. The best plan would be to get Klaus as far as the tower, where he could get out of the wind, and then to go for help. It took a long time, but after several months of illness Klaus was incredibly light, and Imre eventually got him to the top. Klaus refused to go inside the tower and sat in the snow facing west with his back to the wall as he had once done in the pouring rain of a July evening. Then the wind had driven the rain into his face but now it was from the east, so the tower gave him a little shelter.

Imre decided to head for the phone box down below at the corner of the main road. It shouldn't take long to reach the bottom of the Tor, so he took off his heavy jacket, wrapped it around Klaus and fastened it in front. It was only as Imre set off on the downward journey that he noticed that his flashlight was fading.

Klaus was fading, too. He couldn't recall what he had been thinking about when Imre appeared, but he knew that on some previous occasion he had sat where he was now and received some kind of enlightenment. Now he was sure that there was something good in the universe, although he couldn't remember what it was. He began to speak and didn't know that he was saying the Lord's Prayer.

(72)

Alison sat in front of the roaring fire. She had refused brandy and was drinking a cup of hot chocolate provided by Halcyon, who was sitting on the rug and looking into the red-hot embers. This time Tom called 999 instead of the police station. When given the choice of police, fire or ambulance, he opted for the ambulance. He explained the situation and told the operator that Klaus was stranded and very ill. He said that he and his wife had already brought one person down to safety and couldn't do it again. He gave his name as Lord Leyford and his address as Stone Down Cottage. Fortunately the operator had kept up with the news well enough to find this believable.

"All the lanes round there are impassable", she said, "but we'll try to get someone up there from the Chalice Well side."

Soon an ambulance and a police car stood by the Chalice Well while men with powerful flashlights climbed to the Tower and down the other side to the place where Alison had left Klaus. Finding nothing but a faint depression in the snow, the searchers concluded that the sick man, if ever there was one, must have got up and walked away. When Sergeant Howells telephoned Tom he was not polite.

"Lord Leyford?"

"Speaking."

"This is Sergeant Howells. I believe you made a 999 call a couple of hours ago."

"Yes, I did."

"Well, I want you to know that two ambulance men and three police officers have just spent nearly two hours on the Tor in this bloody weather and there's nothing to be found. I expect you know that there's a penalty for making frivolous 999 calls."

"It wasn't frivolous", Tom said. "There's man up there. Didn't you find anyone at all?"

"No one."

"Then I'm afraid there may be two."

"Well then, Sir, perhaps you'd like to go up and look and let us know when you find them."

"I don't understand it", Alison said when Tom reported the conversation. "He was lying across the path and I was sure he had died. And what's happened to Imre? I want to go up there again as soon as it's light."

Halcyon looked up and realized that she was no longer afraid of Alison.

"Klaus is all right now, dear, and I expect after Imre missed you he walked all the way to the top and down the other side. And I'm not sure you'll be well enough to go anywhere tomorrow. Would you like to go to bed?"

"I must go and see for myself. Can I just stay here by the fire until it gets light again?"

"Yes, I'll get you a blanket and Tom can bank up the fire."

But Tom was stretched out in the other armchair, snoring very gently, so Halcyon brought a blanket for Alison and a pillow for herself, added some logs to the fire and lay down on the rug. An hour later, she was awakened by the sound of the end of a log falling onto the hearth and she saw that Alison was sitting up.

"Did it wake you too?" she asked.

"No, something else did—like something passing through the room. I don't know what it was."

*

The wind died down during the night and the sun rose into a clear sky. Halcyon decided that she had better not go on another trip up the Tor, but for reasons that she would have had difficulty in explaining, she insisted that Tom should accompany Alison. It was not only that Halcyon could draw some strength from her possession of a house and a title, and her knowledge that she was carrying Tom's child. Tom's performance on the previous evening had made a deep impression on her. It seemed to her that he had gone about his business with calm determination and no sign of emotional involvement beyond the desire to save a fellow human being from almost certain death. If she had been able to perceive the feelings that Tom was trying to cope with as he walked along the lane with Alison, she would not have been so confident.

It was even colder than it had been the previous evening but the going was much easier. Tom was afraid that Alison would want to go over their past history, to ask him to explain how it was that he had bounced so quickly from her to Halcyon, but hardly a word was spoken until they reached the point where Alison had last seen Klaus.

"What could have happened? I was sure he had died."

"He must have woken up, tried to move and slipped off the path", Tom said. "It snowed for several more hours and he might be anywhere down there."

"I want to go up to the tower. We may be able to see something from there."

Klaus was still sitting with his back to the west wall of the tower. He was almost completely submerged in snow.

"No wonder they couldn't find him", Tom said.

Alison brushed the snow away from his head and shoulders.

"Look, someone put an extra jacket on him."

"Imre", Tom said. "It's the one he was wearing yesterday. He must have found Klaus, given him the jacket and gone for help."

They stood in silence, thinking about Klaus and trying to suppress the thought that Imre might not have made it to the bottom of the hill. Alison looked at Klaus's face. There was no sign of the ecstatic embrace of death that he had hinted at when she had last seen him alive, and there was no pain or fear. It was just the old Klaus with his great strengths and strong weaknesses, ready to meet as best he could whatever situation confronted him. So, Alison thought, he met death and accepted it, but he wasn't crazy about it. She bent and kissed him.

"We must try and find Imre", Tom said. "I'll have to phone the police again. Would you like to stay here while I go down to the call box? Are you warm enough?"

"Yes, I'll stay with Klaus until they get here."

"OK, I'll come back as soon as I've phoned.

As he started down the hill, Alison said, "Tom—I'm sorry."

Tom turned, ran back and took her in his arms. She held him very tightly and their tears mingled.

"Don't say anything, Tom."

"There aren't any words."

They released each other and looked across the town of Glastonbury into the far west, where the Welsh mountains were faintly visible.

"Alison, you're not going to . . ."

"Kill myself? No, don't worry—I think I'm going back to Peoria, but now I'm not sure. Anyway, I won't be staying here. Be happy, Tom, and don't cry any more."

Tom thought that once Alison had left Glastonbury it was almost certain that he would never see her again, but he smiled through his tears.

"Maybe I'll see you in my next life."

"Yes, and you'll probably be my sister."

"That's the way it goes."

*

The police were very kind to Alison. As the deceased's wife she had identified the body, and if she would just call at the station the next day all the necessary formalities could be taken care of. Klaus's body had been taken away, but the search for Imre was still going on. Tom and Alison went back to the cottage, and Alison was about to leave when Sergeant Howells telephoned to say that Imre had been found. He had lost the path, strayed on to the steeper slopes and slipped into a deep snowdrift. Without his jacket he couldn't have survived long. The sergeant was very apologetic.

"You did all that you could", Tom said, "and you're not to blame for anything. Klaus must have died long before you got to the top, and there was never any chance that you could have found Imre."

"Do you know if Mr. Takacs has any relatives in this country?"

"I don't think so but I believe his father lives in Ulm in West Germany."

"They've found Imre's body", he said as he put down the phone. "They wanted to know if he had any relatives in this country and I told them I didn't think so. What's the matter?"

Alison had gone very pale, but now her pallor was slowly giving way to a deep flush. Tom took her arm and led her to one of the armchairs. Halcyon knew the traditional remedy for shock and went to the kitchen to make a cup of hot sweet tea.

"What is it?" Tom asked again, but Alison didn't speak until Halcyon had brought the tea.

"It's something about Imre, isn't it?" she asked.

"I've been so frightened about everything", Alison said, with her usual talent for apparent irrelevance. "Like the poor man in *Showboat*, I suppose, 'Tired of living and scared of dying.' He's been helping with Klaus and letting me use his car, and I've been smuggling liquor into the house. The night before last I got drunk and let him sleep with me."

"Imre?"

Halcyon was stupefied.

"Yes—well, I kind of goaded him into it.

"I don't suppose it took much goading. But . . . But why?"

"I kept telling myself that things couldn't get any worse, but they always did, so I thought, why not go all the way and make myself ultimately filthy—then maybe I could start coming back."

Alison paused for a long time and Halcyon and Tom were silent, sensing that something else was coming out.

"And now he's dead and Klaus is dead and it's all because of me. Klaus left in disgust and I asked Imre to go and look for him. And Imre's father is dead too, but Imre did have a relative in this country. I'm probably his half-sister."

There was another long pause before Tom said incredulously, "Your mother and Imre's father?"

Alison nodded.

"It must be a bit like murder—incest I mean. They say when you've done it once it's easier to do it again. Only if I'd been thinking properly I'd have realized it was one or the other and not both."

"I haven't the faintest idea what you're talking about", Halcyon said.

"Klaus and I were really the only people in his life", Alison went on, as if trying to explain things to herself. "Klaus was his hero for a long time. Even after he tried to blackmail Klaus into giving me to him, he still seemed to look up to him as if he was some kind of superior being. And nobody knew my mother had been making out with Imre's father until Imre read his father's old letters. First he wanted me for a lover and then for a sister and then probably both, and he never quite let go of his old feeling for Klaus. I had got so used to the idea that I'd done it with Klaus, and I was so drunk and confused that I forgot that if he was my half-brother, Klaus couldn't be my father. So now I've really done it, haven't I? Unless, after all, my father—I mean Phillip . . . I mean, maybe my mother wasn't completely truthful."

"You know about Phillip?" Halcyon asked.

"Yes, Dr. Ginsburg told me. Nothing's ever certain, is it, but I think my mother was telling the truth—it just seems like the way it would have happened. And now I can't blame anyone else for anything—not after what I did with Imre."

"Listen, Alison", Halcyon said, "Klaus and your Mum and Imre and his father—they all made this mess and you're not to blame if it was too much for you."

"You're a sweetheart, Halcyon and I think you must be getting like your Mum. Can I have some more tea?"

As Halcyon returned to the kitchen, Alison murmured to herself, "I ought to have done better", and repeated it several times.

"What are you going to do?" Tom asked.

"I don't know. I was going to go back to Peoria, but now I don't think I can face Billy. He already called me a slut once, and now I'm something worse."

"Well, what do you really want?"

Alison looked up with a wry smile.

"Something I can't have."

Tom was fairly sure that he knew what Alison meant, but there were other possible interpretations. Halcyon, who had been standing at the door while she waited for the kettle to boil again, called Tom into the kitchen.

"Do you think we should let her . . ." she began but Tom shook his head before she could finish her question.

"You're very wonderful, my darling, but no—definitely no. And I don't think she would accept even if we asked her. You don't want me to explain, do you?"

"No—I get it."

Alison finished her second cup of tea and stood up.

"Thank you. I'm feeling a little better."

"That's good", said Halcyon, "'cause you know what? You're a wealthy young widow and you can do whatever you like."

"Wealthy?"

"Yes, wealthy. Klaus told me that although we were spiritually united he was intending to leave most of whatever he had to you. He said I'd be OK but you were still his earthly responsibility."

"It never occurred to me—I thought he was going to leave everything to the Society."

"Well, listen. Since you mentioned my mother, I'll tell you what I think she would say. Don't do anything rash—in fact don't do anything at all until the dust has begun to settle a bit. Just enjoy having plenty of money and no responsibilities."

Alison shook her head and smiled ruefully at something inside her. As she set off down the lane, Halcyon said, "Well! She never even thanked us for saving her life."

"Maybe she wasn't grateful", Tom said.

(73)

When Alison got back to the Trathgannons' house she saw Klaus's suitcases still standing in the hall, so she knocked on the living room door.

"I've been up to your flat", the old lady said, without giving Alison the chance to speak, "and you ought to be ashamed of yourself. The place stinks of whiskey and there's a cupboard full of empty bottles. And I suppose you've been out all night with that Hungarian. Disgusting! Well, you can't stay here and I don't expect your husband wants to see any more of you . . ."

Alison couldn't stand any more so she turned and ran up the stairs. When she got to the first landing she stopped and called down to her landlady, "My husband is dead and so is Imre." As she continued up the next flight, Mrs. Trathgannon's final comment reached her.

"Well, I'm sure you drove them to it."

*

Alison found room for her few possessions in one of Klaus's suitcases. Money was not a problem since they had set up a joint account when Klaus became ill, so she went down to the hotel, booked a room and arranged for Klaus's belongings to be retrieved. It was a sleepy Sunday afternoon and she was relieved to find that the name Hübel didn't mean anything to anyone. Halcyon's words returned to her as she sat on her bed and wondered what she would do next.

I'm a wealthy young widow and I can do anything I like. The trouble is I don't like anything. And now it's come to the point, I don't want to kill myself, although I'm not sure why, and it would have been very convenient if I'd died in the snow. I really don't want to go back to Peoria but maybe I will anyway. The only thing I really must do is arrange Klaus's funeral.

This was a problem, as Goerner had never said anything about funerals. CW people generally liked to be meditated over, sent on their way with a musical accompaniment and buried intact, but Klaus and Alison had agreed that they wanted to cause as little trouble as possible. They would be quite happy to be cremated and leave it to anyone who wanted to to organize a memorial service later on. At this point no one in the CW movement knew that Klaus and Imre had died, and Alison felt no inclination to tell anyone, since it would mean a lot of sympathy cards and conversations with people she had no desire to talk to. So it was left to the *Evening Star*, which had an unofficial hot line to the police station, to spread the news. Bill Graveney and various other people connected with the Glastonbury Archway School saw it on Monday evening, and by Tuesday afternoon it had reached Harry Grainger, who very importantly telephoned Jane Malone and Anne Weston in America and Carolina Ende in Germany. He didn't know where to find Alison, but being a man of great resource, he called the police in Glastonbury and told them that he was Klaus's closest friend, that there were no relatives apart from Alison, who obviously needed help at this terrible time, and managed to wheedle her present address out of them. He arrived in Glastonbury on Wednesday morning and tracked Alison down at the New Avalon. When he arrived there he was horrified to learn that the police had released Klaus's body, and that it had already arrived at a crematorium in Bath.

"But my dear Alison, you know as students of Cosmic Wisdom we have a duty to the dead, to assist in the first stages of their return to the spiritual world. Surely it would still be possible to find a burial plot and arrange a vigil."

Alison, who had never liked Harry, looked at him with weariness and distaste.

"I suppose this is kind of you and maybe you mean well, but it's really none of your business and I wish you'd go away."

Harry was too thick-skinned to take any notice of this. Now he was at his most avuncular.

"Now Alison, I understand that this has been a terrible shock to you. Let's go into the lounge and have some coffee and talk it over."

"There's nothing to talk over, and I want you to know that the last time I had coffee with a man in the lounge I slapped him, and now he's dead."

Harry smiled at what seemed to him to be an obvious fantasy.

"Come, come now, Alison. Surely at this time you need a friend, especially someone who has experience of dealing with these melancholy events."

"I have found that I get on better without friends, and in any case, I understood that you had lost your wife under different circumstances."

This was a nasty blow that finally penetrated Harry's epidermis, since his wife had divorced him twenty years previously on several grounds, including neglect and infidelity. He flushed a deep red and left.

Later that day, Alison watched Klaus and his coffin disappear into the furnace. If she had been a vengeful person she might have taken some pleasure in the fact that Klaus and Imre were gone and the rapists were in jail; but all she could feel was an unutterable dreariness and a complete lack of motivation to do anything.

*

There were some letters waiting for Alison when she got back to the hotel. One, which had been delivered by hand, was a request from QTV for an interview in which she could tell the viewers the truth about her relationships with her late husband, his late secretary and, especially, Lord Leyford. There would be no fee but she could expect a generous allowance for expenses. She threw it into the waste paper basket and then, after another moment's thought, fished it out again. What an opportunity to get everything off her chest—she could let it all hang out, and if she told the truth no one would believe it anyway. The next letter was from Candy, hoping that Klaus was getting better and giving the latest news about Billy and the diner. Billy had begun to express regret for what he had done and whether this was genuine or merely in the hope of an early parole, Candy didn't say. The third letter was from Billy.

> "Dear Alison,
>
> I think about you all the time, specially at night when I can't sleep. Jackie is very nice but I don't feel that way about her. She has gone back to school and the diner is not doing so well. Mom and Dad are very worried about it. I wish you could come back but I guess you have to look after your husband. I have spent a long time thinking about it and I'm sorry I hurt him.
>
> Love from Billy."

It seemed to Alison that there was something very funny about the way money was distributed. The CW's and Archway were always begging for it, and yet all around her there were people with plenty of it. Klaus had been wealthy and had passed it on to her. Imre had inherited a bunch from his father, Tom had a ton and was sharing it with Halcyon, and Harry Grainger lived in a lavish style that didn't go very well with his spiritual pretensions; but on the other side of the Atlantic, Pete and Candy were uncomplainingly trying to keep their heads above water while their son endured his jail sentence. Alison discarded the QTV letter again, looked around her room, and decided that most of Klaus's belongings could be sent to the Salvation Army. She arranged this with the management, packed her bag and checked out of the hotel. She was pretty sure that she would come back to Cosmic Wisdom at some point, but she was never seen by anyone in Glastonbury again.

X

Epilogue: Opening Ceremonies for the Peoria Archway School July 1995

(74)

Iris, Duchess of Brueland and Street, sat between her two grandchildren at the back of the auditorium. James, who was six, looked like a smaller edition of his father and grandfather, and the four-year-old Victoria showed every sign of continuing the female line of gorgeous blondes. There was a vacant seat on Victoria's left.

Iris looked at her program.

"Peoria Archway School—Opening Ceremony and Festival of Dedication: thanks to the generosity . . ."

Her reading was interrupted by the arrival of her husband.

"Hello Jim, I thought you'd never make it."

"So did I. Everybody under the sun wants to talk—you'd think they'd never seen a duke before."

"Maybe they haven't."

"Who's that, grandma?" James wanted to know, as an expansive gentleman with a red face and a mop of wavy brown hair took the stage.

Iris looked at her program again.

"That's Charlie Oaks—he's one of the local big wheels."

"He doesn't look like a wheel."

"Looks like a proper Charlie", said Lord Otterill.

"Hush", said Iris.

By this time Oaks had already welcomed the audience, which consisted largely of parents, teachers and guests from other Archway Schools. Virginia Reddick was there to represent the Pittstown Archway

375

School, together with Diana Davies, head of music at the school, and Diana's eight-year-old son Mickey. With them was a very reluctant and surly Elwyn, who still regarded Goerner as a subversive charlatan and, even after seven years in Pittstown, still refused to set foot in the school.

Oaks outlined the evening's agenda, speaking enthusiastically about Tom Dexter, the evening's principal speaker, who was the well-known science correspondent of the London *Daily Sentinel* and *New Observer*. Fortunately Elwyn's loud groan was drowned by the applause.

"As I'm sure you know, Mr. Dexter is the son of the famous owner of those publications and many others, and it is with great pleasure that I announce that Lord and Lady Otterill have honored us with their presence this afternoon. (Gasps and great applause.) I also have the privilege of welcoming the world's greatest euphonist, known to everyone as Halcyon, but in private life as Lady Leyford or, as she prefers to be known, Mrs. Tom Dexter (More applause). Tom is going to talk about . . ."

Charlie stopped and looked at his notes.

"Well, he'll tell you what he's going to talk about."

This time Elwyn's groan was audible and he received a painful corrective from his wife's elbow.

"And then Halcyon will end the evening with one of her wonderful performances. First, however, I want to emphasize that this is not only a great day for Peoria—it is also a great day for the whole Archway Movement. It gives me great pleasure to welcome many representatives from schools all over the world, including two honored guests who are sitting in the front row. Carolina Ende is the Science Coordinator for the European Archway Schools, and Anne Weston, who is the Faculty Chair of the Manhattan Archway School, has recently become President of the Archway Schools Association of North America. Carolina claims that she has no talent as a public speaker, which we don't believe, but as you know, everyone has the right to remain silent."

This remark was felt to be in poor taste, so the audience exercised its right and Oaks plunged on.

"So before we come to our principal speaker, Anne will begin the proceedings by talking about what it means for the Archway Movement to have a new school here in the American heartland . . ."

Anne, who had abandoned purple for the occasion and was wearing a long maroon dress with a high collar, stood up, but the preliminaries ran on, so she sat down again.

". . . and then I'll introduce the person who has made this whole evening possible, and who has been instrumental in the erection of this wonderful school building and bringing the Archway Movement to our great city—the talented, lovely and, if I may say so, extremely well-heeled, Alison Bigley."

Alison wasn't visible. Preferring to remain out of sight as long as possible, she had found a chair at the side of the stage. As she waited for the introductions to end she was still wondering what she was going to say. She had certainly accomplished a lot since coming back to Peoria. She had brazenly returned to her former job at the diner, and this had done wonders for Pete's business. Thanks to this and her financial support, he was now the proud part-owner of three restaurants in the southern Peoria area, Alison owning the other part. With Klaus's money and her income from the restaurants she had made the foundation of the Peoria Archway School in a brand new building possible. She had married Billy when he got out of jail, and this had been only a qualified success. He was still beautiful, charming and devoted, and a great comfort to go to bed with, but there was an unspoken feeling that they were not giving each other all that they really needed. Billy's main interests were still cars and sex, and Alison did her best to keep him happy, but he had gradually discovered that there was a big part of her mind to which he had no access, and that it wasn't possible to stay on cloud nine all the time. Billy wanted children, but so far Alison had felt unable to take on the responsibility.

Alison peeked at the audience. "They don't get it" she thought. "They probably mean well but they don't get it. If they knew what Cosmic Wisdom really meant, they'd be running as fast as they could in the opposite direction." Candy and Pete were at work in the diner, but Billy was sitting in the far right corner of the auditorium, and Alison could see the Duke and Duchess, with a small boy and a smaller girl, sitting at the back next to the center aisle. Tom's children, she thought with a huge surge of jealousy. She had been planning to be very brief, so Tom and Halcyon were waiting in the wings behind her, but now she was thinking, "I can't do this." What could she honestly say that would be cheerful and uplifting, that would welcome everyone to a bright future?

The complimentary remarks continued on stage, but the restrained applause quickly died away. There were plenty of people there with vivid memories of the two trials in which Alison had appeared, and many of those who were happy to profit from her generosity still thought of her as a shameless hussy who had married a jailbird. Not wishing to disappoint them, Alison had put on the briefest mini-dress she owned, but now she was wondering whether it had been a good idea, or whether, in fact, it had been a good idea for her to appear at all.

Oaks finally remembered whom he was supposed to be introducing.

"So a warm welcome, please, for Anne Weston."

Anne stood up again and climbed the steps up to the stage. Like many Archway people she was allergic to microphones, so she stood among the flowers at the side of the lectern and spoke without notes.

"It's a great honor to be asked to assist at the opening of the Peoria Archway School . . .

Alison wondered what Anne was really thinking. She was a good person—a bit gruff and rigid, but trustworthy, unpretentious and more knowledgeable about the world's affairs than the average CW.

"People who come from Europe often get as far as New York, Boston, Philadelphia or Washington and just stick there, but Dr. Goerner believed that the true center of gravity for the Cosmic Wisdom Society and the Archway Schools should be in what Mr. Oaks has just referred to as the heartland of America. This is not just a matter of geographical centrality. We hope that this will be the land where the forces of the human heart come to their full potential, where all our thoughts and deeds are brought together in a realm of true human feeling, feeling that has been purified and freed from selfishness, egotism and mere carnality so as to become an active force for good in the world."

"One of the great goals of the Archway schools is to foster a healthy life of feeling . . ."

It doesn't seem to have worked for me, Alison was thinking. *My life of feeling is a total mess, my thoughts are horrible and my deeds . . . Well, never mind. And I'm going to have to go out there and say something after this.*

"And now I'd like to say something about our next speaker. I had the pleasure of working with Alison when she taught euphonics in New York for a year. She is a fine artist and a wonderful teacher and I hope she will give your new school the benefit of these talents; but above all, she is a person of enormous courage. I wouldn't mention this if it weren't a matter of public record of which the people of this city are well aware but . . ."

Alison stood up, with the blood rushing to her face. How could Anne be so inept? And how could a person with a public record like Alison's go and face an audience expecting a nice uplifting little speech about the wonders of Archway education? She began to walk rapidly in the opposite direction but her path took her directly between Tom and Halcyon.

"Where are you going", Tom said in a loud whisper."

"Out", she said. "I can't do this. They have no idea."

Halcyon got in front of her.

"Yes you can, dearie. You can do it."

She took Alison in her arms.

"You're a good, good, good person and you can do it. And maybe it's better if they have no idea."

Anne was now descending from the stage to modest applause. Charlie Oaks took the microphone and thanked Anne for her fine, uplifting presentation.

"And now, ladies and gentlemen, here is Alison Bigley."

"Here, Tom, you hold her for a minute", Halcyon said and beckoned Charlie to the side of the stage. "Tell them Alison's not feeling well and we're doing the program backwards. Get the podium out of the way and give Irene a minute to get to the piano and then I'll start. Tom can speak when I've finished and Alison can say something at the end if she feels up to it."

Halcyon had scandalized the euphonics world by choreographing jazz and rock, but for Peoria she had gone back to the old staples, so while Tom held on to Alison she did Mozart and a verse by Goerner.

Tom hadn't seen Alison for seven years and it came as a shock to feel his body reacting to her, especially when she whispered in his ear, "Let's fake them all out and run away together."

He looked at her face, to see if she was serious, and was surprised to see a vestige of the old cheeky grin.

"Come on", she said, "Make up your mind."

Tom was mortified to find himself dithering. He ought to be saying, "Don't be ridiculous", and giving all the obvious reasons, but for a few moments it was almost as if the last seven years hadn't happened and he was back in Mrs. Barrington-Smythe's kitchen trying to decide whether to run after Alison or wait and see what happened.

Alison broke away and tugged his arm.

"Come on while there's still time."

"Don't do this to me . . . I have children and . . ."

Loud applause broke out in the auditorium and Halcyon left the stage. Looking into the wings she had the impression that Alison was trying to get away and Tom was restraining her.

"Hold on, Tom", she called, and went back for a bow.

Tom, in total confusion, thought Halcyon knew what was happening and was telling him not to run away.

"I can't, Alison. I love her and it would kill her."

Halcyon had dressed to look like a young schoolgirl for the Turkish Rondo and had simply covered the whole thing up with a long, deep purple robe for the verse by Goerner. Returning from the stage she removed the robe and once again looked like a sixteen-year-old rather than the twenty-five-year-old mother of two.

"You're right, Tom" Alison said. "Off you go and give 'em hell."

Halcyon found some folding chairs and she and Alison sat in the wings to listen to Tom.

"What was Tom right about?" Halcyon asked.

"That I should stay here and not run away."

*

Tom had been invited to speak not as an expert on Archway education but as a deeply interested public figure, whose presence would impress the sceptics and lend importance to the event. In the past seven years he had kept his readers informed about the rapidly multiplying families of quarks and the tantalizing possibilities of string theory. He had also given them as much of Goerner's scientific method as he thought they could stomach, but his plan for this event was to keep it simple, emphasizing Goerner's insistence that every child should be given a thorough education in science, and his own belief in what he called "dirty hands science." Diagrams, models, movies and TV science were all very well and useful, while mathematical formulation was essential, but there was nothing like getting in there with the raw substance of the earth and finding things out for yourself. Unfortunately he was so overwrought that he wandered onto the stage while the podium was still being replaced. Most of the audience didn't realize who he was and thought he was there to help with the podium. With a great effort he pulled himself together. He still couldn't raise a smile but he managed to turn to the audience and say,

"Everything's backwards tonight, so I'll introduce Charlie Oaks and then he'll introduce me."

This produced a chuckle and Oaks entered from the opposite wing.

"Keep it short", Tom muttered, but Oaks had already switched on the microphone and it was heard all over the auditorium, to the great delight of everyone present, especially Lord Otterill.

As Charlie Oaks's mouth opened and silence fell, a small boy's voice was heard to exclaim, "That's my Daddy", and another minute of buzz and laughter ensued.

The voice of his son brought Tom back to his senses and it was only then that he realized that he had no idea where his lecture notes were. He had had the folder in his hand before his encounter with Alison, and he thought he might have put it down somewhere at the side of the stage. He looked into the wings, where Halcyon and Alison were sitting, and raised his hands, palms upwards. Halcyon looked around and spotted the folder just as Charlie Oaks was saying something about a warm welcome for Tom Dexter. The applause increased as she walked onto the stage and handed the folder to Tom, who took it, seized his wife and kissed her vigorously. The applause was deafening.

By the time Halcyon got back to her seat, Alison was gone and Elwyn had left the auditorium.

(75)

Alison walked aimlessly along a corridor with doors on each side and a skylight above. Eventually she stopped, opened a door on the south side and went into a classroom. The walls and ceiling, all freshly painted, sparkled in the afternoon sunshine, and twenty-five brand new wooden desks stood in ranks before teacher's chair and table. Not exactly like the Garden of Eden, Alison thought, but the teacher is a sort of tree of knowledge and probably one of the kids will bring her an apple. Or him. That doesn't fit either way. Maybe it's just an empty body waiting for someone to incarnate, and it would be safer all around if no one did. Probably the teacher who belongs to this room is somewhere in the audience, and hasn't realized that she's going to come down to earth with a bump when she gets in here with the kids.

Alison sat down at the teacher's table. This was just idle association of ideas and it wasn't getting her anywhere. The only thing she had figured out was that she really must go back and face all those people, who were there because they had accepted or been persuaded of the benefits of Wolfgang Goerner's ideas on education, or thought the school would be a nice safe place for their kids. But Goerner's view of the human future was so frightening that it had driven Alison to drink, and in spite of Halcyon's words she felt bound to let everyone know what they were in for. She had managed to get over her dependence on the bottle, but at this moment she wished ardently that she could find something, anything with alcohol in it.

Alison had never felt sorry for herself, but she still had the residues of her anger, and now it wasn't directed against anyone in particular but against the design of the universe. She, Klaus, Imre, Phillip, Maria, Tom, Halcyon, Billy—they were all caught in the same mesh, and it went all the way back to Adam and Eve, who had only ever had one decision to make and had got it wrong. Now everybody had to make decisions all the time, and it wasn't surprising if most of them were wrong, like most of hers. And the crowd in the auditorium, getting the impression that CW and Archway would provide all the answers—that wasn't what Goerner had said, but public presentations of CW usually left out the difficult bits. His message was like Little Orphan Annie's; times were bad and they would get worse and the gobble-uns'll git you ef you don't watch out. The obvious thing that CW's sometimes forgot was that you can't do it on your own—even the good powers that fought against the demons were not assured of the outcome. As she had remembered on the night of the rape, Goerner had placed Christ as what real believers call the Savior of the World, although he had expressed the matter in different terms. Although Goerner was demonstrably fallible over some of the details of human existence, Alison was still convinced that he was right about the big picture. Well, I can't explain the whole of Cosmic Wisdom to them, she thought, but these people have got to know that the road to heaven is paved with landmines and that CW isn't there just to make you feel good. But I also have to give them some reason for hoping that things will turn out OK in the end, and maybe I'll even manage to convince myself. She returned to the side of the stage just as Tom was wrapping up his talk.

*

"Like many scientists and philosophers, Wolfgang Goerner thought that when it comes to trying to understand the problems of perception and consciousness, atomic science isn't much help and may actually get in the way. The fact is that in spite of its obvious usefulness and applicability, we still don't know why the quantum theory works, and people are still wrangling over the reality of things like electrons and photons. We know how to manipulate them but we don't know why they exist or what they are. The things we know and the things we can make are wonderful and terrible, but they haven't brought us any closer to knowing how to live. I'm not suggesting that problems like this should be tackled in Archway schools—only that a deep love and experience of the earth will help people to keep their feet on the ground and their heads on straight. You can take all this any way you like, but sometimes it's very simple. I have a friend with a Ph. D. in physics who can't repair a bedside lamp because he's never learnt how to strip the insulation off the end of a piece of wire."

This struck Alison as being extremely significant but she couldn't think what it was significant of—surely not just circumcision. She got so involved in thinking about it that she didn't hear Tom's final sentences, or the applause or the thanks from Charlie Oaks. The next thing she heard was her name.

"And now at last let's welcome Alison Bigley."

Alison picked up Halcyon's purple robe and made her entrance. The polite applause died down as she draped it over the lectern and plunged in without preliminaries.

"If I were sitting where you are, I'd be sick and tired of hearing about my generosity and the wonders of Archway education. I'd rate my generosity as about average for this planet, and I think it's only right to tell you that although some people are generous out of sheer goodness of heart, I actually have an agenda. And the Archway schools really are wonderful, but maybe we say it a little too often without mentioning what we're really up against. So I want to tell you why I'm being so goddamn generous and what the schools are really for, besides giving your kids a decent education."

Lord Otterill, who had dozed through most of his son's talk, sat up and took notice. This looked like being interesting. People in the audience who thought that Alison would just make a few graceful remarks and let everyone go home were shocked by her coarse bluntness, and wondered if it would be possible to leave unobtrusively.

"Many of you probably still think of me as a baggage. My figure doesn't fit the tits and ass description so you'll probably have to settle for legs. I've been told that mine are quite nice."

This produced a lot of murmuring and a significant number of people headed for the exits. It also brought Charlie Oaks halfway across the stage. He coughed loudly but Alison went on.

"That's why I borrowed this from Halcyon."

She held up the robe and slipped it over her head. She was a little shorter than Halcyon, so it came all the way down to the floor.

"Now you'll know that I'm not speaking as a trollop or a whore. I want to tell you what it's really all about, and it's not going to make you feel comfortable."

Oaks seized the microphone and told the audience, "I'm afraid Mrs. Bigley is not well and won't be able to continue."

He took Alison's arm and tried to escort her from the stage but she struggled free and slapped him. Billy was already halfway down the side aisle and gave a loud hoot.

"Hit him again, Allie", he yelled.

"Do something, Tom", Halcyon muttered, so Tom ran over and pushed Oaks off the stage. Meanwhile, Lord Otterill had risen from his seat and walked to the front of the auditorium. He was used to taking command of situations and had a very loud voice.

"I believe that Mrs. Bigley has something important to say. If you don't like the way she's saying it you have every right to leave, so I suggest that we pause for a couple of minutes and then we can go on with those who want to stay."

He glared ferociously around the room and several people who had started leaving sat down again. Billy worked his way along the front of the stage.

"Are you OK, Allie?"

"Yes, but stay close in case I need you."

"Are you Mr. Bigley?" Lord Otterill asked.

"Yes."

"You should be proud of your wife."

"I am."

Meanwhile, Elwyn, wandering around outside and trying to get a grip on himself, saw people leaving and decided that he'd better go back in.

*

Alison was trembling but still determined. She walked to the very edge of the stage and almost tripped over the hem of the purple robe.

"Damn this thing", she said and started pulling it off. As she did so, her short dress rode up with it and the audience had a good sight of her panties.

"Come and help me, Halcyon", she called.

The two of them managed to get the robe off and Halcyon returned to her seat. "Well, now you've seen the real me", Alison said.

There were a lot of empty spaces in the room, so she asked the audience to come forward and fill up the front rows. Sitting on the front of the stage with her legs dangling over the edge, right in front of Billy, she said, "OK, now I can talk to you like people. Has anyone here got anything to drink?"

Most of the people in the room thought Alison was talking about things like coffee, tea or water, but this was something that Charlie Oaks did understand. He pulled a small flask out of his hip pocket.

"Give her this", he said, removing the lid and handing it to Tom.

Tom took it to Alison and returned to his seat next to Halcyon, who was feeling very shaky and climbed onto his lap. He closed his eyes, held her very tightly and tried to picture her walking with him through a field of buttercups.

Alison took a generous gulp of Oaks's brandy without coughing or spluttering.

"Just what the doctor ordered", she said, "Only not Dr. Goerner, although you know there was alcohol in his family and the first Archway School was founded on beer. He used to make a lot of jokes about cow shit, but I think I may have to say something about bullshit and it won't be a joke. Anyway, to go back a bit, it wasn't supposed to be like this. I mean what they call the human condition. We're supposed to be on our way back up to the spiritual world, but when you come right down to it we're really a bit of a mess. You name the seven deadly sins and we've got them all—yes, and that includes the CW Society, with pride and sex at the top of the pile. And to hear some of us CW's talk it's all onward and upward until we reach the status of angels, and at the same time, out of the other side of our mouths, it's the great peril of the human race, the evil powers that are going to turn us all into little robots. Only somehow that just applies to all those other people. And believe me, I'm not saying anything against Goerner. I think he was right about reincarnation and karma and a whole lot of other stuff too, only maybe he didn't really grasp what it was like to be just an ordinary person. Well, let me tell you, I was up on a hill near Glastonbury in England one day . . . Excuse me a minute."

She took another swig of brandy.

"That's better. I was up on this hill with the remains of something spiritual that had been going on in 3,000 BC. That's five thousand years ago. Well, for average Joes like us five thousand years is about ten incarnations and when I look inside myself I think, Gee, I don't seem to be making much progress—in fact I seem to be going backwards. How much longer do I have to keep on doing this? I mean, Goerner says that what you go through in the spiritual world is even more exhausting than what happens down here so that after a while you're longing to come down to earth again. And then it's so terrible that you want to get away, only you can't. I heard some drunks singing in a pub one night and the chorus went, "Round and round went the bloody great wheel." It was really about sex, and the guy who made the machine forgot to provide a way of switching it off, but it got all mixed up in my mind with reincarnation and wheel of karma—there's no exit and no hiding place, only the wheel, and you can't switch it off. I thought of that and I was so scared that I ran all the way down the hill, and that was when I took to drink. Goerner told us that we have to be alert and know what's going on, but when we do know it's so frightening that we wish we didn't. Maybe you're different, but I sometimes get the feeling that whoever's in charge gave the evil spirits a bit too much latitude. You may have been surprised that I put pride ahead of sex, but everyone has problems with sex. I mean, don't I know it? But not everyone thinks that they know so much about meditation, the spiritual world and the meaning of life that they can not only transform and purify themselves but they can also tell the rest of the human race exactly where they're going wrong. And you can't blame Goerner for that. It's exactly what he kept warning us about. It's called egotism."

Alison employed the bottle again and looked at her diminished audience. Nice, serious people with good intentions, she thought. They hadn't had to deal with Klaus and Imre and have incestuous relationships and find out things about their mothers that they didn't want to know. And most of them hadn't been raped. Maybe it would be a good idea not to tell them any more. Nothing much had happened to improve Alison's view of her own future, but maybe these people had brighter prospects, and she couldn't leave without saying something positive.

"OK, I know I'm not being fair. I'll stick to it that there's a lot of spiritual pride and a lot of we-know-something-you-don't-know, and that there are people using their spiritual pretensions to justify behavior that regular folks find hard to tolerate. But there are also thousands of CW's out there who are sincerely working their butts off, reading lectures and going to study groups and trying to understand, and being perfectly ready to admit that it's all too hard for them. And it *is* too hard for most of us."

"That's why I think that people who go to church and pray for forgiveness and don't expect to be moving up among the hierarchies have just as good a chance as we do. I mean, if the angels can get in a muddle and get it wrong, what do you think our chances are? In spite of everything that Goerner said, we're apt to forget that Jesus Christ came into the world to save sinners, which we all are—but some of us have realized we need a priest as well as a guru. Or maybe instead of . . . Well, that's another story and maybe for some of us it's a better one, but now I want to explain about the money. My grandfather Walter was the cousin of the owner of the Schmidt Brewery, and there was money in our family from that. My late husband Klaus, who taught at the first Archway School, had a lot of money in his family and eventually most of that came to me. When I came back to Peoria I helped my parents-in-law with their business, and I want to tell you they're great people and did nearly all the work, so there's money there now. So my money comes partly from Archway and partly from Peoria, and that's why I want to spend it on Archway in Peoria. Ignorance is bliss, but only temporarily, whereas knowledge is a form of punishment that might come in handy later on. If we put our children in an Archway school we're exposing them to the risk of knowledge, but Goerner thought it was important, and if he got it right, which I think he did, they're getting something that might help them survive the 'bloody great wheel.' There may not be many places where they can get it, but just don't assume it's going to give them all the answers. Most of it they'll have to find out for themselves. That's really all I want to say, so I'll leave you now and try to set a good example."

To most of the audience this seemed to be an abrupt and unsatisfactory end, and the only people who applauded were Billy, the Otterill family and Elwyn—Billy because he was proud of his wife, the Otterills because they had just seen a display of unusual courage, and Elwyn for no reason that he could clearly distinguish. He found his way back to his wife, said, "I'm sorry" and added, "But don't expect me to get mixed up in this Archway rot." Alison looked down at her husband. She thought she would probably never be happy again, but there was a sure way of bringing some joy into Billy's life and maybe even making some new karma, so she added a tailpiece.

"This is my husband. He knows nothing about Goerner and when he dies he'll go straight to heaven. Come on Billy, let's go home and make some babies."

"Sure thing!" Billy scooped her up and carried her triumphantly up the aisle, straight out to the parking lot and into his beautiful, shining black 57' Ford V8. Doing a hundred down the interstate, Alison felt she had got something right.